The Prophecy of the Yubriy Tree

Book One of The Song of the Burning Heart

Ben Spencer

KNOCK-KNEE

BOOKS

ISBN-13: 9781732038066 (Hardcover)
ISBN-13: 9781732038073 (Paperback)
ISBN-13: 9781732038080 (Ebook)

KNOCK-KNEE BOOKS

About the Author

Ben Spencer lives in Concord, NC, with his wife and daughter. Please sign up for his newsletter at benspencer.substack.com or visit his website at benspencerwrites.com for more information. Ben's novelette, *Last Performance at the Three Dragons Inn,* is available for free to newsletter subscribers.

ALSO BY BEN SPENCER

The Song of the Burning Heart
   Last Performance at the Three Dragons Inn (Novelette)

Many Savage Moons

THE DEER KING (Novellas)
   The Deer King
   The Sundering
   Last of the Baronites

For Beth, for always

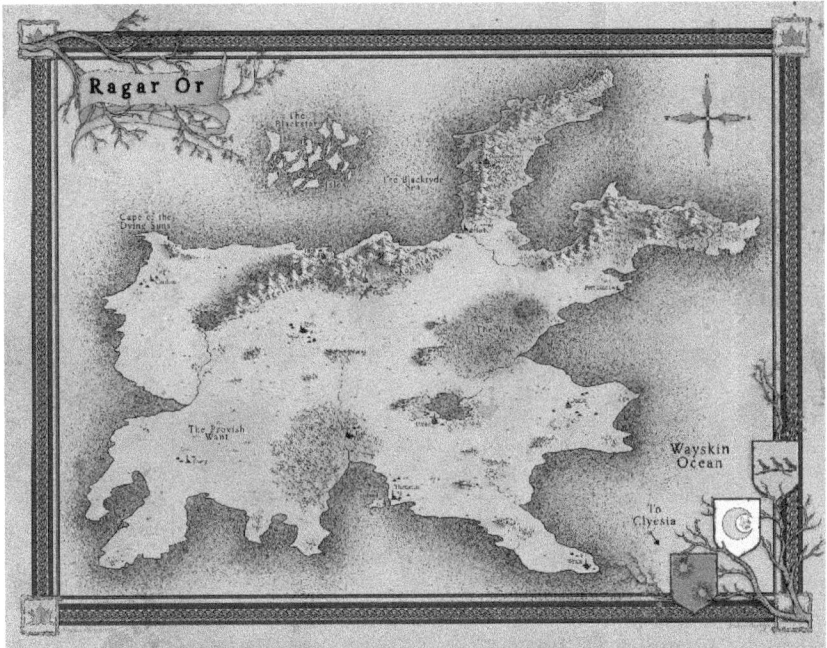

Prologue

The future was falling from the sky.

The rich orange leaves of the Yubriy tree.

Holy creatures watched the leaves fall. The sons and daughters of Stavus. Here Winged Women clad in the purest white tracked a swirl; there a Hawk's-Eye made note of a far-flung leaf spiraling to the ground. A priest of the faith of the Twins was present, but only one. The Gorgostrine sat his old and bony ass on an outcropping of rock, leaving it to the servants of Stavus to track the thousand falling portents.

A handful of soldiers, king's men, stood to the side. Bored.

When at last the leaves landed, the pious collected them. Unlike their dried and decaying counterparts, the large leaves of the Yubriy tree remained supple even after their descent, so that when the hands of the holy gathered them up, they remained intact. A dark, honeyed orange, the seven-pointed leaves were a testament to the wonder of Stavus's—or, if you were a believer in the Twins, Beoliotius's—design. Dutiful eyes did their best to ignore the veins of spider-webbed silver that sometimes spelled out words on the leaves' skin, but even the most devout found it difficult to be entirely pure. The thrill of sinning, however, was short-lived. What was written on the leaves was either nonsensical, mundane, written in an unfamiliar language, or, most common of all, not words at all, but rather a design that was merely word-*like*, the mischief of a deity with too much time on their hands. It was said that the king's bastard brother could see messages in the leaves that others could not, but he was not here, and even if he were, it was widely known that he did not share his findings. Disappointed, the holy men and women put away their ungodly wonderings and went back to collecting the leaves, growing increasingly less curious about what they might see.

Their charge was to collect, if possible, every leaf. Fortunately, once the Yubriy tree began shedding its bounty, it rarely took more than eight hours for the remainder to fall. There were trying years when the great abscission began in the dark of the night, but this year—two hundred and forty-two years after the great union of the Struvan and Ontish peoples— the leaves blessedly began falling in the middle of a clear and cloudless day. A gentle wind pushed a few of the leaves outside the great circle of the gathered, but, all in all, the collecting was a simple ordeal. After a time, the number of people on hand began to seem excessive. Ten would have sufficed. Perhaps as few as five. There was no need for the forty who were present.

By late afternoon, it was possible to count the number of leaves that remained attached to the tree. The tally dwindled as the great molten sun settled into the horizon, the skyline blurring into a smoldering palette. Five holdouts could be seen at the onset of the gloaming, silhouetted against the incipient starry sky.

A soldier offered to climb the Yubriy to harvest the remainder. *No,* said one of the Hawk's-Eyes. *A plucked Yubriy leaf tells no tale.* The soldier nodded, abashed that he had forgotten this simple truth: the silvery scrawls that foretold both past and future didn't appear on the leaves until the moment of abscission. To that end, the forty stood and patiently waited while the dark took hold.

A bright and glorious moon ascended into the heavens. Another gift from Stavus.

One of the leaves fell. Every eye followed its descent as it drifted gently into the waiting hands of a Winged Woman.

Then, without warning, a mighty wind kicked up out of the west. Leaves from the nearby woods blew into the ranks, while high in the branches of the Yubriy tree the four remaining leaves took flight, gusting upward before spiraling, twisting, swirling, and ultimately joining a happy chorus of baseborn leaves from lesser trees. Together the leaves sang a papery song on the wind, and together they flew Stavus knew where.

The search promptly began in earnest. Lanterns were lit in the deepening dark as the holy men and women spread out to find the Yubriy leaves. Almost immediately, a Hawk's-Eye located one of the leaves on the edge of the woods. Hope blossomed that perhaps all four would be found in the short grass. But fruitless minutes soon became fruitless hours. Around midnight, the Gorgostrine, lantern-less, produced a second leaf from an area well clear of where the others were looking. A few of the sons and daughters of Stavus were silently suspicious that the Gorgostrine had simply produced a leaf found earlier that day, but none gave voice to their doubt. Bone-tired, all agreed that it was best to stop and resume the search in the clear light of day.

The lot retired to the staked tents where they had kept watch over the Yubriy tree for nearly a week, waiting for the leaves to fall.

In the morning the search resumed. The third leaf was found at midday, bedded down fifty yards deep in the woods. Heartened, half of the group concentrated their efforts near the spot, fanning out in ever-widening circles while the other half roamed far afield, mindful of the manifold potentialities of the wind.

But it was to no avail. Hours passed, and the last and final leaf still wasn't found.

At dusk, the pious men and women reconvened. The Gorgostrine, sensing that a Stavusian prayer was in the offing, returned to his rock. The soldiers approached the group and swore to attest that the holy men and women had fulfilled their vow to the best of their ability. A consensus was quickly reached. But before ending the search, the sons and daughters of Stavus felt it incumbent to make a show of their good virtue. They turned west, knelt, and asked for reaffirmation from the setting sun.

To the surprise of no one, Stavus gave the go-ahead to stop.

The tents were used one last time. In the morning, the Gorgostrine, a Hawk's-Eye, and a Winged Woman divided the burden of carrying the three leather bags in which the Yubriy leaves had been collected. Together with a few of the soldiers, they began making their way south toward Union—the capital city of Ragar Or and the seat of King Micah Dayborn.

The remaining servants of Stavus packed up the tents and returned to their homes, Stavusian temples spread throughout the Vake.

The Yubriy tree, its twisting silver-brown trunk blossoming into a hundred newly bare branches, watched from nearby. Dormant prophecies rested in its timeless soul, waiting to manifest the following autumn.

In the nearby woods, fallen in a tree hollow, lay the undetected leaf.

Johanna Salk

From her place on the raised platform, Johanna could see that the evening had turned. Wine that once filled pewter cups now bloomed angrily on men's cheeks. Voices grew boisterous as conversations became snarled in passions. Eyes cut like knives toward the guest of dishonor— the captured Blackstar prince. Even the songs had soured: the lutist summoned dirge after brooding dirge, stoking the discontent.

They're angry at King Micah, Johanna thought, looking at the empty seat at the center of the table. *When he got stuck in the snow, he spoiled their fun.* Against her better judgment, Johanna risked a glance at the Blackstar prince at the table's end. To her chagrin, Axton Boil looked as hale as he had when her father's men first marched him into the feast. *Why are you still alive? I gave you the means to end your life. What are you waiting for?*

Needing a distraction, Johanna turned to her sister, Wulfess, who was sitting beside her. Wulfess sat loftily in her seat, holding her spine the way a skilled archer holds a bow: with a perfect, steadied tautness. Her dark blonde hair poured off her head like a golden waterfall against a backdrop of slate. Johanna knew that Wulfess was as aware of the changing mood in the hall as she was, but, if anything, Wulfess seemed more at ease than before.

The Twin Ascendant, indeed.

"The men want to kill the Blackstar prince tonight," Johanna leaned over and whispered to Wulfess. "They don't want to wait for the king."

"Of course they want to kill him," Wulfess responded. "They're Ontish, aren't they?"

That they were. Johanna scanned the hall. Nearly all the great Ontish houses were present. The Coffyns. The Garstrings. The Mocks. The Dyerhelms. The Burntrees. The Qorls. Ontish surnames all, although, in most cases, enough Struvan blood was mixed in as to make no difference. Except for the Ollspaers, of course. They were the only clan that had never interbonded, not even after Union.

A tradition that would soon come to an end.

"Do you think—" Johanna started to say to her sister, but Wulfess had turned away from her to talk to Cato Ollspaer, the overgrown man-bear from Kalandragote. The heir apparent to the wintry kingdom had bent his ear to better hear his betrothed, and though there wasn't a grin on his rough-bearded face, he did appear amused. *She isn't the least bit scared of him,* Johanna thought, watching with awe as Wulfess worked flirtatious fingers into the brown-and-white fur of Cato's great wolfskin coat. Wulfess had always possessed a fearlessness in keeping with her position as the Twin Ascendant, but even Johanna was amazed to see her sister take so adeptly to the task of beguiling her future bonded, a man whose savage exploits were known throughout Ragar Or. Johanna had wept for Wulfess the night she heard her sister was to bond a man who had participated in the twin-death rite when he was only a boy, but if Wulfess had shed tears, Johanna hadn't seen them.

Johanna settled back into her seat, trying her best not to look the way that she felt, like a traitor to her family. *I'm not a traitor,* she told herself.

It's only...I knew Axton. We kissed once, on the banks of the Dezoe River. He followed me there. He called me the twin of his choosing. Frustrated, she bit the inside of her cheek until she tasted blood. Why hadn't everything gone according to plan? She had slipped the Blackstar prince pearl dust, a painless and fast-acting poison, in the hopes that he'd be dead within minutes of her leaving his cell. But no. He was still alive, apparently determined to die in the grand barbaric fashion. *I never should have slipped him the poison. It was a rash and stupid thing to do.* She had had her reasons, though—reasons other than repaying the debt incurred by the Blackstar prince's young affections years ago. Since entering Low Osgood, Johanna's father and sister had monopolized the family business of politics, leaving her out entirely. Every day, she could feel the promises and pacts they were making hovering around her like unclean spirits. Giving Axton Boil an easy death was Johanna's way of balancing the scales: lesser twin or not, she would not be shut out of the story of her own life.

"The braised elk isn't to your liking?" queried Egros Coffyn, interrupting Johanna's worrying. Egros was the man in whose castle they were staying. Despite this fact, Egros was seated to Johanna's right, even farther from the seat of the absent king than she. Not that Egros was cowed by Johanna. He made that apparent by poking at the food left on her plate with his own dirtied fork, and, in doing so, making true the suggestion implied by his question.

"It's delicious. It's only...I'm full."

Hearing that, Egros brought his knife into the mix, cutting off a choice piece from the largely untouched meat. He stuffed it into his mouth with an indelicate gusto. "My nephew Darry felled this very elk on

Coffyn grounds three miles east of here," Egros explained, retelling a story that Johanna had already heard from Egros's own lips. She was tempted to spoil his fun by reminding him, but the truth of it was she was grateful for the distraction. "Enormous beast. Darry dropped him with one arrow straight to the heart. A natural hunter, my nephew. He is the heir to Coffyn Castle, you know, and all of Low Osgood as well." Egros was sterile—all three of his wives, two of whom were widows proven fertile, had failed to produce an heir—but unlike most men, this didn't cause him to avoid conversation that referred to the fact.

Johanna knew where Egros was heading. Johanna might have been newly widowed and the lesser twin, but she was still a Salk, which made her a choice match for Darry Coffyn. No doubt Egros thought Johanna might hold some sway over her father when it came time for the selection.

He was wrong, of course. But she didn't have to let him know that.

"The future lord of Low Osgood," Johanna cooed. Her sister wasn't the only one who knew how to flirt. "Whoever bonds your nephew will be fortunate indeed." She more than half meant it. She knew little of Darry Coffyn, but chances were he was as good a choice as any of the men her father might bond her to, and she could do worse than becoming the lady of Low Osgood. There were worse fates than spending the remainder of her days sailing on the glimmering magnificence of Lake Wyglass. Low Osgood was the gem of the historically Ontish cities, civilized and tourist-friendly; plus it attracted enough visitors from the south that it genuinely felt like a city of the realm, and not merely an Ontish enclave. *I might choose your nephew for myself at this very moment if I could leave my father out of it,* Johanna thought. Not that leaving Daguss Salk out of it was an option. Johanna might have been the lesser twin, but she was still a *sennequi* piece in her father's larger game, which meant, ultimately, that she would be played.

"Yes, yes, they will be fortunate!" Egros agreed, forcing the words past a stout defense of masticated meat. "I've been meaning to broach the matter of finding Darry a suitable bonding with your father, but there's hardly a minute where he's indisposed. If the Qorls don't have him cornered, then it's the Dyerhelms. If it's not the Dyerhelms, it's the Mocks. If King Micah ever arrives, I imagine he'll have to queue up for a word with your father as well."

"Father is in high demand," Johanna agreed.

"He is Lord Daguss Salk, I suppose," Egros continued. "Everyone knows the power of the Salk name. You know it yourself, don't you, young lady? All those Salk kings and queens of yore. I would bet half the men with their nose up your father's ass would make him king of all Ragar Or for two shakes of a Qorlish donkey."

Without turning to look, Johanna could see her father in her mind's eye farther down the table, sitting on the other side of Cato Ollspaer. He was no doubt holding his familiar pose: white-forest chin in hand, body listing to the left, ever scanning, ever surveying, like a raptor high in the limbs. Johanna's uncle told her that when her father was a boy, he was called the crow-hawk—the Salk family crest was three crows perched on a tree limb—but when Daguss ascended to the head of the family, he put an end to the nickname, on account of the hawk being one of the chief symbols of the Stavusian faith. The Salk kings and queens of yesteryear might have paid homage to the god of the hawk and the sun, but Daguss Salk was an adherent of the faith of the Twins.

"Father is a loyal servant of the Dayborn king," Johanna replied carefully. For all she knew, he was. Treason wasn't a matter that Daguss discussed with Johanna.

"As are we all," Egros responded. "But between you and me and the Yubriy tree, any dynasty not named Salk will always be illegitimate in the eyes of some."

Johanna wondered if Egros Coffyn was drunk.

"Please forgive me if I speak too freely, Lady Johanna. I am a little drunk. But, as you can see, I'm not the only one."

Johanna followed Egros's nodding forehead to the benches, where Reginal Burntree was staggering to his feet. Like all the Burntrees, there was a haunted aspect to Reginal's character, an effect seemingly produced by the amalgam of his lean build, wiry beard, and pale green eyes. The effect was intensified by Reginal's drunkenness: Reginal stumbled toward the platform like a specter intending to petition the gods to address grievances from a past life.

High above Reginal, in the great glass dome above the hall, the snow clouds momentarily parted, permitting a bone-sickle moon to shine through.

"Your highness!" Reginal shouted, raising a wine-filled cup toward King Micah's empty seat. The assembled took great pleasure in Reginal's mocking toast. Coarse laughter spilled from what moments ago had been pursed, angry lips.

"Our king is not with us," Daguss replied from the platform.

Reginal nodded dumbly, like he had only now realized. "Oh. Aye. The snows. I had nearly forgotten."

That scornful laughter again. Wulfess joined in, but Johanna couldn't summon the spirit.

Reginal continued, "Do you think His Grace would mind if we carried on the feast without him? And by carry on, I mean gutting and spitting that sea rooster sitting at the end of the table." Reginal suddenly produced a dirk and pointed it menacingly at the Blackstar prince. "The sight of that proud little shit offends my eyes."

"Axton Boil rose in rebellion against the Dayborn kingship," Daguss calmly replied. "Therefore, he is King Micah's captive."

Reginal Burntree hocked a great gob and made as if to spit, but didn't. Instead, with his head turned, he began to solemnly nod, giving the impression that he had come around to Daguss's way of thinking.

Then he abruptly stopped.

"The Blackstar prince may have risen in rebellion against the Dayborns, but it wasn't Dayborn blood that was shed bringing him to heel. No. It was Garstring blood. Qorl blood. Mock blood. Dyerhelm blood. Coffyn blood. Burntree blood. Salk blood." After each surname, Reginal gave a pause, letting each house shout in turn. After *Salk*, he paused the longest, letting the tension build. *"Ontish blood,"* Reginal finished at last. With those words the entire hall joined in, every soul shouting and stamping their feet.

Daguss waited until the ruckus died down of its own accord. He was playing the calm man now, Johanna knew, the great Lord Salk. Daguss the Unruffled, his admirers liked to call him. *But you're not entirely at peace, are you, Father?* Johanna thought. Since the death of Johanna's bonded and her subsequent return to High Osgood, Johanna had seen firsthand the strain her father was under. He had played a long and patient game with the advantages his surname had to offer, and, at long last, it seemed his pieces were in position. But reaching this moment had brought him no peace. In private, he was a coil of tightly wound nerves. Johanna knew that better than anyone.

"True," Daguss admitted, a sly smile spreading across his face. "It was Ontish blood that brought this oath breaker to heel. Nevertheless, he is not ours to kill." A smattering of grumbles. "But I *am* of the mind that he is ours to bleed."

The men raised a cheer so loud that Johanna wondered if the glass dome might shatter.

Amid the hubbub, Johanna risked another glance at the Blackstar prince. Axton Boil sat alone at the table's end, his legs bound to the chair with heavy rope, his arms and hands free. He looked the same to Johanna as he had when he was a devilish teen, hunting her down for a kiss. His hair was a sea of black waves, his eyes a pool of light, his expression twisted with dark amusement.

He may look like the boy I once knew, but now he's a man in full, and dangerous. He showed me that in his cell. Beneath the long sleeves of Johanna's blue samite gown, her right wrist was raw with pain, a present from the Blackstar earlier that day. "Take the vial," she had commanded him, refusing to give in to the fear that Axton might reach through the cell bars with his opposite hand and choke the life out of her. "It's pearl dust. A painless poison. Use it to end your life. If not, they'll serve you an Ontish supper, and you'll wish you had." Still, he held her captive a moment longer before plucking the vial from her fingers and releasing her wrist. Free, she turned and fled, knowing the guard would soon return from his morning constitutional. Leading up to the visit, Johanna had imagined all manner of words the Blackstar might gift her in exchange for the poison, but in the end she won no prize from his lips; instead, he left her with only a burning ring of flesh around her wrist.

The men in the hall pressed forward, eager to see the Blackstar suffer. A rope was tossed onto the platform to loud cheers. *Father said bleed the Blackstar, not strangle him, you fools.* Daguss stood and unsheathed the dagger on his hip, a Clyesian beauty of a blade that he had named Talon. Cato, Daguss's future son-in-law, stood in turn, cracking his knuckles. Together they made the short stroll to where the guest of dishonor was seated at the table's end.

The Blackstar prince watched them approach with characteristic insouciance. Then, to the surprise of all, his voice boomed across the hall.

"Have you served me my Ontish supper, Lord Salk?"

Daguss weighed the Blackstar's words. Johanna understood the question behind the question. What Axton really wanted to know was if he had been served his last meal.

"You may sit another meal, once King Micah arrives. But I can't promise that after tonight you'll be able to eat it."

The Blackstar nodded. Johanna thought he possessed a terrible beauty in that moment, some combined effect made possible by his aquiline nose, impenitent voice, and steely, fatalistic demeanor. She had heard the men talk of his unsettling prowess in battle, the way he transformed into an entity that seemed near inhuman. *He warred like one of Werring's demons, escaped from the Sky Ends to bring death to the sons of the Twins.* But to Johanna he looked closer to a Stavusian angel than a demon. *We might have been together in a different life,* she thought. *I would have been the twin of your choosing. You, my Blackstar prince.* But in this world the choice had never been theirs.

Shortly after their teenage kiss, Johanna had been sent south by her father to bond the ill-fated Nicolas Raleigh, while the Blackstar prince had returned home to be groomed by his father to lead a doomed rebellion.

"Then I trust that you'll keep to Ontish custom and honor my last request while I'm of sound body and mind to make it."

Daguss Salk narrowed his gaze at the Blackstar. The many candles in the hall cast soft notes of reflected light off Daguss's clean-shaven skull, before disappearing in the dense morass of his frosted white beard. "I'll hear your request. As to whether I'll honor it—well, that depends."

"It's a simple request. I want to make a proper Ontish toast. In honor of the highest lord in the hall."

Bells of warning sounded in Johanna's mind. *A proper Ontish toast. He'll drink from the same cup as father.* She had no way of knowing if pearl dust had been mixed with the grape.

Daguss turned his palms to the sky, managing to look both munificent and powerful. A silver-gray moonbear coat hung from his shoulders, while a silver chain of ponderous weight dangled from his neck. "By all means then, let's hear it."

To Johanna's right, Egros Coffyn leaned in, still chewing on elk. "Can't say I'm not curious to hear what the sea monkey has to say." He wasn't the only one. Looking around the hall, Johanna could see that the men's bloodlust had returned to a simmer, no longer boiling.

When the Blackstar began speaking, his voice was a strong peal of thunder. "One month ago, I sailed my fleet around the Cape of the Dying Suns, returning in glory from our western raids. My father was already dead, but I didn't know it at the time. What I knew was riches, glory, victory. The Blackstar ascendant."

A handful grumbled at this bit of sacrilege, but no one interrupted.

Johanna stared hard at Axton's cup, trying to see through pewter.

The condemned man continued, "We were sailing within sight of the coasts, our sails bearing us back east, when, to the south, a monstrous shadow swallowed one of the black cliffs along the cape. I turned, nearly stumbling on deck, while all around me men bellowed and shouted. When I saw with my own eyes, I thought I had died. There, high above the cliff, flew a dragon."

A dragon? All around, the news was unevenly received. Johanna furrowed her forehead, dubious. One of the Qorls shouted, "Liar!", but the majority of the men simply murmured to one another, trying to parse the rather strange direction the toast had taken. Where was Axton going with this? It had been sixty-eight years since a dragon had been sighted on Ragar Or—the year the last Salk king died. Ontish ears weren't simply going to accept news of a dragon sighting from the guest of dishonor at an Ontish supper.

Which, Johanna knew, made the dragon no more or less real.

"I thought the dragon a sign," the Blackstar prince continued, unfazed by the doubt. "A sign of the rightness of the Blackstar cause. They say the last dragon, the Ice Ghost, visited Kalandragote because he favored the Ontish line. This, I thought, was my father's dragon, come to usher in the Blackstar era. The beast was even black and green, the colors of the Blackstar Isles."

Axton Boil's expression turned wistful, resigned. The hall grew quiet. It was evident that the Blackstar prince had won a few believers.

"But the dragon flew on," Axton continued, returning to the here and now. "Storms swept us ashore at Pecking Knot, where I lost half my fleet and learned that my father had perished swimming the Night Channel. Grieving, I made mistakes. I ordered the raid on Dunning Harbor. I kept my eyes to the skies, searching for the dragon, instead of peeled to the shoreline, scanning for my foes. The Ontish knot closed. And now I sit here before you, a dead man, with naught left to do in this world but make a final toast."

The Blackstar prince raised his cup. But not to Daguss Salk, as Johanna had expected, but rather toward the shadowy back of the hall, where the benches blurred into gloom. "To the family for whom the dragon soars. To the good graces of Stavus, and the cleansing forgiveness of the sun. May I be judged fairly and swiftly by a son who knows what it means to honor his father. To Prince Easton—I dedicate this toast, and submit my life, to you. The highest lord in the hall."

He jests, Johanna thought. But, along with a hundred others, she whipped her head across the great hall to where an alcove harbored the back benches.

Sitting beside Johanna, Wulfess gave a nasty little laugh.

A young man emerged from the darkness of the alcove into the glass dome's soft late autumn light. He wore a snow-dusted blood-orange cloak over a quilted doublet of dark gray wool, and gray woolen breeches atop high leather riding boots. A brooch made of two suns pinned the cloak in place. His head was covered by a sensible cap of somewhat intemperate brown hair. He stood a little taller than most men, and he carried himself with a lightness of being that looked unsuited to the moment.

He was Easton Dayborn, the second son of King Micah Dayborn, and second in line to the Union throne.

"A dragon, you say?" Easton declaimed once the hall had drunk their fill of him. "I'll drink to that."

The assembled parted in a seemingly delayed display of deference as Prince Easton approached the platform. Daguss Salk sheathed his dagger. Here and there men found their knees, but most of the Ontish remained standing, befuddled spectators. With a spry leap, Easton bounded onto the platform. To the prince's right, the Blackstar sat offering his toast, while across the table and to Easton's left, Daguss Salk worked hard to master his expression.

Johanna stood up without thinking. Beside her, Egros whispered, "Sit down, child. I cannot see!"

"Prince Easton, when did you—" Daguss began, but the Blackstar prince interrupted, his eyes afire with the urgency of the moment. "To the king's justice!" he exclaimed. He knocked back half the contents of the cup, then extended the pewter chalice to Easton.

Johanna watched. The Blackstar's eyes betrayed him. When Easton took the cup, Axton's eyes flitted in her direction.

"No! Don't drink it!" Johanna's own voice sounded foreign to her, a madwoman's shrill singing, and yet it sounded again and again as she rushed down the length of the massive oak table to where the Prince of Ragar Or stood, cup in hand.

Easton Dayborn, his eyes perched above where his lips rested on the rim of the cup, paused as Johanna approached. Keeping the cup on its vertical plane, he slowly pulled it back from his lips and returned it to the table.

All eyes went to the Blackstar prince. Johanna, breathing heavily, saw that Axton's gaze—so sparing all night—now fell on her in full. It was bright, steady, the first star in the firmament on a crisp and cold eve. "I had hoped that you might grant me the gift of your silence, in honor of the kiss we shared years ago," he said. "But still, I thank you for the kiss." He turned to the room, his lips hardening into a sneer. "My story of the dragon is true. May he devour you all."

Then, as if a winter storm had started up inside of him, the Blackstar's liquid blue eyes froze over, and he breathed his last.

Slowly, the gaze of every person in the room turned toward Johanna.

Silas O' the Songs

"Listen to me, Silas."

Silas's name sounded like a reproach on Gay Gracie's tongue. He preferred it when she said his name like a prayer, the way she did when they were intertwined in the throes of passion, but it had been a long time since he'd heard his name used in that fashion. *She pities me for my stubbornness,* Silas thought. *And pity makes for a poor aphrodisiac.*

Gay Gracie continued, "Sing 'The Pickleberry Wench.' Sing 'The Good King, The Bad King, The Dead King.' For Stavus's sake, sing 'She Loves Cream, He Loves Pie,' but, for the love I once bore you, don't sing one of your songs." She took his face in her hands and gave him a heartfelt look. "It's not that they're bad. But they're not fit for the Swans. They don't have enough...life."

Silas acknowledged Gay Gracie's barb with a pained smile. His ever-diligent left hand kept at the tuning pegs on the lute, while the right teased music into the air. "You wound me, Gracie. But as I've told you before, I see no purpose in spending the remainder of my days playing the parrot. Look around the room. There are parrots a' plenty as is." Silas thumbed at the other hopefuls in the room: a handful of wretched fiddlers, a lyrist and a flutist, a lutist he didn't know and a lutist he did (but wished he didn't), and an unnervingly beautiful woman holding a half harp. "They will all play and sing passingly good, and they will all play and sing one of the standards. I'll play and sing better than most, but I won't outshine Felix Fingers. So if I want to join the king's own musical and acting company, I had best give them something original. Something that's mine. And *that* is what I intend to do."

Gracie released Silas's face and put her hands on her hips. She gave him a look like she was about to bid him a bittersweet goodbye—one slightly more sweet than bitter. "Which song do you intend to play? 'Ballad of the Cruel Sister'?"

"Yes." He did his best not to wince.

She reached out her hand once more and gave his face a quick caress. She had the hands of a serving wench: strong, thick, with flour-frosted fingers, but caring, too, full of genuine affection. "It's a good song, Silas. One of your best. But it's not a song for tonight. And it won't win you a place with the Swans."

Silas withdrew his cheek and turned away. "Leave me, Gracie."

When he faced forward once more, she was gone. Back into the dark of the kitchen, where half of the village was working to meet the night's demand.

Silas took a deep breath. Resumed his tuning. Humming a note from 'Ballad of the Cruel Sister,' he cast his gaze hither and yon, observing the myriad differences tonight's audition had wrought in this most familiar of taverns. Silas had played in The Golden Pear a hundred times, but never on a stage, never with multiple musicians in the room, and never to an audience of greater than twenty-five people. Earlier in the week, Gracie's brother Sawyer had fashioned a gorgeous cedarwood platform for the performers to stand on, and now scores were crowded around the circular stage, waiting for the show to begin. More tallow candles than Silas could count burned black shadows on the tavern's back walls. And up front, seated at a table stage right, sat three talent scouts for the Swans, clad in cloth of black and white.

"Are you nervous?"

Silas turned to find himself face-to-face with one of the wretched fiddlers, a pox-scarred gent he'd never seen before. That was another difference about tonight. Usually, The Golden Pear was full of familiar faces. But tonight, the familiars were making coin in the kitchen, and the common room was packed with visitors from all over the Vake, like the fellow before him.

Silas made his voice as calm as a moonlit pond. "I am."

"Ha ha!" the man chirruped, his face scrunching into a most unattractive spasm of joy. He had a beard that looked like the fur coat of a gangrenous vole, and silver-brown hair that hung from his scalp in ragged ropes. "As am I! Honesty befits you, I believe. The name's Wyn Dunkin. And you are?"

Silas extended his playing hand. "Silas Rowbry. Also known as Silas O' the Songs."

Wyn's eyes widened, revealing a bramble of red arteries. "Silas O' the Songs, he says! Would those be the same songs we'll all be singing, or are you inferring that the Melodies speak to you directly?" The Melodies was the name given to the spirits that inspired songwriters. Silas had always heard that the spirits were Struvan in origin, although there were those who claimed that the Melodies originated from an Ontish legend about two sisters named Gia and Blue.

"Directly. I write and sing my own songs." Silas kept his eyes and voice level. He was twenty-five years old, hardened enough to know better than to equivocate when speaking about his talents to a fellow musician. He had a good voice, but there were better singers. He played the lute with aplomb, but he'd come across those whose fingers finessed a tighter tune. What made Silas different was his songs. He would not deny them, even if others would.

"And will we be hearing one of your songs tonight?"

"Yes." Silas squirmed uncomfortably on the wooden bench. He could sense his tongue yearning to say more, overpowering the voice in his head telling him to shut his mouth. It was a failing of his. "'Ballad of the Cruel Sister.' It's a song about the daughter of the first Salk king."

Wyn clapped his hands and danced a little jig. "I've heard of her! A hellion, that one! Aris…no, Abi…no, what *was* her name—"

"Anis."

"Anis! Yes, Anis Salk! Oh, my boy, that's a doozy of a tale, if you don't mind me saying. She was a jeyedoshi, wasn't she? Killed her sister and bonded the son of her father's mortal enemy and seduced a dragon, am I right?"

The sheer amount of incorrect information pouring out of the fiddler's mouth was difficult to process. A truth had slipped in there somewhere, but now, in the aftermath, Silas struggled to parse it. "No, I mean, yes. I mean…look, my friend, you've made a mess of it. Anis *tried* to kill her sister Rebecca, the one who bonded Brogan and later became queen. But she wasn't successful."

"Brogan the First! The fellow on the golden coin! A brogan's-head goes to the winner tonight, you know," Wyn said, tapping his foot.

"Yes, I do know." Silas was flustered. He knew an inordinate amount about the history of the realm, and it made him feel panicked when false information needed to be set to rights. "Listen—Anis Salk wasn't jeyedoshi. If she had been jeyedoshi her attempts to 'tame' the dragon they called White Morning might have been successful, but, as it was, the dragon burned her to a crisp. You *were* right, however, in saying that she bonded the son of her father's mortal enemy. She bonded an Arc."

Wyn squinted at Silas, all the while keeping an imaginary beat with his feet. "Arc? Like our liege lords?"

Silas felt a pang of regret at having ventured down this path. The memory of his time spent playing for the Arcs at Castle Greenwell still rankled, enough that the mere mention of the dominant family in the Vake made him agitated. Even when he had been the one to mention them. "Yes. Like our liege lords."

Wyn's foot-tapping changed over into a sort of all-body twitching. He took his bow and fiddle—which until now had swung from his left hand like an afterthought—and quickly moved into a musical position, slashing a series of strangely compelling notes into existence. Finished, he bore a wild smile. "Gratifying as this conversation has been, I fear I need to take my leave of you. Inspiration strikes, and so must I while the iron is hot. All the best to you, Silas O' the Songs." And with the pretend doff of a nonexistent hat, Wyn Dunkin hurried away, possibly going outside.

The exchange with Wyn left Silas feeling unsettled. *There was something of the rat about him,* Silas thought. *A manic, jittery, thieving rodent.* In a sudden panic, Silas patted at his ankle, where he kept a coin purse tied tight beneath his woolen breeches. The coins were still there, but it didn't dispel Silas's anxiety the way he had hoped. Before he could ruminate further on the reason for his disquiet, one of the Swans stood and moved to the cedarwood stage.

The crowd hushed. The musicians, scattered in the back, stopped worrying at their instruments. Silas surveyed the candlelit crowd. They were a cheery, ale-addled lot, many of them friends of the musicians, but a sprinkling of lesser nobility was likewise present, minor lords and ladies of the Vake who had caught wind of the Swans' arrival and were present for entertainment's sake. The Lady Ghent and her bastard half brother, known carousers, stood near the front, their faces shiny with drink; while standing to the right of the stage with bowed shoulders was Philemon Yurk, the estranged trueborn son of Lord Delton Yurk. It was said that Philemon continued to make money in spite of the fact that his father had disowned him: he knew a sorcery for accruing wealth, and, from the look of his rich velvet cloak, had yet to stop dabbling in the arts. *No doubt he has money on the night's winner,* Silas thought moodily. He could only assume that Philemon had placed his bet on Felix Fingers.

Onstage, the Swan addressed the crowd. "Good evening." The man was tall and skinny with a large beaked nose. He wore a sumptuous white cloak offset by a black hem, and he spoke with the effortlessly deep baritone of a god. "I am Adolphus Morto, of King Micah Dayborn's own acting and musical company, the Swans. While the king progresses north to put an end to the Blackstar rebellion, we players three are scouring Ragar Or in search of true talent to add to our ranks. By day, we hold auditions for prospective actors, and by night we frequent the halls and fair inns of our glorious realm in the hopes of hearing a musician gifted enough to bring back to court. Our successes, as you might imagine, are few and far between."

He paused, permitting a downcast beat. "But hope springs eternal. By the munificence of His Majesty King Micah, the most talented musician to step foot on stage tonight will be rewarded with a brogan's-head. If we truly like what we hear—and, to be clear, we rarely do—we will extend an offer for the musician to return south with us and join the Swans."

Adolphus paused, permitting the electric murmur in the crowd to dissipate. "Before we begin, I would like to speak directly to any prospective thieves in the audience." He stared sharply down at the audience from the towering heights of his beaked nose. "The Swans travel with three knights of the king's own guard"—he paused once more, allowing three swordsmen in the audience to bark out the Dayborn motto: *The Sun Forever Rises*—"as well as two very silent and stealthy assassins"—another pause, this time followed by an eerie silence—"so, if you're of a mind to lose your life this evening, by all means, do try and steal from the king's own purse." Adolphus smiled, a long, curving scythe of a grin that distracted the audience from the sleight of hand that produced a mean dagger in his right palm. Seeing the dagger, the audience ooooohed, then broke into a round of applause.

Adolphus gave a little bow. "Let the show begin."

Silas took a deep breath, trying to suppress the sudden churning of butterflies in his stomach. Having drawn seventh position, his turn on stage wouldn't come for some time, but that knowledge did little to quell the rising fear that tonight, like so many prior nights, would end in professional failure.

The night's first player took the stage. A flautist. Silas put down his lute and took a sip of ale, hoping to temper his nerves. As good as the ale was, its calming effect paled in comparison to hearing the first notes of the performance: a series of charmingly trite sounds issued from the flute, the opening notes of "The Pickleberry Wench." The crowd, happy to hear the familiar melody, instantly fell under the song's spell; together, they swayed contentedly in the mild haze of collective inebriation. *Good, Silas* thought. *A gratified crowd is better than a restless one. It will make them more amenable to what I have to offer.* The flautist's talent was average at best, not that the crowd appeared capable of such subtle discernment. The assembled sang raucously along, eagerly providing the vocal accompaniment. It wasn't long before the sound of the singing grew so loud that the flute was drowned out. Silas could no longer see the Swans sitting near the front of the stage, but he trusted that they were unimpressed by what was transpiring. *Stavus bless them, they've likely suffered through a similar rendition in every inn they've visited.*

At last, the flute became audible once more, finishing out of time to the audience's drunken singalong. This in no way diminished the cheers once the song ended. While the flautist took his bows and soaked in the applause, Silas let his eyes wander, searching for his true competition. He found Felix Fingers sitting on one of the back benches on the opposite side of the room. Predictably, Felix was cradling the Wrainish lute in his arm like a mother holding a swaddled babe. The instrument was doubly protected by the curtain of Felix's long, dark tresses, which fell around the lute like gentle vines.

Silas forced himself to look away. *Put Felix from your mind. Felix will play what Felix will play, and you will do the same.* Oh, but he knew what Felix would play. Not an original. No. Felix would take a well-known song and transform it into something transcendent. Silas could see it now: the crowd watching with a hushed reverence as Felix worked a myriad of subtle changes to embody the song's new spirit—grace notes and tempo changes and unexpected stops gathering together in a storm of delicate grace—until, once the crowd was in Felix's thrall, the song would unexpectedly reclaim its customary form, and the response would be all the wilder for it.

Silas knew because he'd seen Felix do it before. At Greenwell Castle. On the day Anna Josephine Arc dismissed Silas from the Arc family's service.

Onstage, the first of the fiddlers took up her bow. She was a local lass by the name of Jia Brinks, a kindhearted soul who looked exceedingly nervous. Silas was familiar with her talent—Jia could play half a hundred songs on command, and often did so at village dances—but tonight she appeared hard-pressed to remember one. She started up an unrecognizable tune. When it was time for her voice to join in, the words wouldn't come. Whatever goodwill had been fostered by the flautist's performance was soon squandered as boos began to rain down on poor Jia's head. She rushed from the stage in tears before the song had even reached the chorus.

Silas considered chasing after Jia. There were few familiar faces present; he knew that if he didn't comfort her, no one would. He was rising to his feet to go after her, when, in a blur of ratty vigor, Wyn Dunkin passed by Jia from the opposite direction and made for the front of the house. *Has he been outside this entire time?* Silas wondered. His impulse to kindness quickly forgotten, Silas shifted his attention to the dirty little man who was next on the stage.

Wyn bounded onto the cedarwood platform with a spry little hop. He held his fiddle by its neck with all the care one might impart to a strangled tomcat. Quickly taking his measure of the crowd, Wyn graced the assembled with a gap-toothed grin, and then, sensing that they needed additional encouragement, he danced the same impromptu jig he'd danced in front of Silas. This won him a quotient of laughter. Satisfied, Wyn lifted his fiddle and bowstring into the air, bugged his eyes, and bellowed his introduction.

"Good evening, ladies and gents! The name's Wyn Dunkin, and tonight I mean to perform for you a song of an original nature, one that the Melodies communicated to me only minutes ago. It's a song inspired by the evil doings of King Daguss the Unifier's daughter, the one who seduced a dragon and killed the queen- to-be."

Wyn peered out into the dark of the crowd. Silas could have sworn the little man was looking directly at him. "I call it 'Ballad of the Cruel Sister.'"

Silas struggled to process what was taking place, but try as he might, there was no way to deny the proof of his ears and eyes: the fidgety, scruffy, pox-scarred fiddler whose acquaintance Silas had made no more than fifteen minutes earlier was onstage playing Silas's song.

It wasn't *actually* Silas's song, of course. Wyn's composition was an altogether different animal. Silas thought of his version as elegant, somber, and historically accurate. In contrast, Wyn's was colorfully frenetic, unapologetically bawdy, and riddled with near as many factual inaccuracies as words. Not to mention that it was no longer a ballad! Worst of all, however, was that Wyn's version was…more enjoyable than Silas's. Silas was generally reticent to think about songs in such simple terms, but the truth of it was undeniable. Wyn's version wasn't as technically difficult, nor did it have Silas's melodic grace, but even after listening to it for less than a minute, Silas knew in his heart of hearts that Wyn had crafted—in the space of fifteen minutes no less!—the more compelling tune.

The crowd certainly liked it. Upon hearing the refrain once—*"that witch Anis, seduced the beast!"*—the audience chimed in the second go-around, freeing Wyn to elaborate with the fiddle. Wyn, for his part, played the instrument with a studied recklessness: he drove the song's narrative with short, percussive strokes of the bow, only to draw out a series of intriguing notes the moment the singing stopped. Angry as Silas was, the musician in him was impressed. Fiddlers weren't typically known for singing and playing at the same time, and here this fellow was making hay of a belter without turning his instrument into an afterthought. Wyn's singing voice sounded like Silas expected: it was screechy, but the quality wasn't as off-putting as one might have thought—Silas thought it rather like listening to a gifted rodent sing. All in all, Wyn's talent was impossible to deny. The bedraggled little man was by no means Silas's musical equal, but neither was he a joke.

"Now *that* is a song with spirit."

Silas turned to find Gay Gracie at his ear, her eyes on the stage. Two tankards of ale filled her hands. She wore a joyful smile on her face. The smile made Silas frown. Gracie had listened to him play a hundred times, and not once had she smiled at his playing like that. He opened his mouth to make a snide remark about the source of the fiddler's inspiration, but stopped for fear of losing the song's thread.

And with a gleaming blade, she raised
The hand to end her sister's days
A hand blessed in an unholy blaze
By a dragon born in the sun's own rays
Foooooooor, you see.........
(That witch Anis, seduced the beast!)

"He's torturing both the history and the lyrics," Silas complained while the fiddle slashed, but Gay Gracie was gone, out into the dark of the crowd to deliver the two tankards of ale. Silas furrowed already distressed eyebrows, recalling his Ragar Or history. In reality, Anis Salk hadn't attempted to find the dragon named White Morning until after she'd been exiled for trying to kill her sister, but damned if Wyn's wasn't the more compelling sequence of events. Silas had spent months polishing the lyrics to his ballad to a historically accurate sheen, but if he played the song now, he'd only confuse the few patrons willing to give the repeated subject matter their attention.

The newest version of "Ballad of the Cruel Sister" ended in a jagged frenzy of fiddling. Wyn hopped a good four feet at the song's finish, as if forced to flee the overheated spot where he had been playing. The crowd roared its approval. Wyn bowed, then departed the stage.

Silas drew a bead on the little man. Visions of violence danced in his thoughts. As a general rule, he tried to avoid fisticuffs—a lutist's hands were more valuable than his instrument—but tonight he was beyond caring. *A little roughing up is the least the thief deserves. And if I break a finger, what of it? My chance at the Swans has come and gone with that song.*

Coming off stage, Wyn navigated a gauntlet of good-natured backslaps, but, scurrying thing that he was, he quickly tunneled through, emerging unscathed near the back of the room. Silas rose to his feet and homed in on his prey.

He was halfway to Wyn when a hand caught him on the shoulder and turned him around.

Philemon Yurk stood before him. The son of Lord Delton Yurk had his father's ears, outgrowths of spongy flesh that reminded Silas of the fungi that sprout on trees. The ears, however, were where the similarities ended. Unlike his father, Philemon had bowed shoulders: weak, rolling mounds held in place by a lolling spine. (In contrast, the aristocratic Lord Delton's spine was so straight that his shoulders looked as if they'd been pinned in place by a brooch.) Philemon's intelligence was self-evident. He had sharp black eyes that missed nothing, and he carried himself with an air of expectation that suggested all would work out well for him in the end.

"What madness separates Silas O' the Songs from his lute?" Philemon asked, gesturing back at the bench with a cup of wine.

Silas had been so intent on harming Wyn that he hadn't realized he had left his lute behind. "I may not play tonight."

His truth-telling tongue again. Always offering additional information, always answering questions that hadn't been asked.

"Not playing? Why in the Bottom Black not? Stavus help us, but if the most Holy Deity of Light and Air didn't intend for Silas O' the Songs to showcase his skills to the king's own acting company, then I don't know why he blessed you with such unnatural talent."

Silas was surprised by the flattery. Knowing Philemon as he did, he wondered if the man was working an angle. "Thank you, Philemon. It was my intention to play. But the scoundrel who just left the stage stole my song, and at the present moment I'm more concerned with cracking his skull in two than I am performing."

"That was…your song?" Philemon asked, befuddled.

The rich man's confusion stung. *He doesn't think me capable of writing anything so catchy.* "The pox-scarred fiddler stole the title and the subject matter, if not the song itself. Regardless, I can't go onstage and sing a second song about Anis Salk. The crowd will think it hackneyed."

Philemon nodded. "Ah. Now I understand your predicament. But surely you have other songs? Or perhaps you can showcase your skills by playing a standard? The fiddler's song was fine, no doubt, but there are only three musicians present tonight who have a legitimate shot at the brogan's-head."

Silas thought he had misheard Philemon. "Three musicians?"

"Yes. Yourself. Felix Fingers. And the beauty on the high harp. Isbel Wicker."

Isbel Wicker? Is the Vake overflowing with people who would wrest from me my position as the area's preeminent musician? But Silas knew even that wasn't true. Felix Fingers had stolen the title from him sometime back.

Silas checked over his shoulder for Wyn. The little man had wrangled a large tankard of ale from the kitchen staff and was taking hearty gulps. Beside him stood one of the backslappers. When Wyn finished the tankard in record time, the fellow rewarded Wyn with an additional slap.

Philemon followed Silas's gaze. "Let me buy you a drink, Silas O' the Songs. Your nemesis isn't going anywhere. Not with a brogan's-head on the line."

Silas didn't budge. "It'd be more gratifying to fight him now, while my blood is up."

"If your blood hasn't cooled by the time your drink is finished, you can be confident that the beating is warranted. Besides," Philemon continued, a knowing smile playing on his lips, "the beauty is taking the stage."

Silas wrenched his eyes away from Wyn and looked to the cedarwood stage. The unnervingly beautiful woman that Silas had seen at the outset of the evening was positioning herself to play the half harp. She had a spine like a trellis around which her delicate frame ascended to the heavens. Her arms were likewise long, giving her easy access to the harp strings. Unlike poor Jia from earlier in the evening, Isbel Wicker looked supremely confident onstage. Once positioned, she paused and assessed the audience with a cool, even stare.

Philemon grabbed Silas by the elbow and directed him away from Wyn. The rich man hailed a serving wench along the way, and, without saying a word, signaled their order with two raised fingers.

The Golden Pear grew silent. Silas, hypnotized along with the rest of the audience, listened as Isbel's first plucked string stirred a butterfly swarm of notes, the many delicate sounds taking flight before lighting in the respective ears of all who were present. The melody was mesmerizing. Silas was soon lost to the music. He was trying to place the name of the song, when, like the sun emerging from behind a cloud, Isbel's voice cut in, brightening the room with an aria so clear and pure that she might have been mistaken for one of Stavus's heavenly creatures. *It's a temple song,* Silas registered at last. "On Wings of Light." Isbel had taken the Felix Fingers route and reworked the tune to make it her own.

Philemon pressed a cup of wine into Silas's hands. "Three musicians," he repeated under the music. Silas could only nod.

The song ended in a fitful trio of elusive arpeggios. When it was over, the crowd held their collective breaths for a full second before exploding in applause. Silas didn't know whether to clap or cry. He took a sizable gulp of the grape and turned to Philemon.

"She may be better than Felix Fingers," he admitted.

"She's certainly better than you."

Silas was taken aback. What Philemon had said was probably true, but the rich man's earlier flattery had left Silas unprepared for the cut. He looked down his nose at the disinherited Yurk. A dark grin was spreading on Philemon's face.

"No doubt you've wagered money on tonight's outcome," Silas said. "From the sound of it, your coin is on the harpist." Silas was angry at Philemon but also confused; why had Philemon wasted breath encouraging him to play if his money was on another?

Philemon laughed, a splintery cachinnation. "Ah, musicians. You see as far as your string-lusting fingers. Stavus bless you for it. I do have money on tonight, Silas O' the Songs, but I stopped making bets on uncertain outcomes sometime back. You are right in one regard, however. Crossbolt to my chest, I would have wagered my coin on Isbel. Not Felix Fingers. And definitely not you."

Silas finished off the last of the wine in lieu of biting his tongue. *Philemon's playing a game,* he told himself. *Enacting a ploy of some sort. Either he has bought off the Swans or he does in fact have money on the harpist. This conversation was all a ruse…his goal is to rattle me before I perform.* He contemplated slamming his empty cup into Philemon's chest, but, estranged son or not, Philemon was still the offspring of a lord. The repercussions for hitting a rich man, Silas knew, could be dire. *I should be bashing the fiddler's head in, instead of being provoked by a man I can't retaliate against.* "Thank you for the drink, my lord. But I've delayed my previous engagement long enough." Silas bent over and placed his cup on the floor. A delightful rush of blood alcohol greeted him on his return to upright. It stirred both his anger and his nerve. He whirled away from Philemon Yurk, hoping to find Wyn where he had last left him.

To Silas's delight, Wyn hadn't moved an inch. The fiddler's only apparent activity during the course of the harpist's song was to switch roles with the backslapper: now Wyn was administering the slaps, and the jovial backslapping bear was downing a tankard.

Silas rushed the pox-scarred fiddler. Wyn saw him coming. Strangely, the little man's expression was all innocence and unconcern. He wore a half-mad grin like he was about to greet an old friend.

"You stole the idea for your song from me!" Silas said.

"I know!" Wyn replied, black eyes dancing. "I am obliged to you for the inspiration!"

Onstage, a lyre gave voice to melancholy, but it was nothing to the three men. The backslapping bear lowered his tankard and pinned Silas with the stink eye. He appeared to be the only one who had noticed that Silas was angry.

Silas clarified. "You stole the idea for your song from me, you ass!"

A light flickered in the depths of Wyn's cavernous pupils. "Oh," he said with dawning understanding. "Yes. Yes, I did." Then he fixed Silas once more with the same irritating smile.

Silas countered with a mean frown. "Listen. This competition may be a joke to you, but to some of us, it's not. I've played for nobility before. And I meant to use tonight as a means for doing so again. This is how I make my living! But now that you have…soiled…the subject matter of my song, my chances are shot. Do you hear me?"

Wyn stuck with his grin. "*Soiled* is a strong word, no? It's not like I stole your song away for an illicit ride in the hay on the night before her bonding day."

Silas decided that trying to carry on an honest conversation with this fellow was an exercise in futility. "I'll have you outside," he demanded.

Wyn's eyebrows jumped. "Fair recompense for the inspiration, I suppose. But before you have me, I need to drink a few more ales."

The backslapping bear caught Wyn's meaning a split second before Silas did. The big fellow made his cognizance known by snorting ale out his nose.

Silas had had enough. He grabbed Wyn by the neck of his worn brown tunic. But before he had a firm hold, Wyn slipped free, using some lightning trick of his hands and body. Silas tried to grab Wyn again, but found, to his chagrin, that the backslapping bear had hold of *him* by the shirt. In response, Silas attempted some approximation of Wyn's extrication maneuver, only to find his version wanting.

"Let him go, my friend," Wyn said to the big fellow, interrupting the tussle. A few curious faces turned in their direction, but, by and large, the majority of the crowd were too busy watching the lyrist.

Silas readjusted and straightened his jerkin, all while staring daggers at the big man. He was angry to the point of being enraged, but he wasn't so out of his head that he had gone blind. The backslapping bear outweighed him by at least two stone.

"All right, outside then," Wyn said in a mock doleful tenor. The pox-scarred fiddler turned to the big man. "I trust you'll have another tankard of ale waiting for me when I return?"

The bear frowned. "There's no need to go outside. I'll smash this annoyance against the wall and we'll continue with our revelry."

"No," Wyn insisted. "I may not be a man of honor, but even men without honor feel the need to honor certain types of requests." The backslapping bear looked confused, but he didn't argue. "After you," Wyn motioned to Silas, extending his hand toward the door at the back of the common room.

Together they walked outside.

Outside, the gloaming was collapsing into night. High in the sky, the sentinel stars rushed to their duty: to the east the Jailer took up his station near the Sky Ends, while in the northern plains the Moonbear's eyes kept watch over the natural dominion.

"I wrote a ditty about the Jailer once," Wyn said, seemingly forgetting the reason for their outdoors excursion. He held his fiddle and bow in his left hand like a dead goose. "Good source material there. But I pity the star, I truly do. Who wants to guard a randy demon for all eternity?"

Only steps outside The Golden Pear, they were already closing in on woods. There were villages spread throughout the Vake, and plenty of farms, but, compared to the rest of Ragar Or, the forest reigned supreme. A thousand varieties of trees stood cloaked in darkness. They exerted a pressure and a power not easily defined.

"You are a thief," Silas declared, ignoring Wyn's divagation. He balled his fist. "I'm of a mind to strike you."

Wyn shrugged. "Go ahead, then. If you must."

Silas had been in fights before. His line of occupation being what it was, he tried not to make a habit of it, but, when things kicked off, he liked to think that he acquitted himself fairly well. He sized up Wyn, and, stepping forward, took a swing. The little man slipped the punch easily, and, pretending as if nothing had occurred, continued with his exposition on the eastern star.

"I had a line in the song that won a laugh every time. What was it? Oh yes…*For the Jailer was a man of honor, and mighty were his deeds, for what greater task, might the Twins have asked, then to protect mother from demon seed.*"

Silas felt a sudden weariness come over him. The sensation was physical, but his first thought was that he was simply exhausted listening to the fiddler's ahistorical butchering of the past. "No," he said, pulling his second punch. "The Twins didn't ask the Jailer to guard the demon. It was Beoliotius, you frzooooool…"

Silas's slurred speech segued to a spinning world. The ground sprung up to give him a slap on the face, but before terra firma could land its punch, the fiddler caught him.

"Whoa! Keep your legs, Silas O' the Songs! I thought perhaps you'd had a drink or two, but I didn't take you for sloshed."

Silas cocked his head and squared Wyn between the moonbear's eyes. "I'z ornly haard the wuuuun." For reasons that he didn't understand, his tongue was flopping like a beached fish.

Wyn squared Silas in turn. "Tell me—what color do you see?"

Silas wouldn't have noticed the change in his vision if Wyn hadn't called his attention to it. "Itzzz ggrayye. Arllll ggrayye."

The fiddler's ever-present smile morphed into a concerned variation. It was still a smile, though. "You've been poisoned, Silas O' the Songs. Graywater Ghost in your wine, I'd guess. You'll be dead within the hour if we don't purge that belly." The fiddler looked to the woods. "The trees are your salvation. Come."

Silas stumbled into the woods alongside Wyn, one arm draped over the fiddler's sinewy shoulders. It was a fantastic night for traipsing through trees: the gray sheen through which Silas viewed the world was illuminated by buckets of stars quickly filling up the sky, as well as two waxing moons. They trekked about thirty yards deep into the forest, where, with tender ceremony, Wyn lowered Silas to the trunk of a scaly-bark tree.

"Toad maple," Wyn announced. Silas watched through the prism of a monochrome-colored pain as Wyn set his fiddle and bow aside and began peeling strips of bark from above Silas's head. When he had a fair amount in hand, he set to grinding it between his palms. He talked as he worked. "I have neither the time nor the tools to make a proper paste, but, so long as you don't choke, the effect will be the same. Just force it down, and we'll get what's inside you right back up. I've ingested toad maple bark many a time after a roaring drunk. Woods witches will tell you that the bark has both antidotal and purgative properties." He stopped and studied the barky crumbs in his palm. "As they say, offal is a feast for the beggar. Open up and swallow, Silas O' the Songs."

Silas was too out of sorts to do anything other than comply. He tipped his chin back, and Wyn poured the tree crumbs into his mouth.

He swallowed too quickly. A wedge of bark lodged in his esophagus. Within seconds, the pain from the poison couldn't compare to Silas's desperate need for air. He jumped to his feet and started to retch, a violent and hopeless heaving.

He was on the verge of passing out when his stomach summoned a mighty wave that washed his esophagus clean.

When at last Silas recovered his bearings, Wyn was standing behind him, patting him on the back. "Stomach acid is hell on the vocal chords," the fiddler commented.

Silas weighed whether the life debt he now owed Wyn precluded taking another swing at him. But before he could make a decision, he heard a noise that sounded like grounded thunder. *Horses,* he realized. Wyn heard it too. The clopping suggested ten mounts, maybe more.

Silas took his hands off his knees and rose to his full height. He exchanged a questioning look with Wyn. Wyn mirrored Silas's expression in the moonlight. It went without saying that now wasn't the time for a conversation.

Together, they quietly worked their way back through the woods, peering through the trees at the shadows gathering outside The Golden Pear. Their glimpses became ever more alarming. The shadows morphed into men armed with steel. Some of the shadows were dismounting, some were shouting, some were crowding the door. Torches materialized. Firelight flashed off mean steel helms. Silas had thought from the sound of the horses that there would be ten men, but there were closer to twenty. His attempts to discern what he was seeing were thwarted time and again by the trees both protecting him and blocking his view. At last, a crystal-clear vantage emerged. Atop one of the helmets a large silver eagle with an open beak bared angry wings. Beneath the helm, a man with a charred beard barked orders of the bloodcurdling variety.

"What are they—?" Silas whispered, pretending as if he couldn't hear with his own two ears.

Bodies spilled out of the inn. Strangely, the men let one or two pass, then they took their swords and began running the others through. A few of the men spread torch fire onto the roof, where it ran wild. Smoke muddled the night's pristine emptiness. Silas struggled to comprehend what he was seeing. It seemed as if the poison had left his body, turned into a nightmare, and ran amok.

A handful of men emerged from the inn with swords in hand, intent on putting up a fight. *The king's knights,* Silas thought, remembering the Swan's speech. The helmed invaders fell on the resistors with a ready savagery, dispatching their lives with brutal gusto. Silas watched for the assassins. If in fact they emerged from the inn, they were killed with the same speed as all the others.

"Silas," Wyn said from nearby.

A woman ran out of The Golden Pear screaming, her dress on fire. She ran straight into a blade, causing her scream to modulate, then stop. A long-haired man followed the woman, coughing, cowering, futilely trying to protect an object in his arms. *Felix Fingers,* Silas realized. The bearded killer with the eagle helm wrenched Felix Finger's Wrainish lute from his grasp, then spilled Felix's entrails on the ground. The killer tossed the lute onto the roof, where it caught fire. Felix's long and elegant fingers reached for the instrument even as he crumpled to his death.

"Silas O' the Songs. We must leave. Now."

Gay Gracie, Silas thought.

A helmed man on horseback cut down an onlooker standing in the street.

Bodies piled up near the inn's door. From deep within the bowels of the inferno, a banshee screaming.

The men on horseback spread out, searching for anyone alive.

Wyn grabbed Silas hard by the arm, spinning him around with a fierce strength. "You can only stare death in the face so long before he spots you. Follow me into the woods now, Silas O' the Songs, or stay here and die."

The pox-scarred fiddler turned and made for the thick of the forest.

Silas O' the Songs followed after him.

Gregor Thorn

A glimpse.

Gregor was buried in the mushroom's mind. He had been there many times. When he was young, the plant would laugh and laugh at him, but now, in Gregor's old-middle age, it quietly, if begrudgingly, gave him the space to be. To live, to die, to see.

Sometimes it even gave him a little nudge.

Look. Over there.

What did he see? A tower of flame, a sorcerer writing riddles in the sky. His eyes burned at the sight. The silver-brown god—surely it was a god?—twisted, sensing who Gregor was, now smiling, now gnashing its tree-bark teeth, now laughing like the mushroom had once laughed, until the mushroom in its begrudging goodness covered Gregor with its coffin cap and he was exposed no more.

Gregor knew what he had seen. He had glimpsed the Yubriy tree.

When morning arrived, Gregor was still half buried, but it was time to go and see the king. Outside of his tent, the snow had stopped falling. Gregor could hear the powder's faint beating heart. High above, a wan sun bid Gregor a weak good morning.

Sickly Stavus.

"Uncle Bones!"

Gregor turned at the sound of his sobriquet, and for his compliance, was awarded a snowball in the chin. He heard his nephew laughing, and another who didn't laugh but smiled loud enough for all the world to hear. Wiping the snow from his chin and ermine-lined red cloak, Gregor indeed saw Ajax Dayborn, and beside the crown prince his newly bonded, the willful Greta Worrint.

Gregor could tell from the looks on their faces that Greta had thrown the snowball as a good-natured joke. Nevertheless, Gregor didn't smile.

"Nephew. My lady."

Ajax gave Gregor a disappointed look. "Don't worry, my love," Ajax said to his new wife. "Uncle Bones isn't mad. He's merely weary from his dreamwork."

"I'm headed to see your father," Gregor said, ignoring the comment. "I need to speak to him before we reach Coffyn Castle. Would you care to join me?" A tree in the near distance shook snow out of its branches.

Ajax grimaced. He was still technically on sweetmarch with his newly bonded, but, after the stunt his brother had pulled last night, Ajax's presence in his father's tent would no doubt be welcomed. *If your father hadn't caved to your request to bond a commoner, your sweetmarch might have been truly special,* Gregor thought. *You might have sailed to the coasts of Clyesia, or traveled to the Cape of the Dying Suns. But when you bond a woman like Greta— and in the midst of a rebellion, no less—you get what you get.*

"Yes," Ajax said at last, defeating his inner lovebird. He turned to his wife. Greta had the good sense not to pout, although Gregor didn't like the look of her narrowed eyes. "I know it's our sweetmarch, but after what Easton did, my father needs me. Now that the snow has stopped, you should go riding. I'll find you when we're through."

Greta said not a word. Instead, she rose on her tiptoes and gave her royal husband a chaste kiss. She was a short but buxom woman, in stark contrast to the long and lean Ajax. *She'll be fat when she's older,* Gregor thought ungenerously. *The commons will call her Queen Cake, or Her Royal Lardness, or some other such nonsense. They'll claim to hate her for being fat, but what they will actually hate her for is being a common. Just like them.* The kiss over, Greta turned and faced Gregor. She was an attractive young woman, in truth, with straight coal-black hair and rose-colored cheeks and eyes like fractured blue ice. Gregor couldn't help but like her, ungenerous thoughts aside.

Greta gave Gregor a crisp little curtsy and a dry smile. "Uncle Bones," she said, then turned and left. Gregor had no idea whether she was being sardonic or playful.

Ajax fell in step with Gregor as they continued toward King Micah's pavilion. The camp was alive with the excitement of completing the last leg of the journey. For a week the king's party had slogged through a snowstorm, pushing toward Low Osgood, but yesterday, in the face of a punishing whiteout, they had made camp only two miles from Coffyn Castle. Now the snow clouds were gone, and the road to Coffyn Castle was clear.

"Any chance my brother perished in the storm last night?" Ajax asked, his tone cheekily hopeful.

"Doubtful," Gregor replied. "The snow let up after nightfall, and your brother has a way of skirting misfortune. If he's dead, the deed will have occurred inside the castle walls. That's where the real danger lies."

"Humph," Ajax snorted. "These Ont—" he stopped, reconsidering his word choice. "These *northmen* will soon see that we bring dangers of our own. The Heron rides at our rear, and with him the greatest army Ragar Or has ever seen."

Gregor was inclined to snort in turn, but he desisted. Dante Heron was the puissant man of the moment in the south, a young lord with a vast amount of wealth, and, now that he had ingratiated himself with the royal family, a vast amount of influence. Gregor knew that Ajax thought of Dante as a boon companion in the making, and the king was too enamored with Dante Heron's coffers to form an objective opinion of his character. Only Easton Dayborn shared Gregor's instinctual distrust of the young lord.

I may as well be in accord with a wild stallion, for all the good having Easton on my side will do me.

They continued their walk in silence. Now that the snow clouds had lifted, Gregor could see the knobby spine of the Edgeling Mountains in the distance. The city of Low Osgood was nestled near the coccyx, but Coffyn Castle was a little farther west, at the base of one of the lower peaks. Higher up the spine and closer to the sea was High Osgood, seat of the Crimson Salks. *Though you should keep the word* crimson *to yourself, Gregor.* Down south, it was the fashion to malign the family that bore the name of the previous dynasty by calling them the Crimson Salks, due to the prominence of the Redd family features among the descendants. There were those—King Micah among them—who would have you believe that the remaining Salks weren't Salks at all. But Gregor and the king were no longer in the south, and the purpose of the trip certainly wasn't to offend Lord Daguss Salk.

A pair of Dayborn standards flew just outside King Micah's large, golden pavilion. *Two suns, doubled. Do we mean to honor the Twins, or mock them?* Gregor nodded at the guards, who let them pass. Inside the tent, King Micah and Queen Anjay appeared to be sifting through the rubble of yet another fight. Their relationship had always been passionate, which was generally to the good, but when their passions turned dark, they were no more capable of concealing their feelings than when in the throes of affection.

King Micah skipped the pleasantries. "Your mother seems to think that I should tie your brother up like a dog to keep him from running off," Micah said, greeting Ajax. He gave Gregor a cursory nod.

Anjay wore a scowl strong enough to harrow the Bottom Black. The crescent-moon shape of her face made the scowl look extra severe—her lips seemed to be digging into the tops of her shoulders. "Spending a night in the kennels might teach Easton a lesson."

The king pointed a belligerent finger at his wife. Micah Dayborn wasn't an overly large man, but his frame was substantial enough to give those on the receiving end of his finger a primal pause. "My son is not a dog."

"He doesn't appear to be a prince, either," the queen shot back. "Princes don't sabotage their father's plans on a lark. Our eldest wouldn't have," she continued, pointing a finger of her own at Ajax. "Though Stavus knows this one has made his own poor decisions of late. But that's what happens when a king refuses to set limits for his sons. The reckless one begins to think there isn't a line he can't cross, and the responsible one decides he can afford to make mistakes of his own."

Prince Ajax smarted, but he kept his mouth shut. Gregor didn't know whether to cheer the queen on or to point out her hypocrisy. Greta Worrint might have been a commoner, but, unlike Anjay, at least she had been born in Ragar Or. If ever a king had made an error in his bonding choice, it was when Micah Dayborn disregarded his father's dying wish and imported his bonded from across the Wayskin Ocean.

"Men aren't made under their father's thumb!" Micah bellowed. "I was their age when my father died. If destiny hands my sons the same burden it handed me, at least they'll have had practice making their own decisions."

Our father, Gregor thought.

Anjay's voice turned cold. "One wrong decision can destroy a king."

King Micah gave a rough, hearty laugh. His thistly, gray-black beard looked like a quivering hedgehog's back. "A weak king, maybe. A strong king refuses to be defined by his errors. He learns from them and moves on."

The queen's eyes bulged. Gregor worried what she might say to her bonded. Thinking better of it, however, she turned to Gregor.

"Did you dream last night?"

"Yes, my queen."

Anjay waited for him to expound, but, as always, Gregor hesitated. His dreams were dangerous things. They were vivid and colorful and powerful and frightening, but that didn't always make them real. And even when they were real, they could easily be misinterpreted.

The queen persisted. "*What* did you dream?"

Gregor paused, remembering. *A disturbing dream, my queen. Then I stole away with the mushroom, and it gave me a glimpse of the Yubriy tree. I saw a tower of flame, a faceless sorcerer. The tree knows who I am. What that portends for Ragar Or, I could not say.*

"I did not dream of the lutist, my queen," he said instead.

49

Anjay smiled at his understated insolence. Long ago they had been adversaries, combatants even, but over the years their relationship had aged into something more agreeable. Interacting with the queen was like playing a lifelong game of sennequi against an evenly matched opponent, one whose playing style was far different from Gregor's own. Gregor was a master of defense and deflection, but the queen's brute charges still managed to occasionally catch him unaware.

"Speaking of this lutist, where is he?" the queen parried, electing to indulge Gregor's gambit. "For a man as stingy with his prognostications as you, you were rather bullish about the lutist's appearance, as I recall. You read of his arrival in the Yubriy leaves. And what is it you say about the Yubriy tree? Oh yes. *It may deceive, but it never lies.*"

Gregor grinned. He knew what his grin looked like. How had his half brother the king described it? *When you smile, you look like a skeleton celebrating the end of the world.* "The Yubriy leaves do not lie, my queen. And if they deceive us, it is only because we deceive ourselves. If there is a fault in the interpretation of the leaf, it will be mine, and mine alone."

"And if you *have* made a mistake, will I pay for it with my life?"

Perhaps. Sephery certainly paid for it with hers, Gregor considered saying, but before he could, the king interjected. "Leave it alone, Anjay. We do as the Sagekind says. As the Yubriy leaf says."

The Yubriy tree. In the fecund dreamscape of Gregor's mind, he saw the Yubriy tree once more, turning, twisting, brown twining over silver twining over brown, looking, laughing, tree-bark teeth gnashing…

He needed to forget the Yubriy tree for now. He needed to tell them why he was here.

"I did have a dream last night." He looked at the three preeminent members of the Dayborn dynasty, letting his gaze fall on each in turn. "Will you hear it?"

King Micah, Queen Anjay, and Prince Ajax nodded, their expressions wary and expectant.

Gregor's training as the Sagekind had skilled him in the art of accessing visions. He did so using three different methods.

The first was through meditation. He knew tens of different ways to breathe, scores of different ways to sit, and a hundred different ways to not think. The not thinking was, of course, the most difficult. The Sagekind before Gregor, a Hawk's-Eye by way of Clyesia by way of Thralk-Braktur (the man was, of course, no real priest; holy men made piss-poor Sagekinds) could fall into an unthinking trance with astonishing speed, a skill he tried without success to pass onto Gregor, who, despite his best efforts to not think about not thinking and thereby not think, continually found his thoughts snagging on his inability to not think.

Gregor had improved over the years, learning, as meditators do, that forgiving oneself for not thinking, was, in the end, perhaps the most important aspect of not thinking. But that forgiveness had its limits, and, for that reason, Gregor's meditative visions were the most elusive of all. Which isn't to say they were entirely unfruitful. Occasionally, while meditating, a vision would materialize from the depths of Gregor's not thinking, and Gregor, stunned into consciousness, would grasp the vision by the tail as he returned to the surface.

The second way that Gregor accessed visions was by communing with the plant world, most commonly by ingesting or inhaling psychoactive vegetation. This, Gregor had found, was the most productive method, and, as the years passed and his comfort level with the plants increased, the method that most naturally suited Gregor's...unique talents. He found mushrooms the most reliable vessel, but gumroot and the Delilah herb also helped him cross the bridge to the realm where the visions lay. On more than one occasion the plants had assisted Gregor in verifying prophecies foretold by the Yubriy tree. But the plants, like all living things, had motivations of their own, and Gregor had to be careful not to interpret every vision shown him as a reflection of reality.

The third way that Gregor accessed visions was through his dreams. He dreamed no more or less than other men, and, like all men, the majority of his dreams were meaningless. But there were times when a dream would hit Gregor with such force that he instantly knew the dream was more than a dream—it was a vision.

He had experienced such a dream early the previous night. It was so powerful that he had awoken with a start. Upon awakening, Gregor had ingested mushrooms in the hopes of clarifying the dream's rougher details, but instead the mushroom had shown him the Yubriy tree, and now his thoughts were doubly troubled.

"In my dream there were three crows—"

"—Salks," King Micah interrupted.

Gregor sighed. His half brother could be a bull with his interruptions. "Most likely, yes. There are three crows on the Salk banner." He considered deviating from the dream to resume his ongoing lecture on the dangers of dream interpretation, but he knew that it would fall on deaf ears. Besides, the king was most likely right. The crows represented the Salks. "They flew into a snow-covered field and picked a crown from off the ground."

"My crown," the king stated with unease. It wasn't a question.

Gregor continued. "With the crown in tow, the crows flew north, deep into the snows. One of the crows pecked at the other two as they flew, before peeling away. At last, the crows lit upon the ground, and laid the crown to rest so that it encircled a blue frostflower."

"Stavus save us," Prince Ajax whispered. The queen looked like she had swallowed something rotten. The king was so disturbed that he couldn't speak. Gregor understood why. The symbolism was ill-omened. Frostflowers grew in Kalandragote, the northern city-state that for more than two hundred years had resisted joining the kingdom of Ragar Or. The city was Ontish to the core, keepers of not only the faith of the Twins, but also (rumor had it) the twin-death rites. Word was that Kalandragote had been of great assistance in bringing the Blackstar Rebellion to heel—Daguss Salk and his Ontish friends had convinced the Ollspaers to unite against a common enemy—but, now that the fighting was over, the old threat loomed once more: that the Ollspaers would make an alliance with the Ontish houses, for the purposes of fomenting a civil war and forming a breakaway kingdom.

There was no use dallying here. Gregor pressed on. "It's difficult to describe what happened next. The dream became less visual and more…auditory. I heard what sounded like a chorus of birds. It started off as cawing, but the cawing was soon joined by shrieks, whistling, birdsong, screeches, hoots, and more. I could see the shadows of the birds reflecting off the snow. The sound grew into a cacophony of madness, until, in an instant, the noise was snuffed out by the roar of a dragon."

"A dragon?" the queen asked. She brought her long, brown fingers to her bottom lip, uncharacteristic for a woman who prided herself on being in full possession of her every movement.

"A dragon," Gregor confirmed. "Unlike the birds, I saw the dragon. Like the crows before it, the dragon descended and plucked the crown from off the ground. Then it rose into the sky and flew toward a dawning horizon." He paused. He knew that the dream's symbolism had unnerved the royal family, so he wanted to deliver the next line to full effect. "In the sky, there were two suns."

King Micah's face, which had grown bone-white during the dream's telling, revived with color. "Two suns," he said, and laughed a little. He pointed a gentle finger at Gregor. "You might have told us that the dream ended well at the outset, Sagekind."

Gregor tried to keep his expression neutral. His half brother would incline toward a positive interpretation of the dream—he always did—but Gregor didn't want to encourage him. There were a thousand possible interpretations to the dream. As Sagekind, Gregor was a firm devotee to the uncertainties. Ultimately, they were the only real truths.

Anjay's face showed no such relief. "What else did you see in your dream? What else did you hear?" She was struck with full force of a dawning thought. "The dragon? Did it have a rider?"

Gregor grimaced. Even the most vivid dreams had blurred edges. "Yes. But I only saw the rider from a distance. I could not see who it was."

The queen tsked. She approached Gregor, dissatisfied. She wore an orange and white-sleeved surcoat that made a swishing sound as she crossed the Wrainish rug. Upon reaching Gregor, she looked at him with hard hazel eyes. "What else, Uncle Bones? Think."

Gregor flinched. The Uncle Bones moniker was a term of affection used by the royal family, but it pained Gregor to hear it on Anjay's tongue. It reminded Gregor of the way his departed wife Sephery—the queen's cousin—used to say it. Sephery had known how much Gregor hated the Uncle Bones nickname, so she had made it an intimacy between the two of them. She would tease him with the nickname when she called him to bed.

Come to bed, Uncle Bones. Show me your skeleton.

"That is all, my queen. When I awoke, I searched for the dream's meaning with the mushroom, but it showed me naught."

Anjay raised her eyebrows. "The mushroom showed you naught?"

"Naught of the dream," he answered honestly. Of the Yubriy tree he kept quiet. Anjay was skittish enough about the lutist prediction without Gregor detailing his vision of the Yubriy tree.

"Enough, Mother," Ajax intervened. "You are surrounded by liars and sycophants at court, and yet you question honest Uncle Bones more than you do any of them."

The queen was lightning-fast with her reply. "I've made allowances for their lies. But our family can ill afford a mistruth from the Sagekind."

Gregor ground his back teeth in lieu of replying. Anjay had neatly summed up the trouble with being the Sagekind. The Dayborns wanted to know his every vision, but, if he misinterpreted any of them, they were quick to make sure that he was the one to shoulder the blame.

The king harrumphed. He could be an impatient man when his mind was settled. As it was now. "Ajax is right. It's enough. We need to get moving, besides. Lord Salk promised me the honors of executing the rebel, but after all our delays, I wouldn't be surprised to find the Blackstar Prince's head waiting for us on a spike outside the Coffyn castle gates. If we're delayed much longer, they'll stick Easton's head beside him for show."

The king meant it as a joke, but no one laughed.

"But first," the king continued after the awkward silence, "I'll have a word with the Sagekind. Alone."

There were only two people in Gregor's life who had ever spoken to him in the language of intimacy.

His departed wife Sephery. And his half brother the king.

The language Gregor had shared with Sephery was the sweeter. Their tongues could scarce contain the joy of inventing it. Gregor had marveled at its creation, overjoyed by the wonder of words that connected him to this intelligent, beautiful creature. When they had first met, their attraction had been instantaneous, but after their bonding ceremony, it was the intimacies of their ever-flowering private language that made their relationship…expand. It was a connected root system, tying them together beneath the surface. It was an unspoken understanding, spoken out loud. It was the secret of their bliss transformed into poetry.

But then Sephery had died, seven years after their bonding. Because of a vision that Gregor had misunderstood. And to Gregor's immeasurable sadness, the language they had shared died with her.

The language Gregor shared with his half brother the king was an entirely different beast. It was older and deeper, dating back to childhood. It was a language partially invented, and partially taught: King Orius, their father, had given Gregor and Micah the vocabulary for communicating with one another, a lexicon that was at once familiar and an ever-constant reminder of the differences in their station. It was a language intended to make the brothers reliant on one another. A language meant to ensure their survival. A language designed to reinforce a story the half brothers were duty bound to believe.

"Who are you?" King Micah asked him.

"A bastard half brother. Bound to serve."

"And who am I?"

"King Micah of House Dayborn, the first of his name, Holy Son of the Air, the Twin Ascendant, and the Rightful Ruler of Ragar Or."

Every time they were alone together, they repeated the same words. To the untrained ear, it sounded like an exercise in King Micah's insecurity. But the two half brothers both knew that it was something else entirely.

A necessary lie.

With their ritual completed, the king relaxed.

"There are times when I'm inclined to believe that your visions aren't worth a bucket of horse piss. Not because they aren't true. But because you won't explain their meaning."

"I could keep them from you, if you like?" Gregor suggested.

"What? And miss out on your cringing when I interpret them for you? No, no. You have your pleasures, I have mine."

"It's risky enough relying on the Yubriy leaves like I do. When it comes to the fallibilities of my own mind, it's better if we have a sense of what to be on the lookout for without drawing definitive conclusions."

"This from the man who used his prophetic skills to defeat the Dagish Prophet of Wrath. Play what game you will, Sagekind, but don't withhold crucial information from me before it's too late. Not when we're about to enter this nest of vipers."

Gregor forced himself to hold his tongue once more. His hated it when his half brother the king referred to the Dagish Prophet of Wrath as if defeating him had been a simple thing. Gregor had barely escaped with his life that day, and, ever since, he'd had to live with the knowledge that even with his prophetic skills and powers combined, there were those whose abilities rivaled, if not surpassed, his own.

The king, sensing that he'd gone too far, retreated to the problem at hand. "It's a damn shame Salk put an end to the Blackstar Rebellion so quickly. An exhibition of our strength might have quelled the conversations these Ontishmen are no doubt having behind my back."

By our strength, you mean the Heron's strength, Gregor thought. He took a moment to study his half brother. Micah looked tired, as if anticipatively weary from the political ordeal that lay ahead. An unambiguous battle against a clearly defined opponent would have done him a great favor. The Boils had been gracious in that respect: declared rebels were always easier to fight than ones working in the shadows. But now the king had to deal with the matters that led to the Blackstar Rebellion in the first place. For three generations Ragar Or had been held together both by the memory of Cedric Dayborn's heroics during the War of the Three Brothers, and by the legends that had grown up around it—legends that allowed the Dayborns to claim that they were the true descendants of the Twin Ascendant. But those memories were fading, and Micah's recent string of mistakes had brought the country's fault lines back to the surface.

"You must embrace Daguss Salk as a brother. He subdued a rebellion in your name."

"He subdued that rebellion for his own damn self, and you know it. The Blackstar Isles would have been a threat to High Osgood and every other Ontish city so long as they were an independent state. What I need now is a show of faith from Lord Salk. And the expedient recovery of tax revenue from the Blackstar Isles wouldn't hurt either."

"What does he need from you?"

"Besides a lesson in humility?"

Gregor refused to indulge the king's ill humor. "Daguss Salk is humble enough, for a lord with his last name. What he needs from you is a seat at the Union Table. There is a paucity of Ontish houses represented in Union. That needs to be rectified. And it shouldn't be just any seat. He should sit to your right, as first among equals."

The king made a mash of his eyes and nose. He rested his right hand on the pommel of Spirit, the most celebrated sword in the history of Ragar Or. "This is your advice?"

"There's more. You must bind him to your house."

Micah's deep-set eyes had the look of volcanic rock. "Ajax is bonded now. To Greta Worrint, the woman of his choice."

"But Easton is not. No doubt Lord Salk has heard of Prince Ajax's…union, but the hand of the king's second son is no small offer."

The king huffed, then gave a little growl. In court he played the part of the mannerly monarch, but around Gregor he relieved stress however he desired. "My boys will bond who they want. You saw what my father's—"

"Our father's," Gregor interrupted, out loud this time.

The king pulled Spirit halfway up its sheath. "You saw what *my* father's arranged bonding was like to *my* mother. A waking nightmare. It sent him to an early grave. I swore not to make the same mistake, which is why I put aside the Garstring girl and bonded Anjay. The lords of the realm bitched and moaned, but they eventually made their peace with it, as they do with all my decrees. They will do the same for my sons."

Peace keeps until it doesn't, Gregor thought. He voiced a different sentiment. "Easton is not Ajax. He has different…motivations. It is said that Lord Salk's daughters are striking. You may need only introduce Easton to the Salk sisters and let nature take its course. Although you will have to explain to Easton that Lord Salk's daughters are to be bonded before they're bedded. If not, he'll skip straight to the second part."

Spirit slid back down into its sheath. The king's expression was still a mash, but now it was one of contemplation, not ire. "Perhaps you're right." He brought his sword hand to his chin. "The one daughter is a widow, no? But the other—"

"Wulfess."

Micah smiled. "Yes. Wulfess. She's aptly named, from the rumors I've heard. A strong, wild beauty. Like my Anjay." The king began nodding in that pulsating manner of his, looking like a half-mad horse. "Who knows, with Easton stealing into Coffyn Castle last night, perhaps they've already met?"

Both brothers' smiles quickly turned to frowns. "All the more reason we should hurry to Coffyn Castle," Gregor said.

The king continued nodding, now in agreement. But still neither brother moved. Gregor had said all that he had come to say. But he served at his half brother's pleasure, and it was evident that King Micah still had something on his mind.

"We're in the north now, Sagekind." The king modulated his voice, growing quieter. "Gregor." Calling Gregor by his given name meant that Micah was transitioning to the intimate language used between two men born in the fog of deception. "Down south, the rumors of your true nature are kept quiet. Confined to private conversations. Up here, I'm sure the discussions are considerably freer. And seeing you in the flesh will only…" The king momentarily trailed off. When he spoke again, his voice was gruff. "Keep your shoe on your foot, is what I'm saying. At all costs."

Gregor smiled in response. He was long practiced at managing his half brother's worry. But behind Gregor's smile resided his body, a body where bones supported muscles strung against meager flesh, the skinny want of his form manifesting in a power that pooled on the sole of his left foot. There the cosmos came to life, in the form of a whorled birthmark.

The telling mark.

The sign of the jeyedoshi.

Johanna Salk

They had confined Johanna to the Cherry Tower on the far western end of Coffyn Castle. She had assumed that part of her punishment for helping the Blackstar prince end his life would be her exclusion from King Micah's welcoming party, but midway through the following day she saw Lord Egros Coffyn below the tower window, ordering servants to tidy up the garden. When the servants secured torches in the ground, she realized what was afoot: *after sunset, they intend to say prayers with the king.*

As predicted, the Ontish lords filed into the snow-blanketed gardens at twilight, looking well dressed and sober. Johanna was thrilled with her vantage: from the window she could see everyone and everything. Lord Garstring's son Mactus noticed Johanna gazing down and gave her Werring's own eye, but when she returned his stare with a cool and level one, he grew flustered and looked away.

The parade of notables began shortly thereafter. Johanna's father Daguss led the procession. He looked every bit the pious warlord, stately in his moonbear coat with a sharp, white-trimmed beard. Behind Daguss came Wulfess, beautiful and tall, and behind Wulfess her newly betrothed, the Kalandragote man-mountain otherwise known as Cato Ollspaer. But these were familiar faces to Johanna, so she paid them little heed as they took their spots beneath Coffyn Castle's famed cherry trees.

At last, the king and his retinue entered the garden. Johanna hoped she might recognize some southern lord from her time in Thistleton, but in the shadowy cast of the torchlight it was difficult to discern distinct personages. She guessed at a couple, a game that was stopped short by the appearance of a man she had never seen but knew at once: the walking wraith wearing a cloak of burgundy was the king's bastard half brother and Sagekind, Gregor Thorn. Johanna almost expected Reginal Burntree or one of the other Ontish lords to step forward and run the demon through with a sword, but, to her relief, they let him pass. Following in the Sagekind's wake was a lean young man and a short, curvy woman. *Prince Ajax and his common bond,* Johanna guessed. *But where is Prince Easton, whose life I saved?* Next came a woman who could only have been the queen: Anjay Vint Dayborn. She was dressed in a heavy coat, but underneath the hood her Clyesian face with its upturned chin cut like an obsidian blade. And finally: King Micah Dayborn, first of his name. From the tower window it was difficult to tell if the king was burly or simply roly-poly; he called to mind a half-tamed boar. Flanking the royal procession were three armed knights. One was dressed in a patterned light blue and white surcoat, the colors of the Stavusian faith. The other two were dressed in the colors of the twins, one in a brocaded deep forest green, the other in midnight black. One was emblazoned with a golden *D,* the other a golden *R.* Southern styling. Johanna could only imagine what her father and Cato Ollspaer thought of their foppery.

But where did the styling originate if not from the Ontish? Certainly the Struvans didn't pull it from thin air?

Johanna was so absorbed by the procession below that she didn't realize someone had sneaked into her room.

"It's a shame that your father ended the rebellion before mine arrived. Otherwise, they might have all held hands and recited the prayer for vengeance together."

Johanna whirled at the sound of the voice, her heart hammering in her chest. Standing beside the bed was Easton Dayborn. Somehow, in Johanna's distraction, the king's second son had managed to not only steal inside the room, but also make his way halfway across it.

Johanna collected herself. She had been around power long enough to know that the worst thing a person could do was show surprise or weakness in the face of it.

"Is sneaking into places your only trick? It's good, I'll admit, but already it runs thin."

Easton laughed, loud enough that Johanna worried they would hear him in the gardens below. She moved away from the tower window. Easton moved with her, a prowling counterclockwise step that seemed equal parts playful and predatory.

Johanna decided it best to cut to the quick. "I saved your life last night. Are you here to rape me as thanks?"

She was glad to see a frown brought to his face. "You mistake me for one of your savage northern cousins, my lady. I am here for curiosity's sake. Pure and simple. And perhaps, in the course of sating my curiosity, I thought I might offer you my thanks as well."

She decided there might be some truth to that. She took a moment to study him. Easton had a peculiar sort of handsomeness. There was a chimerical quality to his looks, as if he wasn't quite real. He had none of his father's paunch. Instead, like his mother and brother, he was made up of sharp angles and long, lean lines. On Easton, however, the effect wasn't nearly as severe as it might have been; his puckish expression and unruly head of brown hair diluted the effect. He was wearing the same orange cloak and gray quilted doublet that he had worn the night before, and the same woolen breeches. The materials were of a princely quality, but, to Johanna's surprise, they also looked like they were due for a wash.

She noticed Easton studying her in turn. Johanna tried to see herself through his eyes. She imagined that the prince saw her the same as most men did: through the prism of Wulfess. Johanna was not as tall or as beautiful as her sister, nor was she the Twin Ascendant. Her sister wasn't the only prism through which men viewed her, of course. Some saw her as a widow, spoiled goods, while others were mesmerized by the lore of her last name, the power of her father. Easton, though…she studied the prince's dancing green eyes, searching for his impression of her. If he had one, he hid it well. It was off-putting. Her early impressions of him was that he was a young man who had mastered nothing so well as the art of enigmatic devilry.

"If not vengeance, which prayer?" Easton asked, raising an eyebrow and motioning to the tower window. "Health or wealth?"

Johanna bent an ear toward the window. There were four prayers practitioners of the Faith of the Twins might offer to the night sky: the prayer for wealth, the prayer for health, the prayer for vengeance, and the prayer for death. The prayers for vengeance and death were uttered sparingly, and only under certain conditions. Health, however, leaped from lips daily, and wealth, while supposedly reserved for the noble classes, found its way into the firmament as much if not more often than its quotidian counterpart. "They're not praying yet. But I know my father, and I've heard tales of yours, so I'm assuming that the Twins will soon have their ears stuffed with petitions for coin."

Easton laughed a little and shook his head. "How...direct. It's done much more subtly in a Stavusian temple. The way to pray for wealth there is to—"

"Place a brogan's-head in the open mouth of one of the begging statues. The cloaked stranger, to be specific."

Easton flashed a delighted smile. "That's right! You are northern born, but a southern widow. I had forgotten. Tell me—did your deceased bonded feed gold to the cloaked stranger often?"

Johanna didn't appreciate the offhand way Easton referred to her former bonded. It was true that she had never truly loved Nicolas Raleigh. But Easton Dayborn didn't know that. "My bonded was a pious man. Of a kind."

Easton slapped his knee. "He was one of those, then? Ha!" The prince screwed up his mouth in a funny way. "*And Stavus said: Feed mine statues gold, and I shall multiply thy bounty.*"

He's goading me, she understood. To her surprise, she found herself willing to be goaded. "I don't recall reading that verse in The Illuminated Scrolls. Or is this your droll way of informing me that you don't keep the faith of your fathers?"

He didn't correct her, choosing instead to plow ahead with his point. "The cloaked stranger's long tongue leads straight into the temple's coffers, you know. Coins placed on the tongues of the orphan and the beggar statues go to the poor, but the temple doesn't redistribute brogan's-heads. But what is it to you, daughter of Lord Daguss Salk? Don't tell me Nicolas Raleigh turned you to the light?"

She opened her mouth and instantly closed it again. *Who are you to pry at my truths?* And: *What is the truth?* The Faith of the Twins and the worship of Stavus were so dissimilar that it had always seemed to Johanna that belief in one didn't preclude belief in the other. Indeed, the union of Ragar Or was founded on that very premise. Johanna had been raised a child of the Twins, but on the day she held Nicolas Raleigh's hand in a Stavusian temple with the sunlight streaming around her, she felt a love that had been cruelly missing from her existence in High Osgood, a love that flowed not from her soon-to-be-bonded's hand but rather from a god who accepted her as the lesser twin she was. And yet…soon after the bonding ceremony, she couldn't help but feel a vital emptiness in the Stavusian worldview, a missing…wildness. Ever since she had felt adrift, tethered to both religions but belonging to neither.

One moment Easton was all ears, waiting for a reply, and the next he was prowling toward the window. He brushed past her with a feline insouciance, their arms grazing. "Do you hear it?" he asked.

She did. Down in the gardens they were praying to the Twins.

Easton drew close to the window but didn't show his face at the glass. Instead, he turned and slid his back down the stone wall. Seated, he withdrew a leather flask from his cloak. He tipped the flask at Johanna. "Listening mead," he explained. "It's honeyed, if my lady is so inclined."

Johanna decided that she was. She strode toward Easton, and, standing far enough away from the window that her face wouldn't show, she reached out a hand and accepted the flask. She took a deep pull, the honeyed bite like a gentle sting. From the gardens below she heard the intonations of dozens of men and women, asking the Twins for that most sacred of blessings.

Wealth.

Whole, we shall be cleaved
And full of longing, chained to life
Burning with want
As a condition of our existence
Mother Beoliotius
Daguss, Ropske
Gift us the fruits of the material world
As recompense

Johanna passed the flask back to Easton and stepped to the window. In the gardens below, the many noble men and women stood like statues in the snow. The only sign that they were alive was the sound of their prayer.

Easton took a long pull of his own from the flask. Then he spoke. "I saw a commoner whipped once in Union for saying the prayer for wealth. Down south we try to ignore malfeasances of that order when possible, but this particular fellow kept flouting his defiance in public, daring—my father, I suppose—to stop him. Truthfully, I don't think father cared. Micah Dayborn is sufficiently Stavusian to feed statue tongues, but he only prays to the Twins when protocol demands it. Still, something had to be done. The City Protection tied the commoner to a post and whipped him in the same marketplace where he'd been attracting crowds for thumbing his nose at nobility. But it was a light whipping, all in all." Easton took a quick pull from the flask. Smiled a shit-eating grin. "What do they do to offenders in the north?"

You know exactly what they do to offenders in the north, Johanna thought, refusing to respond. She found, all at once, that she had been goaded too far.

Down in the gardens, the noble men and women were taking their leave of the cold. Their many footprints made a mess of the snow; what pristine white remained rested on cherry tree boughs.

Easton sighed, disappointed that his provocation had borne no fruit. *He sounds like a bored little boy,* Johanna thought, refusing to look at him. She decided then and there that she didn't like him. *How old is he? Twenty-one to my twenty-four?* She wanted another taste of the honeyed mead, but not at the cost of asking Easton for the flask. It was time, she thought, for the prince to leave.

"Is your curiosity sufficiently sated?" she asked coldly.

"Almost." He nodded at the door on the opposite side of the room. "I imagine your sister will be here soon."

This jerked Johanna's attention. "My sister? Why would you say that?"

Easton had stoppered the flask and was swinging it on his finger by its cord. "I was there when your father spoke to her. He thought it best that she be the one to tell you."

"Tell me what?"

He released the flask into the air, and, one revolution later, caught it on the upright. His mischievous smile had returned. Or had it ever left? "Hearing the news from me would be improper, I think. And besides, part of why I'm here is because I'm curious to be in the room when word is delivered. Hidden out of sight, of course. But I digress. *Before* your sister arrives, I would like to properly thank you for saving my life."

Johanna felt off-balance. She watched Easton transition from the floor to his feet with a svelte quickness and ease. And then, in the blink of an eye, he was on bended knee before her, wearing an expression that might have passed for solemn. "My lady, though I can scarce repay you the debt I owe, I hereby swear that if you should make a request of me, I will fulfill it." He lifted his right hand; for a moment Johanna thought he was reaching for hers. But instead, his irritating smile returned, and he lifted one finger in the air. "But one request only. It's important that I am clear about that. And it would be best if you make the request sooner rather than later, as I don't intend to stay in Low Osgood for long." He moved his finger to his chin and struck a quizzical pose. "Though we may have wiggle room with the time frame, depending on how the conversation with your sister proceeds."

"Where are you going?" It was a ridiculous question to ask, all things considered, but it was the question that sprung to Johanna's tongue.

A jag of light caught in Easton's green eyes. "West. To find the dragon the Blackstar prince spoke of." The light in his eyes fired like a burst of flame. "Perhaps I'll take my newly bonded there on our sweetmarch."

Confusion concealed the dawning light of comprehension like a bank of dark tufted clouds. Before Johanna could zero in, Easton pricked his ears at a faint sound. Without saying a word, he moved to his feet, and, with the stealth and speed of a cat, made for the silver drapes that guarded the tower bed. In an instant he was swallowed in the fabric. Try as she might, Johanna saw no sign or trace of him.

Steps sounded on stone. Johanna's eyes went to the door.

The heavy oak swung open. Wulfess Salk, the Twin Ascendant, stepped inside.

Wulfess looked like she always did: like an empress on her coronation day. A pearl and onyx necklace encircled her neck. Kalandragote colors: black and white. Wulfess's bonding pledge from Cato Ollspaer.

"Could you hear us saying the prayer?" Wulfess asked Johanna without saying hello.

"Wealth, not health," Johanna responded. She fixed her gaze on her twin, studiously keeping her eyes away from the silver bed drapes. "I watched from the window. Mactus Garstring gave me a look like he wanted to serve me my Ontish supper."

Wulfess dropped her chin and raised tsk-tsk eyebrows. "He would if he could. And he's not the only one. Father has done you a favor by locking you in the tower."

"Father only does favors for himself. If anyone else benefits, it's merely circumstantial." She wanted to say more, but there was the matter of Easton in the drapes. She hadn't quite reached the place where she would betray her family outright.

But she was getting there.

Wulfess sidestepped Johanna's anger. It was a dance Wulfess had gotten quite good at, a nimble one-two that allowed her to stay on good terms with Johanna while continuing to reap the benefits of being the Twin Ascendant. "In this specific case, I'm siding with father. You stopped the Ontish lords from sating their bloodlust. It's better that you're safe in the tower than their consolation prize."

"The tower must not be *that* safe. You broke in easily enough."

Wulfess furrowed her brow. "That's true. I was told that Father's man Rolphus was on guard duty, but he's nowhere to be seen."

Johanna assumed that the answer to that particular riddle was wrapped in the drapes, but it was a question that would have to wait.

Johanna studied her sister, searching for clues as to why she was there. Like Daguss and Ropske, Wulfess and Johanna were fraternal twins; and, like the legendary founders of Ragar Or, they were close to one another, despite the many tensions that might have driven them apart. Their bond had been forged in the years that they had relied on each other after their mother's death. They had made promises to each other back then that Johanna would rather die than believe could be broken. Promises made in anticipation of the day they both knew was on the horizon—the day Father named one of them the Twin Ascendant. And in the years since her naming, Wulfess had done nothing to lead Johanna to believe that she would be unfaithful to her vows.

But every day was a new day. And every day, while Wulfess worked closer with their father to bring his worldview into existence, Johanna fell further and further from the family orbit.

"How did the king receive the news of your bonding pledge to an Ollspaer?"

Wulfess smiled. "With a fat fake grin and a long drink from his cup. What *could* he say? His own son has bonded a commoner."

"I saw—Greta, isn't it?—from the tower window. Do the prince and his bonded seem in love?"

Wulfess arched her eyebrows. "I suppose. Love doesn't interest me the way it once did. Father has trained me for too long to see bonding as a war that must be won." She grinned. "The goal, of course, is for both sides to emerge the victor."

"Bonding isn't a war. Love isn't a war."

Wulfess replied in a voice that suggested she felt sorry for Johanna. "My dear sister. Everything is a war."

They disagreed in the space of a restive silence. Johanna broke the peace. "Surely the king protested. It's not only Cato you're bonding. It's Kalandragote as well. There are…political ramifications. I understand that Father needed the alliance to quell the rebellion, but now that it's over, now that the Blackstar prince is dead—"

Wulfess's waterfall blues roamed the room. She looked dreamy, distracted. *What I don't know could fill a book,* Johanna understood. She waited until her sister's eyes settled once more on hers. "Go on," Johanna said. "Enlighten me. At least to the extent that Father will allow it."

Wulfess stepped closer. She was taller than Johanna, but only slightly so. When they were teenagers, it was unclear who the Twin Ascendant would be; there were days when Johanna believed in her heart of hearts that their father would name her. But now, watching Wulfess at the height of her powers, it seemed as if their futures had been written in stone from the first day of their existence.

"The king *was* upset, at first. But then Father told him what my bonding pledge to Cato Ollspaer had won. Kalandragote has agreed to join the kingdom."

Johanna thought she had misheard. "You can't be serious. Kalandragote has been independent for more than two hundred years. They fought a war over it. I recognize that you are the Twin Ascendant of Lord Daguss Salk, but surely your hand in bonding alone can't change the course of history."

Wulfess fake-winced. "You wound me, Sister."

"Come off it, Wulfess. What else is at play? You have father's ear, and he has yours. Tell me: what understanding has he struck with the Kalandragote king?"

Too late Johanna remembered Easton Dayborn in the drapes. For a nervous second, she worried that Wulfess might in fact be privy to their father's maneuverings. *Beoliotius bless us, if she spills the beans, we'll have to murder the prince together by stabbing him through the drapes.* But if Wulfess knew something that Johanna did not, she covered it well.

"I am no small prize, Sister. Everyone knows father's power. And the Blackstar Rebellion reminded Horos Ollspaer just how isolated Kalandragote is. In this new age, Kalandragote realizes that the time to fulfill the promise of Union…is now."

"An Ontish lady bonding a Kalandragote prince, novel as it may be, hardly fulfills the promise of Union."

Wulfess's face lit up like a struck match. "What if there were two bonding ceremonies? Our father has two daughters, after all. As King Micah has two sons."

Easton appeared. Like a specter materializing from the ether, he was suddenly standing at Wulfess's back, a magician's grin on his face. Wulfess, seeing Johanna's eyes catch behind her, spun around.

The second son of King Micah Dayborn gave a deep bow. Johanna realized with relief that for all Wulfess knew, he had just snuck in the door.

"The sisters Salk! Speaking of king's sons and whatnot. I knew my ears were burning for a reason." He stood upright, and, making a go-ahead motion with his hand, gestured that Wulfess should continue. "Go on, you were about to reveal the good part."

Wulfess laughed. Johanna couldn't tell if it was a mean laugh or an amused one. Wulfess looked for a long moment at Easton, and then turned back to Johanna. She gave an elegant little shrug of the shoulders. "He'll keep you entertained, at least."

Him. They want me to bond him. Johanna felt a black surge of anger at both Easton and her sister. She thought of the Blackstar prince, downing the contents of his poison cup. *Axton called me the twin of his choosing. And I betrayed him to save this jackass.* "This is what father wants? To bond me to the king's *second* son?" She put extra bite in the word *second*.

Easton's response was whip-quick. "This coming from the *lesser* twin. And who says I want to bond you? Father may think it's for the best, but as for me, I'm undecided. You may not know this, but Dayborns bond who they want. It's a family tradition."

Johanna readied another retort, but before she could launch it, Wulfess reached out and grabbed her by the arm. She pulled Johanna close and whispered fiercely in her ear. "Careful. It's him or no one. If you fail father in this, he'll make you a Winged Woman."

A Winged Woman? A wave of sickness overtook Johanna. She knew the dreary and mundane existence that awaited every woman sent to a Stavusian temple, and she wanted no part of it. "Father worships the Twins," she whispered back. "He doesn't even—"

"It doesn't matter. After what you did with the poison…" Wulfess's grip was both softness and steel. "Listen to me, Johanna. You are out of options. Be of use to the family. Bond this boy. Then you'll have power of your own. The fact that you are a lesser twin won't matter as much down south."

She knew that her sister was right. Northern life held no hope for her. Her future, if she hoped to have one, was far from any place where lesser twins were held in contempt.

Johanna looked at the Dayborn prince, standing in the background. She expected to find an expression of condescending curiosity on his face. The curiosity was there, but, to her surprise, his smirking smile was gone. In fact, he almost looked like a man who had undergone a revelation.

Johanna steeled herself. Jerked her arm away from Wulfess. She realized that she was standing at a crossroads. It seemed that there were only two choices, but perhaps that wasn't the case. The boy before her wasn't bonding material, but he was a man made for adventure, and that could be put to use. Plus, he had promised her a favor.

It was time to see if he would be true to his word.

"Leave me alone with him," she said to Wulfess, loud enough for Easton to hear. "We need time to get to know one another."

Wulfess nodded. She released Johanna's arm and walked toward the door with an unsettling grace. On her way, she stopped and gave Easton a head-to-toe appraisal. "Be nice to my sister, Dayborn, or I'll sic my bonded-to-be on you. He has practice killing inferior men, you know." And with those words, she left.

The room felt smaller after Wulfess was gone. The prince pretended that he was unfazed by the threat. "Cato Ollspaer *is* a big son of a bitch," he said with a smile. "Bigger than me. But I can assure you that I'm quicker. That being said, I will try my best to follow your sister's suggestion, and be nice."

"I don't want to bond you."

To Johanna's surprise, the prince looked hurt. He quickly hid his pain behind a paring-knife smile. "I couldn't hear what your sister said to you. But based on your reaction, I'm guessing that maybe you don't have a choice."

Johanna gave Easton a look of contempt. "Oh, you've decided that you want to bond me? That certainly wasn't my impression." She sneered. "Or did I mishear you?"

A mischievous glint shone in Easton's eyes. "I enjoy keeping my family on their toes. They expect me to rebel, so maybe, just this once, I'll do what's asked of me. Also, bonding you would be a thumb in my brother's eye, especially now that he's bonded a commoner. That's another plus." He donned a gallant smile. "See, I've talked myself into it. Make your request, and I'll say yes."

He's playing games with me. He's a stupid boy, and he thinks this is a lark. She could only imagine what type of husband Easton Dayborn would be. He was too young to be faithful, too obsessed with himself to be an equal partner, and too full of wanderlust to stay in her company for long. Not that she wanted to be around him. No, she wouldn't bond him. But she wasn't about to become a Winged Woman either.

She closed the distance between them. "I'll say it again. I don't want to bond you. But I am going to hold you to that favor. Right now."

He looked surprised. And perhaps a little disappointed. Still, he recovered quickly enough, and offered Johanna his most insouciant smile. "As you wish. A bonding pledge from the son of a king doesn't grow on trees, but I suppose you have your reasons, however ridiculous they may be." He tugged at his quilted doublet, as if physically readjusting his purpose. "Okay then, let's settle our debts. Name your favor."

Johanna took a deep breath. She knew that once she spoke, there was no going back. "We're not bonding one another, second son. But I want you to tell everyone that we are. Then, when you find the opportunity, steal me far away from here."

Silas O' the Songs

A sword-wielding brute chased Silas and Wyn through the nighttime forest. Glints of moonlight flashed off the swordsman's hawk's-head helm, informing Silas's repeated over-the-shoulder glances that the fellow was, in fact, closing the gap.

Up ahead, Wyn steered a path through the trees. Hungry tree limbs raked at the fiddler's clothes, but each time Silas thought the path was on the verge of closing, Wyn would find a way through. *He is aware that we're being chased, isn't he?* Silas wondered, unable to recall a time when Wyn had looked back. Not that it mattered. The little man's efficient pathfinding made following him a foregone conclusion, regardless of whether Wyn was cognizant of the peril.

"Gaaaaaaarrrrrrrr!" the swordsman bellowed, either out of bloodlust or growing frustration at being unable to bridge the distance. Wyn paid it no mind. Silas, satisfied that his fiddle-playing counterpart was now aware of the danger, glanced over his shoulder once more to check on the swordsman's advance. When Silas turned back around, he discovered that he was following air.

"Wyn!" The little man was nowhere to be seen. Flustered, Silas stumbled, tripping over a tree root. Upon recovering, he shot for a gap between two trees, only to discover at the last moment that there were thorny vines underfoot. The swordsman's charging footsteps sounded out Silas's error. Silas tore through the vines, but it was too late. Death was upon him.

He turned to meet his end.

The swordsman's arm was primed, set for the thrust, when from behind a nearby tree Wyn Dunkin emerged, a dagger at the ready. Quick as a cat, Wyn slipped the blade between the swordsman's ribs with a no-nonsense élan, and then, while the swordsman worked Os with his mouth, the fiddler withdrew the dagger and redeposited it in the exposed portion of the swordsman's neck.

The swordsman slumped to the ground, dead. His hawk's-head helmet tumbled onto the black of the forest floor.

Silas was too stunned to speak. To his utter amazement, Silas realized that Wyn was still holding onto the fiddle and bow with his left hand.

Wyn began rummaging through the dead man's clothes. He came away with a handful of silver. "To the victors, eh?" he quipped. He retrieved the bloody dagger from the dead man's neck, wiped it clean, and sheathed it. Satisfied, he hop-stepped a few feet away and picked up the hawk's-head helm. "Worth coin and contemplation, don't you think?" He pointed the helm in the direction from which they'd came. "Let's keep moving. I imagine there will be no more murder birds, but all the same, I'd rather imagine it from a safer remove."

They continued, traipsing ever deeper into the woods. Silas had no idea where they were or where they were going, but Wyn seemed confident enough. Silas had always thought that he knew the Vake like the back of his hand, but now he realized that what he actually knew were the roads that ran through the Vake, not the woods that made up its ligneous core.

They walked in silence for a long time. All around, the forest sung its nighttime song, a soporific symphony of late-autumn stillness. The two men joined in with the percussion, crunching leaves underfoot. Silas could feel the effects of his adrenaline rush wearing off, while at the same time the numbing horror of what he had witnessed at The Golden Pear came crashing in. *They killed them all,* he thought. He stopped short. *No, not all,* he remembered. *Not everyone.*

Thirty minutes passed. An hour. The night, chilly at the outset, settled into a teeth-chattering cold. Silas's bones began to ache. He needed warmth. He needed rest.

"We should stop and build a fire. We should get some rest."

"You need a new lute, Silas O' the Songs. Your old one is turned to ash."

Why is he talking about my lute? In the midst of Wyn's heroics, Silas had forgotten he was dealing with a crazy person. "Yes. Eventually. But it's not at the top of my priority list at the present moment."

Wyn sniffed the air, rising on his hind legs like a rat. "I know a woods witch who lives nearby. Last time I visited, she had a lute lying around. I feel confident that she would part with it for a price."

"Are you paying with the silver you took from the dead man? I'm short on coin."

"No worries. She doesn't trade in coin. A taste of your blood or a ride on your cock will suffice."

Silas laughed, in spite of himself. "I choose the latter."

Wyn raised his eyebrows. "Blood is the cheaper price. But it's your decision."

They fell back into a silence. Continued walking. When on occasion Silas lifted his head, he could see the Moonbear constellation stalking them from high in the sky, peering through the forest glut.

Twenty minutes later, they arrived at the woods witch's abode. It looked less like a cabin than a mangled grave of rotting trees. Silas felt a chill run up his spine. Only an unholy creature would live here. Of that he was certain.

"Do you mean to wake her?" Silas started to ask, but even as the words left his lips, he saw a woman with straight long hair emerge from the dwelling. She stared at them from behind the veil of her hair without speaking. After a moment, the woods witch stepped to the side of the door, indicating that they should come inside.

The fireplace had dwindled to embers. Otherwise, a single brooding candle burned inside the cabin. The light the candle produced was more adept at casting shadows than illuminating the interior. Silas strained to follow it, trying as hard as he could to better glimpse the witch.

"I heard you coming," the witch said, surprising Silas. Her voice was softer and more feminine than he had expected. "Such a ruckus tonight. Dirty doings. And the two of you, running and killing, crunching leaves."

Wyn laughed. It was difficult for Silas to tell in the dark, but it looked like the little man had found a place to sit. "You have a good ear, Merjy! But I suppose a witch that isn't a good listener isn't a witch at all."

"Very true," the witch responded, a coy note in her voice. "Tell me, O—"

"Wyn. Call me by name, Merjy. Wyn Dunkin."

The woods witch perambulated back and forth slowly, the candle flame failing to find her face. When she spoke next, her voice had a hint of humor in it. "Tell me, Wyn Dunkin, why did you come here?"

Wyn responded with glee. "My dear, I am traveling with none other than Silas O' the Songs, the greatest living lutist in all of the Vake! But sadly, he no longer has a lute!"

"Lost it, did he?"

"Yes, he did! During the dirty doings."

"That's no excuse. The greatest living lutist in all the Vake should never abandon his instrument. He could learn a lesson from you. Dirty doings or not, you still have your fiddle."

"Not everyone can be like me, Merjy."

Silas felt punch-drunk from the repartee. The conversation wasn't at all what he had expected. For one, the woods witch, though shrouded in appearance, had a sense of humor. And for another, the subtext passing between Wyn and the woods witch suggested that all was not as it appeared. Silas felt trapped in a dream.

The woods witch worked her way over to the corner of the cabin. The parsimonious candle flame exposed images in the gloom: a cast-iron skillet hanging from a wall nail; dried and bundled herbs; wicker baskets; a tree-stump chair; the empty stare of a skinned and scowling fox. And last, where the woods witch was leaning: a gorgeous lute. Merjy picked up the lute and brought it to Silas. Then she led Silas by the arm over to the tree stump and bade him sit.

"Play," she suggested.

Silas plucked one string, then the others. All in tune. Without thinking, he started playing "On Wings of Light," trying to recreate the same magic Isbel Wicker had conjured in The Golden Pear. But almost as soon as he had begun, the witch shot out her hand and grabbed Silas by the arm. "None of that," she said. The flame bled onto her face, revealing an alabaster chin and lips like strips of rose petal.

"None of what?" Silas asked, confused.

Wyn's voice bounded through the dark. "What Merjy means to say is that we're not in a temple, Silas O' the Songs. Play us something…different. Something personal."

Something personal. Silas nearly scoffed. But his fingers were already going to work, outpacing his thoughts. He slowed the song's tempo, allowing his fingers time to find their mark in the dark. The end result was a version of "Ballad of the Cruel Sister" that was both elegant and haunting. Silas laced his voice with a bitter edge when he sang the parts told from Anis Salk's perspective. There were moments when he felt like he was summoning her ghost.

When he had finished, silence fell. Wyn clapped, while Merjy reached over and stroked the hair on the back of his head. "That was damned fine. You make a good magic, Silas O' the Songs," Wyn said from across the room. "I wager that's the best you've ever played it."

It was true. He had never played it better.

Merjy put down the candle on a nearby table and began tracing fingernail shapes on the nape of Silas's neck. Wyn's voice poured through the gloom like a mesmeric smoke. "Still, it was missing something. Help me, Merjy. What was Silas's song missing?"

Merjy was working the lute from Silas's fingers. He was sad to see it go, but when she leaned in close to his face with her breasts, he made his peace with it. "The common touch," she replied.

"The common touch," Wyn echoed. "The indefinable indelible. That which causes lips to hum long after the evening song is sung."

Silas's pride stirred him to a response. "I don't compose tavern music. I compose for lords and ladies. My song—" The woods witch had begun unlacing his breeches, which made Silas lose his train of thought.

"'Ballad of the Cruel Sister' would not have won you the brogan's-head. Nor a place with the Swans. But at least your song was *yours,* which is more than can be said for the maid with the harp and Felix-fried-in-the-fire."

Merjy interrupted with a whisper in his ear. "I'll give you a song to sing." She had him undone, out; she was hiking up her shrouded garb, readying to settle on the want of him.

"Has Merjy made you an offer?" Wyn asked from across the way, laughter in his voice. "Tell me, what is it?"

Merjy stilled, hovering above Silas, the night hanging in the balance. It took Silas a moment to realize that the question wasn't rhetorical. "She said she would give me a song to sing."

"Insist that she include the lute in the bargain as well. And remember, she'll settle for a taste of your blood if you're so inclined."

The present bargain seemed well struck to Silas. But, hard as his cock was, he didn't want to pass up the chance at a new instrument. "The lute then, as well?" he asked her.

"Agreed," she answered. "But don't lose this one." And then she was on him, opening, and he was hers, and she was his. Together they danced the timeless dance.

Across the room, Wyn began to play the fiddle. The song was unlike any Silas had heard before. Silas drifted in and out of the darkwoods melody as the woods witch rocked above him. The song sounded like the springtime engaged in a cryptic conversation with autumn. All the while Merjy poured into him, and he into her. They drew closer to one another, his face finding its way through her veil of hair. And there she was before him, not unholy at all, but a beckoning shadow, a refuge. He searched for her rose petal lips with his own, but at the last moment she pulled back and held him with her dark-lit eyes. And then, and then...

She took something from him. A needle-sliver. It drifted out of his body like a stinging wisp. As she extracted it, he saw the underbelly of the world, the deep dark soil, the begging question asked of everyone at the end. He fell headfirst into a tiny death. She buckled above him, coming.

As her shuddering body settled back into solid ground, she leaned forward and whispered the gift of her song into his ear.

It sounded like nonsense.

They left early the next morning after a simple breakfast of scrambled eggs and skillet potatoes. Outside, a Stavusian dawn held sway, the sun glorying in its proximity to all living things. Wyn left as he had arrived, with a loose hold on his fiddle and bow. He wore the hawk's-head helm atop his head for convenience's sake. Silas, conversely, carried the witch's lute in a worn leather case given to him by Merjy (free of charge, unlike the lute). The lute was made of rosewood and had a quality that suggested lofty origins. Silas couldn't help but speculate on its genesis as they walked through the forest.

"Where do you think she got it from?"

Wyn was walking with his customary bounce. As he walked, he stared at the sun with a smile, suggesting cahoots with the celestial body. "The better question is: who did she get it from? Woods witches aren't known for their travels."

"Who, then?"

"A man. Or a woman. A person, I think."

"A person from whence?"

Wyn shrugged. "What you're really asking is if the lute is Wrainish. You want it to be a Wrainish lute. A *true* Wrainish lute. Personally, I say believe it is if you're so inclined. Who would know otherwise? It certainly sounded Wrainish when you wrung that song from its neck."

Silas frowned. *I haven't wrung a song from a lute's neck a day in my life.* He did suppose Wyn had a point about the lute's origin. The meaning of what constituted a *true* Wrainish lute had changed since the early years of union. For a century and a half, the only lutes that passed through the port city of Wrain were ones that had been crafted by a guild of master luthiers out of Clyesia. But in the last one hundred years, inferior Clyesian luthiers had gotten in on the trade, thereby diluting the definition. Lutes that passed through Wrain these days remained superior to those crafted in Ragar Or, but true Wrainish lutes were more difficult to identify than they had once been.

"Felix Fingers's Wrainish lute had a *Fruy Teech* guild label visible through the sound hole. I should check the witch's lute for the same."

Wyn laughed so heartily, it made him dance a little jig. "There are luthiers in Dunning Harbor who spend more time fashioning a plausible *Fruy Teech* label than they do crafting their instrument. The only way to know if you have a true Wrainish lute, Silas O' the Songs, is to know what a true Wrainish lute sounds like. And then compare it to your own."

Silas's face flushed red. He didn't appreciate the pretense implied by Wyn's statement—namely, that the little man knew more about lutes than he did. "And you, song thief, know what a true Wrainish lute sounds like?"

Wyn tugged thoughtfully at his chin. The hawk's-head helm wobbled atop his noggin like a precariously placed bolder. "Might be I heard one last night. It's difficult to say. You played multiple songs, if I recall correctly. The sloppy sounds of your second number certainly didn't suggest Wrainish quality."

The red on Silas's face crimsoned. Sex with Merjy had seemed a splendid idea at the time, but in hindsight, the memory unsettled. He still wasn't sure what the woods witch had taken from him during the act. Not to mention that he could make little of the song she had given him. Not that you could call it a song; it was more like a nonsensical suggestion.

Still, his endeavors had won him the lute, which wasn't nothing.

"How do you know Merjy?" Silas asked.

"I'm familiar with many of the woods witches in the Vake. We walk the same path."

"What path is that?"

"The trail of the trees."

Silas didn't know what to make of that. "She seemed to suggest that she had heard us coming. That she knew about your…um…dealings with the hawk's-head soldier."

"No surprises there. Woods witches are superb listeners. The Stavusian faithful have been trying to eradicate them from the Vake for years, but the witches always hear them coming."

Silas remembered Merjy's reaction to his playing of "On Wings of Light." "Most woods witches worship the Twins, do they not?" he asked Wyn. Even though he had lived in the Vake all his life, Silas was more familiar with the concept of woods witches than the reality of them. From his perspective, a woods witch was a woman that lived in the woods. Simple as that. It was common knowledge that women who took to the woods didn't worship Stavus, the Struvan god of light and air, but that was no crime. Many across the Vake worshipped the Twins rather than Stavus. Others worshipped both; others neither. It was often said that worshipping Stavus was a science, while worshipping the Twins an art. If the woods witches made an art of worshipping Daguss and Ropske, what of it?

"Woods witches certainly claim they worship the Twins, if ears need tending. But their worship is too peculiar for Hawk's-Eyes and the like. And this being the Vake, Hawk's-Eyes are particularly attuned to worship of an aberrant variety. Especially if that worship involves the glorification and deification of"—Wyn spread his arms wide, as if hugging the forest—"trees."

Silas nodded. "You mean the Yubriy tree?" Silas knew that there were occult worshippers of the Yubriy tree scattered throughout the Vake. No doubt woods witches numbered among them.

"Among others. The Yubriy is a glorious tree, but it's difficult to worship properly. The king's soldiers are always guarding it. The woods witches say their high prayers to the Yubriy, but they're not above muttering low prayers to lesser timber—your oaks, your ashes, your willows, your toad maples."

"I've always wanted to see the Yubriy tree."

Wyn cocked his head at Silas. "You've lived in the Vake your entire life and you've never seen the Yubriy tree?"

"That's not uncommon. I'm from the southern Vake. Ragknot. And I don't pray to trees, so there's not been a compelling reason for me to travel north."

"Ragknot, you say? I *thought* you had the look of a riverboy. As for the Yubriy, we're walking in the right direction if you would like to fulfill a lifetime wish. We could make it there in two days. There's a knoll in a nearby field where the soldiers guarding it will let you gaze upon the Yubriy unmolested." Wyn gave Silas a roguish grin. "I wouldn't mind seeing it myself, truth be told. The Yubriy would be a calming sight after all the dirty doings."

Silas shook his head. "No thank you. Soon as we cross a road, I'll be on my way." He gave Wyn a mean look. "I'm appreciative that you saved my life, but I don't keep with song thieves."

"I've saved your life twice, if we're keeping count," Wyn sallied. Apropos of nothing, the little man skipped, kicking his heels in the process. The hawk's-head helm slipped to the right when he jumped, covering his entire ear. "Suit yourself, Silas O' the Songs. I had hoped we might write a song together before our paths parted, but if you must leave, then leave you must. Where will you go?"

An inadvertent sigh escaped Silas's lips. *Where will I go?* he pondered. With the passing of Felix Fingers, he could once again claim to be the greatest living lutist in all the Vake, but he doubted there was a locale in the region where he could make decent coin off his talents. Perhaps Castle Greenwell, but he'd be damned if he gave Anna Josephine Arc the pleasure of groveling for a second residency. Fail or succeed, the tryout for the Swans was meant to be his ticket out of the Vake. He supposed all that had transpired didn't change the fact that there was no future for him in the area.

"South," he said. "To Dagon. Union perhaps. Someplace where the nobility will appreciate my talents."

"Merjy appreciated your talents. There are other woods witches, Silas O' the Songs, if you would like to be appreciated closer to home." That laugh again, hearty and hollow. "But in all seriousness, I wouldn't venture south just yet. Merjy and I shared a word after you nodded off last night. She says the murder birds are migrating north. Best to stay ahead of them for the time being."

Is that true? Silas would have dismissed it as a ploy to keep in his company if he hadn't witnessed Merjy's soothsaying abilities firsthand. Perhaps the little man was telling the truth. Perhaps the murder birds were heading north. Perhaps going south meant death.

Wyn capitalized on Silas's uncertainty. "You should visit the Yubriy tree with me, Silas O' the Songs. We can write a song together along the way. Make the trip and I'll forgive you the debt you owe me for saving your life. Twice." He grinned a gap-toothed grin.

Silas gritted his teeth. All things even, he would have rather been rid of Wyn Dunkin, but he didn't know his way out the woods, and the little man's company was a good idea with murder birds afoot. "All right. But don't forget that you owe me a debt as well. If we happen to write a decent song together, it's mine."

Gregor Thorn

The Ontish lords watched Gregor with a discomforting openness. They watched him, and as they watched him, they whispered the many names they had fashioned for him. *The Wraith in Red* was a popular one, as was *Skin 'n Bones, Bad Magic,* and, simply, *Struvan Bastard.* There was another name that they held on the tip of their tongues but never spoke aloud, though their expressions screamed it, and Gregor could hear its echo in the hollow of their thoughts.

Jeyedoshi.

Jeyedoshi.

Jeyedoshi.

While the Ontish watched and spoke of Gregor, Gregor was watching and listening too. Most of the talk centered on the Blackstar's dragon. The traitorous prince whose head now resided on a spike had, in the moments before his death, proclaimed the arrival of the first dragon seen on Ragar Or in over sixty-five years. There were those who believed the prince's story, and there were those who did not. Although Gregor had not been there to hear the prince, the story so closely mirrored Gregor's dream that he was convinced.

Dragons had returned to Ragar Or.

What no one could agree on was what the arrival of the dragon meant. In an attempt to find meaning, the old histories were penned and butchered like hogs.

"Remember what the dragon Teriquay did to King Reuel's family? Dragons mean calamity."

"Not always. The Slumberer did little but sit on his fat lizard arse and gobble up anyone who dared come close."

"That's only because it wasn't approached by the right person. Dragons come to Ragar Or looking for a rider. It's searching for a son or a daughter of Coros. For a Jeyedoshi."

And then the Ontish lords would cast baleful eyes at Gregor and whisper of quieter things.

The talk wasn't only of dragons. Everyone was curious to know what accord King Micah and Daguss Salk would reach. The negotiations were ongoing, but Gregor had a sense of where they were heading. It wouldn't be long before the entire host was heading to Kalandragote.

The king had implied as much that first night. After saying the prayer for wealth in the cherry tree garden with the Ontish nobility, Gregor was admitted to Micah's chambers, where they rehashed the revelations of the day.

"Who are you?" King Micah asked him.

"A bastard half brother. Bound to serve."

"And who am I?"

"King Micah of House Dayborn, the first of his name, Holy Son of the Air, the Twin Ascendant, and the Rightful Ruler of Ragar Or."

The ritual completed, Micah chuckled. "We are in Daguss Salk's world, are we not? He greets us with the Blackstar prince's head on a spike and his eldest daughter's hand lounging in the crook of an Ollspaer elbow." He sighed. "But what can I say? My own firstborn arrived at the castle flaunting his common bond."

Gregor kept an impassive face. "We will pin our hopes on Salk's other daughter. And on your younger son."

The king's chuckle became a laugh. "From the sound of it, they're meant for one another! Tell me, Sagekind. Do you believe that this girl poisoned Axton Boil?"

Gregor's voice remained flat. "Easton believed it to be true. He said that he witnessed it with his own eyes. He said that she saved his life."

This set the king to huffing and puffing. "Ah, yes. My second son. The escape artist. He's so trustworthy that he vanished before prayers." After a moment, Micah calmed himself. He waved his hand as if dismissing his son. "It's irrelevant. My son will do what he will do. And I will do what I will do."

Gregor addressed his half brother with a soft tongue. "Be wary, my king. Kalandragote refused to join Ragar Or when a Salk sat on the Union throne. The fact that they are offering to do so now is…surprising. I know there were rumors of a near uprising against Horos Ollspaer during the rebellion, but—"

The King waved his hand once again, dismissing Gregor this time. "Not that surprising. It fits with your dream, doesn't it? Kalandragote has troubles. I have troubles. But together…" He yoked his fingers in lieu of finishing the sentence. "Besides, you have told me how the dream ends, Sagekind. Two suns! If I go this route, I will go down in history as the king who brought Kalandragote into the fold. That's well worth the price of a trip north to watch the lovely Wulfess Salk bond a man-bear. Ha!"

Gregor simply nodded. Everything the king said was true. By the simple act of witnessing a bonding ceremony Micah Dayborn would be transformed from the king who nearly lost Ragar Or into the king who made Ragar Or whole. The only question was how to ensure the king's safety during the trip. He supposed they would be forced to rely on Dante Heron. Despite Gregor's misgivings.

"But for now," Micah continued, bringing a pointing finger into the fray, "we'll settle in and allow Daguss Salk to twist in the wind. In the meantime, I have chores for you."

Per Micah's instructions, Gregor selected the most antagonistic of the Ontish to humble.

Reginal Burntree, he of the sneering leer and wolfish face.

There were other Ontish present as well. Grocian Mock, a great swine of a man who seemed incapable of drinking his fill. Seydron Qorl, a man who, given his surname, Gregor might have thought would have been friendlier than the others, but instead had done nothing but stare daggers at the Dayborns since his arrival. And Darry Coffyn, Lord Egros's nephew and the heir to Coffyn Castle. They were part of a delegation chosen to ride out and meet Dante Heron, which also made it a ripe opportunity to humble Reginal. *Only prick the Burntree's pride,* the king had commanded. *But make sure a sufficient number are there to bear witness and spread the word.*

Gregor gathered them together in the yard midmorning. Prince Ajax and a handful of the king's guard were with Gregor, making it a balanced delegation. The Ontish wore their customary surly aspect, but there was a hint of pride as well: everyone in the castle knew that Dante Heron rode at the front of a magnificent host. To be chosen to ride out and greet him in Low Osgood was a great honor, even if the honor had been bestowed by a Struvan king.

Gregor studied the men atop their magnificent mounts. They looked proud and puffed up in the cold, bright sun. He sighed on the inside.

I am a bastard half brother, he reminded himself. *Bound to serve.*

"Good morning." His voice wasn't booming, but when he spoke, his tone had a harshness that gathered ears. The men turned to him. "In a moment, we ride out to meet Dante Heron. But before we go, King Micah has requested that the severed head of Axton Boil be retrieved from the ramparts and turned over to his possession." His swiveled his head and found his man. "Reginal Burntree, I have heard tales of your prowess on the battlements. Would you do King Micah the honor of retrieving the traitor's head?"

Reginal's neck snapped; his eyes bit. Gregor's praise of Reginal was disingenuous, and everyone knew it. Reginal had been selected because he had been the one to sever the Blackstar prince's head from his shoulders after the poisoning and parade it up the gatehouse battlements. The act had been permitted by Daguss Salk, of course, but Daguss Salk was above making an example of, as were most of the lords. Reginal, on the other hand, was merely the heir to Port Black. He would suit fine.

Reginal worked his tongue around his mouth, searching for the right response. His pale green eyes were full of anger. Still, Gregor could see that Reginal was keenly aware of who he was talking to. Reginal's hatred of the Wraith in Red was real enough, but so was his fear.

"I don't know, Sagekind," Burntree said at last, pausing to spit on the ground. "He looks content on that spike. I say we let him be."

No one laughed at the joke. A wind kicked up in the courtyard, stirring the silence. Gregor glanced up at the gatehouse battlements, where the Blackstar prince stared out at the great expanse of snow-covered land that poured into the Edgeling Mountains. He wondered if the Blackstar prince was dreaming. He wondered if even in the afterlife it was impossible to escape one's dreams.

He turned back to Reginal. *Time to play the part.* His eyes were obsidian hard.

"The King of Ragar Or has commanded that he come down. I've asked the man who put him there to retrieve him. Are you refusing?"

His words were direct, his voice calm. Gregor was the king's bastard half brother, yes, but there wasn't a soul in Ragar Or who didn't understand that when the Sagekind spoke in the king's absence, he was speaking with the king's voice. To defy Gregor Thorn was to defy the king.

Or, to put it in terms the Ontish understood, to defy Gregor Thorn was to defy the Twin Ascendant.

Reginal snorted through his black prickle-bush beard. But, all the same, he dismounted.

To Gregor's great relief, Grocian Mock, Seydron Qorl, and Darren Coffyn held their tongues.

Up on the ramparts, Reginal worked Axton Boil's head off the spike. When the severed head was free, Reginal carried the Blackstar prince back by his stormy-sea tresses, swinging the head with deliberate carelessness: more than once the dead prince's face scraped against the stone walls of Coffyn Castle. Reginal's ire must have grown during his labor, for when he reached the ground, he tossed the Blackstar prince's head at the feet of Gregor's horse. Gregor's mount was as steady as they come, but even so the horse nickered when the severed head bounced against its leg.

"Tell the king he's welcome to it." Reginal sneered. "Tell him that Reginal Burntree brought him the Blackstar prince twice. First from the battlefield. Then from the ramparts."

Gregor remained motionless atop his mount. He summoned the look of a demon emerging from the hellfire of the Bottom Black. "I will give him my account. Though I can assure you that the king already knows who you are."

Prince Ajax, mounted beside Gregor, gave a little laugh. Reginal steamed but said nothing.

A young knight nearby named Deglan Whisk jumped into action, swooping down into the dust to transfer the severed head into a felt-lined wooden box. Now that the Blackstar's forces had been crushed, the prince's head served better as a bargaining tool than it did a war trophy. King Micah had every intention of returning Axton's remains to the Blackstar Isles once the tax revenue resumed pouring in.

"Well done, Uncle Bones," Prince Ajax said into Gregor's ear as he moved his steed to the front of the group. Gregor backed up his horse, fading behind his nephew. It was a pre-orchestrated arrangement: the prince taking command, the hated Wraith in Red receding into the background. It had all been planned beforehand. One of the Sagekind's primary duties was to suffer arrows of hate on the Dayborn dynasty's behalf. Gregor was hated already for his position, his powers, and his suspected nature. Ajax, on the other hand, would be the king one day. There was no need for him to engender needless ill-will.

"Open the gates!" Ajax commanded. The great iron bars gave way, revealing a tableau of blinding white. After days spent cowering behind snow clouds, the sun was at last on the offensive. "The Twins and Stavus are getting along well this morning," the prince said to the men. "And why wouldn't they? Our deities have always smiled on the union of the Struvan and Ontish peoples. When we are joined together," the prince continued, looking at each and every man, "all of creation smiles on Ragar Or. Now let us ride out and welcome Dante Heron to the north."

The prince kicked his heels into the ribs of his horse, and off the delegation went. Gregor hung back, watching the Ontish with discerning eyes, curious to see how they divided themselves. Mock's massive brown destrier fell in with Burntree's dappled-gray steed. Coffyn and Qorl rode alone.

Gregor kept his eyes on Seydron Qorl as the procession rode through the gate. *I should have a word with him,* he thought. *He's something of an outsider, even among his own.*

"Revered Sagekind."

Gregor turned. Hannibal Luthrow, the king's young squire, was standing aside the horse's flank, a grin like a comet shooting across his face. "The king bade me find you before you departed. He said to tell you that Prince Easton has pledged to be bonded to Johanna Salk."

There was little that could catch Gregor Thorn off guard, but this news certainly did. For all his positive preaching on the subject, Gregor had held scant hope that Easton would ultimately bond the Salk girl. Following convention simply wasn't Easton's way.

"Good," he replied. His thoughts were already churning, trying to predict what might go wrong. One possibility came to him straight away: a bonding pledge was not a bonding ceremony, and a promise from Easton Dayborn was far from the fulfillment of his oath. "Tell King Micah that the sooner Easton and Johanna are bonded, the better. Tell him that if Egros Coffyn will permit it, he should bond them now on Coffyn Castle grounds. Ceremony be damned."

Hannibal made a serious face. The young squire was the guileless type, ideal for delivering messages. "I will, Revered Sagekind." Hannibal turned on his heels and left.

Facing forward again, Gregor Thorn saw that he had ground to make up of his own. Fortunately, his horse was strong, and Gregor had always been a good rider. He gave the horse a little encouragement and made for the gate.

The army—meaning the king's army, or, perhaps, Dante Heron's army (Gregor hoped it was the former, but feared it was the latter)—was so prodigious that it was almost impossible to tell that the ground beneath the thousands of tents was covered with snow. Low Osgood, the gem of the north, lay curled within the grasp of the tent city slightly to its south. If the city wasn't captive to the army, then, clearly, that was at the army's discretion.

Despite himself, Gregor smiled when he saw it. Riding near the back of the delegation, he watched the Ontish to see their reaction to the sight. Reginal Burntree and Grocian Mock sat up straighter in their saddles, their sphincters tightening. Darren Coffyn blanched. And Seydron Qorl,

Gregor's project for the day, cast a nervous glance at his fellow Ontish, finding, to his dismay, that they were too overwhelmed by the sight of the troops to notice his attentions.

The delegation entered Low Osgood by way of the Serpent Road. The winding thoroughfare meandered along the shimmering beauty of Lake Wyglass before working its way up into the city's higher elevations. Gregor was entranced. He had heard about the city his entire life—primarily from Struvans who had traveled north for a taste of the Ontish life—but, now that he was here, he understood that their exuberance for the city was, if anything, understated. Lake Wyglass, a slim and silvery chimera of water, wove through the valley floor like a quicksilver dragon, while, high above, the diminishing tail of the Edgeling Mountains framed the city's celebrated architecture with aplomb. Here, Gregor thought, was a place where history and dream-weaving walked hand in hand, a place where legends begged to be born, and often were.

Like every newcomer to Low Osgood, Gregor's eyes went first to the water, and then to the sky above. He felt a little guilty, but, like many before him, he found it impossible to look at Lake Wyglass without recreating in his mind's eye the event that had taken place there nearly two hundred years before. He could almost see the dragon Teriquay descending from the mountaintops with its slow wings beating. The young girl, the dragonfeeder, riding on its back. King Reuel Salk and his young family looking skyward, thrilled to see the reclusive third dragon in the trio gracing them with its presence. And then, the flame upon the lake. The history of Ragar Or writ in the span of a heartbeat.

At last, the Serpent's coil guided the procession away from the water. The wealthier parts of the city, nestled in the mountains, loomed above.

Gregor immediately identified Simstone. What other mountain had three dragons carved into its stone face? Gregor was delighted to see that the stone sculptures were every bit as impressive as he had heard. The winding road up Simstone led the procession by each dragon in turn. Mooncalf lay curled at the mountain's base, heavy with sleep. Comet, his wings half open, prowled the road's bend, his long body stretching across the rock. And finally, above the storied Three Dragons Inn, Teriquay spread her wings wide, a menacing ridge of teeth suggesting the fire residing inside her gullet.

Deglan Whisk pulled his horse alongside Gregor's. "This is it? The famous Three Dragons Inn?"

"The third incarnation of it, yes," Gregor responded. "It's also the least famous incarnation, because it is still standing. My intention is to keep it that way during our brief stay."

The young knight nodded knowingly. "That's why the king—"

"Will never step foot in the Three Dragons Inn, or Low Osgood for that matter, so long as I have a say. King Micah may be a Dayborn and not a Salk, but only a fool would tempt fate by entering this graveyard of monarchs." Gregor nodded toward the front of the procession. "It's worrying enough with the prince being here."

Deglan nodded solemnly. Gregor couldn't help but like the young man. In a world full of sycophants and ladder-climbers, Deglan Whisk was refreshingly focused on duty and honor. Gregor had roped him into taking the trip north for this very reason. The boy's sense of the larger world needed broadening.

"Should it come to it, I will lay down my life to save the crown prince's."

Gregor nodded in kind. "Should it come to it, that's why you're here. But let's hope that Low Osgood is kinder to the Dayborns than it was the Salks. The Three Dragons Inn is one of the great tourist attractions of our kingdom. If at all possible, we should try and enjoy ourselves."

Deglan dutifully looked up at the inn, trying to appreciate the sight. Gregor gave a silent chuckle. But then, like Deglan, he craned his neck and did the same.

The third incarnation of the Three Dragons Inn was made of jaltwood, notable because, unlike the majority of the buildings in Low Osgood, the construction wasn't stone. The jaltwood had been hauled up from the Vake nearly a hundred years prior, permission having been granted to Wyros Coffyn by Queen Johanna Salk to rebuild what had twice before been destroyed. The current Three Dragons Inn was nearly as popular with visitors as the original had been in its heyday, due, in no small part, to the reintroduction of live theater for paying guests. The owner of the inn—no longer a Coffyn, but a transplanted Blackstar Islander by the name of Doxius Brine—had wisely refrained from reviving *The Flame,* the play that reenacted the death of King Reuel Salk and his family upon the lake. (Queen Portia Salk had infamously died in the fire that burned the first Three Dragons to the ground while attending a performance of *The Flame*, and it was years afterward before another member of the Salk dynasty permitted the inn to be rebuilt.) Gregor had heard through the rumor mill that the new plays were sometimes satirical in nature, and, occasionally, poked fun at the Dayborns. He had to believe, however, that Doxius Brine wouldn't be so stupid as to show one of these plays during their stay.

They were greeted at the inn's great jaltwood door by Doxius Brine and a retinue of stableboys. Doxius wore his beard in the style of the Blackstar Isles: tied into four different sections with colored string. A handful of the men damned Doxius beneath their breath, but that was the extent of it. The Blackstar Rebellion was now officially over, and, hard feelings notwithstanding, the men knew there was a decided difference between Axton Boil's army and the many transplanted Blackstar Islanders who made a living on the mainland.

Once the stableboys had taken away the horses, Doxius, exuding good-natured joviality, escorted the delegation inside to the eating hall. Three tiers of platforms scaled the hall from its center to the far wall, looking like terraces cut into the side of a mountain. On the third tier, against the far wall, a single setting on what was arguably a fourth tier jutted above the remainder. Sitting on this fourth terrace, neatly dining on what appeared to be a rather oversized cut of an unspecified meat, resided Dante Heron.

Seeing the delegation enter the room, Dante dabbed at his slim, seemingly nonexistent lips with a pristine white cloth. Then, donning a wormwood smile, he rose from his seat, and, upon executing a slight bow, addressed the prince. "Welcome to the Three Dragons Inn, Holy Son of the Son of the Air."

Prince Ajax gave a riotous laugh. The Struvans in the room joined in. Gregor used the opportunity to better assess his surroundings. Most of the men seated at the tables were loyal to Dante Heron, as evidenced by the myriad avian-themed surcoats on display. Once, the many ornithological-named families of eastern Ragar Or had been at each other's throats, scrapping for the seat at Dagon, but, now that the Heron house was the undisputed master of the east, the birds had fallen in line.

"What are we eating, Dante?" Ajax asked. "From the looks of it, you've killed the king stag."

Dante lifted his eyebrows, highlighting pale blue eyes. He had something of a trouper's look, intermixed with that of a lord's. With a restrained dramatic flair, Dante turned and reached for the plate, grabbing the strange piece of meat. "My prince, since the Ontish stole our glory on the battlefield, my men and I sought a little glory of our own." He held the meat aloft. "Have you ever supped on dragon?"

Silence exploded like an inverse thunderclap. *He can't possibly be serious,* Gregor thought. But, before the silence drew on for too long, Dante confessed. "I am joking, of course. We have not seen this newly rumored dragon. Besides, I haven't the bow for bringing down such a creature. Even if I did, I'm not sure it would be fitting for a heron to kill a fellow flying creature of the divine."

Once again, Ajax and the others responded with laughter.

Gregor made mental notes. *"My men," he says. And how did Dante learn news of the dragon so quickly?*

Without discussion, it was agreed that the performative banter portion of the program was over. Dante swept down, while Ajax swept up. The two men embraced like brothers. A great reshuffling ushered Prince Ajax's party onto the third terrace's table of honor. Gregor used the benefit of the commotion to run his fingers inside a leather pouch sewn into the inner pocket of his burgundy cloak. Residue from the Delilah herb stuck to his fingertips.

He drew a bead on Seydron Qorl.

Within seconds, everyone was seated. Gregor struck an advantageous position between Seydron Qorl and Deglan Whisk. When the wine was served, Gregor took charge and transferred the cups from the serving girl to his seatmates. At first, he thought only to tamper with Seydron's cup, but, trusting some gut instinct, he allowed his fingertips to brush the respective rims of both. Satisfied, he licked his fingers dry. Then, grabbing his own wine cup, he proposed a toast to the men sitting to his left and to his right.

"To the feast. May it be a revelation."

Within minutes they were swimming the Delilah herb's dark currents.

Gregor expected Deglan to pipe up first, but, surprisingly, it was Seydron. "Owoervyrn's great bloody sky souls!" the Ontish malcontent whispered. He grabbed onto the table as if he was slipping off the end of the world. Wild-eyed, he turned to Gregor. "I've been poisoned," he said.

Gregor grinned at the drowning man. His own boat was upright, but to be fair, he had more experience navigating the Delilah herb's choppy waters. "Keep your shit together, Seydron. I'm the one who poisoned your cup. Make a fuss and I won't share the antidote."

Seydron's eyes grew wide with fear and loathing. "I'll kill you for this, jeyedoshi," he hissed.

Gregor knew from the hushed hiss that he had chosen the right man. Seydron possessed the sort of quiet pride that prevented a person from making an audible stink about being drugged by his dining companion. "You'll do no such thing. What you will do is have a decent conversation with me while we eat our…" He cast a puzzled look at the exotic meat in his hands. Dante had riffed off the dragon entrée without divulging what, in fact, they were eating. "…whatever this is."

Gregor felt a tapping on his shoulder. He turned to find Deglan looking at him with moon-sized eyes. "Something has happened, Revered Sagekind. I'm…floating. Between this world and another."

Gregor patted the young man on the shoulder. "Nothing to fear. I put a substance in your wine called the Delilah herb. I have ingested the herb as well, as has the Qorlish gentleman to my left. Together we will swim the herb's currents, and perhaps stumble upon a revelation or two."

Deglan took the news in stride. "As you say, Revered Sagekind. I have only one concern: if Prince Ajax is attacked by his enemies, I won't be of much help."

"Nonsense. The Delilah bonds you to another world, but it doesn't divorce you from this one. Tell me, can you see the prince?"

Deglan nodded. "The Heron is trying to cover the prince with his wings, but yes, I can see him."

Gregor glanced at Prince Ajax. He saw the same thing: the Delilah version of Dante Heron had sprouted beautiful pearlescent feathers and was shielding Prince Ajax from view. "Good. The Delilah will be out of your system within the hour, but, in the meantime, should someone attack the prince, be they human or heron, hack their arms—or, if need be, their wings—off. To that end, nothing has changed. Understood?"

The young knight wagged his stone-cut chin. "Understood."

Gregor returned his attention to Seydron. Upon the swivel, an under-the-table dagger tickled his ribs. "Listen, you skeletal Struvan bastard," Seydron hissed. "Hand over the antidote this instant or I'll make a skewer of your beating heart."

Gregor rolled his eyes. "You'll do no such thing. Stick me and the favor will be returned upon your person twenty times over." He checked the room to see if their exchange was drawing attention. Everyone else was too distracted with making conversation and eating to notice. For safety's sake, he decided to come clean. "If it will calm you, Seydron, I'll have you know that the poison isn't a poison at all, but an herb. A hallucinogen. I'm under the influence myself. The effects will pass soon enough. Between now and then, I'd like to have a conversation with you."

Gregor watched with amusement as Seydron Qorl tried to bite his tongue. But one of the effects of the Delilah herb was that it spurred speech, even among reluctant talkers. "I have nothing to say to you, jeyedoshi. You are an unclean spirit walking among us. You sully the king's court with your presence. Nothing you can say or do would ever convince me that you are naught but a contagion upon Ragar Or."

Gregor saw an opportunity to ask a slippery question. "You are suggesting that if I did not exist, you and your Ontish brethren would put aside your scheming and support the king."

Seydron flinched. A deep furrow gullied his brow. "This herb is dark magic, wraith. My tongue is a loosed hound, while my mind conjures strange visions." A curl of black hair repositioned itself on Seydron's forehead. He involuntarily glanced down the bench to where Reginal Burntree and Grocian Mock were sitting. "If there is scheming against the king, I take no part in it."

Seydron's aura was dusted with blue, the color of truth. A vision of snow clouds rolled in above Seydron's head, but, when the snow fell, it changed to sand that gathered round the Qorlish lord's feet.

Gregor smiled. "I believe you." He stuffed his smile with a bite of the mystery meat, letting the juices drip down his chin in the Ontish fashion. Seydron, seemingly put at ease by Gregor's display of barbarism, followed suit. *And now to press the advantage.* "Of all the Ontish, I singled you out for the honor of the Delilah herb, Seydron. The Qorls and the Dayborns have a history together. As you well know, your great-aunt, Tiatris Qorl, was bonded to Cedric the Redeemer, the first Dayborn to sit the Union throne." He paused and made a forlorn face. "If I am the cause of your estrangement from the king, then we must make it right. Come, share your visions with me. Tell me what the Delilah shows you, and I'll interpret it, *speyetwu sfomu.*"

Gregor took great delight in seeing Seydron's reaction to his saying "debt free" in Old Ontish. Settling, Seydron made a show of chewing on Gregor's suggestion, though his wild eyes suggested he was having difficulty bearing up under the Delilah's visions. "You mean to trick me, jeyedoshi," he said at last. "You will make my visions your own. Feed me lies, and keep any real insights to yourself. I won't do it. I still see you for what you are. The lesser twin. A descendant of Coros. Your mother should have snuffed you out—"

Seydron startled and went quiet. Gregor followed his gaze. Delilah visions, he knew, sometimes overlapped when two people were in the same setting, a phenomenon that suggested shadows or spirits inside the room. But if Gregor saw the same thing as Seydron, he only caught the tail end of it. Literally. The long, burnished orange tail of a lithe, muscular creature whipped out of sight, leaving only the rocking black waves of the Delilah-tinged here and now.

"Beoliotius bless us," Seydron said, gawping.

"Was that—?"

No answer was forthcoming from Qorl, but, to Gregor's relief, young Deglan had seen the same. "It was a cordrix, Revered Sagekind," the young knight offered, leaning in from the right. For his first time hallucinating, Deglan had retained a considerable bit of poise. "It was…incredible. I have seen pictures of a cordrix, but never one in real life. Though I suppose that one wasn't real either, was it? Merely a vision. It entered through the doorway like an uninvited guest, took a look around, then turned and sleeked away." The knight gave his chin a thoughtful tug. "The king's Clyesian brother-in-law sent him a cordrix last year as an anniversary gift. Only King Micah hasn't brought it to the capital yet. He left it in the port city. He left it in—"

"Dagon," Gregor replied. *Though I fear it's no longer there,* he thought, tasting the meat stuck in his teeth.

Seydron heard them talking. He pushed his head into the fray, their three skulls bunching together. "This is jeyedoshi magic. Woodkin work. You saw it," he said, pointing at Deglan. "The Sagekind summoned a monstrous beast out of thin air."

"I have no such powers, Seydron," Gregor responded. "Truth be told, I would have missed it altogether if it hadn't been for your gawping."

Seydron grabbed at his wine cup and drank it dry, the way a man might drink away his present circumstances. Finished, he leaned across Gregor and pulled Deglan close, red droplets dripping off his coarse black beard. "We are under an evil spell, young knight. For the good of the realm, let's run this jeyedoshi through. Struvan and Ontish, together."

Deglan laid a hand on the pommel of his sword. "You are too casual with that word, sir. The Sagekind is a blessing to this realm, and a good man, besides. I would run you through without a second's thought before I let you touch a hair on the Sagekind's head."

A menacing quiet enveloped the trio. Gregor let it stand. He had learned from his years dabbling in the hallucinogenic arts that uncomfortable groupings sometimes led to surprising revelations; to that end, he was willing to see what would happen. He used the opportunity to check in with his senses, hoping that he might catch another glimpse of the cordrix. He hated that he had missed the sight of it. He, too, had only seen pictures of the Clyesian creature in books, detailed drawings that suggested an animal suspended between states of being. In the pictures, it was impossible to discern if the beast was lumbering or spry, contemplative or savage, ancient or newly made. Once, he had asked his departed wife Sephery about the cordrix: as a child she had seen one in the wild, roaming the interior cliffs of her childhood home, Dedringbone. She had been coy with her answer, speaking to him, for the only time in their relationship, like their respective countries of origin were an impediment to understanding. "The cordrix are nature's shadow children," she had told him. "Beyond description. Beyond morality. To describe the cordrix is to diminish it. And that, I refuse to do."

Gregor found Dante Heron. He took a long, hard look at him. Then he turned back to the cut of meat on his plate. He would need evidence, of course, but, until then, he saw no reason not to draw the obvious conclusion.

There were moments when Gregor thought he could feel the weight of his soul resting inside of his body. This was one of them.

He forced himself to break off from his line of thought. "You must understand where Seydron is coming from," he said to Deglan matter-of-factly, moving the evening along. "A true jeyedoshi, in the eyes of the Ontish, is a great danger to the realm. The greatest danger. For Seydron to believe that I am a jeyedoshi and then not try and find a way to kill me would be treasonous."

The silence shifted to stunned. The masticating sounds of a hundred men filled the void. Gregor was fighting off queasiness, but he made no outward expression of it.

"It's true," Seydron admitted, his temper cooling. He looked like he wanted to say *thank you* to Gregor for clarifying the matter.

"Tell me, Seydron," Gregor continued, putting a hand out to stop Deglan from taking another bite of the meat, "do your northern brothers not harbor similar concerns about Johanna Salk? Unlike me, you know for a fact that she is a lesser twin."

Seydron scoffed. "Daguss Salk would never nurture a jeyedoshi in his own keep. And from what I hear, she has no telling mark. Besides, you cannot fault a man for loving his own daughter. We Ontish keep the faith of the Twins, but we are not monsters."

"They say that in Kalandragote the twin-death rite is still practiced." Gregor hoped the rhetorical nature of his statement made it unnecessary for him to ask the obvious question.

Seydron harrumphed. He grabbed at his cut of meat and tore off a shred with his incisors, the juices glistening. Gregor fought the urge to smack the food from his mouth. "Kalandragote is a different place. It always has been. It always will be."

The gentle rocking of the Delilah suddenly changed over to a great swell. Gregor, familiar with the sensation, rode the wave with his eyes wide open, looking for revelations. To his disappointment, what truths presented themselves were either minor or universal. Dead men and women wandered in and out of the hall, keeping tabs on their long-ago murderers. A dragon materialized, hovering above the room; one glance at its purple scales and Gregor knew that it was Comet, one of the lesser dragons from Low Osgood's storied past, and not a vision of the Blackstar's beast, as he had hoped.

His attention was drawn to a pair of greyhounds sitting in the corner of the hall. For a second, he thought that they, too, were a vision, but then he remembered seeing the dogs when he had first arrived at the inn. They belonged to the innkeeper, if he wasn't mistaken. He was on the verge of turning away from the greyhounds when both dogs turned and looked at him, studying him with the same frankness with which he had been studying them. To add to the strangeness, Gregor noticed the other visions in the room halting their business and turning their attentions to the dogs, as if they were of vast importance. After a second of this, the visions turned to look at Gregor, and he could somehow hear their whispering thoughts: *Do you see? Do you see? Do you see?*

But Gregor did not see. He kept listening and watching, hoping that apprehension would dawn. But instead, the wave of the Delilah herb crested, and the visions and their voices faded into the walls. Seconds later the greyhounds loped away, leaving the hall.

Gregor turned back to his dinner companions. From the astounded look on the men's faces, it seemed that they, too, had ridden the wave. Deglan, for the first time all evening, appeared disturbed. The young man drew a deep breath, and, with a specificity that flabbergasted, cast light on one of the great mysteries of Seydron Qorl's life.

"You are a falconer?" he asked Seydron.

The Qorlish lord nodded warily. He looked like a man who had seen one too many ghosts. "I am. Or, I was."

Deglan nodded. "Your bird. What happened to it?"

Seydron's eyes turned to beads. All around them the great hall continued with its clattering. "Dead. An accident. The dogs killed it during my nephew's visit. The door to the falcon's room was left open, and the hounds knocked its cage on the ground." Seydron put down his cut of the meat and made a trailing motion with his fingers. A wistful look crossed his face. "I loved that falcon. Reyist, I called it. It was a magnificent creature. To see it hunt was to witness the beauty of Beoliotius's design."

"It's possible that Reyist isn't dead. I saw…" Deglan looked uncertain, but he plunged ahead. "Your nephew, does his hair come to a point in the middle of his forehead?"

"Yes," Seydron replied. His eyebrows collided in anger.

"I saw him in a vision. Standing across the table from you. He was switching falcons between cages. Once the more majestic of the birds was secured, he left the door of the other cage open. As he walked away, I heard barking—"

Seydron smirked. "That little rat bastard. His jealousy on the day of the hunt was palpable. I should have known."

A good idea, this, Gregor thought. *Truly, I should drug people more often.* He decided it was time to contribute to the conversation.

"And you, my lord of Qorl. Will you make an offering of your visions as well? In the spirit of all that young Deglan has shared?"

Seydron tapped thinking fingers on the table. His pupils remained swollen from the Delilah herb, but his manner suggested a growing comfort level with the experience. Finally, he sighed, suggesting he had arrived at a decision.

"Your herb has shown me much, jeyedoshi. I thank you, and I curse you for it." He paused and stuffed a bite of the meat on the plate into his mouth. When he resumed talking, bits of cordrix spewed out on the table. "If I tell you what I have seen, you will not like it."

"All the more reason I need to hear it."

Seydron nodded. "Never let it be said that the Qorl family betrayed the realm." He stopped staring into the middle distance and gave Gregor the full brunt of his drug-addled eyes. "I saw the ghost of Axton Boil, the Blackstar prince. He walked into the hall, looked around, and made an announcement. He said that the Blackstar Rebellion wasn't over. He said that on the morrow Low Osgood would once again become the graveyard of royalty. Then he approached Prince Ajax, put his ghostly fingers around the prince's throat, and squeezed."

Johanna Salk

Word reached Johanna in the tower midday. Rolphus, the oafish tower guard, brought in her lunch wearing a grin so wide, it could have been pinned behind his ears.

"You're the talk of the castle today, you are," he said as he presented Johanna with a plate of rosemary chicken garnished with slices of pear. "When you're not killing princes, it seems that you're wooing them."

"Whatever do you mean?" she asked, feigning ignorance.

"The Dayborn prince has declared his intention to bond you. The whole castle knows." Rolphus worked his thick, nubby fingers into his chin, curious of her reaction. For Rolphus's sake, Johanna did her best to act surprised.

"My father? He's agreed to the match?"

"I would think so!" Rolphus grabbed a hard wedge of cheese from his pocket and began gnawing on it. "One daughter bonded to Kalandragote, the other to Union. He will be a man with options!"

I soon mean to have options myself, Johanna thought. Once Rolphus was gone, she went to the cherry tower window and looked out at the snow-covered expanse beyond the castle gates, frustrated that she couldn't be the deliverer of her own independence. *Easton is key. They won't send anyone after me if I've absconded with the king's son. Especially if we're pledged to be bonded.*

Once we're away, I'll make my own plans. She felt wild with boldness. *Perhaps I'll sail to Clyesia, live out the rest of my days in exile. Or...*she remembered the way one of the household guards used to look at her when she lived in Thistleton, an audacious knight by the name of Theaster Long. She might have claimed him as her paramour, but back then she was still playing the part of the dutiful daughter, the faithful bonded. No more. *I'll find Theaster, and we'll live as the commons do on the southern coast, shacked up in a stilt house on the marshy tides. We'll make a living netting crabs.* She smiled. In truth, she hadn't been attracted to Theaster. He had only been intriguing at the time because he wasn't her stiff and uptight bonded. Still, he might suffice, if it came to it.

I need to start seeing men the way Wulfess sees them, she thought. *The way they see me.*

As a means to an end.

The day ground along. Johanna spent the hours prepping for the coming escape. She donned riding leathers, then covered up her clothes with a heavy coat so that only the boots were exposed. She was a practiced enough rider to know what hardships lay in store: the best of journeys left one saddle-sore, and this, a flight from a castle with a prince known for his brash comings and goings, promised a bit of pain. But she was ready for it. She refrained from packing anything extraneous. She would have secreted a poison or two in the coat pockets, but, after assisting the Blackstar prince in departing the planet, Father had swept her rooms and removed the remainder of the pearl dust, as well as a dried sprig of gloaming green. Poisons were difficult to procure, but Johanna considered herself a resourceful young woman; she would find a way to obtain more. She stored an empty glass vial for this eventuality. Last but not least, she loaded one of the coat's multitudinous inner pockets with a pouch full of brogan's-heads, enough that, when the time arrived, she would have no problem leaving Easton and paying her way wherever she wanted to go.

By midday she was growing restless. She sat down at a sennequi board on the edge of the room. She tried summoning the discipline to play against herself, but the carved wooden pieces proved more interesting than her opponent's too-familiar stratagems. *These are custom-made,* she realized, studying the oversized dragon representing the whites. The dragon was monstrous, nearly twice the size of a standard sennequi piece, with a set of teeth that, even in miniature, looked prepared to devour the world. The red dragon, conversely, was lissome and serpentine; it wore a grin that suggested a deportment more cunning than ferocious. *They're specific dragons from Ragar Or's history,* she realized. Frustratingly, she didn't know which ones; her dragon lore had always been spotty. Setting down the dragons, she studied a few of the other pieces, and soon reached a similar conclusion. *Every piece on the board represents someone real.* A handful were obvious. The white king was Daguss I, also known as Daguss the Unifier; she had seen enough statues of Daguss I to recognize him anywhere. The white queen was equally easy to identify: Portia I, the most famous of Ragar Or's four female rulers. Going down the line, Johanna was able to name a fair number of the white pieces, included among them Cedric Sparrot, the Struvan who, had he survived the Crow and Arrow Rebellion, might have been Ragar Or's first king. On the sennequi board, Cedric was positioned as a knight on Daguss the Unifier's right, which, Johanna supposed, was where an Ontish lord commissioning carved sennequi pieces would want him.

When she turned her attention to the red pieces, identifying the pieces became more difficult. No, not more difficult…impossible. *Who are all of you?* Her eyes combed over the pieces one at a time. Unlike the white pieces, which had a formal staidness about them, the reds looked a rather puckish lot. The red king, for example, had the size and physical makeup of the ideal monarch, but his kingly characteristics were undercut by upturned palms and a smile that suggested subversiveness. The queen didn't look like a queen at all: for one, she was a girl, *and* she was clothed in a tattered dress. Her smile, however, matched the red king's. More startlingly, the woodworker had embedded tiny pieces of cobalt in place of her eyes. Johanna found her mesmerizing. She picked up the piece and studied it in detail. *You're like me, aren't you? Restless. Reckless.* Johanna traced the girl's wooden contours lovingly with her thumb.

The sound of the door opening interrupted Johanna's musings. She turned, expecting Rolphus or perhaps even the prince, but instead, to her surprise, she found her father.

Johanna speedily placed the sennequi piece back on the board. Then she stood and faced Daguss Salk.

Daguss looked askance at her, his eyes lighting on what she thought were her boots. But if he noticed what she was wearing, he didn't mention it. From the look on his face, he seemed on the verge of either great anger or great sorrow. She couldn't tell which. But when at last he spoke, his voice was devoid of emotion, producing an alien, disembodied effect.

"You've heard the news? From Rolphus?"

She tried to match his disembodied tenor. "I have."

Daguss nodded. Johanna studied her father standing in profile: the rounded skull, the portly nose, the boulder-like build. *He's why they call us the Crimson Salks,* she thought, and not for the first time. In High Osgood there was a sculpture of Theron Redd in the eagle garden. As a child, Johanna had thought the statue was of her father; it wasn't until adolescence that she came to understand that the sculpture was of an ancestor from long ago.

"You know, then, that I've agreed to the match?"

When Johanna opened her mouth, Rolphus's words came out. "One daughter bonded to Kalandragote, the other to Union. You will have options."

Daguss's hard, brown eyes found her own. He gave a little nod. "Options, yes. But in the end, options must evolve into decisions, mustn't they? That's what life is, ultimately: a series of decisions. It's a lesson I tried to teach you and your sister when you were young."

Dangerous words leaped to Johanna's tongue. "I recall you saying something to that effect. But, as you know, I've had little opportunity to make decisions of my own. As the lesser twin, you've always made the most consequential decisions for me."

Daguss squinted at Johanna. Then he stepped deeper into the room, a brisk one-two. Johanna held her father's gaze as best as she could, trembling with the difficulty of it. Ever since Daguss Salk had named Johanna the lesser twin, he had kept her at arm's length, and from that distance Johanna had cultivated, through much hard-won life experience, the skill to think and act for herself; but up close her father was still the imposing Daguss Salk, Lord of High Osgood.

"There is truth in what you say," he said at last. "I had hoped, when I sent you south to bond the Raleigh boy…" His words trailed away, leaving Johanna clueless as to how he might have finished the sentence. He gave a little sigh. Johanna used the opportunity to peel away from her father's gaze, following the crow's-feet at the corners of his eyes to the less intense tableau of his glabrous dome. Daguss continued. "But all that is over and done." He found her eyes again and locked in. "Just like your decision to poison the Blackstar prince. That decision damaged my standing among the Ontish houses. Not irreparably. But until you are out of the picture, I can't win back their trust completely."

"So that's why you agreed to bond me to the Dayborn prince. Because you want me gone." She felt a hard nugget of resistance forming in her soul. Perhaps she wouldn't abscond with Easton after all.

Daguss looked at her with a sudden vulnerability. It was like watching her father transform into a different person. "Do you know that I wept the day you and your sister were born? I knew what it meant to be the father of twins in the north. I knew what it would cost me. What it would cost one of you. For every Daguss a Ropske, for every Onto a Coros. The other Ontish considered it a blessing. After all, a Twin Ascendant cannot be born without there being twins in the first place. But for the other, for the lesser twin…" Johanna watched her father's gaze harden, returning him to the man she knew and feared. "…you don't have the first idea what I've done to protect you. What I've done to shield you from harm. Had you been born in Kalandragote—"

Johanna cut in, quick as a knife. "Wulfess would have killed me in the twin-death rite. Is that what you're trying to say, Father? Have you ever stopped to consider that you chose the wrong Twin Ascendant? Perhaps

I'm the one who would have emerged victorious in a twin-death rite. Perhaps my entire existence as the lesser twin is predicated on a mistake made by *you*."

She expected a scoff, a sneer, perhaps even a slap. But instead Daguss rubbed his right hand over the surface of his face, starting at his forehead and moving it slowly down to his white-forest chin. His recast eyes revealed an unexpected expression. A haunted expression. It seemed that he was on the verge of sharing something revelatory, but when he spoke, his words were simple and straightforward.

"I did not make a mistake."

Time stood still. The unspoken implication lingered in the air like a miasma. *I did not make a mistake…because you are a jeyedoshi.* But that wasn't true. Johanna had always known that she wasn't a jeyedoshi. Had she been a jeyedoshi, they would have killed her in her crib. Had she been a jeyedoshi, she would have a telling mark on her body for the whole world to see. Had she been a jeyedoshi…

"Father—"

Daguss interrupted, his voice once again iron. "You will agree to bond Easton Dayborn. That is nonnegotiable. King Micah is arranging for a party to escort you to Union so that you may begin preparing for your life there." His eyes flickered, revealing some unfathomable depth. "The rest of us, the king's party included, will travel to Kalandragote for your sister's bonding ceremony to Cato Ollspaer."

Johanna was thrown by the change in the conversation. She put the ridiculous thought of her possible jeyedoshi nature out of her head. "The king's party?" she responded, remembering to protect her sister's confidence.

"Yes. I…we…have reached an agreement. Kalandragote is casting off its independence and joining Ragar Or. King Micah is traveling north so that the Ollspaers can recognize him as their king in front of their citizenry. While he is there, he will take in Wulfess's bonding ceremony. Then, the entire host will travel south to Union for a repeat performance, only this time the bonding ceremony will involve you."

A man with options, she thought again. "Our family will be the glue that holds the entire realm together."

Daguss said nothing.

Johanna thought of an angle to work. "I would travel to Kalandragote to see Wulfess bonded. She is my sister, and I should be there."

"You will not travel north. As I have said, you will travel to Union. The king and I have arranged it so that you will leave later today."

"Will my bonded-to-be accompany me to Union?" She thought she had been clever in talking Easton into stealing her away from the castle, but it was beginning to appear that a less thrilling abduction had been in her father's plans all along.

Daguss frowned. "I don't know." The frown grew deeper. "Actually, I do know. Prince Easton has a touch of wanderlust. My sources tell me that he slipped away from the castle about an hour ago. His father wanted him to return to Union, but I have it on good authority that he means to travel out west. He intends to find the Blackstar's dragon."

Johanna's heart dropped. *That selfish, lying little prick. He promised me that he would take me with him. He swore an oath.*

She realized too late that her father had mistaken the look of disappointment on her face for something else.

"You're disappointed? Is it because you're taken with the boy?" He looked at her with a keen interest, as if waiting to organize her answer on one of the many shelves in his mind where he ordered his knowledge of the kingdom.

Johanna's tongue faltered. *Yes? No?* It dawned on her that the lie of love provided more options. "Yes." The word felt false falling off her tongue, so she tempered her response. "I'm not sure. There's…potential."

Though the effect on Daguss's expression was slight, Johanna could tell that he was pleased. Seeing the change, she committed to the track. "I will bond Prince Easton. Willingly." She pursed her lips to stop herself from saying more.

Her half-haughty expression seemed to satisfy her father. *He thinks me equal parts compliant and defiant. Good. Let him.* They held their uneasy détente, studying one another. At once Daguss Salk broke away his gaze and unsheathed his dagger, Talon. Looking around the round room, his eyes settled on the table where Johanna took her food. A crisp red apple, the untouched remains of yesterday's midday meal, caught his attention. He walked over, picked it up, and, with a clever, unshowy skill, used the dagger to core the fruit and divide it into four segments. Returning to Johanna's side, he handed her half of the yield.

Daguss bit into the apple. The crisp fruit crunched between his teeth.

Johanna followed in turn. They ate the snack together in a strange, holy sort of silence. It was as if a tender, familial spell had been cast. But when Daguss swallowed the last of the fruit, the spell was broken. The Lord of High Osgood wiped Talon on his shirt. Just when it seemed that he would turn and go, he pointed the tip of the dagger at his daughter like an admonitory finger.

"You complain that I have made all your decisions for you. You complain that I named you the lesser twin. You blame me for your woes. Fair enough. If I were you, likely I would feel the same. But hear me when I say this. If ever there comes a day when a consequential decision is yours to be made, I advise you to side with your family. Your true family. The Salks. If you love your bonded-to-be, encourage him to do the same. If you do that, I will rush to your aid, and I will protect you the same as I have protected you your entire life. But if you defy me…if you once again betray me, the way you betrayed me by poisoning the Blackstar prince…know that I will not forgive you a second time. You will become my eternal enemy. And from that position, daughter, there is no recourse."

And with those words, Daguss Salk turned and walked away.

With her father gone, Johanna returned to the sennequi board. She tried to stop herself from thinking about the conversation with her father. In lieu of this discomfort, she moved one of the white footmen, as if starting a game. The move was bland, milquetoast, the most predictable of predictable openings. She reflected upon it for a moment, and then stood up and moved to the opposite side of the board.

She had no more sat down in front of the red pieces than she sensed a shift in the room. She looked to the window. The glass was ajar, and cold ribbons of air were streaming inside.

"Do you prefer playing the red pieces?"

She jerked her head to the left. Easton Dayborn was standing by the canopy bed, wearing a tomcat smile.

In her heart, Johanna was thrilled to see him. *I guess he didn't abandon me after all.* But she forced herself to look unsurprised. "I have no preference," she replied. "Besides winning, that is."

Easton moved closer and studied the board. Seeing white's position, he rolled his eyes good-naturedly. "White's opening move was rather…quotidian."

Johanna ground her back teeth. During her short-lived bonding to Nicholas Raleigh, their one shared enjoyment had been playing games of sennequi together. Nicholas was a strong but unimaginative player; the move she had made with white, commonly known as *deference,* had been Nicholas's go-to opening, the standard salvo when one wished to settle into a protracted war of attrition. Johanna, raised on reckless games with Wulfess, had at first struggled against Nicholas's methodical style, but, once she became familiar with it, she won more often than not. Still, to hear Easton disparage the move—it grated.

"I was told that you had left the castle. That you had gone dragon hunting."

Easton presented himself with upturned palms. If it weren't for his rapscallion quality, Johanna could have almost imagined him a pious Hawk's-Eye. "I keep my promises."

So you say, she thought. She turned her attention back to the board. "*Deference* is a fine opening move for the sensible sennequi player. Going forward, you can play either offense or defense. Nicholas, my first bonded, was a master from the position."

"Really?" Easton took a seat in front of the whites. "You're saying that when the two of you played, he usually emerged victorious?"

She met Easton's eyes. "No."

Easton broke out in a broad grin. "That settles it. Let's play." He looked at the board. "I rarely open with *deference,* but out of respect for the dearly departed, I'll stick with it."

Johanna was equal parts interested and agitated. The agitated part of her wanted to flee Coffyn Castle straight away, but, as had been the case since she first met Easton, he held the upper hand, and she was loath to make requests of him from a position of weakness. After a moment, she thought of a different tack.

"Okay. I'll play you. On two conditions."

"Yes?"

"One: We play a speed game. No more than ten seconds per move."

That smug tomcat smile again. "And?"

"If I win, you'll defer to my judgment in all things once we've escaped the castle."

The prince grimaced. He ran a hand through his wayward hair. "Dangerous bargain, that. If I'm to accept, the conditions will have to be offset by similar assurances on your part."

"You mean that if you win, I'll defer to your judgment?"

"Exactly."

Her stomach twisted at the thought. Recent happenings aside, breaking her word didn't come easy to Johanna, and she had no real knowledge of Easton's strength on the sennequi board. She thought it best to qualify the conditions. "Why don't we put a limit on it? Whoever wins, the other will defer to their judgment for the first two days of the trip." There was a decent chance that she would dump him within two days' time regardless.

"Deal," Easton replied. "Your move."

She opened with the piece that was meant to represent the Sagekind, only on this board the red piece was represented by a gnarled tree with a man's face. Her first thought was that the piece was meant to be the infamous Yubriy tree, but before she could ruminate on it further, the game accelerated at a rapid-fire pace. Easton, to her disconcerted chagrin, moved his pieces with a speedy self-assuredness, taking far less than the permitted ten seconds for the majority of his moves. Johanna's posture on the board quickly turned defensive. She backtracked for multiple moves, cursing softly under her breath. Her position grew more untenable by the moment. Then, at once, she saw a weakness on Easton's back line that she could exploit with her queen. Picking up the girl in the tattered dress, she moved the piece to a square where it exposed Easton's overextended ranks. Instantly, the game flipped. Easton, now the one murmuring profanities, tried to close ranks, but the merciless red queen slashed his line to pieces. The end came when the gnarled tree and the girl with the tattered dress trapped Daguss the Unifier in the board's far-left corner.

Easton sighed the sigh of the defeated. "Two days, you say?" Johanna noted that his ever-present grin didn't slip, and there was a light in his face that suggested that losing wasn't the worst thing that had ever happened to him.

She had never seen a male of the species take a loss so well. For the first time since Johanna had met the prince, it crossed her mind that she might learn to like him.

"Two days," she confirmed. "And for my first directive, I say it's time to leave. No more diversions until we are far from here."

"As you wish." He took a step toward the window. Glanced back at her. "Can you climb down a rope?"

She snorted with contempt. "I'm from High Osgood, aren't I?"

"I'll take that as a yes." His expression turned quizzical. Ironic. "Should I lead the way? This being your show and whatnot."

She took back the thought that she might learn to like him. "Stop being a jackass. Go."

Easton gave one last jackass grin and climbed out the window.

Johanna readied to follow him. But when she reached the window, a thought crossed her mind. Quickly, she hurried back across the room to the sennequi board. Once there, she picked up the red queen and stowed it in the same inner coat pocket where she had stashed the brogan's-heads.

Emboldened by the thought of the sennequi piece safe in her pocket, she returned to the window and made her escape.

Silas O' the Songs

They made it to the Yubriy tree in two days' time. Along the way they stayed at the home of a second woods witch, tried their hand at a musical collaboration, and foraged mushrooms. The mushroom meals were the highlight. Wyn had an eye for fungi: while walking the woods, he spotted and collected chanterelle, lion's mane, lactarius, oyster, bat harvest, and morels. After adding a touch of forest floor seasoning (Silas didn't pry), Wyn cooked the respective mushrooms in the hawk's-head helm over a fire, differing the time and temperature for each. The results were mouthwateringly delicious.

The second woods witch wasn't as welcoming as Merjy. She swallowed her tongue at the sight of them and kept it swallowed throughout their stay. Wyn swore that he knew her; he said her name was Dryis. Silas was inclined to believe him on both counts: Dryis appeared unsurprised to see them, and she responded to her name readily enough. But she treated Wyn with a prudence that suggested either reverence or terror. Silas, she ignored completely. He had no issue with it, he was only surprised after Merjy's...hospitality.

Their songwriting collaborations were an exercise in frustration. Silas's every attempt at working with Wyn ended in a madcap jam session that failed to produce a song. Silas's style was to craft a song into being; Wyn slashed at his fiddle until it gave him what he wanted. It was the same with lyrics. Silas coaxed words out of hiding, whereas Wyn clubbed a few hundred over the head and took his pick of the dead. On the evening of the second day, lost in the labyrinth of a monstrous creation that sounded to Silas as if it was screaming for a mercy killing, Silas begged that they stop.

"Enough. We sound like a minstrel act in the Bottom Black."

Wyn sharpened his ever-present grin. "Yes! You hear it too!"

"You misunderstand me. We're bringing to life an abomination."

Wyn screeched his bow across the strings. Startled birds took flight. "Your songs are too smooth, Silas O' the Songs. I'm trying to roughen them up."

Silas sighed. He leaned his lute against a log. "You say we will arrive at the Yubriy tree by morning?"

Wyn lowered his fiddle, appearing to accept defeat. "In the morning, yes. From a knoll far afield, our eyes will alight on one of the wonders of the world, a tree that foretells the future." He wagged his eyebrows at Silas. "Perhaps we will stumble across a Yubriy leaf. Then, after divining its meaning, we will go and make our fortunes in this world."

Stavus save me. Tomorrow will be my last day with you. Murder birds be damned. "They don't allow the likes of us to get our grubby hands on Yubriy leaves. Those days are no more. Besides, it's too late in the season. The tree has already dropped its leaves."

Wyn sucked his teeth. "It's a damn shame. I could do with finding a good fortune. When do you think was the last time a commoner stole away with a Yubriy leaf?"

Silas knew the historical answer to that. His uncle Krayton had studied history at the White Walls in Thistleton, back when he thought to make his living as a Wandering Tongue. When Krayton abandoned his dream and returned to the Vake to work the land, Silas, rather than the multitudes, became the beneficiary of his education. "Legend claims that Cedric Sparrot discovered a leaf that convinced him to come to the aid of the first Ontishman he crossed, who, as we know, turned out to be Daguss the Unifier."

"The first king of Ragar Or?"

He loves to play the fool, doesn't he? "Yes, the first king. After Daguss unified the Struvan and Ontish realms, he started sending holy men and women to collect the leaves. But the Salk dynasty didn't send soldiers to guard the Yubriy tree until the reign of Caeress I. After Caeress's mother the good queen Portia died in a fire at the Three Dragons Inn in Low Osgood, word spread that a leaf poached by a common woman named Breta Barton had predicted the queen's death. Breta was captured and hanged, and the leaf was confiscated. For a time, the common folk of the Vake discussed cutting down the Yubriy tree as a show of loyalty to the crown. Caeress sent soldiers to the Vake before the tree was lost, and ever since the crown has both protected the Yubriy and collected its leafy bounty."

Wyn slapped his own hands together one-two. "And nary a leaf has fallen into the hands of a commoner since!"

"If so, they've been wise enough to keep their mouths shut. There are tales of blabbermouth Hawk's-Eyes who have lost their tongues for spreading rumors about what they read when collecting the leaves. Baron the Redd actually went so far as to preemptively remove the tongues of the holy men and women sent to collect the leaves, but his niece Johanna stopped the practice when she took the Union throne."

Wyn nodded his head maniacally. "I hear you, Silas O' the Songs. If we find a leaf, I'll be sure to cut out your tongue. For mine own safety."

Silas laughed uncomfortably. It was difficult to tell when Wyn was joking.

The Yubriy was a god among trees. Even stripped to its winter bones and devoid of leaves, its twisting, silver-brown form awed.

"Therein lies eternity," Wyn whispered. His ever-present smile was absent from his face.

Silas soaked in the sight of the Yubriy tree. There was no guarantee he would be in its presence again.

Nearer to the tree, a small group of soldiers kept a lazy watch. The sight of the armed men made Silas nervous at first, but their clear disinterest in his arrival soon calmed him. Turning his attention to the Yubriy, he soon forgot that the soldiers were there. But moments later, looking up, he saw that two of the soldiers were approaching at a leisurely clip.

Silas turned to Wyn. He had forgotten that the little man was still wearing the hawk's-head helm. "What do you think they want?" he asked as the soldiers approached, trying to temper his urge to reach over and snatch the helmet off Wyn's head.

"Either blood or company." Wyn nodded in the soldiers' direction. "We will know soon enough."

Returning his attention to the approaching pair, Silas noticed, to his surprise, that the smaller of the two was a woman. Her gender, however, was the only striking thing about her. She had a plain face, strong limbs, and a short thatch of black hair atop her head. Her male companion was an imposing-looking fellow. With his lively dark eyes and coal-colored beard, he reminded Silas of a very large black bull. But as Silas was thinking this very thought, he noticed the arms on the man's beige surcoat: three crows on a tree limb.

He's a man of the Salks.

"Good day to you!" the woman said, affable and bright. She was dressed in a dull brown top and breeches, and she wore a short sword on her hip. "I hope that you'll forgive us for intruding on your visit, but from a distance it looked as if…ah yes, I see Madrig's sharp eyes were not mistaken. You do have musical instruments in tow."

Silas nodded. Wyn did the same.

The big fellow wore a pleasant smile, similar to the woman's. The woman continued, "Music is a rare treat at the Yubriy tree. We would be ever so grateful if you would honor us with a song. Madrig especially. He is a music enthusiast to his very bones."

Madrig nodded in agreement. Turning to the woman, he made a series of signs with his hands. Perhaps it was because Madrig was large and imposing, but it took Silas an inordinate amount of time to grasp the reason for the gestures.

Madrig was a mute.

The woman nodded agreeably at Madrig. "Madrig requests that you join us at the tree," she said, turning back to Silas and Wyn. "When you're finished playing, you may lay hands on the Yubriy, if you like." It seemed as if she was finished, but then Madrig elbowed Jacy in the ribs good-naturedly, and she continued talking. "My name is Jacy. Madrig says that I should tell you that he and I are newly bonded. He says that you must play for us, because we are on our sweetmarch."

Silas was taken aback. And skeptical. The two of them did not look the likely pair. For one, they looked too old to be newly bonded, and, for another, the fact that they were on duty guarding the Yubriy tree undercut the story of their sweetmarch. He was tempted to pry, but Wyn started speaking.

"I knew the two of you were bonded from the moment I saw you!" the little man lied. "Lovers' eyes, a visible disease. The two of you afflicted. There's no hiding it. Of course we will play for you. Tell us, what would you hear? 'The Sweetmarch Shine'? 'Broken Arrow'? 'She Loves Cream, He Loves Pie'?"

Madrig smiled and shrugged. He signed something to Jacy. She relayed his message. "What Madrig loves to hear most of all is music that he's never heard before. Do either of you compose?"

Wyn laughed so hard that the hawk's-head helm fell from his head. "As it so happens, we've both written a song about that cruelest of princesses, the dragon-lover Anis Salk. Perhaps we'll play both versions, and you will tell us which one you like more?"

Silas went first. Beneath the thousand grasping hands of the Yubriy tree he played Ballad of the Cruel Sister to an audience of song-thirsty soldiers. He closed his eyes at the song's midpoint, losing himself in the melody. When he opened them at the end, a hushed stillness had fallen.

Madrig broke the quiet by clapping; the other soldiers quickly joined in. Silas's song had awed, but it was clear by the expression on the soldiers' faces that it had not hit the mark. Only Madrig looked satisfied by what he had heard.

Then came Wyn. Within seconds of his bow touching the strings, a handful of the soldiers took to their feet to dance. As in The Golden Pear, the lot were soon singing the refrain—*That witch Anis, seduced the beast!* A general euphoria set in. The song ended in a crash of joy and laughter, with Wyn slashing the bow in a slapdash manner and the soldiers cheering for him until he bowed.

But even as the soldiers clapped and cheered, their eyes went to Madrig. He was sitting silently at the base of the Yubriy tree with his eyes closed and his hands still at his side. When the soldiers saw him, their clapping quickly died.

The big man opened his eyes. Smiled. He made a pronouncement with his hands. Jacy duly translated it.

"Madrig says that the songs were like beauty and joy. Related concepts. But not the same. He says that he prefers the beautiful song"—Jacy pointed at Silas—"but that in no way detracts from the joyful song." She pointed to Wyn. "He also says that there was beauty in the joyful song, but little joy in the beautiful song. Instead of joy there was melancholy, and, he thought, a discordant note of anger. The melancholy added to the beauty, but the anger did not. Madrig only notes this. It is not a criticism. Or, if it is, the criticism is beside the point. He says that critiquing a beautiful song is like critiquing a beautiful bird. A bad habit at best, a personal flaw at worst."

Silas was taken aback. He hadn't expected such poetic discourse from the imposing-looking mute. But looking at the big man sitting meditatively on the grass with puffs of winter weed lolling at his sides, he wondered how he could have missed the man's true nature.

It's the fucker's size, an internal voice whispered.

Silas gave the voice a nod.

While he was staring at Madrig, the big man's hands wove additional words out of the air. Jacy interpreted. "Madrig thanks the both of you for your songs. He says that if you would like to touch the Yubriy tree, you are more than welcome."

Wyn hopped to it. With a sprite-like spring in his step, the little man lowered his fiddle to the ground and hurried over to the tree, nearly bowling into Madrig. Madrig moved amiably out of the way, closer to where Jacy was standing.

It took Silas a moment to realize that Wyn had left his fiddle behind. *First time I've seen him do that.* Silas fell in step behind Wyn, curious to touch the tree, but not nearly so eager as Wyn. When the little man laid his hands on the tree, a serene look came over his face. It threw Silas seeing Wyn look this way, but he decided to simply chalk it up to another of the fiddler's strange behaviors. Silas moved further around the massive trunk, and, feeling a bit on display, placed his hands on the disparate sections of bark; the left he placed on smooth, dragon-skin silver, the right on ropy brown. Hands on the bark, he followed the colors with his eyes. Coils upon coils of silver and brown snaked into the soil and streamed into the heavens, separating into roots on the one end and merging into branches on the other. *This is no mere tree,* he understood. He surveyed the leafless branches, imagining the rich orange abundance that had been there only weeks earlier, wishing he had been present to see the future fall from the sky.

All at once a wild and strange laughter seemed to emanate from somewhere deep inside the tree. Startled, Silas removed his hands. As he did, he realized that the sound was coming not from the tree, but from Wyn. He turned to the little man just as Wyn jumped back from the Yubriy like he had received an electric shock. The fiddler's half-singed smile poured out laughter.

"Did you hear that, Silas O' the Songs?" Wyn said finally, turning to Silas. "The Yubriy says that it preferred your song, too."

They were persuaded to stay. For the day, at least. "The two of you will play and sing more songs," Jacy said on Madrig's behalf. "In turn, we will honor you with food, cider, and a place to sleep." The big man confirmed Jacy's interpretations by conferring an amiable grin on the two men.

Silas still wasn't entirely at ease around so many soldiers, but Madrig and Jacy's easygoing natures kept him from protesting. Wyn accepted on their behalf. "We're happy to stay, happy to play! And perhaps, in-between songs, we can swap stories. I, for one, would love to hear the story of how the two of you came to be together."

Jacy's grin was enigmatic. "Of course. But first…more songs."

They played the sun-dappled evening away. Songs begat stories and the stories begat food and food begat drinking and drinking begat more stories. All beneath the boughs of the leafless Yubriy tree. Silas nurtured a fine and creeping drunk, sipping on apple cider at a speed that enhanced both his musical prowess and his ability to converse with others; soon he was chatting up Madrig and Jacy with ease. Madrig, it was discovered, was a cousin of *the* Daguss Salk of High Osgood; although, to see the offhand manner with which the big man discussed his noble roots, Silas would have thought he was indifferent of the connection. Further discourse revealed that Madrig was a recent hero of the Blackstar Rebellion, and that, for his exploits, he had demanded of his famous cousin both the right to bond Jacy and to visit the Yubriy tree on their sweetmarch. "Lord Daguss wasn't pleased," Jacy explained in a short little speech. "But Madrig is no dummy. He made the request in front of half the Ontish army at the outset of the victory celebration, not two hours after spearheading the charge that brought the Blackstar prince to heel. Madrig pulled me from the ranks, removed my helmet, and, with ten thousand Ontish looking on, planted a kiss on my propers."

"He pulled down your pants in front of the army?" Wyn asked, deadpan.

Silas was embarrassed on Jacy's behalf, but she thought it hilarious. "No doubt he was tempted!" she exclaimed, looking to Madrig, who, though chuckling, appeared to be holding his comedic judgment in reserve. "But no. By propers I mean lips, and the lips sufficed."

"Women fight in the Ontish ranks?" Silas thought his question considerably more suited to the moment, but, to his surprise, it drew an irked response.

"I do," Jacy said. She gave Silas an unsettling *try-me* look. When she saw his well-meaning face, however, she softened. "Truth be told, there aren't many. But if a woman of martial appetites proves she can hold her own, she is accepted."

Madrig's fingers started flurrying. Jacy, blushing, looked reluctant to interpret. She shot back a fast-hands reply, only for the big man to respond in insistent double-time. She frowned in seeming acquiescence. "Madrig says that I should tell you my nickname."

A handful of the soldiers sitting next to the fire bent their ears. "They call me *bear dancer*," Jacy said. She then cocked her head to the side, refusing to say more.

Madrig shook his head with puppy-dog dismay. With a warrior-like intensity, he moved into the epicenter of the proceedings and stomped his right foot twice hard on the ground, clearing a sizable space. All eyes turned to him. Slowly, Madrig rotated his head, soaking in the stares. Then, using his entire body as a fulcrum, Madrig fired up his fingers and began to talk. He moved his fingers with such vitality that Silas thought fire might sprout from their tips. He stopped only once, long enough to scowl at Jacy, who, when Madrig resumed his performance of the hands, at last began interpreting.

Her voice was begrudgingly theatric. "In the village of Tonhit, when the winter winds begin to howl and Lake Loma has frozen over, moonbears roam the ice. The villagers there believe that winter will not relent until a brave soul crosses the frozen lake and makes it safely to the fishing cabin on the opposite shore.

"Tradition dictates that at least one villager per year must successfully cross to stay winter's cruel hands. And without the use of a weapon, no less. The year that I arrived, the villagers were losing faith, on account of an aggressive, fleet-of-foot moonbear, who it was said had devoured the last four men to try and cross the ice. No one else would take up the task, so all had resigned themselves to a harsh winter.

"The evening of my arrival, the villagers made their way to the banks of the lake at dusk. Out on the ice, I could see the feared moonbear, a long and lean creature that looked evilly equipped for the purposes of running down humans. Still, yours truly was tempted. Opportunities to burnish one's legend don't often present themselves, and, as such, they shouldn't be glibly dismissed. Besides, although the villagers held that a crossing only counted if it was accomplished without a weapon, I was not a villager of Tonhit, so if it became a matter of life and death, I could always use the dagger hidden in my boot.

"At last, I made up my mind. *I'll do it,* I said through my translator, and the villagers all cheered. Or, nearly all of them did. A woman's voice rose above the din. 'Shame, you cowards!' she shouted. I paid the woman no mind, supposing her the village loon (Jacy spat good-naturedly in Madrig's direction after translating this), but the voice continued to grow stronger, until, turning to my left, I saw that the woman had worked her way down to the shoreline, and was stepping foot on the ice.

"She was a wonder, this woman. She looked like answers to questions you would never think to ask. She looked like the carvings of weather. She looked like a fever dream. She also looked much like the woman speaking to you now. (Jacy smiled.) Then she pointed a finger at me and uttered a curse. '*Sfos, fiy klirthir,*' which, in Old Ontish means *Leave, foreign scum.* I consoled myself with the knowledge that my ability to translate her insult meant that what she said wasn't true, but before I could relay a fitting reply to my interpreter, the woman started sprinting across the ice.

"There was nothing to do but watch. Within seconds, the moonbear began loping her way. The woman, majestic in her ice boots, showed no fear. In fact, she appeared to be heading directly toward the beast. As the

142

distance between the two decreased, the woman sped up. Her approach was arrow-straight. *Beoliotius bless her, she means to jump directly into the moonbear's mouth,* thought I. But, when the beast was within ten yards, the woman feinted hard to the left. The moonbear, its mouth slavering, adjusted course, only for the woman to plant hard on the second step and pivot to the right, leading her across the moonbear's listing left side. For a heart-stopping moment it was unclear if the gambit had worked. But then the moonbear, waving its paw like a forlorn lover, swiped ineffectually at the woman, who, in a sublime showing, dipped beneath the moonbear's reach, like a dancer of the highest order."

Silas listened, his attention rapt. Beyond the story, the interplay between Madrig's signing and Jacy's interpreting was spellbinding. Silas knew that the big man could hear what was being said, but, all the same, putting his story in Jacy's care was an act of trust. He wondered whether she took liberties in the telling. Madrig's storytelling style, after all, wasn't cut and dry. She was interpreting for a man with a poetical sense.

Or was she the one with the poetical sense?

Madrig, by way of Jacy, continued. "Once the moonbear had recovered from its spill, it went loping after her in the hopes of requesting a second dance, but by then the woman had crossed the ice and was safely locked away in the cabin. The beast wailed at the door, hungry and hurt. It might have persisted the entire night had not a second suitor arrived on the scene."

"Ha!" Wyn interrupted, laughing and slapping his knee. The gloaming shadows of the Yubriy tree had settled around the little man's shoulders. "You dog, you."

Madrig paused long enough in his storytelling to give Wyn a searching look. It wasn't a hostile gaze, per se, but all the same it made Silas uncomfortable. Wyn, of course, was unfazed. After a moment the big man broke into a gap-toothed grin, and his fingers resumed the tale. "Think of me what you will. All I knew was that I needed to meet this woman, and I had no intention of waiting until the ice thawed to do so. As a result, the moonbear and I had our own little dance in front of the cabin. My dancing skills not being equal to the woman's, I was forced to draw my dagger, but before I could do any damage, the woman opened up the cabin door and berated me for resorting to steel. Duly chastised, I sheathed my blade, and, as a consequence, caught a moonbear claw across my chest."

Jacy paused. All eyes went to Madrig. With a dramatic flair he removed both his surcoat and the brown shirt beneath. Then he stepped closer to the firelight. Claw mark scars colored his chest, comets racing across a hirsute sky. He gave everyone time to drink their fill. Satisfied, he fired up his fingers once more.

Jacy resumed interpreting.

"The woman, feeling guilty (Jacy cocked her head to the side, implying disagreement), distracted the moonbear by stepping outside and clanging pans together. The bedlam made it possible for me to bolt for the cabin. Once inside, the woman and I at last made our acquaintance."

Wyn tee-heed. "She nursed you back to health, did she?"

Madrig made a simple gesture. Jacy interpreted: "Yes, she did."

Jacy continued talking, but her tenor had changed. It took Silas a moment to recognize that she was speaking for herself. "You're a wicked little man, aren't you?" she said, addressing Wyn.

"I'm as the gods have made me."

"You're an acolyte of the Twins, then?"

Wyn put a finger to his nose. "I didn't say that."

Silas hurried to interrupt. His fiddling friend had a unique intelligence, but Silas worried it didn't extend to comprehending how others might respond to his pagan sensibilities. "The two of you have been together ever since?"

"We have. By the time we left the cabin, Madrig had taught me his language. We lived and traveled as a bonded pair for over a year until the Blackstar Rebellion. When Madrig informed me that he intended to fight, I insisted that he take me with him. Now we are bonded in the eyes of Stavus and the Twins, and the only ones who rue our union are those unfortunate enough to cross paths with our swords. As many a Blackstar Islander can attest."

Silas gulped. He caught Madrig's fingers in his peripheral vision.

Jacy smiled. Interpreted. "What the woman from the story says is true."

And with those words, the storytelling ended. A contented silence descended, the only sound the hungry licking of flame on firewood. The gloaming gloom had deepened into darkness. Silas relaxed long enough to remember that he wasn't supposed to relax. His eyes went to the woods.

Where oh where are the murder birds?

"It's a fine hospitality you've offered us," Wyn said, breaking the quiet. He raised a cup of cider to the group. Madrig, Jacy, and the other soldiers returned the gesture. "But it's time to turn in. Out of respect for the Yubriy."

Funny looks crossed the soldiers' faces, but no one argued. "We'll tent you," a clean-shaven soldier from Oseiy said, and with those words four of the soldiers stood and went about the business of readying Silas and Wyn a nighttime abode. There were already two tents standing in the accompanying field, one for the soldiers who guarded the tree at night and one that belonged to Madrig and Jacy. There was a stone house a quarter mile away that the soldiers used for daily living, but only five slept there at a time.

The soldiers, though cider-sloshed, pitched the tent with an impressive efficiency. Silas noted that they placed the tent at the edge of the field, against the tree line of a dark and foreboding woods. "Figured you boys would appreciate proximity to the pisser," one of the soldiers joked, but Silas had already deduced the real reason. To get to the Yubriy tree, they would have to pass the soldiers' tent. Amiable atmosphere or not, the soldiers had not forgotten their duty.

A final round of goodnights ended the evening. Silas and Wyn retired to their tent.

"You made a good magic today, Silas O' the Songs," Wyn said, tucked away in a tattered woolen blanket lent to him by the soldiers. "The Yubriy is particular when it comes to songs, but it liked yours. It already knew that it would like your song, of course. The memory of it was stored away in its infinite roots." Wyn's voice was strangely plaintive, as if steeped in a rich nostalgia. Hearing it, Silas couldn't help but feel as if the fiddler was speaking from a deep wellspring of knowledge. "That's the thing about the Yubriy tree, Silas O' the Songs. Its memory is so long and so deep, it remembers events before they've even happened.

"And today, it remembered you."

Silas awoke with a song in his head and a deep, urgent need to piss.

He stumbled out of the tent into the bracing night air. The song's melody, a twisting fishhook of a thing, rang in Silas's skull, but, all the same, he couldn't place it. He continued humming the melody as he ventured into the forest, in search of a suitable tree to piss against.

The soft edges of his earlier drunk were hardening into a hangover. But he didn't mind. It had been a memorable day, the sort of day a man might reminisce on at the end of his life. Well worth the price of a few too many drinks. *I've seen the Yubriy tree. Touched it too.* With his young man's arrogance, he had always assumed that the Yubriy's significance was overstated, but now that he'd stood beneath its branches and laid hands on its future-conjuring form, he grasped its power. *The divine lives within its branches. Even a skeptic such as myself could sense that.* It crossed his cider-addled mind that perhaps he should compose a paean to the tree, but, when he tried to summon a melody, the one in his mind insisted upon its primacy. *Okay, okay,* he laughed, while pulling out his member to piss. *I won't drive you from my skull.*

As the hot stream of his piss turned to steam, he paid closer attention to the melody. *Where did this melody come from?* As a songwriter, he was always forgetting and later remembering half-realized melodies, which made it difficult to ascertain if he was remembering his own work or someone else's. *Is this a gift from the Melodies? Or perhaps from Gia and Blue?* He wanted to believe that it was an original, but he couldn't fight the nagging sensation that he had heard it before.

Piss on it, he thought. He gave a little laugh. His thoughts were all a scuttle. Cider-soaked. He sensed the melody fading, drifting away. *A gift to the gods.* He was the munificent, magnificent Silas O' the Songs, after all; he was talented enough to afford losing this one. There would always be another, and another, and another, for a composer such as him. For a brief moment he didn't even begrudge Wyn the song he had stolen. Silas took his hand off his cock, and, raising his arms to the heavens, bequeathed the gods the gift of his genius.

The gods gave it right back. The sound of a loud *CRAAAACK* stunned Silas to his bones, rendering him immobile as a large tree branch crashed to the ground not five feet in front of where Silas stood. He jumped when it landed, sending warm piss across his hand. In that instant, the melody bounced back into his brain, and along with it, the words.

STICK YOUR HAND IN THE HOLLOW, STICK YOUR HAND IN THE HOLLOW.

Merjy's song.

He waited for his heart to settle. *Too many near-death experiences in the woods,* he thought, but he could hardly think for the song, now booming in his brain. He remembered what he had forfeited to the woods witch. The needle-sliver. The stinging wisp. STICK YOUR HAND IN THE HOLLOW. He wondered if any of the soldiers would come running to ascertain the source of the sound, then laughed at himself. *Stavus knows they're accustomed to the sound of a falling tree branch.* He thought of Wyn, tucked away in the tent. "What path do you follow?" The little man's reply: "The trail of the trees." STICK YOUR HAND IN THE

HOLLOW. He studied the contours of the tree branch in the darkness, its pointing fingers. *Over there.* He followed with his eyes and feet.

Ooooooooh.

A tree. Long. Gnarled. Damaged. At its compromised core, a deeper darkness, an aperture to the world within.

A hollow.

The song swelled, transforming into the mythic, the chorus of the gods. Silas a slave to its message.

He stepped forward. His heart thump-thumping.

His hand trembling, he reached deep into the black.

He pulled out a large, orange, seven-pointed leaf.

Gregor Thorn

Unlike its predecessors, the present incarnation of the Three Dragons Inn included the theater as part of the main building, rather than as a separate setting. A passageway of white marble on the southern side of the inn emptied into the grand auditorium. Upon entering, Gregor noted the tapestry hanging from the theater's back wall, a gorgeous vista of Low Osgood as seen from the perspective of someone standing at the front doors of the Three Dragons. The mesmerizing Lake Wyglass parted the fabric, resulting in a dazzling spill of blue. "Did you know," Gregor said, drawing Prince Ajax's attention to the tapestry, "that a similar tapestry hung from the walls of the first Three Dragons Inn, during the days of Queen Portia? That one was lost in the fire. When this one appeared in the Wrainish marketplace, there were those who swore it was one and the same."

Prince Ajax gave the tapestry a passing glance. Ever since Gregor had shared his concerns with the crown prince that his life might be in danger, Ajax had been understandably edgy. "Queen Portia? Stavus save us, Uncle Bones, must you invoke the one monarch who was assassinated here?"

Gregor supposed Ajax had a point. "Apologies, Nephew. The history of Low Osgood intrigues me. As for preventing your demise, short of leaving the premises, I can assure you that we have taken every possible measure to ensure that you make it through the evening unscathed. However, if you would rather we return to Coffyn Castle…?"

As expected, the prince bridled at the suggestion. "No. Of course not. I would not be thought a coward. Besides, it was only a—" The prince stopped short before saying *vision*. The heir to the throne of Ragar Or gave Gregor a look of apology before changing over to a serious expression. "I trust you, Uncle. You'll steer me through the evening. I'm sure of it."

Gregor nodded. *What a luxury, to put one's trust in others. I'll have to try it myself, someday.*

They made their way to the center-front of the theater, where Dante Heron and his cohorts were sitting. *Birds, birds, and more birds.* Ajax greeted Dante with gusto, reprising their meeting at lunch. The men surrounding Dante, a consortium of eastern upstarts whose power was derived almost entirely from their fealty to the Heron household, rose for Ajax and gave awkward half-bows. Gregor made note of one in particular: Jakastor Weylcoin, the martial prodigy and minor son of the famed Weylcoin family. Jakastor wore a mustache like a stiff broom. Ajax waved away the men's displays of obeisance and took a seat beside Dante Heron.

Gregor sat beside the prince, ignoring the many flitting glances directed at him. He searched instead for Deglan. Not seeing the young knight, Gregor assumed that he was still shadowing Doxius Brine as commanded. Shortly after the meal—and once the effects of the Delilah herb had diminished—Gregor and Deglan had sought out the innkeeper, and, with polite insistence, requested that the young knight be allowed to tail the innkeeper for the remainder of the day. They offered the pretext that Deglan's father was a well-connected innkeeper in Union, and Gregor would consider it a personal favor if the young knight was allowed a behind-the-scenes look at Doxius's routines. Doxius, without a real say in the matter, obligingly agreed.

"Sagekind." Gregor turned to his left. Dante Heron was leaning forward, speaking across the crown prince. Gregor waited for the young lord to say more, but instead Dante held his tongue and graced Gregor with a rather insipid smile.

"Lord Heron," Gregor replied. While waiting for Dante to continue, Gregor took note of the Heron's attire. The man was dressed, as was often the case, in the purest white, from white felt-lined boots to white breeches to a snow-colored cloak pinned at the shoulder by a silver heron brooch. The only other color in Dante's ensemble was a whisper of blue stitching that lined the cuffs. *We're of a size,* Gregor noted. He worked his way back to the young lord's eyes. *Though I fear we're not of a mind.*

"Care to venture a guess as to what the subject of tonight's play might be?"

"Guessing is tedious work. It seems, however, that you may be privy to that information. Would you enlighten me?"

Dante smiled, a thin-lipped grin that somehow looked more like a moue. "If it's the same performance that my men and I were treated to last night, you're in for quite the surprise."

My men and I, he says. They're all the king's men, you arrogant ass. "Interesting. What was last night's play about?"

The Heron gave a quick, conspiratorial glance at Ajax, as if including the crown prince in an inside joke. "Why…you."

Gregor held his face in a still, impassive expression. "Me?"

"Yes. You. And me, as well. It seems the tale of our encounter with the Dagish Prophet of Wrath last year has made its way north. We must hope there's a repeat performance this evening. I would consider it criminal if the Three Dragons Inn deprived you of the pleasure."

Gregor kept his expression stone-still. He wasn't accustomed to being caught off guard. He had doubted Doxius Brine would be so stupid as to show one of the plays that satirized the Dayborns with a member of the royal family in attendance. But a play that featured Gregor? That was most unexpected.

And…most worrisome.

Gregor decided that a direct tact was the best one to take. "Should my portrayal concern me, Lord Heron? There are Ontishmen in our company who already take too northern a view of my…person. As a faithful servant of our king, I hope that you will tell me if this is a play that we should stop before it starts."

Dante brought his right hand to his chest. His smile was a shining knife. "You will find that I am ever prepared to defend the interests of the Dayborn dynasty."

Gregor wasn't keen on Dante's nebulous response, but, before he was able to push for a more definitive answer, an actor appeared on stage wearing a dark cloak stitched with tongues of red flame. The real Dagish Prophet of Wrath had been larger and uglier, and his flame-covered black cloak considerably more ragged, but, by and large, the effect was accurate.

The actor's voice boomed out from the stage. "Sons and daughters of Stavus. Hear me now. For thirty days and nights I have prayed beneath a blistering sun. On the thirtieth day, Stavus spoke to me through a hawk screaming from on high, and this is what he said: Go forth and cleanse

Ragar Or of the foul contagion that is Twin worship. If false priests and weak-kneed kings resist you, baptize them with fire. The Bottom Black awaits those who refuse the one true god. And so it is spoken. And so it will be done."

A chill ran up Gregor's spine. The real Dagish Prophet of Wrath had been a nasty piece of work, single-minded in his purpose. Seeing the actor brought back memories of the fear Gregor had felt in facing the prophet down. *He nearly killed me,* Gregor reminisced, remembering the heat from the prophet's unseen flames. *If I hadn't seen him for what he truly was, it's likely that he would have.*

The Prophet of Wrath was joined on stage by a bearded man wearing roughspun. *The Dagish Gorgostrine,* Gregor guessed. He looked at the performer's hands. *Two brands on the player's fourth and fifth fingers. Impressive attention to detail.* The actor playing the Gorgostrine started heckling the Prophet, only for his taunts to turn into screams of anguish and pleas for mercy. *Same as in real life. This can't be sitting well with our Ontish friends.* Gregor wished for a moment that he had a head like an owl, so that he could take in the entire theater. He used his peripheral vision as best as he could. At the front-right of the theater he spied Grocian Mock and Reginal Burntree, sitting together with scowls on their faces. *I wonder if Reginal ever wears an expression other than one suggesting he's on the verge of stabbing somebody.* Gregor started to look away, but then, sitting beside Grocian and Reginal, he saw a most unexpected person: Betrard, a Gorgostrine of the southern provinces. Gregor knew Betrard well because he was the representative of the Twins at the collection of the Yubriy tree's leaves.

What in the name of the Fire Mother is he doing here?

Gregor tried to clear his head. *That's a mystery for later.* Onstage, the play was transitioning to a new scene. The Dagish Prophet of Wrath had disappeared, and a new player had taken his place. The actor was covered in red from head to toe, making him instantly recognizable. Even so, Gregor thought him a pale imitation of the real thing. *I'm two inches taller and a half-stone lighter. And much less handsome, to boot.* Scattered applause and a sprinkling of boos filled the theater. The actor looked at the crowd directly and gave a rakish smile. The expression was so unexpected, so out of character for the character, that everyone laughed, including Prince Ajax.

That's not fair. I smile. Only I'm not so stupid as to do it in front of others.

The imitation Sagekind was joined on stage by a beautiful woman playing the part of a comely young traveler.

"Pardon, milord. May I ask where you're traveling to?"

"Dagon, dear girl." The actor spoke in a jaunty voice that Gregor would never use. "There's bad doings afoot, and I'm the man to put a stop to it."

The woman moved closer to Gregor's counterpart. "You mean to confront the Prophet of Wrath?"

"I do."

The actress brought her hand close to her mouth. "Do be careful, milord. I've only just come from Dagon. The Prophet of Wrath possesses a terrible magic. If someone challenges his teachings, he burns them alive from the inside."

The Sagekind on stage gave yet another of his winning smiles. Reaching behind his head, the actor pulled at a hairpin, and a glorious cascade of chestnut-brown hair tumbled to the midpoint of his back. The juxtaposition to Gregor's baldness was blatant. The audience howled with laughter. "As you can see, dear girl, he'll have met his match with me."

The actress's open palm changed to a questioning finger, contemplative on her chin. "And who are you? Exactly?"

"Surely you recognize me?" He made a show of his red apparel.

The actress's chin-touching finger tap-tapped. "A handsome man with a headful of hair, genial and kind, and wearing red. Why, you're the king's half brother. The Sagekind!"

The audience exploded with laughter. Gregor thought that he even saw Reginal chuckle.

"In the flesh."

"And how will you defeat this prophet? Do you have a magic of your own?"

Gregor leaned forward, along with the rest of the audience. This was dangerous territory.

"I have the favor and the blessing of King Micah of House Dayborn, the first of his name, Rightful ruler of Ragar Or, the Holy Son of the Air and the Twin ascendant. That is magic enough."

A few people in the audience muttered, but most applauded. Prince Ajax nudged Gregor with his elbow. "A good answer that, eh, Uncle Bones?"

Gregor nodded, but otherwise didn't respond. He was trying to stay attuned to the temperature of the room. If an assassin was lurking, even a split second's delay in response could make the difference. At the present moment, however, he sensed nothing.

The play continued. When the Prophet of Wrath was onstage, the play made no bones about his supernatural abilities: time and again those who stood against the prophet found themselves screaming in pain, victims of internal immolation. The Sagekind, however, was too handsome and humorous to be taken seriously as a sorcerer. It appeared that the playwright had decided to bypass the matter of Gregor's powers altogether by creating a character who clearly wasn't intended to represent the real Sagekind. For the purposes of the play at least, it appeared to be working. *But what will happen at the play's end?* Gregor wondered. *I certainly didn't kill the Prophet of Wrath with a wink and a smile.*

The play moved steadily toward its denouement. As different from reality as it was, Gregor had difficulty watching it without feeling like he was reliving the experience. The prophet especially unnerved him; every scene reminded Gregor of how confounded he had been by the prophet at the time. *Why did it take me so long to realize what in retrospect was so obvious?* Onstage, the imitation Sagekind made similar efforts to learn about the prophet. But, as Gregor anticipated, the actor in the play arrived at the wrong conclusion, the one Gregor and King Micah had purposefully spread to deceive the realm.

"This so-called Prophet of Wrath is using shadow magic that he learned in Thralk-Braktur," the Sagekind on stage assured the actor playing Dante Heron, who, at last, had entered the play. "I'm sure of it. I'll need your assistance in bringing him to heel."

The Dante Heron on stage was part dashing young lord, part deliberate decision-maker. He in no way resembled the man Gregor had found when he arrived in the city: a plodding hypocrite trying to have it both ways. The real Dante Heron had slow-played squashing the prophet because he was waiting to see whether the prophet's popularity with the Stavus-worshipping sect proved greater than the crown's willingness to put him down. It wasn't until Gregor arrived with an edict from the king that Dante decided he had been opposed to the prophet all along.

"And my assistance you shall have, Revered Sagekind," Dante the actor exclaimed. "The prophet has amassed a great many followers. Give me the word, and I'll cut out the strength from underneath him. It's only his shadow magic that makes me uneasy."

"Do not worry, Lord Heron. You deal with his men, and I'll deal with his magic."

The real Dante Heron leaned across Prince Ajax and whispered to Gregor, "The actors have captured us quite nicely, don't you think?"

Gregor didn't respond. Something was wrong. He had only now detected it. He slowed his pulse rate and tried to slip into a meditative state. *Quickly but slowly. Halve your mind. One half to stay in this world and look, the other half to travel into the mind and see.*

Onstage, Gregor and the Prophet of Wrath prepared for their confrontation. A makeshift army of actors engaged in a skirmish, half representing the Heron's soldiers and the other half the acolytes that had sworn allegiance to the prophet. At center stage, the actor playing Gregor stood alone against the prophet. The real Gregor, sitting in his seat, surrendered to his meditative mind as he drifted back to the events of that fateful day.

The rising sun. A morning walk, toward the hill in the center of town where the prophet held sway. Hundreds of the prophet's followers cloaking the knoll like an army of ants, prepared to die. The Heron's army moving in by my side. Everyone on edge, waiting, waiting…and then the first man cries out, screaming because of the invisible flames burning his insides. Then another. And another. The soldiers losing heart. The Heron retreating, falling away. On top of the hill, I see the prophet, terrible in his power, looking down at the army, looking down at me. His acolytes frenzied in their belief, screaming. And then I feel the prophet's heat licking at my organs, ready to burst into flames.

Who am I?

Who is he?

See. See. See.

Gregor opened his eyes. Onstage, the prophet was screaming, calling the wrath of Stavus down on the Heron's soldiers. But instead of looking at the other actors, the prophet was looking at the audience. *No, not at the audience,* Gregor realized. *He's looking at Prince Ajax.*

Gregor understood in a flash. He turned to the prince, who was silently gasping for air in his seat.

The actor is a jeyedoshi. Just like the real Dagish Prophet of Wrath, and just like me.

On instinct, Gregor reached for what was available: the many dancing heads of flame in the sconces lining the theater wall. He took a deep breath and channeled his energy. One moment later the theater went dark, and the actor playing the prophet screamed.

A great commotion ensued. Beside Gregor, the prince continued to struggle for air. Gregor couldn't help him. The jeyedoshi onstage, while less formidable than the Prophet of Wrath, was trying his damnedest to fight back. But Gregor knew the scope and the limitations of a jeyedoshi's powers. He knew that once a jeyedoshi had taken possession of an element, it was no simple task to switch, especially in the middle of a fight. And while Gregor was fighting with fire, his counterpart was stuck flailing about with the wind he had stolen from Prince Ajax's throat. Every attempt the actor made to snuff the fire with wind only fanned the flames, so that his suffering increased.

Gregor wished that he could make time stand still. This jeyedoshi wasn't nearly as formidable as the Prophet of Wrath had been, but overpowering him was still no easy task. Around Gregor, a hubbub was brewing: there was movement at the periphery, shadowy rushings with evil designs. The Heron and his men were shouting, beneath which Gregor heard the unmistakable sound of sharp steel being extracted from wooden scabbards. But Gregor could do nothing until the jeyedoshi had been dealt with.

At last, the onstage jeyedoshi succumbed: his body combusted, and the stage was momentarily ablaze with flame. Gregor quickly redirected the flame back to the sconces, and light filled the theater once more. To Gregor's left, Prince Ajax gulped in desperate lungfuls of air. Further down the aisle, two men rushed at the prince, their swords drawn. Gregor turned—unsteady from his exertions but ready to help—only to find Jakastor Weylcoin making short work of the unfortunates who had been foolish enough to launch an attack at the prince using conventional methods. With a savagery of purpose that was as efficient as it was brutal, Jakastor cut down both men with two successive blows, transforming their corpses into flowers blooming blood on the theater floor.

A shocked silence fell. But only for the briefest of moments. From behind the stage curtain, a curdling scream spilled out into the room. Buried beneath it a shout: *Vengeance for the Blackstar Isles!* All eyes went to the stage. Moments later, a figure stumbled through the slit in the curtain's middle, his belly red with blood.

Gregor's long-hardened heart cracked. *This is my doing,* he thought.

Deglan Whisk raised a blood-painted finger and looked out at the crowd. Then he slumped over and fell to the floor.

Johanna Salk

They rode south and west, the warmth of a brilliant winter sun falling on their backs. No words between them. Easton, leading the way, kept to the main road. Johanna considered demanding, per the conditions of their agreement, that they choose a less conspicuous route, but, seeing none suitable for horses, she remained quiet. Once, they passed a commoner leading a mule laden with bitter-black apples, but he kept his eyes straight ahead. So did they. Occasionally, Johanna would turn her head to see if they were being followed. But no one emerged from the castle, and, within twenty minutes of riding, they were out of view of the castle walls.

The land, for the most part, was flat, snow-covered, and devoid of character. Johanna had traveled the southern route out of the Edgeling Mountains before, so the landscape was familiar to her, the only difference being that, traveling west, she wasn't personally acquainted with the terrain. Shortly after they lost sight of Coffyn Castle, the main road branched in two different directions: one route curved serpentine-like into the Edgeling Mountains, whereas the other dove south into a pocket of evergreens. When the roads appeared, Easton dropped back with his horse and fell in stride beside her.

"Do you have a preference?" he asked, gesturing at the fork.

She thought back to her geography lessons as a child, responding to the Wandering Tongue as he pointed to place after place on the map. "Are you pretending to give me a choice? We are not equipped to travel into the mountains."

Easton nodded. "If we venture south—"

Johanna interrupted him. "We'll come upon a village. Doakmont."

The prince smiled. He gestured back in the direction of Coffyn Castle. "I doubt my father has the heart to send anyone after me. He knows from past experience that it's a fruitless effort. Your father, on the other hand, will likely insist that a genuine effort be made to track down his daughter." Easton tilted his head in a way that made it clear that he was asking a question.

I wouldn't be so sure, she thought. But to Easton, she said, "He might."

Easton's smile widened, secret-style. "I left a note explaining that we had…um…absconded together. I suggested we were going on a *mivay kliye lorwenflil* before our sweetmarch proper."

She raised her eyebrows. "You speak Old Ontish?"

He laughed. "Not as well as you do, I'm sure. But, being a prince, a certain amount of learning was hammered into my skull before my wildness and wanderlust ran amok."

Johanna pondered this, permitting a small gap of silence. "This isn't, you know? A *little sweetmarch* before our sweetmarch proper."

Easton grinned again and gestured once more at the fork in the road. "For the next two days, it is whatever you say it is."

In lieu of replying, Johanna dug her heels into the horse's ribs. Trotting ahead, she veered left, away from the mountains. She expected Easton to catch up, but, when a minute passed and he hadn't joined her, she twisted her neck to find him following at a respectful distance. The second time she looked behind her, he gave a little wave. When she found herself wanting to look back at him again, she slowed the horse to a slow walk and waited for Easton to make up the ground.

She continued the conversation without looking at him when he drew beside her. "I have no doubt that my father is glad that I'm gone. He might send someone after us for appearance's sake, but, believe you me, he has no desire to bring me back." She paused. "His intention was to send me to Union, to wait there for our bonding ceremony."

Easton half laughed, half scoffed. When he spoke, a mischievousness colored his voice. "I have no desire to bond someone who wishes to sit around like a pampered princess. I want a woman willing to ride with me into the wild. A woman unafraid to speak her mind, who forges her own path."

Johanna felt a blush creep into her cheeks. Worried that Easton would notice, she snorted. She tried to think of a witty reply, but, when nothing came to mind, she decided on a different course of action.

The horse beneath her was a Rugarder. He was a beautiful creature: bold, muscular, and colored a deep auburn red, which was characteristic of the breed. She had had a sense of its power from the moment she mounted up outside the castle walls, but now she unleashed the horse's potential in full, urging the beast to a quick, hard gallop. She felt giddy at its responsiveness: Johanna had ridden many a horse in her lifetime, but the creature beneath her possessed a vitality that made it seem a species apart. He ate up the long, flat road like a famished demon. She laughed in delight, and then laughed again at the thought of Prince Easton Dayborn trying to catch her.

By the time she reached the pocket of evergreens, the wind was playing at her thick, brown hair like sprites. She gave a quick glance behind her, and saw, to her amusement, that Easton was giving chase. Facing forward once more, she settled into position, absorbing rather than fighting the horse's movement. The snow-covered road was in surprisingly good condition, but, all the same, she kept an eye out for slicks of ice. Her prudence, however, could not allay the joy swelling in her soul. For the first time in forever, she felt alive, free. In her mind's eye she envisioned riding the Rugarder ever further south, out of the snows and into the Qorlish plains, through the grasses and into the Provish Want, on and on and on until the magnificent creature beneath her plowed into the sea.

And if the prince follows you the entire way?

She couldn't help but smile at the thought. *Then perhaps I will grant him the favor of a kiss.*

Forever soon ran out. Up ahead, the pinewood thickened, and the road narrowed. She wanted nothing more than to continue charging forward, but the horsewoman in her resisted. Fighting every fiber of her being, she pulled on the reins and slowed the Rugarder to a walk. The horse, frustrated at having to stop, neighed churlishly, which lightened her mood somewhat. She reached out and stroked his neck. "Don't be bitter, boy." She liked the way the b's rolled off her tongue.

Bitterboy. And thus you are named.

Easton drew beside her seconds later. "Who knew I had stolen for you the fastest horse in Egros Coffyn's stables?"

"Stolen?"

He laughed. "Yes, stolen. Lord Egros will pretend that the horse was borrowed once he learns the identity of the thief, but, truly, I have no intention of returning him. It does beg an interesting question though, doesn't it? Can a member of the Dayborn family ever truly *steal* anything?"

She snorted again. She liked the unladylike sound of it; it was a noise for keeping stupid boys at bay. "I'm sure you've done a fair bit of research on that account."

"So says my accomplice."

She brought Bitterboy to a complete stop. "You're a prince! Your father's own horses were housed in Lord Egros's stable! Why didn't you take one of those?"

His answer was simple. "When I saw this horse, I thought it suited you."

She found herself unable to argue with his logic. "You were right."

Easton accepted his victory with uncharacteristic grace. Together they continued into the forest's thickening knot. The evergreens gave way to trees of a deciduous variety, their bare-bones branches grasping at the sky like the outstretched arms of towering skeletons. The forest floor displayed the aftermath of the first snowstorm of the year's war with autumn: the snow was thick and white, but here and there the drifts took the unstructured form of autumn's leavings, corpses of leaves compressed under the snow. Weak sunlight weaved through the tree branches. Johanna, despite her heavy coat, shivered.

"Oooh."

The sound was a precursor to a surprise. Easton, spotting something, directed his horse off the road. Johanna, curious, brought Bitterboy to a stop. Seconds later, the Dayborn prince dismounted with the stealthy aspect of a predator stalking prey. He led his black mare by the reins through a maze of trees, stepping slowly, keeping his eyes peeled on a prize that Johanna had yet to identify. Finally, he stopped in front of a shriveled tree, his body blocking a low-hanging branch.

When he turned around, he held a silver-gray flower in his hand.

He strode back through the woods in triumph. Johanna tried not to appear impressed, but, having spent years tending the Eagle Garden in High Osgood, she knew what he had found.

"Milu Sfal," she said. "The forever flower."

"I can't believe I spotted it. They're so—"

"Uncommon," she finished for him. "We have a kunlu tree in High Osgood that hasn't produced a bloom since before I was born. The blooms keep for close to a year, infinitely longer if you rest them in a pool of cold water." Her thoughts returned to High Osgood. There were two *milu isfal* in the cold-water spring that originated in the Eagle Garden. One had bloomed in Daguss Salk's youth. He had gifted it to Johanna's mother. The other was from the time of Theron Salk, grandson of Theron Redd.

Easton nodded. With horse reins laced through his fingers, the prince cupped the forever flower in the palm of his cold, red hand. He glanced up at Johanna with wild, impulsive eyes, then returned his stare to the flower. She grew worried by the look on his face. As all good Ontish knew, there was no higher declaration of love than when a man gifted a woman with a forever flower.

He looked at her once more. Longer this time. He appeared to be working his tongue around the right words.

She beat him to the punch. "Don't you dare."

It was the worst thing she could have said. Easton puffed out his chest like a Thistleton peacock and presented her with the bloom. "For my bonded-to-be. On our *mivay kliye lorwenflil.*"

She considered knocking the flower from his hand, but the haunting beauty of it arrested her. Instead, she looked Prince Easton hard in the eyes from high on her Bitterboy perch.

"Toying with my affection is no way to win it." She thought of a way to press the attack. "Tell me true. How many women have you lain with?"

The question appeared to surprise the prince, but he answered it all the same. "Four," he said, without bravado or shame.

It was less than she had expected, for a prince. But she continued, determined to make her point. "And would you be content having only lain with five when they lay you in your grave? Because that's what it means to give someone a forever flower. It means fidelity. Devotion. Commitment. *Pla milu sfal* is a symbol of love's transcendent powers. You dishonor it and dishonor me by offering it on a whim."

Easton squinted. Then he shook his head. "No."

"What do you mean, no?"

He returned the flower to his side, but he didn't put it away completely. "I mean 'no, I do not dishonor you.' This isn't a whim. This is serendipity. There's a difference."

She laughed so loudly that a startled bird took flight from a nearby branch. "Serendipity? Ha! You're not in love with me, you're in love with the moment. Yesterday you weren't even certain that you wanted to bond me. Remember? What, bless Beoliotius, has changed between now and then?"

"Nothing. Everything." He gave a small frown. "A feeling. A voice."

"A voice?"

"Yes." He grinned again, but for once the smile on his face was distracted rather than roguish. "A voice spoke to me when you were talking to your sister. It said: 'She's your queen. The true love of your life.'" He paused. "It was then that I made the decision."

Johanna felt a little dizzy. She took tighter hold of the reins. "And what decision was that?"

"The decision to commit. To you." He gave the wider world a glance. "To this."

He's telling the truth. The voice in her head sounded like a whisper from a ghost. She pushed it away.

"You forget yourself. And who's to say that I would commit to you? In fact, I believe I've already made it quite clear that I have no such intention. Remember?" She leaned sideways in the saddle and jutted her chin out at the prince. "I saved your life, Easton Dayborn. In turn, you owe me a debt. One that you promised to pay. The fulfillment of said debt is where we begin and end. Understand?"

Easton shook his head, and, with an upward puff of wind from his lips, blew a cold breeze through the curls of brown hair resting on the front of his forehead. "The voice never said it would be easy." He turned back to his horse and opened up the saddlebag. There, in its mysterious depths, he deposited the forever flower with care. Finished, he saddled up once more. "To Doakmont, then?" he asked with a studied nonchalance.

She cast her gaze on the road. "To Doakmont."

Johanna's mind was a blizzard of thoughts the remainder of the way to Doakmont. Decisions had to be made. Before the first of the daub-and-wattle houses appeared, she had concocted a rough plan. *I'll drive the prince south for forty-eight hours. Then I'll insist that he escort me to Thistleton. If he refuses, I'll go it on my own.* She experienced a pang of fear at the thought of navigating through the heart of Ragar Or by herself—*You'll be robbed! Raped! Captured by highwaymen and held for ransom!*—but she pushed the fear aside. *Being on your own has been your lot for some time. You're only now coming to grips with it.* She forced herself to formulate the remainder of the plan. *Once in Thistleton, I'll use the brogan's-heads and my contacts to ensure safe passage to Wrain. From Wrain, I'll sail to Clyesia.* Clyesia was a civilized land, and, based on the stories Johanna had heard, the Clyesians would jump at the chance to entertain a barbarian princess. For a moment Johanna thought of Queen Anjay: the queen's dark skin standing out against the snow in the cherry tree garden, the regal way she held her chin against the foreign clime. *Perhaps I'll bond a Clyesian prince, become Queen Anjay in reverse.*

It wasn't the most finely tuned plan.

But it was hers.

The village appeared like a transition in a fragmented dream; the woods abruptly thinned as the horses climbed a small hill. Cresting the knoll, Johanna realized that the knoll was in fact a plateau that stretched as far as the eye could see. The dark knot of the forest had been a lie. This was a land of wide-open spaces, a land of unbounded potential. The forest had been the gate. Now all they needed to do was keep going.

"Well?"

A question from Easton. She turned to find him looking at her with interrogative eyes.

"Well, what?"

"It's two hours to sundown. We can either prepare for the coming darkness by finding a place in the village, or, if you are so inclined, we can pass through the village and spent a cold night under the stars. Your decision, of course."

Her gut told her to keep going. But that urging was so at odds with her primal yearnings for food and fire that she suggested the opposite.

"We have plenty of time out of doors ahead of us. Let's stop." She thought of another reason for calling it a day. "Plus, it will give us the opportunity to see if we're being followed."

Easton's expression suggested that they were of one accord. "My thoughts exactly." His ever-present grin turned cheeky. "If we go to an inn, you understand that we will have to—"

"Pose as bonded." Johanna exchanged her view of his eyes for one of the far horizon. "So long as you remember that we're not."

"How could I forget?"

The innkeep was an old turkey of a man, wattle-necked and possessive of a nervous energy that made Johanna ill at ease. But when Easton slipped him a few pieces of silver, the innkeep channeled that energy into his work. He promptly served them tankards of ale and a duck stew swimming in root vegetables, along with trenchers of black bread. Throughout the meal, the innkeep kept stealing glances at them like he had a hundred questions on his mind. He may have even asked a couple, but they were murmured so low and under his breath that Johanna had to assume they were for his own pleasure rather than for the purposes of being answered.

Midway through the meal, a man with a beard like a hornet's nest entered the inn. He had a wild-eyed aspect that became even more pronounced when he spotted Easton and Johanna. "Who in Werring's weeping asshole are they?" the man asked the innkeep.

"Travelers. Visitors," the innkeep replied. The old turkey lowered his voice, but Johanna could still hear him. "A lady and her lord, most like." The hush in his voice suggested that he hoped the bearded man would do the same.

"Huh," the bearded fellow responded, looking like the idea of lordly sorts had never occurred to him before. He gave a pondering sort of stare. "First news of the dragon, now this. Why in Werring's weeping asshole are they here?"

The innkeep harrumphed. "Rooster, I've lived long enough to know that some questions are better left unasked," he said sagely, and disappeared into the kitchens.

Rooster considered the innkeep's advice but seemed disposed toward discarding it. He took a seat on the bench directly across from Easton and Johanna. Johanna couldn't tell if he was dull-witted or brazen. When he proceeded to take his fill of her with his eyes, she felt her blood go hot. She sat up straight on the bench and gave him a look for starting wars. The movement shifted her coat, where, deep inside the coat's interior pocket, the sennequi piece brushed up against her ribcage.

She was speaking the words before she had even processed them. "You mentioned a dragon. Do you have any idea where in Werring's weeping asshole it might be?"

172

Beside her, Easton nearly choked on his ale. Rooster, who was running his hands through the ungodly tangle of his beard, processed the question on a delay, until at last his mouth opened to reveal a tooth-deficient grin. An eruption of laughter followed.

"Werring's weeping asshole is a foul hole, deep, and chasmic! And this world, this realm, this king-damn-dom is naught but a bulging red vein on its outer rim. But yes, Rooster has heard rumors of a dragon circling high above our hemorrhoidal hellhole. *And* rumors of one who can coax the creature from the sky."

Johanna didn't know what was more surprising: Rooster's information or his linguistic abilities. Easton, likewise impressed, put down his tankard and leaned forward. "Rumors?" he said with a smile. "Rumors love nothing more than to be shared."

Rooster didn't respond. Instead, he pointed at them with the index and pinkie fingers on his right hand. "You are shitty little lordlings, no? Lordlings and lordesses? Tumbling west from Coffyn Castle or perhaps the Osgood that is Low, searching for dragons and adventure and glory?"

"Yes," Easton replied matter-of-factly.

"Then you will produce the plump purse all shitty little lordlings and lordesses keep hidden on their person and pay Rooster for the information his munificent tongue might produce?"

Johanna bristled at the affront, but in its own way the bristling felt good, like it was a reminder of being alive. *This is far preferable to being trapped in the Cherry Tower,* she thought. She shifted again on the bench. Beside her, Easton did the same. It was a hungry sort of movement: a subtle positioning of the pack, if you will. Here, away from their castles, away from their families, away from the power and the prestige of their names, they were vulnerable. This left them no option but to be fearless. Unafraid. She drew strength from Easton, who, if nothing else, was daring.

That makes two of us.

"The lord and lady before you are neither shitty nor stupid," Johanna responded. "We don't pay for information. But we may choose to reward those who help us."

Rooster took this news under advisement. He furrowed his great caterpillar eyebrows and screwed up his face in imitation of a thinking man. Then he leaned forward on the bench, letting the great ham hocks of his forearms rest on the wood. He shrugged his shoulders as if coming to a realization. "It's strange for the two of you to be alone, together. Something is not right. Something tells me that if I wanted, I could turn you upside down and shake you by your ankles, take all the silver and gold that pours out of your pockets. Something tells me that if I did this, no one would come to your aid." He proceeded to slowly turn his head from left to right, as if looking for their absent retinue.

In response, Easton picked up the black bread trencher on the table. He moved it up and down like a plate, studying its weight. Satisfied, he looked at Rooster and said, "An offering of food for our new friend." Then, with a studied casualness, he tossed the trencher to Rooster, the bread tracing a gentle arc. What happened next happened in a flash. While the trencher was in flight, Easton pulled a knife from his boot and threw it hard across the room. The blade struck home in the heart of the bread at the exact moment Rooster snatched the bread from the air. Rooster, flipping the trencher over, realized what Johanna already had:

were it not for the trencher, the knife would have speared Rooster in the face.

A tense second passed as Rooster considered his response. Giving his eyebrows a slight raise, the commoner flipped the trencher over, and, removing the knife, nonchalantly began cutting the hard bread into slices. "Fine. We'll talk payment later," he said, stuffing a slice of the black bread into the woolly cave of his mouth. Pretending that nothing unpleasant had occurred, the big man began talking through a mouthful of mush. "There is a woods witch lives two days west of here. There are those that say that she coaxed this new dragon from the sky, gave it a pet on the nose, whispered in its ear, and sent it on its way."

"When?" Easton asked, his voice a hard nugget of want.

Rooster shrugged. "A fortnight ago. Twice that. Half that. Time doesn't dance for us common folk the way it does for you lords and lordesses."

"Where, exactly?" Johanna chimed in. The duck stew's aftertaste clarified when she spoke, revealing a subtlety of flavor she hadn't previously detected. *Oh,* she thought. *Oh my.*

"Where the mountains weep. At the far edge of the Edgelings. Many a pilgrimage is made there by the people of these parts. But I'll be honest. This witch keeps with common folk. I don't believe she'd welcome the likes of you."

It unsettled Johanna how quickly the villagers had keyed in on their social status. *It's me, not Easton,* she realized, glancing at their clothes. Easton forged ahead, unperturbed by the warning. "What do you mean when you say she coaxed the dragon from the sky?"

Rooster stopped masticating and gave them a *Bless Beoliotius* stare. "Dragons grow disoriented when they cross over from the Beasting Rock. Prickly, too. Or so they say. When this one wasn't bellowing in the blue, it was laying waste to good land, gobbling good mutton. People were concerned. The pilgrimages piled up quick. Our lady of the blue eyes took pity on the supplicants and spoke to the dragon."

Easton frowned. Johanna stepped in. "What did she say to it?"

Rooster stuffed the last of the black bread into his mouth. "Do I look like a woods witch?"

It was at that moment that the innkeep reentered the room from the kitchens. Picking up on the tension, he tried to hide his nervousness by fixing the room with a mean little glare, but it didn't work. Easton and Rooster had stopped conversing and were engaged in a strange sort of staring contest that appeared destined to end in either friendship or fisticuffs. Johanna left them to it. She rose from the bench and approached the innkeep, donning her most disarming smile. He attempted a small retreat, but, foiled by his fumbling feet, resorted to muttering under his breath, a defense he abandoned when Johanna laid her hand upon his arm.

"The duck stew was delicious."

The innkeep gave a nervous bob of his head and tried to pull away. Johanna held tight.

"It was the seasoning that made the meal. Garlic. Pepper. Basil. And brayosk, if my tongue did not deceive me."

Beads of sweat sprouted like translucent mushrooms on the innkeep's forehead. His eyes darted at Easton. "I make do with what I have."

"You make do well." She relaxed her grip. Coupled that with a lovely smile.

The innkeep, uncertain, glanced at Easton once more. The prince and Rooster had resumed talking. The innkeep leaned in close for a whisper. "I know what I'm doing in the kitchen, milady. If I had wanted you harmed, you and the young lord would be dead as we speak. Most who come here don't have your palette. I use brayosk often."

Johanna held him with a soft stare. She could still taste the brayosk in the corners of her mouth. It took a refined palate to detect brayosk, but Johanna had long been a student of the culinary arts, particularly when it involved edibles that doubled as poisons. "I'm well aware of that," she said. "It's a wonderful seasoning in the right hands, and, considering the fact that I'm still alive, your hands, it appeared, were capable."

The innkeep gave a little nod. Flashed Johanna *am-I-free-to-go* eyes.

She ignored them. "Do you have more? Perhaps some that's still on the bark?"

On the other side of the room, Easter and Rooster were negotiating an uncertain point in the masculine fashion. The innkeeper gave them a wary stare, then pulled Johanna closer to the kitchens. He leaned in close, his breath like a sour, yeasty bread. "Your man will run me through if he thinks I tried to poison you," he whispered.

He's not my man, she thought, although, upon the thinking of it, she didn't feel as dogmatic about the notion as she had assumed she would. "He doesn't know brayosk bark from his butt." She laughed a little for the innkeep's benefit. "Share what you have with me and I'll see that my lips stay sealed." She gave the innkeeper a good-daughter smile, the one she had practiced for years—to no avail—on Lord Daguss Salk.

The old turkey's posture softened. "All right. Make some excuse and come with me."

Beneath the kitchen floorboards, a cellar door. Steps led to a foodstuffs sanctuary, nestled into Ragar Or's preserving soil. Cabbage, pickled fish, leafy greens, rutabaga, autumn-colored preserves and jams, squash, salted meat, beets, broccoli, pears, tomatoes; the bounty hung from hooks and was stored in baskets and jarred on shelves. The highest shelf displayed an impressive variety of seasonings and other miscellanea, including, Johanna noted, the rhizomes of an eclectic number of plants, the blossoms of three perennial flowers, and a sprig of brayosk still on the bark.

Johanna patiently allowed her eyes to adjust to the dark. Once adjusted, she perused the room as her brain cataloged the wonders one by one, matching the abundance before her with the inventory of her mind.

Twice she stopped and turned to the innkeep.

"May I?" she asked the first time. When the innkeep nodded yes, she took a rhizome from the shelf.

The second time she simply said, "As we agreed."

She left the root cellar two times richer than when she entered.

Rooster was gone when Johanna returned. "Show us to our rooms, will you?" Easton asked the innkeep. On the short journey up the stairs, Johanna and Easton gave each other curious looks, but neither said a word.

The room was of middling size. The inn's slanted roof sawed its vertical space in half. A straw mattress suitable for two people on intimate terms rested in the corner. Easton laughed when he saw it, then slipped off his boots and lay face-up on the wooden floorboards, ready for rest.

Dust motes danced in the fading sunlight. A memory surfaced in Johanna's mind: the day of her bonding ceremony to Nicholas Raleigh, the way the late-evening sun had sucked all of the charm from the room in The Goldleaf Keep in which they were to spend the night. She had stolen away there at the outset of the bonding feast, determined to claim a moment for herself in the midst of the celebration, only to grow ill at the thought of consummating the relationship in that same space with the spindly, sickly young man she had bonded only minutes before. Later, awash with wine, the reality of the ordeal had been, if not pleasant, at least less disagreeable than she had anticipated. *He was kind. Being drunk helped as well.* She wondered for the hundredth time if she had ever loved Nicholas. She had worked hard to convince herself that she could love him—and in that labor she had grown to believe that perhaps she did—but in the stark aftermath of her widowhood, Johanna knew in her heart of hearts that at best she had only developed for him a cultivated affection.

Johanna claimed the straw mattress. It was too early to retire, but the day had been long, and a good night's rest seemed the best cure. She took off her coat and turned it into a blanket, being careful to protect the many newfound treasures that she had stored in its pockets. The sennequi piece found its way to her fingers. She drifted off caressing the wooden carving through the fabric.

She awoke to a shadow hovering above her. Her wits told her it was Easton, but, when she saw a second shadow on the opposite side of the room, she panicked and screamed. Slim, princely fingers clamped down on her mouth. Her teeth mounted a fierce defense, drawing blood and a muffled curse. "Stavus fucking save us, woman!" Easton said, smarting and pulling back his hand. His lack of continued aggression cued her in that perhaps she had an incomplete understanding of what was transpiring. They stared at each other for a half-blind second in the dark.

On the other side of the room, Rooster gave a muted chuckle.

"What are you doing?" Johanna tried to ask, but Easton's explanation in progress bounced off it.

"I was trying to wake you, without, you know, touching you." A second eclipsed before Easton continued, descending into a quieter register. "Your father sent someone after us. Not to bring us back, I don't believe, but to watch and follow us. Rooster has graciously agreed to delay our tracker should we choose to make an escape of it tonight. Or we can string the tracker along until we decide to ditch him."

"If he's my father's man then you had best believe that escaping him won't be that simple."

"No doubt my father was forced to humor yours when Lord Daguss Salk assured him the same. I hate to further reinforce your opinion of me as an arrogant sapling, but trust me: when I want to lose this fellow, I will. But the first forty-eight hours are yours. So, what would you have us do?"

Forty-eight hours. Johanna disliked the way their temporary bargain hung over their entire enterprise. She thought back to earlier in the day, when the prince had stood before her in the forest with a forever flower in his hand. *It's not a forty-eight-hours flower.* The thought became a thread that she followed to her reply.

She leaned in and whispered, not wanting Rooster to hear. "I would have us leave tonight and go south. To Thistleton. I would have you make good on your forever flower promise. If I truly am your queen, do as your queen commands. Put aside your dragon. See me to my freedom. Forty-eight hours and beyond. *Flerwa ikril vamiyska.*"

She knew that she had put the screws to him. In the intervening quiet she crowed internally with a sad but certain triumph, confident that he wouldn't comply. *At least,* she thought, *we can put aside this charade.* But then he replied.

"As you wish."

She was tempted to believe that she had misheard him, but his words were crystal clear. "Don't trifle with me," she said. "If you believe there is any chance that you will go back on your word, I would rather you not give it."

She still couldn't see Easton's face in the dark, but his voice, for the first time she had known him, was as solemn as a stone. "I make a solemn vow that I will see you to the end of your journey, Johanna of House Salk. I promise that I will pursue no dragons until our paths are parted. I swear, on the illustrious honor of my ancestors, that I will labor to prove by my deeds and actions what I could not convince you of when I offered you *pla milu sfal.*"

She wanted to trust him, but, like the shadow in the dark before her, she didn't know the real Easton. "Okay, then," she challenged him. "Prove it."

Silas O' the Songs

Silas returned to the forest shortly after daybreak, lute in hand. The Yubriy leaf, which had the texture and suppleness of vellum, he had stored away in his boot, the most secure place on his person. The message on the leaf he had committed to memory. The fear of what might happen to him if he was discovered in possession of a Yubriy leaf had made him consider returning the leaf to the tree stump, but, for the moment, Silas couldn't bring himself to part with it.

Back in the forest, he found a seat on the grand trunk of a fallen red oak. Then he set about scratching the songwriting itch that had been worrying him since he had first read the message on the Yubriy leaf at sunrise. What came to him was powerful, a revelation from the Melodies, but, to his frustration, the song refused to reveal itself in whole. He was lost in the creative process, repeating the words "the queen's burning heart" over and over again against a delicate fingering, when Wyn Dunkin jarred him from his reverie.

"Now that, Silas O' the Songs, is a song to make a young maiden cry. I daresay even Merjy would approve."

Silas stared dumbly at Wyn. He felt exposed. Down in his left boot, the Yubriy leaf pressed against the sole of his foot. Feeling color start to creep into his cheeks, he forced himself to reply. "The Melodies are assisting me. Or at least they were. Before you showed up."

Wyn moved and gainsaid Silas at the same time, rushing the tree and sitting next to him. His fiddle, as always, was in hand. "Nah. The Melodies gave you half a tune and then left you wanting. I've been spying on you for a good ten minutes. You're stuck." Settling into the wood, the little man brought the fiddle to his chin. Dirty ropes of silver-brown hair draped over the instrument like threadbare curtains. "Play that bit again," he commanded.

Fuck off, Silas thought, but his hands went to work as if of their own accord, bringing the half-finished tune to life once more. Wyn swooped in with his fiddle and bow, but instead of the bird-of-prey dive that Silas was expecting, the sound that Wyn Dunkin summoned was more akin to the graceful skimming of a stork over water. Elegiac and powerful, the fiddle served as a counterforce to the lute, creating a natural momentum that swept Silas up into the song's heretofore-unrevealed progression. Silas's fingers took over, transitioning from the ethereal to something more concrete, something more propulsive, though neatly and seamlessly done. Wyn followed, steady for once, content to accent the song rather than take it over. Silas sung the melody, leaving out the words.

The song ended in a stirring hush. The restless quiet of the forest filled the empty space. The usually talkative Wyn let the stillness linger. But then a pressure began to build, a pressure they both sensed. At the same moment, they looked at each other and said, "Again."

They played the song through nine times in a row. Until every note was etched in their memories, until its ineffable spirit was fixed firmly in their hearts. When at last they were finished, Wyn slid forward and arched his spine backward across the tree trunk, sighing in an almost post-coital manner. He laughed good-naturedly. "Now there's a song to earn a man his name! Silas O' the Songs, indeed. Though I daresay this one's so good, you might be remembered as Silas O' the Song!"

It was true. Silas knew it in his bones. The feeling was so powerful that it almost made him feel ill. Like he was a plaything of the gods, and they were channeling him for their own purposes.

Wyn sprang upright. "Tell me, Silas O' the *Song*, do you have any lyrics rattling around in the skull of yours beyond the words *the queen's burning heart?* If so, let's hear them. If not, tell me which of Ragar Or's fair queens you're referring to so we can write more!"

Silas knew the lyrics. But they were not lyrics that he wished to share. There was a terrible power in the yubriy leaf's message, but, meager soul that Silas was, he hadn't been able to make sense of it. The best that he could tell, the message was an answer to a riddle that hadn't yet been posed. And now Silas was the carrier of that message. He shivered at the thought.

Wyn laughed his all-knowing laugh, smiled his *nothing-gets-by-me* smile. "That good, huh? Come now, share with your friend, Silas O' the Song."

Silas looked at the little man. Really looked at him. Beyond Wyn's crooked crow's smile and his ratty silver-brown hair and his rodent-like physique, the fiddler looked entirely unlike any other person in the whole of Ragar Or. Silas couldn't explain it exactly, but sometimes he had the feeling that Wyn was merely posing as Wyn for Silas's benefit. Silas shivered again, and, as he did, he saw the knife-like glint of Wyn's smile dull a little, as if the little man sensed that he had revealed too much of himself.

184

"I don't have the rest of the lyrics figured out, but *the Queen's burning heart* references Queen Portia, the queen who died in the fire at the Three Dragons Inn."

It was a lie—or at least Silas intended it to be a lie, as Yubriy leaves were known to predict the future, not the past—but it was a lie that fit, a lie that Silas could build upon.

If Wyn picked up on the lie, he didn't show it.

"Yes, yes, yes! Now there's a story. Queenie goes to see a play about a brother who died by dragon's fire, only to perish by fire herself while watching the play!"

"Correct," Silas responded. *When he isn't butchering history, the little man is a regular Wandering Tongue.* "The subject matter's been done, of course, but—"

"Not like this," Wyn interrupted.

Silas couldn't help but smile. "No. Not like this."

Wyn sped on. "It's a song fit for the ears of a king and queen. We'll travel north, you and me. Silas O' the Song and his humble fiddling companion. Along the way we'll work out the remainder of the words. Easy as a piece of pie. Then it's as simple as finding the Dayborn king and queen and singing for their pleasure, and we'll be as rich as a Hawk's-Eye who pinches from begging statues. They'll love us!" The little man tossed his fiddle in the air and slapped his knee, then cleverly caught the instrument with his opposite hand. "Better than finding a Yubriy leaf, this is!" he finished, and gave Silas a wink.

Silas nodded in agreement. This time he was unable to keep the color from his cheeks.

They returned to the tent, where Wyn collected the hawk's-head helm. Then they went to say their goodbyes. The soldiers, to Silas's surprise, were gathered around the Yubriy tree in a rough approximation of the social circle from the evening before. For whatever reason, Silas had assumed that the soldiers' mornings were full of industry, but no, here the lot of them sat, Madrig and Jacy too. *While in between I wrote a song to make the world weep.* His puff of pride soon dissipated, however: first, because the lump pressing up against the arch of his foot reminded him that he was more an instrument than a creator of the song; and second, because as he drew closer to the tree, he saw five new faces.

Silas shot out a hand and grabbed Wyn by the arm. Whisper-hissed: "Wyn. Murder birds."

"Too late," Wyn responded before shaking free and continuing forward. The little man was right. They had drawn too close, for every head had turned to watch them approach. Juristic expressions graced every face, save Madrig's, whose countenance was serene, and Jacy's, who appeared deep in thought. The new additions were dressed in surcoats of red and black. Carrion birds were emblazoned on the back, alighting on a barren field. The clothes looked sharper than the men. Most of the new additions looked boorish and mean, their expressions a mishmash of snarls and sneers, but one, a broad-faced fellow with a thunderstorm of black hair, added smugness to the mix. His lips were curled in a way that made Silas guess that he was the designate speaker. Every man wore a short steel sword on their hip.

The smug one motioned at Silas and Wyn as they approached. "Here they are. The rapists two."

The accusation shocked Silas into silence, but Wyn, predictably quick-witted, sallied back. "So sayeth the vulture, that paragon of avian virtue! Go on, friend, tell your story. Then I'll share mine, and we'll see who they believe." Wyn took a seat on a rock directly facing the man, and posed with his fist on his chin.

Wyn's cocksureness momentarily befuddled the speaker. But the vulture soon recovered. "It's a dead man who mocks the Desighart sigil," he spat at Wyn. Then he turned to the others. "It's like I said. Two days past we came across a woman of the woods. She served us squirrel stew and gave us a place to sleep. Upon our leaving, we offered her our thanks and a silver Salk. She became emotional and said that two days earlier, a pair of traveling musicians had visited her abode and had their way with her. She was beyond grateful that we had not done the same." The vulture pulled his sword from his scabbard. "When she told us that they had traveled north, I swore that we would look for the men, for we were traveling in the same direction. Now that we have found them," he said, pointing the tip of his sword first at Wyn and then at Silas, "I intend to see justice done."

"What was her name?"

Wyn's question threw their accuser. The vulture narrowed his eyes in a bid for time. "What's this?"

"Her name. What was it?"

The speaker pretended at anger. "What matters her name?"

With a clever little reach into his coat, Wyn produced his own dagger, and pointed it in turn at each of the vulture-men. "Her name was Dryis. If she has been maltreated, it was by you. Dryis has been my faithful…friend…for many years. Faithful and true. Any injury to her requires blood payment. And since I can only assume that you wouldn't be accusing us of harming Dryis if you hadn't harmed her yourself, every vulture here must die." Wyn tossed the hawk's-head helm at the feet of the men, and then stuck out his tongue and gave the dagger a lick. "We know who you are, you murder birds. We know what you've done."

Silas's sphincter tightened. He had seen Wyn's talent with the dagger, but even he doubted the little fiddler could outfight five men. Silas, for his part, had no weapons but his fists, weapons that would be of little consequence against sharp steel. What mattered—all that mattered—were the responses of the soldiers in the circle. And Silas, who had a lifetime of experience reading rooms, sensed that the other soldiers were disinclined to intercede on their behalf.

The vulture with the black hair gave a nasty grin. "A wild and untrue accusation. But by all means, let's fight to the death and see who emerges innocent of the crime."

"You will not do that here," one of the Yubriy tree soldiers piped up. An Oseiyan from the looks of him. Silas remembered him as one of the ones who had clapped along to Wyn's song the evening before. "We will make no judgment as to which party is guilty," the Oseiyan said, looking to the other soldiers, who gave halfhearted nods, "but neither will we permit you to shed blood in our presence. Take your quarrel elsewhere. Away from the Yubriy tree."

The soldier's proclamation was greeted by an uncertain silence. A few awkward seconds later, the tenuous quiet was broken by Madrig. He thunder-clapped his hands together and began signing. Jacy, of course, was the only one who understood him. When he was finished, she gave a faraway nod. Then she took a deep breath.

"It seems that we have decided to leave. It is time for my bonded and I to travel back north to put ourselves in the service of Madrig's cousin, the powerful Lord Salk." She spoke loudly and clearly, making sure that all could hear. A couple of the vultures furrowed their brows at the mention of Lord Salk. Jacy turned to the soldiers guarding the Yubriy tree. "Madrig and I thank you for your hospitality and fellowship. We could not have hoped for a finer sweetmarch. The memory of the Yubriy tree will stay with us till the end of our days." Her eyes resettled on Silas. "Perhaps the lutist and the fiddler are leaving as well and would welcome traveling companions? Say, two well versed in the art of combat?"

Silas grasped Jacy's meaning in the span of the blink of an eye. "Yes!" he answered, a little too enthusiastically. He looked to Wyn, certain that the little man would concur. But the fiddler was still staring at the vultures while toying menacingly with the dagger.

"Only if these five promise to follow," Wyn said in a cold voice. He made another slow show of pointing at each of the vultures with his blade.

A few of the vultures, stealing glances at Madrig, looked unnerved. But they deferred to the broad-faced, black-haired fellow. "Don't fret, you little rat-haired skink," the man said. "We'll follow you. And once we catch you, we'll send you to the Bottom Black."

They walked toward the tree line in a foreboding silence. One by one every member of the group produced weapons. Madrig unsheathed the largest longsword that Silas had ever seen. In Madrig's hands, however, the blade looked like a toothpick. Jacy held a short sword in each hand.

She sharpened the blades against each other as she walked. Wyn held his dagger in one hand and his fiddle and bow in the other. The fiddler's demeanor was taut, intent, murderous. He seemed to Silas like a stranger.

Silas looked over his shoulder. The vultures were following forty yards back, stalking through the tall grass. They had produced steel of their own, silvery gleams of death, resplendent in the morning sun.

Suddenly, Silas was acutely aware that he carried no weapon. "I have nothing with which to defend myself," he admitted to the others. He felt blasphemous disturbing the sacred pre-battle quiet, but it was a better alternative than being left to defend himself with only his lute.

Madrig and Jacy exchanged a look. "If you are not already carrying a blade, you are no doubt ill-prepared to protect yourself with one," Jacy surmised. That was true, but before Silas could reply, Madrig had riffled through the mountain of clothing covering his body and produced a long knife that was as big as a sword. He handed it to Silas with *good luck* eyes. Silas nodded, grateful. "Thank you," he said. Jacy dismissed his thanks with a shake of her head. "If you don't know how to fight, don't. Keep clear. There's no point in us risking our lives for you to end up dying regardless."

At the edge of the woods, Madrig and Jacy turned to meet the coming kettle. But to everyone's surprise, Wyn, who had been the most eager to fight, continued apace into the forest. "Where are you going?" Jacy asked, her voice snapping like a whip.

"I fight better in the woods," Wyn replied. "And unlike my friend Silas O' the Song, I do have a bit of experience in the killing business." Jacy's expression was a mix of befuddlement and ire, but, before she could protest, Madrig gave a *keep-going* toss of his head, and the group followed Wyn into the woods.

The bare-bones branches of neighboring beech trees made an archway high above their heads, welcoming them to the woods. It was Silas's fourth trip into the forest since sunset the previous evening, but it still took him a moment to get his bearings. All at once everything fell into place. To Silas's right lay the fallen red oak where he and Wyn had composed the song; fifty feet further on was the spot where he had stood at sunup, reading the Yubriy leaf; and, there, jutting out of the ground before a small rise reshaped the terrain, stood the gnarled knot of wood with a hollow in its center, that unsuspected abode of possible futures. An involuntarily chill ran through Silas's body. *What if I die here and now, with the Yubriy leaf pressed against the sole of my foot?* If that happened, in all likelihood a vulture would strip him of his boots, and find the leaf for themselves. *What if,* he wondered with a sudden terror, *the leaf was never meant for me? What if fortune bequeathed it to me knowing I would die and pass it to someone else?*

Wyn stopped, bringing the group to a halt. Then, to Silas's astonishment, Wyn gently lay his fiddle and bow on the ground. Silas followed suit with his lute. With the instruments set aside, they all turned and watched as the vultures continued winding their way through the woods. Once the distance was closed to twenty yards, the vultures stopped. The looks on their faces suggested an unspoken disagreement. Finally, the oldest and ugliest of the vultures spoke. "Who gets the big fucker?" All eyes turned to the scraggliest, most vulture-looking of the bunch, a stooped, acne-scarred, crooked-necked teenage boy. The only one not holding a sword.

The one holding a bow.

The one reaching for an arrow in his quiver.

Madrig and Jacy charged. The twang of the boy's bowstring was muffled by Jacy's banshee battle cry. Madrig, bounding through the woods like a spry bull, raised his arm and then smarted; he gave the impression that he had been stung by an enormous bee. Silas, looking on, couldn't believe his eyes: an arrow was sprouting from the big man's face, just below his left eye next to his nose. Madrig paused for a mere second. Reaching up with both hands, the big man grabbed hold of the shaft of the arrow near his cheek with his free left hand, took hold halfway up the shaft with his sword-laden right, and, on the strength of a silent scream, snapped off the arrow's back half. Then he continued his charge. Had Silas not seen it, he would have never believed it. Wrenching his eyes away from Madrig, Silas searched for Wyn. He found the fiddler stealing thief-like between the trees, edging ever closer to the vultures. Silas watched them all with a frozen wonder. He thought it fortunate that Jacy had given him the order not to get killed, because, at the current moment, he couldn't move his legs.

The teenaged archer was reaching into his quiver for a second time when a flying dagger opened his throat. Down the boy went, futilely trying to stanch the crimson fountain spouting from his neck. Wyn's handiwork: Silas turned to his right to discover the little man posed at kneeling height, his throwing hand pointing at the kill. There was cursing then among the vultures, a great squawking of profanity. But it was short-lived because Madrig had arrived. Three of the vultures stepped forward to meet Madrig—Thunderstorm-Hair among them—but the big mute's first blow was so tremendous, so unbelievably violent, that the trio crashed backward. One of the vultures, dead on impact, gushed blood from a caved-in skull.

Nearby, Jacy dueled with the fourth. That particular vulture, believing himself lucky to have drawn the woman, fought at first with gusto, but as the deadly dance intensified, the look on his face changed from frustration to disbelief to horror as he realized his was the lesser skill. The end came when he tripped over a tree root and Jacy slipped one of her blades in-between his ribs.

Silas inched closer to the fighting. He scanned the area for Wyn, but the little man had retreated to the trees, and was once again dancing twixt timber. Jacy, having delivered one death, hurried to help Madrig. The colossal mute, now squared off against two, was struggling; the arrow-wound, it seemed, was rapidly depleting his strength. At the moment when it appeared Madrig was on the verge of succumbing, Jacy's arrival forced one of the vultures to peel away. Steel rang against steel. Trees, those obdurate spectators, refused to yield their vantage points; in return, they were co-opted as shields by the surviving combatants. *We're winning,* Silas thought, surveying the scene, but almost as soon as the thought entered his head, he grew less certain. The treescape sporadically hid the fighters from view, and each time they reemerged, the vultures appeared to gain more of an upper hand. The broad-faced vulture especially seemed to be getting the better of Madrig. Having survived Madrig's heavy blows at the outset, Thunderstorm-Hair was now giving worse than he got.

Help them, Silas told himself. Moving seemed impossible, but step by step Silas mastered it, forcing his feet toward the fray. His mind was a blank, but his arm, acting of its own accord, gave a couple of practice thrusts with the long knife. *Madrig. Help Madrig.* He maneuvered toward Thunderstorm-Hair, trying to judge the best angle to come at the vulture's kidney. *Go. Do it. Now.* He planted his feet to start his charge. But at that very moment, a shadow shot out of the woods.

The savagery of Wyn Dunkin's attack was a thing to behold: the little man jabbed a dagger into the vulture's back repeatedly and with a terrible glee, pausing only long enough to dodge the dying man's desperate attempt to swing his sword at whatever was behind him. Blood slicked the leaves on the forest floor. When at last Wyn pulled away, the dying man flopped disgracefully to the ground.

All eyes turned to Jacy. Her fight had turned decisively in her opponent's favor; the murder bird was pressing her backward, and she was struggling with her footing. Silas, closer to Jacy than the others, dashed forward. His thoughts were bellicose and black: *kill jab quick now Now!* He reached the vulture on a wave of adrenaline and fear, closing the gap before the murder bird realized what was happening. Silas jabbed the long knife deep into the vulture's back, trying for the same area that he had seen Wyn target. But unlike Wyn, Silas left the knife planted, and then fell back, shocked by what he had done.

The fifth and final vulture shrieked like a soul suffering in the Bottom Black. It was a horrible, gut-wrenching noise, a sound of the utmost anguish, a sound that seemed like it might rise and rise until every creature in the forest went insane. And perhaps it would have. But, before the noise could reach its zenith, Jacy stepped forward with one of her short blades and silenced the vulture forever.

Madrig slumped against a skyward-shooting ash tree. The gaping wreck of his puckered second mouth was a horror. Upon seeing it, Jacy gasped. "They have killed you, my love," she stated, struggling to keep the emotion out of her voice. Silas, however, thought the big mute looked quite alert for a dying man. His optimism was affirmed when Madrig surrendered his sword to the ground and began signing with a surprising vitality.

Jacy's eyes lit up with hope when Madrig finished. "He says the arrow deflected off chain mail before it took him in the face. He says that it's not buried deep."

Wyn kneeled down before Madrig and peered at the carnage. "Buried is buried, and buried is bone." He raised his eyebrows at the big mute. "Can you spin the shaft?"

Madrig reached up and gently tried to rotate the arrow's snapped end. But there was no movement, only sparks of pain in Madrig's eyes.

Wyn nodded like he had expected as much. "Stuck in the skull. It will have to be pulled out, or an infection will finish him off," he said to Jacy.

Rings of distress multiplied around Jacy's eyes. She looked at Madrig, and Madrig only. "I will be with you. Till this bodkin is out, or until I lay you in the grave." He signed his response. Then they pressed their foreheads together and closed their eyes. Silas couldn't look away. They made a mesmerizing scene: the homely warrior woman and the mutilated mute, she with blood covering her face and clothes, he with a gaping cheek wound shot through with the shaft of an arrow.

"How can we get to it to pull it out?" Silas asked. Aware that he had been staring at the couple for too long, he shifted his gaze to Wyn.

The little man took up the position of a scholar: he crossed his legs on the forest floor and brought a hand to his chin. "Jaltwood," he said after a moment. "Tempered, it turns as tough as stone." Wyn gave a strange, shy grin. "There is an instrument that I might make, given a handful of hours. Carving is a skill I've acquired over the years, and, as any child of the woods worth his salt knows, a tempered jaltwood carving has many practical uses." The fiddler scanned the forest. "I would bet my fungused big toe that there's a jaltwood tree north by northeast. Had I an axe—"

Leaves crunching underfoot caught their attentions. Looking up, Silas saw the Oseiyan and one other soldier making their way through the woods. The Oseiyan nodded grimly at the sight of the butchered vultures. When his gaze reached the group, the Oseiyan's mouth made an O of shock at the sight of the arrow protruding from Madrig's cheek. "He's alive?" he asked, but before anyone could answer, he answered his own question. "You're all alive." He spoke with no small bit of wonder, a wonder perhaps magnified by the fact that of all of them, Madrig was the one who was injured.

"No thanks to you," Silas spat. His blood was still up from stabbing the vulture.

The Oseiyan nodded as if in agreement, but when he spoke, he named his excuse. "I'm no lord to pass judgment on claims of rape. For all I know, those now dead were the ones speaking the truth."

Wyn piped up. "These now dead abused the truth the same way they abused women. But we'll forgive you and your brethren, as your duty was to the tree. Assist me in saving Madrig's life, and the deities that be might forgive you as well."

The Oseiyan frowned. "We will help in any way we can. But"—he pointed at Madrig, disbelief coloring his face—"is the bodkin embedded? In his skull?"

"It appears that way."

"Then I fear your efforts will be in vain."

Wyn was unfazed. "I will need an axe, honey, and a blazing fire. As for your doubts, give them to the Yubriy tree."

They extracted the arrow's shaft, leaving only the embedded bodkin. Then, per Wyn's directions, they propped Madrig up against the Yubriy tree. A blazing fire was prepared. Silas sat quietly among the soldiers, who, to a man, appeared pleased that the foursome had survived, irrespective of their earlier refusal to intervene. Together they waited on Wyn to return from his sojourn in search of a jaltwood tree.

One hour passed. Then two. Silas could not help but indulge the unlikely worry that Wyn had absconded with the axe and would never be seen again. *Stavus save me, how did it come to this?* he wondered, remembering how only yesterday he had wanted nothing more than to be free of the little devil. But today they had stolen a song together from the Melodies' own lips, a song that, Silas feared, he would lose the spirit of without the fiddler's accompaniment. More importantly, of course, Madrig's life hung in the balance. If Wyn didn't return, the big man would die.

Two and a half hours in, the little man showed, lugging the axe in one hand and the fiddle in the other, looking as cocksure as ever. After setting down the axe, Wyn approached Madrig straightaway. "I've carved a contraption that will allow us to…um…extract the arrowhead from your skull. But it will involve a considerable amount of digging around in your face. And a lot of pain." He gave a little sigh. "When I start doing what I need to do, some here are going to think me half-cocked. You might be among that number. Before I begin, I need your assurance that you're going to let me finish. Otherwise, there's no point."

Madrig wore an expression of stone. For a moment, Silas thought that he had gone deaf as well as mute. But finally, the big man signed to Jacy. She gave a tearful little laugh, then translated his response. "Madrig says that you will hear no complaints from him."

Wyn nodded in an uncharacteristically workmanlike manner. Then, to Silas's surprise, he sat his fiddle down next to the Yubriy tree and walked over to the fire. Once beside the flame, he unrolled the knot he had tied in his tunic and produced the carving. Silas, wanting a closer look, went and stood next to him. What Silas saw was fascinating. Somehow, in the short amount of time that Wyn had been gone, he had managed to carve what appeared to be a pair of tongs and a long wooden screw. The screw, fashioned independently of the tongs, slid seamlessly down the center of the tongs. Wyn held the carvings about three feet from the flame, and began the process of fire-hardening the wood.

Silas was flabbergasted by Wyn's craftsmanship. "I was worried that you had been gone too long. Now I see the time was…magically spent."

"Trees are magical things, Silas O' the Song." He gave Silas a knowing wink. "But you already knew that, didn't you?"

The carving tempered within minutes. Satisfied with the result, Wyn brought the instrument back to where Madrig was lying against the Yubriy tree. Kneeling beside the big man, Wyn reached into the back of his breeches and pulled out four smoothly carved sticks of jaltwood that were rounded at the ends, each one bigger than the last. Then he called for the honey. One of the soldiers brought over a jar. Wyn coated the bottom half of the smallest stick with the honey, and then, leaning over Madrig, probed open the wound.

Madrig smarted, but didn't move. Jacy, standing nearby, harrumphed with displeasure. "You're a strange man, Wyn of the Woods, which is all fine and good, but if my bonded ends up dead with honey smeared across his face, I swear I will serve you an Ontish Supper of your own testicles."

Moving only his hands, Madrig gave Jacy a sign that needed no interpreting. Duly chastised, Jacy quieted. Wyn kept at his work as if he hadn't heard a thing. Removing the first jaltwood stick, he coated the second, and, going about his business, probed the wound open further than before. He continued widening the wound with successive jaltwood sticks until he could see clean through to the skull-embedded bodkin.

Satisfied with his progress, the little man gathered the tongs and screw. Then, to Silas's surprise, he stopped and stood very still. *He's nervous,* Silas realized. After an awkward pause, the fiddler began humming a familiar tune. It took Silas a second to realize it.

It was Silas's song. "The Queen's Burning Heart." The moment Wyn began humming the song, Silas became acutely aware of their proximity to the Yubriy tree. The tree's thousand grasping branches undulated in the evening breeze like the meditative hands of a sentient creature, reaching for but not touching the humans below. The sight of it gave Silas a shiver down his spine. But even as Silas shivered, he took up the tune and harmonized with Wyn.

Everyone around the tree fell into a trancelike state. All except for Wyn, who now went to work, leaning over Madrig while continuing to hum "The Queen's Burning Heart," angling the contraption over the wound, wiggling and working the tongs and the screw. Madrig harvested beads of sweat on his face but he refused to move, refused to give in to what must have been extraordinary pain. Silas couldn't help but think that the song was making it easier for the big man to endure the ordeal. But even as he thought it the screw latched onto the arrowhead's socket, and the big man's face seized with the fury of his suffering, song be damned. Fortunately, in the next instant it was over: Wyn withdrew the tongs, and there, fitted neatly into the end of the screw, was the offending bodkin.

The soldiers cheered. Jacy gave a war whoop that changed into a sort of strangled sob that metamorphosed into the decision to jostle Wyn by the shoulders before taking him up in an awkward hug. Madrig sat upright, and, waiting until his bonded had finished her embrace, reached out and wrapped a grateful paw around Wyn's ropy arm. The gratification of the moment expanded into an unexpected sort of ecstasy, the entire tableau colored by sunlight racing through the arms of Ragar Or's most celebrated tree.

Silas watched it all with a reverent silence. Or, more specifically, he watched Wyn.

It's time, he thought, *that I start giving Wyn Dunkin his due.*

Gregor Thorn

Some of the Heron's men found Doxius Brine the morning after the play holed up in a small cave farther up the face of Simstone Mountain. Gregor, sitting vigil over Deglan in the Three Dragons, heard the commotion from his room. Judging by the sound, Gregor correctly assumed what had occurred. To that end, he hurried outside to keep the ruffians from killing Doxius on the spot.

The men drove the innkeeper down from the mountain with whips. Doxius was a bloodied mess by the time Gregor reached him outside the Three Dragons' massive jaltwood door: what had once been a beautiful doublet on the innkeeper's back was now a gory amalgam of red flesh and black velvet. The Heron's men, drunk with violence, appeared intent on whipping Doxius into his grave. Gregor moved forward to put a stop to it.

"Desist!" he shouted. And then again, "Desist, damn you!" All but one acquiesced. Gregor stepped forward and grabbed that particular brute by the wrist. The man, not knowing who had taken hold of him, tried shrugging Gregor off. Gregor struggled to stay upright, but he held on. The brute turned on Gregor in anger and readied his whip to deliver a blow, but all at once he recognized who he was struggling against, and his eyes went white with terror, and his whip hand went limp.

Gregor started in on the chastising. There were days when it seemed like reprimanding the citizens of Ragar Or was his primary function in life. "This man's death will occur at the pleasure of the Dayborns. Not yours," he barked at the brute. Gregor took a quick look around and noticed that a crowd of people had amassed: many of the hired staff of the Three Dragons had gathered to witness the abasement of their former boss, and, above, what men of the Heron's that had been left behind during the search for Doxius Brine were now hanging their heads out of the inn's windows to see what could be seen.

No one responded, and the silence, initially wary, turned nasty. Gregor soaked in the crowd's hateful stares the way his cloth of red had soaked in Deglan's blood during the long and dreamless night. What the brutes and malcontents before him didn't understand was that no one wanted to whip Doxius Brine into the dust more than him, for what had been done to Deglan. But being Sagekind meant restraining oneself—and oftentimes, everyone else—from killing people while in the throes of passion. Doling out death to one's enemies should be a civilized business. Especially when it was done on behalf of a king.

On the ground, Doxius rose to his hands and knees, a long spittle of bloody drool hanging from his lips. At that very moment the innkeeper's greyhounds came loping around the front corner of the inn. Recognizing their owner, they started toward Doxius's side, but, halfway there, they appeared to detect that something was amiss, and decided it prudent to sit on their haunches until they could better assess the situation.

Gregor's eyes went to the dogs. They were beautiful beasts. One was tan with a chest plate of white, the other a day-swallowing black. Gregor was always careful to guard his behavior around animals, on account of his jeyedoshi nature, but for the briefest of moments, he let his guard slip, and the two greyhounds, attuned, noticed. The dogs conferred in the manner of their kind and made a decision. Trotting past their previous owner, they took up new positions on either side of Gregor.

Gregor did his best to keep his face steely straight. *That was not ideal,* he thought. Everyone had taken note. Gregor could hear the windows above his head filling with whispers. Jeyedoshi gossip. He remembered his half brother's warning: *We are in the north now, Sagekind.*

If eyes were blades, he would have been stabbed a hundred times.

It was tempting to disavow what had occurred, to move quickly away from the hounds, to further harangue the bird-brutes as a means of distraction. But the way he saw it, the damage had already been done. Experience had taught him that mistakes sometimes turn to victories when you lean into them. To that end, he reached out and fondled a greyhound skull with one hand, while with the other he pointed at Doxius Brine.

"On behalf of His Majesty King Micah of House Dayborn, first of his name, the Rightful Ruler of Ragar Or, the Holy Son of the Air, and the Twin Ascendant, I do hereby command that the traitor Doxius Brine be remanded to my custody until such time as King Micah or the Crown Prince Ajax have the opportunity to determine the traitor's sentence."

No one responded. The whispering in the windows was swept away by a gust of mountain wind. Gregor knew that the compliance was strategic, but decided that he would take what he could get. He swiveled his head and craned his neck one last time in the hopes of finding at least one friendly face in the crowd, but all the Dayborn men had gone down into the city proper with Ajax. *Best I take this into my own hands,* Gregor thought. He stepped forward and brought Doxius Brine to his feet. Then, with all eyes on him, he led the traitor back into the Three Dragons Inn.

The greyhounds followed in his wake.

Deglan was resting on the bed, drifting in the dreamlands of poppy. Doxius, drifting in and out of a hellscape of intense pain, startled into something resembling full consciousness when he saw the young knight. The innkeeper gave a disconsolate sob in response, expecting, Gregor assumed, that he had been brought before Deglan as a precursor to additional punishment. But that wasn't Gregor's intention. The Sagekind simply needed to store the innkeeper away from the rabble while checking in on Deglan, and this room was the only option.

He could use a touch of the poppy, too, Gregor thought, but, now that he had Doxius alone, he knew that he would be remiss if he didn't capitalize on the opportunity to interrogate the Blackstar Islander. To that end, a drugged-out innkeeper would not do. "Sit," Gregor commanded, pointing to a Wrainish tuft chair in the corner. The innkeeper did as he was told, bloodying the valuable piece of handcrafted furniture in the process.

Gregor sighed. For whatever reason, the sight of the bloodied chair drove the inanity of last night's violence home. *The rebellion was over, you fool,* he thought, looking at Doxius. *This was all a waste. You have changed nothing.*

But enough of that, he told himself. It was time to focus. There was work to be done. Sifting through his belongings, Gregor quickly gathered the ingredients for a successful interrogation. Ingredients in hand, he prepared a tea mixed with the sfustu bean (a mind-clearing stimulant), the slightest residue of the Delilah herb, and a tincture of the poppy. He then presented it to Doxius with a drink-up gesture.

The innkeeper waded through his pain to ask a question. "Will it kill me?"

Gregor responded with hard eyes. "No. But make no mistake. You will die soon enough. Though not by my hand." When the innkeeper still refused to drink, Gregor leveled him with the truth. "The drink is to encourage you to talk. It will also take the sting out of the pain. I suggest you accept it. If not, I have other methods at my disposal that aren't half as pleasant."

Doxius downed the tea. Seconds later, his pupils dilated. A look of animal panic shone from the wellspring of his eyes, but Gregor knew that the effect was only temporary. "Breathe slowly. The other ingredients will kick in momentarily." Gregor's words seemed to take the edge off Doxius's panic, for he slowed his breathing, and, minutes later, began to drift into shallower pools of pain. When the innkeeper looked Gregor in the eye and began talking, Gregor knew that all three ingredients were working in concert.

"Ah. Yes. Thank you." The innkeeper thought of a question. "Was the tea a byproduct of jeyedoshi magic, or Sagekind wisdom?"

Gregor had no intention of confirming that he was a jeyedoshi. Not even to a living dead man. "Sagekind wisdom. Or, more accurately, a byproduct of the Sagekind's access to rare ingredients."

Doxius nodded. As if to demonstrate the change in his physical state, the Blackstar Islander stroked his beard, which was tied off into different sections by colored pieces of string in the fashion of the isles. "But you *are* both a Sagekind *and* a jeyedoshi, are you not?"

Gregor said nothing. He wasn't enamored with Doxius's attempt to flip the tables and interrogate him, but he intuited that if he kept his mouth shut, the newly drugged innkeeper might give away information of his own accord.

The innkeeper nodded as if Gregor had made an admission. "Of course you are. The rumors are true. How else could Berak have died, unless at the hands of a stronger jeyedoshi? I had hoped"—Doxius leaned forward, putting his forearms on his knees and looking contemplatively into the middle distance—"that a jeyedoshi of Berak's caliber would have been able to complete the job before you intervened. When I saw what Berak was capable of, I deluded myself into believing that his power was sufficient to the task. And with the subject nature of the play being what it was, I hoped that the distraction would keep you from realizing what was taking place. But you…you are no Berak, are you, sir? No, you are *more*."

Gregor refused to be manipulated. "This Berak? He was from the Blackstar Isles?"

Doxius decided that it was his turn to ignore a question. The innkeeper licked his lips. "Is there Delilah herb in the drink as well?"

Gregor gave a small nod. "A little. Enough."

Doxius laughed through his pain. "Enough to make me talk, is what you mean. I know how the Delilah herb works, Sagekind. You run an inn like the Three Dragons long enough, and all manner of wonders pass through the doors."

Gregor thought of a different tack. "You have been the owner of the Three Dragons Inn for how many years now?"

"Six years." A look of pride shone on the innkeeper's face. "Kelgro Coffyn, the previous owner, didn't know how to maximize the inn's potential. I changed that."

"Indeed. The entire kingdom is aware of your business acumen. I can't tell you how many times the king and I have been forced to listen to some nobleman or noblewoman prattle on and on about their great adventure north to Low Osgood and the Three Dragons Inn." Gregor paused, letting his flattery settle. "But now you have thrown both the inn and your life away. For a rebellion that had already been crushed. Why?"

Doxius found Gregor's eyes. *He's swimming the Delilah's dark currents,* Gregor understood. "You of all people must know that the motives of men are manifold," Doxius answered. "But the motive of vengeance suffices, does it not? You killed my prince. In turn, I tried to kill yours."

Gregor shook his head. "I knew your prince. He was a man for hard truths. You would honor him by speaking the same."

Doxius scoffed. "Here is a hard truth for you, *Sagekind.* You would have been better off being born a Blackstar Islander."

For once, Gregor's silence wasn't strategic.

The innkeeper's eyes danced with mischief. "It's a bastardized faith these northmen keep, don't you think? The faith of the Twins. But do they honor the Twins? No. They honor the Twin Ascendant. Lesser twins live in the shadows, or, in Kalandragote, not at all. But in the Blackstar Isles, many hold to a truer faith." He leaned back in the Wrainish tuft chair, blood still weeping from his back. "I myself was born a twin. No jeyedoshi I, but a lesser twin all the same. We were identical, me and my brother, which did not work to my advantage—when it's the small differences that people use to tell you apart, they are all the more glaring. My father was a wealthy trader, and fell under the influence of those he traded with: northern Ontishmen who preach the glory of the Twin Ascendant and worry that every lesser twin who walks Ragar Or will resume the Corosian line. By my fourteenth year, it was clear that if my father could have his way, I would be tossed aside for my brother's greater glory."

Gregor looked at the flayed innkeeper anew. He, too, understood what it felt like to be a lesser twin, superfluous to the Twin Ascendant.

Doxius continued, "I believe my father intended as much. He made plans to send me on a trading expedition to Kalandragote, on a ship captained by one of his fanatical friends from Dunning Harbor. Had I gotten on that ship, I have every reason to believe I would have never returned. Fortunately, the brave woman that served as our family's Wandering Tongue got wind of it, and, together with an influential Gorgostrine from Pecking Knot, hid me away from my father for a time. My father was a powerful man, and wanted me returned, but I later learned that the Wandering Tongue petitioned Lord Trufish Boil himself, who wrote a letter threatening my father with repercussions if I went missing. I procured the letter years later, after my father and brother had died and I had inherited my father's trading company. 'The madness of the mainland does not extend to the Blackstar Isles,' Lord Trufish admonished my father. 'Here, we hold the Twins as whole.'"

Gregor knew that the Blackstar Isles had long been an oddity; there were Gorgostrines there who didn't preach the power of the Twin Ascendant, and it was said that the words to the Prayer for Vengeance were often altered on the islands as well. But hearing Doxius's account of his life brought home just how different the Islands' version of the Faith of the Twins actually was.

"I respect your loyalty to the Boils, but I don't see why loyalty and mindless stupidity have to go hand in hand. I will say it once more: the rebellion was over."

The innkeeper's Delilah-black eyes flared. He spat on the floor and shuddered with the pain of it. "Don't you dare speak to me of stupidity, jeyedoshi. You and your incompetent *brother* have yet to make a mess that you could not compound. Tell me, what did King Micah think would happen when he raised taxes on the Blackstar islands to help fund the defense of Wrain? The Boils certainly knew how it would play out. The Blackstar Islands were to be sacrificed to the gods of Union, its wealth stripped away because the king was too weak to demand the same of the northern lords who curse his name behind his back. It was only a matter of time before those same northmen exerted their influence over the islands. The day that King Micah raised taxes on the islands was the day the crown doomed the true Faith of the Twins to extinction. And that was the day that I decided I was willing to risk my life to hasten the end of this cursed monarchy."

The harsh sting of the innkeeper's righteous anger nearly compelled Gregor to justify the king's actions. Everything Doxius had said was true, after all. But political decisions weren't always a matter of making the right decision over the wrong one. More often than not—and especially for a king in as impossible a position as Micah—it was a matter of recognizing which decision's consequences could later be leveraged for advantage. The decision to squeeze the Boils and the Blackstar Islands had been an intentional one.

Weighing all the options, Gregor would have advised the king to do it again.

"The union of Ragar Or is what matters most," Gregor said carefully. "Every other consideration is secondary."

Doxius snorted with contempt. "Careful, jeyedoshi. If I know these fanatics the way I believe I do, the day will not be long before they convince the king that preserving the union means sacrificing *you*."

One of the greyhounds—the tan one armored with white—suddenly disrupted their conversation with a *look there* bark. Gregor's eyes went to the bed, where Deglan was stirring from a poppy-induced sleep. The pain of awakening instantly caused beads of sweat to form on the young knight's face, but, stalwart young man that he was, he offered no complaint. Surveying the room, Deglan took in Gregor with grateful eyes. Upon seeing Doxius, however, Deglan's glare turned grim. Gregor assumed that the young knight was simply upset to find the man who had slashed his stomach in the room, but, when Deglan opened his mouth, Gregor discovered that wasn't it at all.

"This traitor..." Deglan struggled to say, "...is in possession of a Yubriy leaf."

Doxius Brine was hung from the gallows in the Heron's military encampment two days later.

An unseasonal thunderstorm swept through that morning, making a muddy mess of the recent snow. King Micah and the traveling contingent from Coffyn Castle had arrived the evening before, and so the scene was quite peculiar, combining, as it did, not only a large group of soldier spectators but also an assortment of lords in the opening stages of a long journey. To add to the dark-carnival feel, scores of Low Osgood citizens tried to make their way into the encampment, believing it their due to witness an execution for a crime committed by one of their more prominent citizens. Reginal Burntree was given permission by the newly arrived Daguss Salk to round up a group of men and turn the Low Osgoodians away. He did so with relish.

The innkeeper looked at peace as he approached the gallows. Queen Anjay, who had wanted the Blackstar Islander drawn and quartered, snorted with contempt as the executioner fitted the rope around Doxius's neck. Gregor did his best to ignore her. The queen believed that an easy execution would only encourage future assassins, but Gregor had given Doxius his word that he would be spared a traitor's death in exchange for information about the Yubriy leaf, and King Micah, to Gregor's relief, had agreed to honor Gregor's promise. As it was, the innkeeper's neck didn't break when the stool was kicked out, and all who were present watched the traitorous Blackstar Islander struggle for air for nearly ten minutes before the strangulation was complete. Near the end, the queen glanced at Gregor wearing a smirk of triumph.

Gregor paid scant attention to the innkeeper's death throes. Instead, he focused on the behaviors of the coterie now surrounding the king, trying his best to gauge their respective loyalties. The mightiest of the mighty stood on the platform with King Micah. Daguss Salk, looking more imposing than the king, stared at the dying man with unflinching eyes. Dante Heron, elegant in white, surveyed the proceedings as if from a snow cloud. Cato Ollspaer, colossus, stood aside Wulfess, his bonded-to-be: together they looked mythical, terrifying, the joining of unholy strength and unsurpassable beauty. Queen Anjay stood on the platform, too, and Prince Ajax and his bonded Greta Worrint, but Prince Easton and Johanna Salk were missing: Gregor had learned yesterday that the two had stolen away together from Coffyn Castle shortly after announcing their intention to be bonded. Whether it was because Gregor was overly familiar with his own family or the juxtaposition between the Dayborns and the others was too extreme, the sight of his Dayborn kin made him feel overwhelmed and helpless.

Somewhere, he thought, he heard the Yubriy tree laughing.

The hanging ended as hangings do, with a dead man swaying at the end of a rope. *Good,* Gregor thought. *It's over.* He moved toward the king, hoping to request a private audience, but the coterie boxed him out. Homing in on Queen Anjay instead, he managed a "Tell the king—" before the queen presented him with a cold shoulder. *That's for the drawing and quartering disagreement,* Gregor knew, recalling the previous evening's discussion. It had been an uncomfortable reunion: the king had begrudgingly taken Gregor's side on nearly every question, and, in doing so, felt the need to punish him afterward. Gregor knew from past experience that the ostracism would not last long. The king needed him now more than ever, and, as pig-headed as Micah could be, he wasn't stupid enough to dismiss blood from his inner circle.

Let's just hope he invites me back in before one of his new friends stabs him in the back.

Stepping down from the platform, Gregor surveyed the scene. A chaotic mix of people had gathered for the hanging: soldiers and lords and the myriad retinues that accompanied the traveling rich. Among the soldiers, Gregor surveyed the three-crow surcoats of the Salks and a heartening number of Dayborn double suns, but, above and beyond all others, what he saw the most was birds. The Heron's men made up the majority, drawing the eye in their gleaming white, but it was easy enough to spot others: at a glance he saw the blazing blue peacock surcoats of House Falade, the red-black turkey vultures of House Desighart, and the proud gold-brown eagles of House Chesterly. *Different houses, but they were all brought north by the same man.* Weeks ago, it had seemed a blessing that Dante Heron could raise such a massive force on short notice. Now, Gregor couldn't help but consider how many birds might be sent home without tipping the balance of power in favor of the Ontish faction.

When Gregor reached the ground, a hand gifted his arm with a tender touch. The gentle softness of it confused his soul; he thought at first that Sephery had somehow returned to him from the grave.

He turned and discovered Greta Worrint looking at him with a rosy-cheeked smile. "Uncle Bones," she said, and hooked her arm inside of his, drawing him closer. Gregor's tenderness vanished. *The foolish girl should know better. Who's to know what the gossiping masses might make of such a display?* He started to pull away, but, to his surprise, Greta held tight. "Tell me," she continued, "who among these are our enemies?"

Gregor leaned in and gave her a piece of his mind. "Let go of me, child. If we do have enemies present, your behavior is only encouraging them."

To his disbelieving surprise, she kept his arm pinned. He found that he couldn't extricate himself without a show of force. Trying another method, he gave her his meanest snake-face, only to be met with a smile so obdurate and sugary sweet that he almost laughed at the unexpected duality of it.

Greta seized on Gregor's softening. "Oh, Uncle Bones. Don't push me away. We are natural allies, you and I. Outsiders pledged to those on the inside, willing to do whatever it takes to protect the ones we love."

The plain frankness of her words brought him to silence. He permitted her to keep hold of his arm, and together they continued around the camp, making ugly footprints in the mud-streaked snow. While they walked, he kept his eyes peeled, and studied, and thought.

"All of them," he said at last. "They are all our enemies. They are our brothers and sisters, our countrymen and countrywomen, and our enemies too."

Greta nodded, as if Gregor had said the most logical thing in the world. "It is more difficult for a Struvan monarch, don't you think? Perhaps particularly so for the Dayborns. The old Salk kings and queens were Ontish, but Struvan enough in their sensibilities that the south never found reason to rebel. But with the Dayborns…the dynamic is different. The Ontish pretend that the king is the Twin Ascendant, but they don't believe it. And the Struvans…why, the Struvans still see the Dayborns as the lesser house they were before the War of the Three Brothers."

It was an astute observation. He gave her the side-eye of the impressed. "You understand the crux of it."

She responded with a knowing little head nod. Gregor saw the deep intelligence in her eyes, and the worry. She looked as if she had more to say, but needed a moment to organize her thoughts. They walked in a pregnant but peaceful silence, threading their way through the encampment. Soldiers from all corners of the kingdom raised their heads to watch them pass, eyes popping at the sight of Gregor's infamous red cloak. Quiet curses followed in their wake. Gregor ignored them. He was busy keeping his eyes peeled for one very specific person.

"This decision to go to Kalandragote." Greta paused after she spoke, as if expecting Gregor to interrupt her then and there. When he didn't, she ventured further. "Do you believe it wise?"

The question made him uncomfortable. He offered an evasive reply. "Wisdom is the application of experience and knowledge. It is not the denial of circumstance. Our circumstances being what they are—yes, I believe it is a wise decision." He paused. "As you can see, our Struvan numbers here are strong. When we travel north, the king will have an army at his back no scheming man would dare welcome inside his city walls. If Horos Ollspaer, Daguss Salk, or any other Ontish intriguer is so foolish as to try and harm the king, why, there will be nothing left of the north when we Struvans return."

"But you don't trust Dante Heron."

Once again, Gregor was caught off guard by Greta's perceptiveness. "I am the king's closest adviser, and an aging man to boot. I don't trust anyone. And that includes you." She cast wounded eyebrows at him. He gave her a *now-you-know* smile, and continued, "Your bonded trusts the Heron. As does the king. It's good that they do. A king who trusts no one ultimately makes enemies of everyone."

Up ahead, a small group of Qorlish soldiers wearing surcoats the color of ripe wheat blocked their path. Gregor gave them a jeyedoshi stare, and they melted away like the disappearing snow.

"I agree that it's important to trust someone," Greta continued once they were clear of the soldiers. "That is why I have decided to trust you. I hope, Uncle Bones, that you will learn to trust me too."

Seconds later they crested a small knoll overlooking the Dayborn camp. King Micah's impressive pavilion lay at the center. Surrounding it were dozens of flags bearing the Dayborn standard, the double suns multiplying into a fiery finery. For the first time that day Gregor felt heartened. While he grappled with these uncommonly optimistic feelings, Greta rose up on her toes and gave him a kiss on the cheek. "You are a powerful man, Uncle Bones, but you cannot save this family by yourself. If ever you need assistance, I hope that you will rely on me. I promise that I will not fail you." Then she disappeared into the Dayborn encampment and left Gregor all alone.

The kindness of Greta's kiss startled him. He felt a sudden welling of emotion; for a moment it seemed that he might shed a tear for the first time since Sephery's death. He turned away from the Dayborn encampment only for his eyes to settle on the person he'd been searching for.

His tears dried like a drought.

There, winding his way between the borderlands of the Ontish tents and those of the birds, walked Betrard, the Gorgostrine who had been in attendance at the harvest of the Yubriy leaves.

The same man Doxius Brine claimed that he had stolen the Yubriy leaf from.

Betrard wore the same badgerlike snarl that he had worn at court, complemented by a grumpiness that bordered on contempt. Had Gregor not made the Gorgostrine's acquaintance once before, he would have been taken aback.

"Revered Sagekind." The Gorgostrine's voice sounded like sarcasm poured over rocks. "You have the look of a tense, taut wolf. I fear that you've come to rip my throat out."

Gregor understood that Betrard was exaggerating, but all the same it made the Sagekind conscious of the expression on his face. While rearranging his facial muscles, he couldn't help but appreciate the way the old priest had put him on his heels. "Not at all, Betrard. I saw you at the play the other day and wanted to speak to you then, but the night had other plans. When I spotted you just now, I hurried to catch you lest I miss you twice."

Betrard nodded, a nod that appeared at odds with his distrusting mien. Gregor thought that the Gorgostrine looked more like an aged warrior than a priest, which, Gregor supposed, was what the ideal Gorgostrine looked like. *It takes little imagination to picture this one presiding over the twin-death rite,* he thought. Gregor's gut twisted just then, because, in his soul of souls, he intuited that somewhere in the deep recesses of the north Betrard had once done just that.

"You *were* awfully busy the other night, weren't you?" Betrard said.

Gregor, back on his footing, gave the holy man a *sure was* smile. They locked eyes for a moment, bony brothers of a sort, playing an old game.

Betrard broke off his stare first. "What do you want, Sagekind?"

"I was surprised to see you in the audience at the play. It made me wonder: where did your travels take you after you helped deliver the

Yubriy leaves to Union?" Gregor asked. Betrard glanced at the rolling infinity of heavy canvas tents flying feather standards. *Fess up,* Gregor thought. The math of miles suggested that Betrard had stayed in the south after delivering the Yubriy leaves to Union, and had subsequently arrived in Low Osgood traveling with the Heron's army. It wasn't the only possibility, but, the more Gregor thought about it, the more it made sense.

Betrard replied as if he had nothing to hide. "I stayed in the south for a time after delivering the Yubriy leaves to the capital."

"And made friends with the birds?"

Betrard snuck a hand into the gray wool robe that he was wearing, retrieved something, and darted it into his mouth. The flash of the Gorgostrine's hand revealed the priestly brands on his fourth and fifth fingers, Old Ontish glyphs. "*Friends* is a strong word, Sagekind. I don't like using it."

Epenklim lonsti, Gregor guessed, watching Betrard chew the pulp. *Messy leaf.* A fast-acting sharpener of the senses. Gregor took it as a sign that the Gorgostrine was rattled, his unaffected demeanor aside.

The Sagekind ignored Betrard's sidestep and continued pushing his case. "I suppose it makes sense, you making friends with the birds. Daguss Salk wouldn't have sent you south as the Gorgostrine representative for the collection of the Yubriy leaves if he hadn't considered you the right person for crossing sectarian lines."

Betrard spat a red-and-white stream of masticated messy leaf onto the ground. Gave an abrasive little laugh. "I'm sure you're right."

He's mocking me, but only because I mocked him first. Gregor thought once more about the multiple missteps and misfortunes of the past few months, and wondered, for the dozenth time, if his failure to attend the collection of the Yubriy leaves in person hadn't been the most consequential. Most years Gregor made the trip to the Vake, but this year compounding crises had kept him in Union: in addition to the problems in Wrain and the incipient rebellion in the Blackstar Isles, it was during abscission season that Ajax startled everyone by claiming Greta Worrint as his common bond. Gregor had assured himself that his contingent of loyal Hawk's-Eyes and Winged Women was more than capable of securing every Yubriy leaf without his being there, but when news reached him that the usual Gorgostrine representative had died, and Daguss Salk had sent another in his place, Gregor's worry increased tenfold.

Meeting Betrard had done nothing to alleviate it.

"Tell me: was that your first time traveling in the south?"

Betrard sighed. "I've always wondered what being Sagekind entailed. Now I suppose I know. You go around interrogating people under the pretense of carrying on a conversation."

Gregor laughed. "That is part of it, I suppose. Mostly, though, I simply try and keep my eyes open."

They met eyes again. Most men wilted under the Sagekind's stare, but Betrard held up better than the majority. *Go ahead, you Yubriy-leaf thief. Send the message that you won't be cowed by the likes of me.* But, as was always the case when Gregor locked eyes with a man long enough, he could see the fear mounting behind the stare: the fear that Gregor would snatch the wind from their lungs, or steal fire from the sun and set their body aflame.

"Traveling in the south was telling," Betrard said. "Up north, everyone thinks that southerners sit around with rubies up their ass, feasting on roasted heartbirds every day. But that's not the case, is it? From what I observed, it appears that these days there aren't enough rubies and heartbirds to go around."

Gregor understood that the Gorgostrine was making what he considered to be a clever observation on the current economic downturn. The damage inflicted on the Wrainish trade market by the privateers from Thralk-Braktur had had ripple effects throughout the areas of Ragar Or where the Stavusian faith dominated. Gregor could have easily turned Betrard's words around on him by ridiculing the poverty of the north, but it would have accomplished little, and, besides, they were standing outside of Low Osgood, the wealthiest of the northern cities.

"To quote the Wandering Tongue Briggs Shroud: 'Wealth cannot buy honor, as poverty is no guarantor of righteousness.' Fitting for today, don't you think? I assume you were in the crowd, watching the islander hang?"

The Gorgostrine's face lit up. "A good hanging, that. I was hoping for a gutting considering the nature of the man's crimes, but I suppose your god of mercy wouldn't allow it. Still, it was a treat to watch him kick for a bit."

He kicked because I paid the executioner to shorten the rope. But Gregor kept that bit of information to himself. "Dead is dead. That's all that matters." He paused. "I interrogated the traitor at some length before he died."

Betrard expectorated another reddish-white stream. "Is that so?" Gregor studied the Gorgostrine carefully, but detected nothing in his reply save curiousness. *Doxius was right,* Gregor thought. *Betrard doesn't have a clue that the innkeeper stole the Yubriy leaf from him.*

"Yes." Gregor took a long, slow breath. Zeroed his attention on the Gorgostrine. "I discovered a Yubriy leaf in his possession."

The Gorgostrine turned a pale, moon-bright white. The distress on his face passed lightning-fast, but not before Gregor noticed it. "Beoliotius bless us," the Gorgostrine pulled himself together to say. He used the excuse of spitting another stream of messy leaf on the ground to obscure his reaction. "Treasonous Blackstar bastard," he muttered. All at once he whirled on Gregor, assuming an air of aggravated righteousness. "That's what you Struvans don't get. You can't show mercy to these sorts. Failing to disembowel the traitor did injury to all of Ragar Or. I swear, if the Dayborns—"

Gregor stole the wind from the Gorgostrine's throat. He gave it back a split second later, so fast that it outpaced the terror flying to Betrard's eyes. By then Gregor was speaking in his stead.

"You are absolutely right. Traitors to the crown deserve no mercy." He stepped in close and loomed over the priest. He only had an inch on the Gorgostrine, but he treated it like a tower. "And there is no traitor so loathsome as one who steals a Yubriy leaf."

Betrard took a step back and nearly tripped over an exposed tree root. The priest quickly found his footing and steadied himself by grabbing hold of his woolen gray robe. There was panic in the priest's eyes, but also hatred, and defiance.

Gregor continued, "The innkeeper led me to believe that he had stolen the leaf from someone in the Three Dragons Inn."

Silence settled between the two of them like a death sentence. While they stood in its wake, a gust of wind blew in a renegade spattering of rain. It smacked them in the face with a short-lived fury.

At last, the Gorgostrine spoke through gritted teeth. "Go ahead and say what you mean to say, jeyedoshi."

Gregor stepped away from Betrard. Laughed a little. He wasn't particularly fond of playing games with other men's minds, but a lifetime of perfecting the art had made him quite good at it. "It's difficult to trust a man when his life hangs in the balance. Wouldn't you agree? And this innkeeper, why, he was a Blackstar traitor to boot. Doubly hard to trust. I'm sure you can appreciate that I took everything he told me with a grain of salt."

Betrard, who had been holding his breath, softened the muscles around his jaw.

Gregor continued, "Besides, I have the Yubriy leaf in my possession now. I know what is written on it. I have a sense of how the enemies of the Dayborns might use the prophecy written on the Yubriy leaf to their advantage. If time proves that no such steps were taken, well, then, politics being what they are, I can't imagine that retribution would be in my, or the king's, best interest."

Betrard gave a hard little head nod. "Politics being what they are, I think that's a wise decision. When all is said and done, I believe you'll find that this Blackstar traitor was filling your head with nonsense."

Gregor mimicked the Gorgostrine with a slower, more deliberate bob of the head. "Time will tell. But believe you me, Gorgostrine, if I ever decide that the Blackstar Islander's warnings had merit, you will be the first to know."

The iron brazier inside of Gregor's tent offered a most welcome warmth. Resting near the brazier were the cedarwood chairs that Gregor preferred, but a plush thistledown was also nearby, placed there for any luxury-loving visitors that the Sagekind might entertain. Gregor had long ago accustomed his bony butt to the unforgiving cedar, but today he slumped unceremoniously onto the thistledown.

You're tired, he told himself. *Tired with a long journey ahead of you.* It was a preemptive sort of tired, he knew, the sort of tired that begs rest before a trial. *Close your eyes. Rest your mind.* He knew that the past few days had taken a toll. Heeding his better instincts, he closed his eyes and allowed his mind to drift into the slipstream.

Sephery was there waiting for him. He found her stepping off the same Clyesian longship that had first brought her to the shores of Ragar Or, wearing a brilliant aquamarine dress. His heart thrilled at the sight of her. For a moment he thought that they were back at the beginning, and had years ahead of them. They embraced each other standing in sands as fine as the grains of time.

"My sweet," he said. "My Sephery."

She answered him with a loving smile. Her eyebrows, delicate arches, called to mind constellations taking shape on the breathtaking galaxy of her face. He wanted to lose himself forever in that infinite space. "Uncle Bones," she said, watching him watching her. The words sounded from her mouth like notes from a musical instrument whose tone he had forgotten. It was the sweetest sound he had ever heard.

The moment passed. Gregor glanced down, and saw that they were no longer standing on the shoreline, but instead were facing each other in a sunlit field. *I know where we are,* Gregor thought. The wind whipped like a cat-o-nine-tails. Sephery's windswept raven-black hair made an obscurity of her face, but even so Gregor caught glimpses of her eyes. She was looking at something behind him, and as she looked, her face grew dark with concern.

"It's the Yubriy tree, isn't it?" he asked.

She didn't have to answer. Stinging currents of wind delivered hundreds of rich orange leaves into Gregor's field of vision. They coated the field with prophecy. Behind him, he thought he heard the Yubriy tree laughing. He wanted to turn around and look at the tree directly, but for reasons he didn't understand, he found it impossible. His vision was Sephery's; only her eyes had been covered by a leaf that was tangled in her hair.

He plucked the leaf from her face and read the message on its surface.

If you would see me, serve me.

When he looked up, Sephery was gone. In her place stood a long and lean king of a man, a man with a smile like the end times plastered on his face. He looked a little, Gregor thought, like the Yubriy tree. The man opened his mouth and thundered: "RETURN FROM THE FAINTING SEA, THAT WHICH WAS STOLEN FROM ME!" Then, a dragon the color of the clouds and sky flew out of his open mouth.

Gregor woke up before the dragon could devour him whole.

He was alone in his tent. The dream was disturbing, but, then again, many of his dreams were. Standing up, he stirred the coals in the brazier with a poker, and then added a few logs of white oak to the diminished fire. Soon the flames were dancing like demons. He stood staring at the flames for a long time, soaking in the heat, revisiting the dream. When at last he was satisfied that he had made of the dream what he could, he reached inside of his cloak and pulled out the Yubriy leaf that he had taken from Doxius Brine. Unlike many of the Yubriy tree's messages, this one was written in simple Struvan, the common tongue.

He read it once more.

a song first sung in the Vake
prolongs the line of the suns

Gregor shook his head. The prophecy—like all prophecies—was problematic. Back in Union, stored in a secret chamber deep inside the Crow Keep, resided a Yubriy leaf from this year's harvest with a prophecy that was possibly connected. Like every Yubriy leaf prophecy that Gregor deemed consequential (there were far less than one might imagine: the majority of the Yubriy leaf messages were either indecipherable, inscrutable, or written in alien languages), he had committed it to memory.

the lutist bears a song for the queen
as his gift lives so lives the queen
as the queen lives so lives the king

Gregor knew that there was a chance that the two prophesies weren't connected, but he also knew it was foolish to dismiss the likelihood that they were. *And now Betrard is privy to the message. And no doubt Daguss Salk as well.* He poked at the fire once more, stirring the soul of the flames. *The Gorgostrine traveled north with the birds. Who is to say that the Heron isn't in the loop, also?* A frown fractured Gregor's face. *Were the north and south working together against the king?* Power and paranoia were steady companions, but often for good reason. *And here I thought it was simply a matter of waiting for the lutist to arrive. For all I know our enemies have been scouring the Vake, killing every musician they come across.*

Gregor tossed the poker to the floor and sat back down, this time on one of the cedars. Putting his head in his hands, he resisted the desire to drift back to sleep. Nightmares awaited him in that realm, but they were no worse than the ones in the waking world, and at least Sephery resided there. But Gregor knew that he couldn't fall back to sleep. Not now. He was in possession of knowledge that needed to be acted upon. Immediately.

Soldiers must be sent to the Vake. Loyal soldiers. The thought of sending loyal men away from King Micah's side under the current circumstances made Gregor feel sick to his stomach, but failing to act was not an option. If there was a musician still alive in the Vake, he needed them brought to the Dayborns at once.

And if all the musicians in the Vake were dead, he needed to know who had killed them.

Johanna Salk

They traveled hard through the night, sticking to the main road. Over the bridge that spanned the shallows of the southern Dezoe. The moon a gleaming sickle in the sky, as sharp as the nighttime cold. Howling wolves urging them on.

Before sunrise, they left the road and headed west. Johanna noticed that they had left the snows behind. The predawn found Johanna walking Bitterboy up a streambed, biting her tongue to keep from complaining about her suffering toes. Easton, lost in his work, lay false trails on one side of the streambed before guiding the horses out of the other. They rode west for a spell before veering south once more.

Shortly after, the morning sun cracked open like an egg, spilling sunbeam yolk all over the countryside. Johanna's exhaustion was a mere annoyance in comparison to the invigorating sun, the feel of Bitterboy beneath her, the adventure at hand. Furthermore, she loved the way Easton had grown quiet in his work. She thought the prince looked more a maturing oak in the saddle, and less an arrogant sapling.

Near midday, they stopped to eat. Easton produced hard bread, figs, and green-grass apples that he had procured from the inn. The two of them sat beneath a beech tree while the horses nickered nearby, contented from their own green-grass apple feast. Easton's horse, a gray-dappled palfrey, looked knackered, but Bitterboy, forever spry, boasted of his stamina by holding his head high.

They ate in an unspoken, agreed-upon silence. The tensions from the day before had dissipated during their flight from the inn, and, with every accumulated mile, the mutual understanding that the quiet was doing them good deepened. Johanna liked discovering that the prince was capable of prolonged periods of noiselessness. His bravado, it appeared, was only one aspect of his character, and not the entirety of his makeup.

They had finished their meal and were preparing to continue their journey when Johanna experienced the strangest sensation: the world to the west, it seemed, was lighter somehow. Instinctually, she turned her head in that direction, and saw, on the far reaches of the horizon, a monstrous creature taking flight. She stared with wonder at the creature's elongated torso, stupendous muscularity, and acre-width wings. It was some time before her mind's eye grasped the reality of what she was seeing.

She was looking at a dragon.

She absorbed what she could of the creature before it disappeared completely over the horizon. Dumbfounded, she turned back to Easton, expecting to find him staring in the same direction, only to discover that he was attending to the palfrey, checking one of its shoes.

Sensing her stare, Easton looked up.

Seeing her expression, he brought the silence to an end.

"What is it?"

She opened her mouth to reply, but the enormity of what he had missed gave her pause. She knew how badly he wanted to see the dragon for himself. For a moment she considered misleading him, but, finding herself unable to conjure a convincing lie, she told him the truth.

"I saw it. The dragon." She pointed west by northwest. "It flew over the horizon."

He gave an uncertain laugh. "From the look on your face, I'm tempted to believe you." When she didn't respond, he narrowed his eyes at her. Then all at once he closed his eyes and gave a long and forlorn sigh. "Stavus save us. You're telling the truth."

She felt a flare of resentment fire up inside of her. If he was expecting her to feel guilty, then he was in for a disappointment. "I am," she answered, refusing to permit any hint of apology in her voice.

Easton took a vain step toward the northwestern horizon, as if hoping he might bridge a sufficient distance to bring the dragon back into view. "It was black and green, then? Like Axton Boil said?"

"It was," she replied, forgoing the sublime specifics, like how the black had been as bottomless and pure as the infinite nothingness of the Sky Ends, and how the green called to mind a verdant blanket of moss stretching across the forest floor. Now that the dragon was out of sight, Johanna felt a portion of her quicksilver soul longing to give chase after its terrible beauty.

Easton sighed, his gaze lingering on the horizon. Then all at once his eyes broke away. "We need to get going." For a second, Johanna couldn't comprehend what Easton was saying, perhaps because his expression was at odds with his lips. But he continued in the same vein. "There's still work to be done before I can be certain that we've lost your father's man for good."

She nodded silently in assent, struggling to reconcile the part of her that now wanted to ride north.

Without another word, they commenced their journey once more, directing their steeds in a south by southwesterly direction, creating an ever-widening V away from the dragon. They rode hard for more than an hour. Bitterboy ran as if he could chase down the sun. The palfrey, on the other hand, labored to keep pace. When they came upon a patch of woods, it seemed a logical opportunity to give the palfrey a break. They dismounted and led the horses through the forest by hand.

At the forest's edge, sheets of widow's moss cascaded from the trees like a fine gossamer. Johanna was watching Easton encourage the palfrey through one of the sheets when a thought occurred to her. "Is your horse stolen from Lord Egros as well?"

Easton turned away from the palfrey, who nuzzled at his shoulder in response. "Yes."

"Why didn't you steal your own horse?"

"My horse, Dark Wind, was under close surveillance. And I, as you know, am a well-known flight risk. It was easier to filch from Lord Egros's stables than it was to steal my own horse from under Father's nose."

And you gave me the superior steed. She stroked Bitterboy's muzzle. The Rugarder permitted it, but was otherwise indifferent. He wasn't the sort of animal that needed assurance from a human. She had never seen Dark Wind, but, from the sound of his name, she had no doubt that his nature was closer to Bitterboy's than the palfrey's.

Another silence fell. Johanna continued stealing glances at Easton, wondering what manner of thoughts were eddying through his mind. *If he wants to say something about the dragon, I wish he would get it off his chest.* But Easton's silence appeared to be the new norm; it seemed that he was dead serious about the oath he had made back at Doakmont. The longer he held his tongue, the more frustrated she grew. She had no desire to goad him by bringing up the dragon of her own volition, but, when the minutes added up and he remained silent, she found that she could no longer resist.

"It's fine if we talk about the dragon. In fact, I'd prefer it if we did."

He screwed on an expression like he thought that was a bad idea, but then changed his mind. "Okay. If that's what you prefer."

She coated her voice in earnestness. "It is. Honestly."

"I only have one question, really. What was the experience…like? For you?"

The question was unexpected. But after contemplating it for a minute, she knew how to reply. "It was…surreal. When I first saw the dragon, my brain wouldn't accept what it was. It felt like I was grasping at an impossibility."

"The Wandering Tongue Philemon Grapple said that to encounter a dragon was to come face-to-face with unreality. He said that once a person saw a dragon, it was inevitable that their mind would break."

The name of the Wandering Tongue registered in the faraway recesses of Johanna's brain. "Wait. Wasn't he the one who—"

"Offered himself up as a living sacrifice to the Slumberer? Yes. The one and the same."

Johanna's stomach rumbled with a queasy disgust. She remembered hearing the story as a girl, how there had once been a wise man who took quinquennial pilgrimages to see the Slumberer, a great yellow-green dragon who had arrived in Ragar Or the century before the founding of Union and then lost the power of flight. The dragon lived for nearly one hundred years in the Qorlish plains, surviving off the munificence of the cult-like worshippers who sustained him with offerings of livestock. Grapple, the most venerated philosopher of his generation, had ended his life on the last of his pilgrimages to the Slumberer, shocking all who were present by suddenly and unceremoniously approaching within striking distance of the crippled dragon, who unhesitatingly gobbled him up.

"And you think he was right, this Wandering Tongue? You think I'm destined to go batty too?"

"I'm sure his philosophy has some truth to it. But what's the alternative? Look the other way when a dragon flies by?" He tsk-tsked. "That sort of life isn't worth living."

"You would risk insanity, then?"

"Without a doubt. It's the only way to live."

Johanna considered this. The idea that everyone who came into contact with dragons went insane was nonsense, of course: the history of Ragar Or was replete with examples to the contrary. Unfortunately, Johanna's short-lived personal experience was proving otherwise: dragon fever was boiling her brain, making her want nothing more than another glimpse of the beast. And knowing that Easton was already infected wasn't helping.

"Why were you…interested…in tracking down the dragon?" she asked.

The prince's mien turned serious. If it wasn't for her own seriousness, Johanna might have laughed at him: Easton's sober deportment was comically at odds with everything about him, from his lean, rascally looks to his insouciant, I-erring-may-care ethos. It made sense, she supposed, that the one subject he was deadly serious about was adventure.

He also looked pretty damn serious when he offered you the forever flower, she remembered. *Don't forget that.*

"When I was nine years old, my brother nearly died."

The unexpected segue jarred Johanna. "What happened?"

"A golku spider bit him. We were playing peek-and-poke in the Crow Keep, and Ajax hid in the dirtiest, darkest corner in the castle. I found him by following the sound of his screams. For the next three days I heard the word *hairsbreadth* a hundred times. As in 'Prince Ajax lies but a hairsbreadth from the grave,' and 'A hairsbreadth separates you from becoming the crown prince.' Late at night, after I was put to bed, I would light a candle and pluck hairs from my head. Then I would stare at the width of them, trying my best to measure the distance between the present moment and fate. At last, I decided that the distance was so negligible that it might as well not exist. Life and death, heir to the crown or second son, safe in one's skin or bitten by a golku spider. A mere hairsbreadth between. Nothing."

The prince's words brought a chill to her bones. Glancing at the treetops, she envisioned one possible fate: the dragon flying overhead, spotting them, sticking its flaming snout twixt the timber, gobbling them up. While she daydreamed, a second vision overlaid the first: a golku spider, crawling up her ankle for a quick bite.

"He recovered, obviously," Easton continued. "Prayers or potions, who's to say. And I became a second son once more. Free to follow my own fate. And that's what I've determined to do. Follow my fate aggressively to the end." He flashed a mercurial smile. "And along the way, if I manage to see a dragon or two, all the better."

Johanna didn't know how to respond, so she gave a little nod and looked at the forest floor. All this talk of fates had left her feeling flummoxed. It felt to her that, since becoming a widow, she had spent most of her time parrying with fate, trying, by means of skill and guile, to outmaneuver whatever destiny had in store for her. But perhaps that wasn't the way. The reason she was driving the prince south was because she preferred the nebulous future there to the one fashioned for her by others. What she didn't have—what she had never had—was a purpose of her own.

"I would see it again."

She spoke the words before she had fully grasped the truth of them. But, once spoken, they rang true as a bell.

Her eyes left the forest floor and found Easton's. His gaze was waiting along with the palfrey's. She repeated and clarified herself. "I would see the dragon again. With you."

The prince looked at her with what she was certain was a mask of judgment. *He thinks I'm insane. Capricious. Fickle.* Snark was in the offing, or worse, a mocking lecture. She felt her dragon-fever blood boiling, hot words rising to her tongue, *fuck off, then, I'll go on my own;* but in the next instant she saw that she was wrong: a trickster's smile had broken out like a plague on Easton's face, and he was turning the palfrey around by the reins.

"Okay. Let's go."

They slowed their pace of travel. Bitterboy communicated his displeasure with a series of impatient neighs, the sounds growing irksome enough that Johanna brought him to a hard gallop on the open stretches, which settled him for short spells. Otherwise, they stayed slow and kept their eyes peeled on the northern horizon, watching for a vast pair of leathery wings to appear.

The conversation centered on two subjects: the nature of dragons, and the likelihood that they would cross paths with the man tracking them. Easton swore on Stavus's sweat-stained brow (Easton's irreverence, Johanna deduced, wasn't indicative that he was unserious about his oath) that he could avoid Daguss Salk's tracker if absolutely necessary, only that it wasn't conducive to their newfound objective. Johanna—her fate-courting frame of mind driving her thinking on the subject—thought it best that they precipitate an encounter with her father's man. That way they could determine, and, if necessary, thwart his business. Both assumed that the tracker had been sent to keep an eye on them, not to bring them in. After talking it over, they ultimately decided against taking a proactive approach. The tracker would find them when he would find them, and they would deal with it then.

Their discourse on dragons was a meandering, if slightly more contentious affair. Neither was an expert on the lore surrounding the creatures, and together they contested the gaps in the other's knowledge.

"The Beasting Rock? Hogwash. That's fiddle-faddle, fairytale nonsense for children."

Johanna gave an unladylike snort, accompanied by a fuck-you chuckle. "Nonsense?! So, I suppose you take the Struvan point of view? Remind me again what it is you southerners believe? Because I'd like to see you keep a straight face while explaining it."

Easton crimsoned ever so slightly. "Dragons cross an ocean to reach us. Why is it so far-fetched to believe that they come from the ocean itself?"

"Say it, then! Let's hear it from your own lips. Say that you believe that dragons emerge fully formed from that piss-pot of a harbor. A harbor you've never seen, I might add. Say that you believe that they erupt out of the watery depths like a geyser, dry off their wings, and then fly a thousand miles straightaway to a foreign land, choosing each and every time to bypass a perfectly good island. Go ahead. Say it!"

"I…you see, it's just that…I suppose it depends on…" Easton's ever-present roguish smile faltered, and an embarrassed grin took its place. "Okay. I wouldn't quite go so far as to say that."

Johanna *"hmphed"* in triumph, and pursed her lips in a proud little manner. Easton, seeing her expression, went right back on the attack. "But you have to admit that it's no more ludicrous than the Beasting Rock theory. Perhaps you could convince me if half a thousand ships hadn't sailed west in search of the place. But after an untold number of failures, the theory simply doesn't hold."

"The Firewalker made it." She spoke the words softly. They were entering *jeyedoshi* territory here.

"The Firewalker," Easton repeated, his voice surprisingly devoid of mockery. "I do suppose that if the Beasting Rock exists, it makes sense that a legendary figure like the Firewalker visited it. When you fly on the back of a dragon named The Wind, I imagine many things are possible."

She appreciated the openness of his tone. "The dragons have to come from somewhere."

"The people who ride the dragons have to come from somewhere as well."

What was he trying to insinuate? She thought of a way to turn the tables on him. "Do you believe what they say about your uncle? Do you believe that he could ride a dragon?"

"You're asking me if I believe that my uncle is a jeyedoshi?"

"Yes." She knew that she had set him up to ask the same question of her, but they were already tiptoeing down that road.

Easton shrugged. "We southerners don't give much thought to concepts like jeyedoshi. And even if we were to think of such a question, we would consider it impolite to ask." His grin once again turned shit-eating. There was no matter, it seemed, that he couldn't make a lark of. "All the same, I'd reason my uncle would be a handy man to have on hand when facing down a dragon."

Facing down a dragon. The reality of the beast that they were pursuing slapped her like a splash of cold water in the face. Johanna had seen the creature from a safe, non-perishable distance. Drawing close enough that the dragon noted their presence was a different matter altogether, one that posed all sorts of problematic potentialities.

"This dragon," she said. "It could kill us."

Easton stroked the palfrey's neck. "Dragons don't"—he chose his next words carefully—"make a habit of killing people."

"Except when they do," Johanna rejoindered.

"Except when they do," Easton admitted. "And, unfortunately, history indicates that they have a predilection for royal bloodlines."

The ubiquitous vision entered Johanna's mind: the dragon Teriquay hovering above Lake Wyglass, enveloping King Reuel I and his family in a great spout of fire.

Her Salk ancestors.

She spoke aloud the thought that had been traversing the hinterlands of her mind ever since they had changed their course of travel. "We should search for the dragon, but we should also travel west."

Easton nodded in agreement. "The woods witch. I agree. If we're going to do this, we should do it right. And seeking out a woods witch that can hail dragons from the sky is the perfect place to start."

A clap of thunder moaned over the distant mountains, sounding like the keening of a distant and wretched god. It took the both of them by surprise. Until now, the day had been seasonably mild, with an atmosphere to match, but in the blink of an eye there was a charge in the air, a charge that gave Johanna the unsettling feeling that forces beyond her ken had sprung into motion.

"Is it a howler?" Easton asked. Howlers were fast-moving storms that swept in from the Blacktyde Sea and cut across the Edgeling Mountains. They usually expired in fits of loud, gusty wind and sporadic, stinging rain. Howlers were different from chuggers, those huge, slow-moving sea storms that managed to make a dent on the interior plains. They were easy to tell apart, but Johanna didn't blame Easton for deferring to the judgment of a mountain girl.

"From the sound of it, yes." Howlers generally weren't dangerous, being fuller of fury than form, but they always had an ominous quality, precisely because they seemed suggestive of something other than themselves. "It will be a quick squall, and nothing more." Having said that, she didn't like the sound the storm made barreling toward them.

They stopped talking. They were riding into the teeth of the storm, and the quiet once again behooved them. Johanna became acutely aware of the landscape. She noted—and not for the first time—that the area south of the Edgeling Mountains had a fractured personality, a feature made even more pronounced by the disquieting advance of the storm. It was flatland upended by the occasional hill; wide, open spaces splintered by desultory trees. It was the sort of land where the horizon feigned transparency, only to shapeshift at the last moment into an unexpected tableau.

Shortly, the land made a demonstration. They were riding north by northwest when the flatland eased into a knoll, and then revealed a copse of trees that required circumvention. They directed the horses around the southern edge of the trees. Circling the copse, they watched the woods, heeding their gut instinct that something in the woods was watching them back. Overhead, the wind howled. So distracted were they by the trees' dark recesses that they were slow in spotting the horror unfolding in the field on the opposite side.

A man stood alone in the middle of the field with his sword drawn. He wore black, or the remains of black: the man's wool cloak was shredded and bloodied, especially near the abdomen, where even at a distance Johanna could see bulges of his intestine showing through. Surrounding the man were three pennywolves, intent on finishing off their kill. Pennywolves were creatures three-quarters the size of their lupine counterparts, but twice as intelligent and equally as aggressive, with coats the color of burnished bronze. Though rarely seen, they left an indelible impression on any human who encountered them: the creatures' faces were oddly shaped, in a way that suggested both a lupine ferocity and a disconcerting intelligence. Besides the name pennywolves, Johanna had also heard them referred to as messenger wolves, the implication being that they were minions of darker forces.

Fear gripped Johanna's heart. Even from a distance she was disturbed by the gleeful way the pennywolves were torturing their prey. Together the wolves took turns rushing in and snapping at the man, being careful to avoid his increasingly futile attempts to withstand them with his sword. On their successful forays, they returned with prizes of blood and black wool. Each time one of the pennywolves won a piece of the man, the other wolves would yip in delight. Johanna hadn't been watching long when one of the pennywolves snagged a link of the man's intestine, and, with a savage fervor, pulled a string of entrails out of the man's stomach.

The storm exploded. Thunderclaps and thunderclouds, bearing brutishly down. Easton, beside Johanna, yelled words that were lost in the wind. Then he left her, spurring the palfrey toward the madness. The wretched god in the clouds screamed again. Bitterboy neighed; in response she turned him away from the awful sights, a purposeless 360, for he quickly reoriented himself facing forward. She screamed in frustration. Or perhaps it was a battle cry; she no longer knew herself. The next moment the horsewoman in her took over, and Bitterboy was thundering forward, a thunder to match the heavens, the Rugarder's hooves eating up the land like a famished giant.

A sudden pelting rain obscured Johanna's vision. The world reduced to Bitterboy's beating hooves: *clop-tromp, clop-tromp, clop-tromp.* Up ahead, through the smear of a world turned wet, Easton arrived at the wolves.

The beasts lunged at the palfrey, wicked yips in their teeth. The yips sounded strange because Johanna expected growls, but for the wolves this was a sport...and in the maelstrom of the sporting sounds the palfrey reared onto its back hooves, too high, too high...fortunately, Easton smartly slid from the horse's back shortly before the equine's verticality rendered his choices moot. The palfrey bolted. One of the pennywolves rushed at the prince...but Johanna could no longer focus on Easton's plight because she had arrived on the scene, and the other two pennywolves were charging Bitterboy. The Rugarder responded by rearing onto its back hooves like the palfrey, only not nearly as high and not in terror: with a forceful kick, Bitterboy divested one of the pennywolves of its consciousness. The other pennywolf, thinking better of its decision, tucked tail and scampered ten yards clear.

Nearby, the pennywolf who had lunged at Easton sung its death song. Johanna turned, still atop Bitterboy, and saw that Easton's left arm was bloody, but the pennywolf was backing away, yelping, dying, howling a song of sorrow to the god in the clouds. Blood seeped from its matted-fur stomach. Everywhere dead and dying pennywolves. Johanna hadn't noticed it until now, but from up high on her Bitterboy perch, she realized that two other pennywolves were dead in the grass, one with its head half decapitated, the other bloodied beyond recognition. *The man in black. He killed them before we arrived.* Turning, she found the man in black behind her; they had passed him in the fury of their approach. He was down on one knee, futilely attempting to contain his entrails, eyes glassy and pained.

The dying pennywolf stopped its song and slumped to the ground. Its sister, the one who had thought better about Bitterboy's hooves, began to look about distractedly, no longer interested in the humans and their hoof-heavy horse. The rain ceased. The howler, speeding south, was already passing them by. All that was left was the business of the standoff with the remaining wolf.

Out of the blue, a new chorus of wolves started up, the sound coming from the copse of trees. The surviving pennywolf perked up its ears. Johanna angled Bitterboy toward the copse and saw, with alarm, that seven additional pennywolves had emerged from the woods. Against the backdrop of the trees, the wolves looked like droplets of molten sun. Together, the pennywolves sang an ancient and inhuman song, crafting a melody both defiant and wild. Wordless though it was, Johanna thought she understood its meaning deep in the tangled forest of her soul.

Then the howling stopped, and the pennywolves began to run.

Straight toward them.

There was nothing to be done. Johanna exchanged a glance with Easton, but no words were shared. The Dayborn prince stood on his feet, sword at the ready. Bitterboy, sensing real danger, snorted in alarm. The pennywolves continued streaking forward like the rays of a slow-moving sun. Johanna closed her eyes, allowing time to bridge the distance between the present moment and her approaching fate.

Except when she opened her eyes, her fate had changed. The pennywolves slowed to a trot and, keeping a safe distance from the quartet of humans and horse, added their sister pennywolf to their number. Then they continued on their way, an octad of departing rays.

The wolves traveled north by northwest, as if getting a head start on the direction Johanna and Easton meant to go.

With the pennywolves gone, Johanna dismounted. Together with Easton, she hurried to the side of the man in black. He was quickly slipping out of existence. Johanna recognized him as one of her father's men, an industrious, no-nonsense fellow by the name of Thacker. A High Osgoodian, smart and capable. She had never spoken to him before, only seen him. "Thacker the Tracker," she said out loud, recalling, from some hidden recess of her mind, the man's alliterative nickname.

"Aye," the man in black replied, a bubble of blood appearing on his lips. Still down on one knee, Thacker gave the impression that he would rather succumb to death than succumb to the ground. "Damned pennywolves," he continued. "Woodkin work." He cast a faraway glance. "My horse," he mumbled, attempting to make a motion with his hand, but the movement carried too high a cost; Thacker spilled to the ground and lost purchase on his guts.

The tracker had entered the gloaming of death before he hit the ground. Johanna thought of a paste that she could make from the rhizome she had taken from the innkeep's root cellar that would alleviate his pain, but it would take too long. Easton, thinking different thoughts, brought his blade to the tracker's throat. Johanna sensed him asking a question with his eyes, but her eyes had moved to the prince's left arm, chewed red.

"You should look away," Easton said. "I'm going to end his pain."

Johanna didn't reply. Instead, she kept her gaze exactly where it was.

The prince didn't argue. Without another word, he drew his blade across Thacker's throat.

A deep, dark red fountained on the ground. Johanna ignored it, and reached over and took Easton by his left hand, the better to study his injured arm. "There's a paste I know how to make," she said, but before she could explain, she was overcome by a distant emotion, rolling in like a tidal wave from the Blacktyde Sea. It was an emotion brought on by Thacker's death…or perhaps by Thacker's death and the decision to chase after the dragon…or to be more specific by Thacker's death and the uneasy mystery of the pennywolves and the loss of her father's good graces and Wulfess bonding that snowbound brute and the decision to chase after the dragon, which felt in effect like a decision to chase after death in the hopes of finding life…but just when the tears were on the verge of beginning to flow, she steeled herself and disallowed it, stripping the emotion from her eyes the way a dog might strip marrow from a bone. She then offered Easton her emotionless expression as a compelling counterpoint to the catch he had no doubt heard in her voice…only to find, to her stunned surprise, that the Dayborn prince was granting her a glimpse behind the same mask that she had just denied him.

No words were said. Easton made no justifications, gave no explanation for his tears. He simply allowed Johanna to see what the ordeal had cost him.

And so it came to pass, with the pennywolves gone and a dragon in the near vicinity and the corpse of Thacker the Tracker of High Osgood lying in the grass nearby, that Johanna of House Salk leaned forward and gave Prince Easton of House Dayborn a loving and healing kiss.

Silas O' the Songs

"You know what that smell is, don't you, Silas O' the Song? That is the smell of land's end, of kraken slime and mermaid puss, of the foul thoughts of briny gods unknown."

Silas was too busy taking in the smell of the sea to respond to Wyn's latest Wynicism. Silas was a woodland creature, a son of the Vake; the thought of life near saltwater mystified him. The smell was befuddling enough, but knowing that somewhere between the rows and rows of dark-lit houses lay a body of water expansive enough to swallow the whole of Ragar Or left him feeling lightheaded. He kept craning his neck between the buildings, hoping to catch a glimpse of the black and briny void, but as of yet his efforts had been unrewarded.

The foursome were stealing into Dunning Harbor at dusk. For the most part the journey north had been uneventful, but a week past a group of soldiers clad in the king's double-sun garb had passed them on the road heading south, and what unfolded then had left them wary of unnecessary encounters. Wyn, heeding an ever-present sixth sense, had whisked Silas into the nearby woods upon the soldiers' approach, leaving Madrig and Jacy to deal with the Dayborn contingent. This turned out to the good, because after the soldiers departed, Jacy informed Silas and Wyn that the men were on the lookout for "musicians of any kind, on the

Sagekind's orders." Ostensibly, the Dayborn defenders had been sent on a mission to protect endangered musicians, but Madrig and Jacy, familiar with Silas's and Wyn's problems with the murder birds, thought it best to personally deliver the fiddler and lutist to their desired destination. Also, being Salks, the bonded pair were naturally suspicious of those wearing double-sun surcoats. The encounter, while unsettling, did have the benefit of informing the quartet of a particularly useful piece of information: the king's party, along with a great number of nobles, were traveling east from Low Osgood, and would pass through Dunning Harbor.

"Okay, there it is," Jacy said, motioning at a tall, unbalanced building in the middle of a busy shadow-growing street. "The Sea Swoon."

Wyn, who had been his usual gregarious self during their sneak into the city, suddenly turned sour. "Aptly named, innit? Any minute now and it will fulfill its destiny."

"Can you see the Blacktyde? From the rooms?" Silas wasn't overly concerned by The Sea Swoon's ramshackle exterior: it had survived plenty of previous nights, surely it would survive one more. What he wanted to know was whether the sea would be in view.

Jacy made a face half annoyed and half amused. "We'll try to arrange a room for the two of you on one of the upper floors."

"Good," said Wyn. "When this mountain of sticks comes crashing down, at least we'll die quick."

They made their way out onto the street. Ill-intentioned shadows lurked in the gloom, but none drew too close, on account of Madrig. Silas had grown accustomed to the safety the big man's presence provided. He felt a smidgen of trepidation at the thought of Madrig and Jacy leaving them at The Sea Swoon to seek out Lord Salk, no matter how many times they had discussed the plan.

Or perhaps what I'm really worried about is being left alone again with this mad bastard, he thought, looking at Wyn. The respect the scrawny fiddler had won from him after saving Madrig's life had been severely strained by their continued time on the road together. Recently, the rascal's behavior had grown contentious, especially in his dealings with Jacy; Silas sometimes had the impression that the little man was scheming for a chance to separate them from their protectors.

They made it inside the inn without incident. The Sea Swoon was a peculiar establishment, a circular tower of seaworn timber cored by a spiraling staircase that climbed from the inn's bottom floor to its penthouse peak. Each level up diminished in size; only the respective change in each level was inconsistent, giving the building a teetering effect. On the bottom level, a crescent-shaped bar ran half the length of the back wall. At the current moment, a dozen soused sailors filled the complementary crescent bench, drinking the local grog.

Seeing Silas and crew enter, a middle-aged woman with strawberry-blonde hair and a glass eye came over to meet them.

"You lot come to Dunning to see the king?"

"How much for a room?" Jacy asked, sidestepping the question.

Glass-eye looked as though she had a snide retort in mind, but, eyeing Madrig, stayed her thoughts. "Five silvers. Though, from the looks of the big 'un, you'll need two rooms. Unless he sleeps standing up."

Jacy counted out five silvers, all bearing the face of King Reuel II. "One room. And we'd prefer something with a view of the Blacktyde."

"The fourth floor is as good as I can do you, but that's high enough for what you're asking."

Jacy looked to Silas. He gave a little nod.

"We'll take it."

Minutes later they were squared away inside their room. Silas, opening the window, whiffed the now-familiar salt and heard the rhythmic pounding of the surf, but when his eyes searched for the sea, all he found beyond the buildings was a black, blank emptiness. It unsettled him. He knew in his mind that the emptiness was a byproduct of the cloud-covered sky, but he also knew that a part of him wouldn't feel settled until he could define the watery void with his eyes.

Jacy spoke. "All right, we're off to find Madrig's cousin. Once we've made the proper arrangements, we'll come and retrieve you. Until then—
"

"Until then we'll sit tight on our respective ass cheeks and twiddle our thumbs till they're worn to nubs," Wyn interrupted. He finished his speech with a salute. "Or not. Guess you'll have to leave to find out."

"You will find me waiting *here*," Silas assured Jacy. "And to be clear, we are *grateful* for your assistance in bringing us this far. Never mind what my friend says."

Jacy gave Wyn a murderous eye. On account of Wyn saving Madrig's life, Jacy had indulged the fiddler's ongoing shenanigans during the journey north, but, it seemed, she was at last reaching the end of her rope. Madrig, on the other hand, still appeared to be making a study of Wyn, and had yet to reach a definitive conclusion. *This break from each other, short though it may be, is for the best,* Silas thought. *Another hour together and the two of them would be at each other's throats.*

The door closed with a glad-to-be-gone thump. Silas turned his attention back to the window, his senses drawn to the sea. Frustrated from staring at the void, he let his eyes wander west, where, to his confusion, an object of indeterminate origin appeared to grow out of the ocean, its black-lit form looking like the large and grasping hand of a giant clawing at the shore.

"What in the name of Stavus—" Silas started, only to remember that Wyn was on the listening end.

Too late. The fiddler sidled up and stuck his head out the window, without waiting for Silas to make room. "Gods of the wicked and wild redeem us," the little man said, following Silas's gaze. "Sea fingers. Now there's an inauspicious sign, if ever there was one. King Two Suns' soothsaying brother will struggle to put a positive spin on that."

"Half brother," Silas corrected.

"Half right," Wyn countered, cracking open his signature smile.

More mindless quibbling. Silas directed his attention back out the window. "Sea fingers? Never heard of them."

"Werring's own work, those of the Ontish affliction would say. It's a fungus that crawls out of the sea to feast upon what have you. From the size of it, it's gorging on a beached whale."

"And it's an inauspicious sign?"

"So *they* say. I say it's merely irregular. Nature has its ways of handling your odd beached fish. Sea fingers are an entity of their own, and appear when they want. Add in the fact that they're poisonous, and smell as sour as a sailor's breath up close, and you start to get your head around why they're associated with ill omens."

Silas narrowed his eyes at Wyn. "How do you know all this? Being a man of the woods?"

Wyn tee-heed. "I know nothing, Silas O' the Song. Every word that comes from my mouth is a fresh fart." He turned and jerked his head out of the window, causing his hair to slap Silas in the face. "Come. We've a ready-made audience downstairs. Let's go and play them a song. One they've never heard before."

Silas speared Wyn with a disbelieving stare. "Surely you jest? You were there, weren't you? When we agreed to sit tight while Madrig and Jacy procured us an audience with a court of nobles? We have practiced 'The Queen's Burning Heart' for days on end, our only audience a mute, a warrior woman, and the birds in the trees, and you would have us risk it being stolen by a bar full of drunks?"

"You fear too much, Silas O' the Song. What better ears than drunk ones to practice upon before we play before a sober king and queen? Like you said, they're drunk! They'll scarce remember what we've played for them in the morning."

"Says the song thief who was drunk when I first met him."

"Aye," Wyn said, smiling. "But as you know by now, I'm not your ordinary inebriate."

Silas determined to stand his ground. "No. I'm staying. *We're*...staying."

Wyn waited patiently to see if Silas had more to say. When it was clear that he did not, Wyn put a mocking, fiddle-free hand over his heart. "A persuasive argument. Truly. And yet..." The little man spun around and headed for the door, the ever-present fiddle and bow swinging freely from his side.

Silas gritted his teeth. *If that fucker plays my song…*

Silas stayed at the window, trying to better understand the sea. The sound of the surf was an effective distraction, subsuming, it seemed, all other noises—except for the sound of "The Queen's Burning Heart," which suddenly struck up in his head. *Or is it coming from somewhere else?* Silas edged away from the window. Craned his neck toward the door. Cupped his ear.

Silas turned back to the window. *You're hearing phantoms,* he told himself. But Wyn Dunkin's threat of singing the song had burrowed like a parasite into Silas's mind. For comfort's sake, he continued humming the song's melody, only to find, to his horror, that in the next instant he could no longer recall the melody; it had been replaced by a version that he was certain Wyn Dunkin was bastardizing this very minute, a caterwauling creation that would no doubt haunt Silas for the remainder of his days.

He gave in. Opening the door, the nightmare became a reality. Issuing forth from the hell spout of the spiral staircase was a song.

Damn it to the Bottom Black!

Silas grabbed his lute and hurried downstairs.

The scene in the bar was decidedly changed. Half of the clientele was standing, dumbstruck by the fiddler in their midst. Wyn was holding court while standing on the crescent-shaped bar, fiddle pressed to his collarbone, crooning a song that both *was* and *wasn't* the one he had written with Silas. Silas strained with his eyes and ears, confused by what he was hearing. When at last his mind wrapped itself around the reality of what Wyn was singing, he nearly gagged at the horror of it.

Wyn had made an amalgamation of "The Queen's Burning Heart" and "She Loves Cream, He Loves Pie." The better to butcher them both.

"Stavus damn you!" Silas shouted across the bar.

Across the gloomy tallow-candle haze, Wyn winked at him.

Rage lit Silas from within like a furnace. He started toward Wyn with the idea of bashing the little man's head in with his lute, but when he closed in on the bar, he found himself pushing aside a patron and commandeering their seat. Then, lute across his lap, his fingers took up the task of reclaiming the song given to him by the Melodies and a Yubriy tree leaf.

The notes grounded Silas. His fingers, clever creatures, coaxed the true rendition from the wood, the music scaling the heights like a magnificent bird of prey, dispelling Wyn's bastardized version in its wake. In an instant, he had command of the room. The bar patrons' befuddled quiet changed over to a reverent hush. And then…at the crucial moment, the moment before the words were to be sung, Wyn's fiddle joined the song, lithe and lovely, urging the lute to plot.

They say, in the flames
Of the Queen's burning heart
Is a story that's long gone untold
A story that screams
For the ending unseen
And the jeyedoshi that took the queen's soul

The song slipped into a timeless space, a place carved from rhythm and tempo and melody and magic. Silas's anger burned off during the playing of it, the joy of sharing the song outweighing his trepidation at playing it for the wrong audience. Even without looking up, he sensed that the room was spellbound. Upon reaching the end, he let his gaze drift into the audience, where he spotted the woman with the glass eye. Her cheeks were stained with rivulets of emotion, water seeping around the glass.

The inhabitants of the bar emerged from the song's trance in wildly different ways. Some wept, others clapped, while more than one simply shook their head, giving physical form to their stupefaction. It took Wyn to give voice to the transition, which he did with gleeful satisfaction.

"Fortune-favored patrons of The Sea Swoon, you have had the honor of hearing the first public performance of 'The Queen's Burning Heart,' a new song by the finest tunesmith in all of Ragar Or, Silas O' the Song...ssss!"

Wyn's proclamation gave way to another round of crying and clapping, along with movement: the drunken spectators were soon pressing around Silas, led at the front by the strawberry-blonde-haired woman with the glass eye.

"My, oh my, what a song. When the big 'un and the she-bear left, I heard a few of the boys in the bar discussing sneaking upstairs and robbing you and the little fellow, but after hearing this, I'm sure they won't. My heart is hurting in the best of ways. Oh, that poor, poor queen. To die as her brother did, and at the hands of a jeyedoshi fiend! Wicked Jezebel. Oh me. Oh my."

The woman leaned over and gave Silas a discomfiting kiss at the midpoint between his cheek and his mouth. It was awkward and uncomfortable, but he understood that it wasn't personal: she simply wanted to kiss the song. And then Wyn descended among them, laughing and chatting, while at the same time those inside the bar pumped Silas's hand and expressed their appreciation for his artistry—unintelligibly for the most part, but he was able to catch the gist of the general bonhomie.

There were calls for an encore. Silas, settled now and reveling in the song's reception, downed the tankard of grog that had been pressed into his hand and agreed. The second performance went over as well as the first, or, even if it didn't, it was impossible to tell; the audience was already won over, and there was no talking anyone out of their joy. When the second performance was finished, calls quickly went up for a third, but Wyn, with his droll quick wit, persuaded the patrons of The Sea Swoon that a third would spoil the first two. To Silas's relief, everyone concurred.

The drinks flowed in earnest then. Silas quickly grew drunk. He was experienced enough that he didn't let his guard down completely, but, after the hard journey north watching over his shoulder for murder birds, it was difficult not to enjoy the moment. Occasionally, he looked to Wyn to see how the fiddler was handling his intoxication, but, as always, the little man's demeanor was such that Silas struggled to distinguish Wyn's inebriated state from his sober one.

Hours passed. Slowly, many of those who had been in the bar area dispersed, stumbling out onto the street or back to their rooms in The Sea Swoon, but not before offering one last heartfelt expression of appreciation to Silas for sharing his song. When the numbers had been whittled to four—Silas and Wyn included—the physical characteristics and personalities of those remaining sharpened. There was the inn's proprietress—the woman with the strawberry-blonde hair and the glass eye—whose name was Freya. And there was a good-natured and exceedingly drunk young man with a crow's-nest of dark hair named Boryl. Freya and Boryl, it was clear, were on familiar terms.

Boryl steered the conversation. "To win a song like that from Gia and Blue. My! Tell me true, songsmith, how did it happen?"

"I—" It dawned on Silas that this was a question he might encounter again. *You had best come up with a convincing answer before you're asked the same in front of royalty.* "I had a moment's inspiration while standing in a forest. Then Wyn here helped me polish my inspiration to a fine sheen."

"Ah. Ah!" Boryl pounded his tankard of grog on the wooden bar. "This life you lead. How I long to live it! Do you think, *Hestrum,* that if *I* went wandering in the woods, Gia and Blue would gift *me* a song?"

Silas learned the meaning of the Ontish word when Freya responded. "I worry, Nephew, that they'd be put off by the tankard you'd no doubt be holding in your hand. I imagine Silas was holding an instrument at the time. But what do I know? Deities work in mysterious ways. Perhaps the goddesses are partial to no-account ne'er-do-wells who spend their days drinking away their auntie's profits."

Boryl laughed, appearing to take no offense. "Har ha! She has the right of me. I am a mirthful, no-account drunkard, unfit for the business of this world. But what she fails to inform you is that the joy-loving gentleman before you also bears a weight of responsibility that surpasses the burdens of most."

Wyn, who was standing uncharacteristically clear of the group, made an observation. "Might it have to do with the fact that you are a Gorgostrine?"

A Gorgostrine? Silas knew little about the northern priests, but, even with his paucity of knowledge, the fellow before him was the last man he would have pegged as a priest of the Twins. But even as Silas thought the thought, young Boryl turned over his right hand to reveal the glyphs burned onto the undersides of his fourth and fifth fingers. "You are an observant one, aren't you?"

"Guilty as charged," Wyn responded, giving a characteristic bow. Silas, making his own observations, thought Wyn's behavior askew. The little man was in possession of his usual panache, but there was also an atypical wariness to him, like he was surveying the room with the guarded instincts of a wild animal.

Freya sighed. She stood and smoothed out the front of her peach-and-cream-colored frock, looking preemptively put out. "Go on, then. Tell them the sad story of your life." She turned to Silas and Wyn. "This is his artistry, as you'll soon see. The telling of his woeful tale."

"*Hestrum* here would make me a pious man, like *Pensta* was."

"*Pensta* meaning his uncle. My dead husband, as it were," Freya clarified. She turned back to Boryl. "These two are southerners, nephew. Or at least Silas is. Not one hundred percent certain about the little man. He looks and acts a breed apart. You'd be wise to go easy on your Ontish."

"Oh. They are Struvans?" Boryl looked suddenly uncertain. "Should I continue?"

Freya gave a curt little nod of the head. "Yes. Silas spoke poorly of the jeyedoshi in his song. All is well."

"Good. Good." Boryl took a long pull from the tankard, then wiped his mouth with the back of his hand. "As I was saying, I might have written a song. Might have learned to play a lute and made my living traveling to the houses of mighty lords and ladies, like you. But when I was a boy—"

"You were sixteen, and not a lick of lute learned." Freya turned to Silas and Wyn. "He had a job at the time gutting and cleaning fish down at the docks. That was where his destiny lay."

"Fine. Though for all you know, I might have been down at the docks practicing my scales on fish bones." Boryl turned back to Silas. "When I was sixteen, my uncle took to his deathbed. He had been a Gorgostrine for years and years, which, as best as I could tell, meant that he had been branded with the glyphs and naught else. But when he was dying, he called me to him, and explained that it was my destiny to be a Gorgostrine too. Next thing I knew, friends of his were holding me down and hot iron was being pressed into my flesh. A special prayer was said over my wounds, and my uncle charged me with a task. Shortly after, he breathed his last. Now I'm stuck in this tavern with nothing to do but drink and ponder the nature of my predicament."

"What task did he charge you with?" Silas asked.

Boryl and Freya shared a look. "That I cannot say," Boryl responded at last. "It's yet another aspect of my predicament. My uncle swore me to suffer my secret alone."

Freya scoffed rather loudly. "And you've done that, have you? Kept your holy oath?"

Boryl shrugged. "For an oath sworn under duress, I would argue that I've done right by my uncle." He gave Silas a wink. "That's not to say that my tongue hasn't slipped once or twice, but no harm has come of it."

Wyn moved closer. He still had a wary look in his eye, but it was also clear that his interest was piqued. "It sounds as if you suffer your secret on behalf of all mankind. As a member of that fraternity, may I say that we owe you a debt, sir? Would that we could repay it."

Boryl drowned Wyn's suggestion in a gulp of grog, then surfaced for air with thoughts on the matter. "You speak truer words than you know, my fiddling friend. If you are serious about repaying that debt, might I suggest that the two of you return tomorrow night? Once word of tonight's performance gets out, *hestrum* could command a full house, especially with the king in town. It won't lighten the burden of my secret, but it will swell The Sea Swoon's coffers. You've seen how I drink away auntie's profits. Help a holy man do right by his long-suffering aunt. What say you?"

Silas could not help but like Boryl. The young man had a natural charisma that was absent from the myriad Hawk's-Eyes he had seen preach in Stavusian temples over the years. Unlike most of those pious buffoons, Boryl was at least interesting. And, to top it off, he was leveraging Wyn's offer to help his auntie, not himself. Silas wasn't overly familiar with the finer points of the faith of the Twins, but, based on this one Gorgostrine at least, it made him want to convert.

Or, if not convert, perhaps do him a favor.

"I don't see why not—"

"This secret of yours," Wyn interrupted Silas, addressing Boryl. "It arouses my interest. Perhaps you might indulge my curiosity in exchange for our returning tomorrow night."

Boryl gave a hardy laugh. He was a meaty fellow, Silas noted, possessive of the type of heft that comes in handy during a fight. "You would have me tell you my secret so that you might repay me for keeping that secret?"

Wyn shrugged his shoulders. "What better way to ease the burden of a secret than to share it? And who better to trust your secret with than a pair of songsmiths who travel far and wide singing stories they pick up along the way?"

There was a slight pause, then Boryl exploded in laughter. Wyn's quip even won a grin from Freya, who was standing behind the bar.

"And what about you?" Boryl asked Silas, once his guffawing fit had passed. "Must I buy you off as well?"

Silas screwed on a neutral expression. He truly liked Boryl, and in his inebriated state was inclined to help him out, but he could tell by Wyn's deportment that there was an undercurrent of the unspoken coursing through the room, one the little man understood better than he. "It would make our performance better on the morrow. Knowing the cause that we were abetting."

Boryl chewed on this. The smile on his face vanished as his wandering, wasted eyes shone a light on the inside of his mind. "This damn thing eats at me. This *secret*..." He trailed off as he tossed a handful of emptiness into the air. "I tried to sell it once. When I was distraught and in my cups. The merchant who took a look at it said that my uncle was lying, said that it couldn't be what Uncle said it was."

Boryl's statement brought Freya to life. She turned on her nephew, good eye gleaming. "Your uncle was a lot of things, but he wasn't a liar. The man was stingy with his secrets, but when he shared them, you'd better believe they were stewed in truth."

The young Gorgostrine sighed. "Uncle *believing* he was in possession of the truth and him *being* in possession of the truth are two different things, *hestrum*."

"The secret is an object, then?" Silas asked, his curiosity intensifying. "Not simply information?"

Boryl and Freya exchanged a glance that hinted at an ongoing disagreement. But the looks were well-worn, the argument's outcome predetermined. Seconds later, Freya threw up her hands. "Do what you will, Nephew. You always do."

If Boryl was joyed by his victory, he didn't show it. "It's a story. Written in Ontish." The young man gave another world-weary sigh. "Uncle said it was written by Greffen, a king of Kalandragote."

"What was it about the story that your uncle wanted kept secret?" Wyn offered the question like a wary supplicant before a shrine.

"Don't know. I don't think my uncle knew either. What little I can read is the shared tongue, not Ontish. And my uncle didn't know his letters from his left testicle. The merchant I showed it to read Ontish, but before he'd finished half the story, he said it was a forgery, and fabricated nonsense to boot. Said it had something to do with the dragon that landed on Kalandragote shortly after the War of the Three Brothers. He offered five silvers for the story as 'a kindness,' and left without a counteroffer when I turned him down." Another sigh. "I should show it to more people, but guilt and sobriety always stop me. Uncle claimed that the story must not fall into the wrong hands."

"What's the wrong hands?"

Boryl's tankard-shaped face filled up with red. "Uncle said to keep it away from jeyedoshi. And…um…woodkin."

Silas had heard the term *woodkin* only a handful of times in his life. They were an Ontish superstition, *magical friends of the natural world* being the best definition, scarce believed in Struvan circles and only mentioned in Ontish circles with an ironic affectation. Silas felt the blood rushing to his cheeks out of embarrassment on Boryl's behalf.

"Smart man, your uncle," Wyn said. Silas jerked, surprised to hear what was coming from the fiddler's mouth. *Aren't you friends with woods witches?* But the little man plowed ahead, sounding out the room with an earnestness that was trying a little too hard to come across as sincere. "I'm a Vake boy, born and bred, but I had an auntie grew up in Port Black that set me straight about woodkin. They live among us, they do."

Freya nodded with the fervency of a Winged Woman at prayer, while Boryl stared straight ahead, lost in thought. Silas kept his mouth shut. Hearing everyone talk about woodkin as if they were a given was a bit much, but, then again, it was also a bit much for Silas to know what he did about his fiddling friend without thinking strange thoughts.

"You're in possession of the story?" Wyn queried the Gorgostrine.

"I am."

Silas asked what he thought was the obvious question. "Why don't you burn it? That way you can be rid of your burden and keep your word to your uncle at the same time?" Silas stole a look at Wyn when he spoke, and caught the tail end of a panicked mien.

Boryl didn't notice. "I can't…burn it. Uncle warned me about the book falling into the wrong hands, but he also said that it wasn't for me to destroy. He said that one day I would need to pass it on. *If the right person shows, give it to them,* he said. Of course, he didn't give me the first idea of who the right person might be before he died. Likely because he didn't have a clue himself."

"What if we're the right persons?"

All heads swung Wyn's way. Silas could sense Boryl and Freya weighing the little man anew, attempting to ascertain if he was salvation or damnation.

"How do you figure?" Boryl asked.

"I'm not saying that we are," Wyn said, showing the room his palms, "only that we could be. That's for you to decide. But from my vantage, it seems that we might meet the criteria. For one, we're here, aren't we? First thing the right persons would do is show up on your doorstep. The second sign is this conversation we're having. Had to be had, hadn't it?"

Silas thought Boryl desperately looked like he wanted to believe, but wasn't sold yet.

"Surely there's more to it than that," Boryl said.

Wyn cut a crafty smile. "Oh, there is. As it happens, I can read Ontish. Same auntie that taught me a thing or two about the woodkin learnt me my Ontish letters. She was a wise one, like your *hestrum* here. If you want, I could read your story for you."

Boryl furrowed his brow, but gave a keep-going nod.

"And last, we're songsmiths. I said it as a joke earlier, but no one's better than a songsmith at carrying a secret in the open. It could be that we're meant to turn your story into a song, one whose meaning will only be understood by the parties meant to understand it."

Boryl thought long and hard about Wyn's argument. A minute of drunken concentration passed, then all at once the Gorgostrine's furrowed brow relaxed and he brought his hands together with a mighty clap. "If there is one thing that a holy man should know, it's when to take a leap of faith." And with those words he stood and walked away.

The room sprung to life. Silas, spinning in the orbit of his lingering inebriation, charted the movements of the other planets: Wyn commenced a little dance; Freya paced the length of the crescent counter, busying herself with private thoughts; while Boryl lumbered away, finding a hole in the wall that Silas assumed served as a downstairs bedroom. *He's gone to get the story.* Silas didn't have the first clue why the story was important, but knowing what he did about Wyn's sixth sense for the extraordinary, he was curious to find out.

Seconds later, the holy man returned, holding a few pages of parchment bound together with wooden boards painted blue. Silas tried to train his eyes on it, but Boryl moved too fast, walking past him and heading toward Wyn.

Wyn looked skittish in the face of the approaching Gorgostrine. He offered an unexpected suggestion. "Let Silas O' the Songs take a look at it first. It's his tune that earned it."

Boryl kept coming, shaking his sizable head. "I've waited years to hear this story in full. I'll not wait a minute longer."

The gap between the two men shrunk to an arm's length. Silas noted a peculiar stillness in the room. Looking out of the corner of his eye, he saw that Freya had stopped her work, and was watching as well.

Boryl extended the story, offering it to Wyn. There was an oddness to the offering, a slight unnaturalness that Silas, to his surprise, sorted out.

Why is he offering Wyn the book with his left hand?

Wyn—his eyes fixed on the book and not the hand proffering it—appeared not to notice; it seemed that in the span of a few seconds the fiddler had reconciled a battle within his own mind, and was setting aside all caution for the purposes of getting his hands on the story. This was why, when reaching for the story, Wyn didn't notice Boryl's right hand sneaking up the opposite side...at least not until the moment the young Gorgostrine grabbed him around the wrist, the glyphs on the Gorgostrine's fingers touching Wyn's skin.

Silas struggled to process what he saw next. Wyn, who on his best days looked like a cross between a half-starved rat and a timeworn piece of leather, aged before Silas's eyes: hard, ridgelike features formed around the little man's eyes and spread rapidly outward, creating fissures that made Wyn's eyes, nose, and mouth look like the vestiges of a man entombed in the face of a tree. Or at least that's what Silas thought he saw...his drunkenness and the room's candlelit, dead-of-night gloom made the surrealness of the scene difficult to accept at face value, so that, like Boryl and Freya, Silas simply stood there, dumbfounded, while Wyn worked himself free from Boryl's grip.

The instant he had extricated his wrist, Wyn's face reverted back to its original form. Then he pretended that nothing was amiss: he wrung his wrist, displayed a larkish grin, and seemed on the verge of setting the world back to rights with the perfect choice of words. And well he might have, had not Freya screamed from the bar.

"Bash his head in, Boryl! He's a Corosian-cursed woodkin!"

All hell broke loose. Silas watched as Wyn grabbed at the book, trying to wrest it from Boryl, but the Gorgostrine, alight with holy fire, jerked the bound parchment away with such violent conviction that he went tumbling to the floor. Behind Silas, Freya screamed again and again, sallying curses the likes of which Silas had never before heard, old Ontish sayings that sounded like the muddled rantings of a demon. Silas gave her his ears, but his eyes were fixed on Wyn, who had pulled his blade but looked strung between two places: there was a part of the fiddler, Silas could tell, that was on the verge of gutting the Gorgostrine and grabbing the story; but at the same time, Wyn held his wrist like it was badly injured, which explained the note of fear in his face, and the fact that he wouldn't move from the spot.

Silas never discovered the course of action Wyn would have taken. Because at that very moment the front door of The Sea Swoon swung open, and a man with a wraith-like appearance stepped inside.

A man dressed in red.

Gregor Thorn

Gregor thought it strange the memory that returned to him as he put the finishing touches on the letter. It was a memory of Zust, the oddly eccentric Thralk-Brakturian who had preceded him as the Sagekind. Gregor had always thought Zust more jester than sage, a foreign affectation meant to enhance the colorfulness of the court of King Orius Dayborn; that is, until the day Zust looked Gregor's way, and decided to impart a lesson to the young man being groomed to take his place.

"Cup your hands. Yes, that's it. Now hold them out to me."

"Why are you pouring water into them?"

"I'm teaching you a lesson. I've been told I owe you at least one. So here it is: this is what it feels like to hold onto power." As Zust walked away, he laughed, and added, 'Now keep it as long as you like!'

Gregor took one last look at the letter in his hands. A part of him was tempted to bypass any discussion with his half brother the king and send the letter to the Raleighs without the royal seal. *Let Micah chastise me later, while I do what is necessary to save his kingship.* He thought for the thousandth time how much easier it would be to hold onto power if he didn't have to keep it on Micah Dayborn's behalf. But how pointless too.

I am a bastard half brother. Bound to serve.

His thoughts flickered back to the day when he had cupped Zust's water in his hands. How he had lasted half a day, by imagining, if he dropped it, that his brother would die.

Half brother.

Remember, you are still in the north, Gregor.

He took leave of his room and headed for the king's apartments. Since arriving in Dunning Harbor the previous day, they had been guests of Grocian Mock at the gloomy monstrosity that was Saltbend, a sad, gray-stoned edifice whose only charm was its sturdiness against the sea. Wherever he went in his travels, Gregor tried to open himself to the experience, but the only knowledge he had gained from Saltbend was a clear-eyed perspective on why Grocian Mock was drinking himself into an early grave.

The greyhounds accompanied Gregor when he left the room. They had been his constant companions since the arrest and execution of Doxius Brine. *I should stop feeding them,* Gregor thought, only to immediately banish the notion, knowing that he wouldn't follow through with it. In truth, he felt that he was indebted to the dogs for depriving them of a master, not to mention that he was still troubled by the look they had given him when he was on the Delilah herb.

For the first time, it was the tan-and-white hound that stayed on Gregor's heel as he walked to King Micah's apartments, instead of the black one. "It's inconsistencies like this that make it difficult to name the two of you," Gregor said while stroking the top of the dog's head. The obvious names for the greyhounds were the Twins of Ontish legend, Daguss and Ropske, but Gregor could not decide which was which. For the time being he thought of them instead as "Black" and "Tan," names so mind-numbingly insipid that Gregor refused to voice them out loud.

The hounds insisted on entering the king's apartments with him. Gregor found the king *and* the queen standing outside on the balcony, looking out at the gray-washed sea.

Anjay saw him, and spoke, first. "Speaking of omens…"

King Micah gave a cross look when he saw the dogs, but he didn't mention them. Instead, he motioned for Gregor to come and join them on the balcony. "Have you seen this?" Micah began, changing his motioning hand to a sea-pointing finger. Gregor followed with his eyes, and found, on the shoreline, a skin-crawling *growth* emerging from the sea that appeared to be laying claim to a bulbous mass on the sand. It was at once captivating and repulsive, the sort of sight that burned one's eyes while begging to be studied. Gregor knew at once what it was, although it was his first time seeing the phenomenon.

"Sea fingers."

"You should know," Anjay quipped. "Considering you're the cause for it."

Ah, this game. Blame the jeyedoshi. Gregor kept an impassive face. "Go ahead. Explain to me how."

King Micah took over, his bristle-brush beard undulating as he spoke. "The Ontish believe it the worst of omens. They think it a complement to evil, and, based on what I can gather, they're certain it's crawled out of the sea because of *your* arrival." He paused. "Grocian says you should leave the city posthaste."

"Be rid of me, then. I am, as always, yours to command."

Micah gave a bitter smile. "And then what? Have them blame me for the next omen?" He gave a bitter chortle. "Tell me: who will guard my back then?" He dismissed the Ontish with his hand. "Let them riot. You and I, Sagekind…we will thread this needle together. Come what may."

Gregor gave only a slight nod in response. Micah Dayborn had been king for so long that he sometimes treated Gregor like he was one of Ragar Or's many gadfly nobles, in need of being courted. The king's favor, however, was irrelevant to Gregor; he was Micah's man in all seasons, and through all of Micah's moods. This was why Gregor insisted on playing the part of the plain-speaking curmudgeon, regardless of Micah's current treatment of him.

Black chose that moment to come over and head-nudge the king in the crotch. Gregor thought Micah might respond with anger, but instead the king's initial grunt turned into a chuckle as the king bent down and gathered the dog's head in his hands.

Anjay used the occasion of the king's distraction to air a personal grievance.

"The lutist? Where is he?" she snapped at Gregor.

"On his way. Hopefully."

"Have you considered taking matters into your own hands? Finding him, perhaps?"

Gregor thought of the men he had sent riding south, looking for living musicians. "I have."

"And?"

Gregor didn't respond.

Anjay looked peeved. "We will be on the peninsula soon. It would be a relief to enter those strange lands with the one prophesied to save us standing by our side. Especially as you seem to believe that there is a conspiracy within our midst."

"If it's a lutist you want, I can find one easy enough. But as for the prophesied plucker of strings, I would argue that he needs to present himself. Wouldn't you?"

"Me? I would argue that we're walking into the mouth of a wolf without so much as waiting on a nod from the fates." And with those words Anjay left the room, her disappointed gaze tacking back and forth between Gregor and the king.

Gregor noticed that King Micah's eyes stayed fixed on the dog's until Anjay was gone. Only then did he look at Gregor. "She takes a different tone in private. It's only with you that she's all spurs."

"I remind her of her cousin."

The expression on the king's face told Gregor that he was right. "She feels guilty that she can't compete with your grief. So she lashes out at you instead." With a look that suggested he had said too much, the king moved the conversation along. "Why are you here?"

Gregor showed Micah the letter that he'd been hiding up his sleeve. *Best to come right out with it.* "We should send for the Raleighs. Tell Lord Wessel to bring an army north."

The king gave Black back his head. "Because of the business with the Gorgostrine Betrard? Or because you don't trust Lord Heron and Lord Salk?"

"No. Because you *shouldn't* trust Lord Heron and Lord Salk." He paused. "I've shared with you my suspicions about Dante serving cordrix meat in Low Osgood. He stole the animal away from you. I'm sure of it. And as for Daguss Salk, the fact that he's Ontish and holds a certain surname, not to mention what I told you about the Gorgostrine Betrard back in Port Black—"

The king waved away the remainder of what Gregor had to say. "You give me too little credit, Gregor. You always have. Stavus save us, I am a king! And a Dayborn king to boot. I know better than anyone that I have no real friends. But the die is cast. Either I am the one to hold this country together, or the Dayborn dynasty falls, and union is no more. It's as simple as that. I trust the Heron because I must. I trust Daguss Salk because I must. But most of all, I trust that both men can be made to see that the alternative to staying loyal to me is having to deal with one another, and that way madness lies."

"Madness is all the rage these days. Look no further than the Blackstar Isles."

"Then why would you have me exacerbate the madness just as I am trying to snuff it out!"

Gregor ignored Micah's question and stuck the letter out at him. "Listen to me. Command Lord Raleigh to hurry north and seize the Brokebone Pass after we have passed through. The army that he was mobilizing for the Blackstar Expedition is likely still intact. The Heron won't learn of the maneuver until we are in Kalandragote. If the Heron is as loyal to you as you say, then he will see fit to rejoice that his Struvan brother has made the trip north."

"He will interpret the Raleighs seizing the Brokebone as a warning to him! You would undermine my position with Dante at the very moment I need him standing with me against the Ontish!"

"No. The Heron will recognize it for what it is: a strong and prudent move by a strong and prudent king. Besides, sending Lord Wessel into the Pass could just as easily be interpreted as a signal to the Ontish lords." Gregor paused. "This realm is *yours* to command. Once we venture into Kalandragote, some will be tempted to forget that. It would be wise to remind them of your strength at the critical moment."

Micah sighed. "Wessel Raleigh is a good and loyal man, but the two of our armies together are no match for the Heron's alone. Most of my strength comes from the Heron. I know that. You know that. *Stavus knows* Daguss Salk and the other Ontish lords know that. It makes no sense risking angering the Heron, especially when we need him most!"

Gregor's voice rose. "The moment you need him the most is the very moment he'll be most tempted to turn on you! But he is a coward at heart. Controlling the Brokebone is the one way to offset his numerical advantages. Once we travel north, the Heron's army will be fragmented; the entire host won't be venturing through the pass. We should capitalize on that. Let Dante know that if he tries to return south without you—"

Micah interrupted, shaking his head and waving his hands. "Careful, Brother, that you do not speak that future into existence."

"My job is to plan for every possible future! Which is why it is essential that you command Lord Raleigh to bring his army—"

Micah's interruption this time was a clap of thunder, issuing forth from the storm cloud of his face. "Damn it to the Bottom Black, Gregor! Listen to me! I will not make enemies out of the men that I must rely upon to rule this country! I will trust them until they see that they must trust me. Come what may! And I will not have you—"

Gregor grabbed the wind from his brother's throat. He returned the royal breath with the same unthinking speed with which he had taken it, his grasping brain desperately trying to catch up with the mad decision his unconscious mind had made. The damage, however, was done. King Micah I of House Dayborn gave Gregor Thorn a look of the utmost betrayal.

"You…you've never…we swore before our father…why?"

Gregor knew that he needed to find the words to set things right. The magic mix of sounds that would explain away this breach in their brotherly contract, and thereby rationalize the irrational impulse that had caused him to do the one thing he had sworn to never do. But, when he looked in his heart, he found that he didn't have it in him.

The tan-and-white greyhound, made anxious by the arguing, loosed a whimper lodged in its throat. The king responded in turn. "Stavus damn you… Get out of my sight."

Gregor responded with a stone-faced nod. When he left, Tan followed him out of the room.

Black stayed behind.

Gregor made his way out of Saltbend Castle and into the streets of Dunning Harbor, with only the hound and his inner turmoil as his companions. It was an impetuous decision, but whatever demon had made him grab the king's breath had to be dealt with, and, at the moment, he thought it best to engage in that battle as far away from the king as possible.

Beyond the barbican, he joined his feet to the road that spilled from Saltbend, gathering eyes along the way. The smell of salt from the nearby Blacktyde Sea filled his nostrils, while in the near distance a chorus of seagulls serenaded the evening sky. The unseen ocean permeated all.

Gregor wanted to blend into the milieu, but his cloak of red made that impossible. Looking around, he noticed that the eyes he had gathered were multiplying. *This will never do.* He needed fresh air, headspace, not the goggling stares of Dunning Harbor's everyman. Looking up, he spotted a building marked with the tell-tale lamp of violet glass hanging above its door. "Speaking of madness…" he said to Tan, but the dog, cheerfully prancing along, appeared unbothered by the notion. Together they slipped inside.

The reaction inside of the brothel to the hound was decidedly mixed. Two of the girls fell upon Tan straightaway with a chorus of cooing, but another, sitting daintily atop a Wrainish reclining chair, twisted up her nose and said, "Dogs aren't allowed in here!"

The girl's comment produced a bosomy woman from the back. The woman, whose attire suggested she belonged to the managerial side of the establishment, looked ready with a cross word on her tongue. But after taking in Gregor, she made a business decision to let the dog slide. At least for the moment.

"Evening, good sir," she said with a slow tongue, her eyes trailing thoughtfully over his red cloak. "Is your business here the business of this house?"

"It—" He stopped talking and motioned to the woman, conveying that he desired a sidebar. She consented, drawing close and offering him a private ear. When she was sufficiently close, he continued in his best approximation of a Low Osgood accent. "I find myself in a most peculiar predicament. I am a trader from Low Osgood, only arrived in Dunning Harbor this afternoon. When the king and his retinue passed through my city, a certain personage belonging to one of the high families requested that I procure a greyhound for them. Now I am arrived with the dog, and intending to close the deal, but upon approaching Saltbend Castle, I find myself attracting an unsettling amount of attention."

"It's your cloak," the woman replied matter-of-factly. "You're dressed like the king's bastard half brother. The hated jeyedoshi."

"Yes." He had summoned the requisite spirit for the performance with his initial explanation, but now, hearing her description of him, his verve faded. "I need…not a girl, but a change of clothes." He produced five shiny brogan's-heads from his pockets, a sufficient amount to make the woman amenable to almost any request.

"You'll have both," she replied. Before he could protest, the madam of the house turned on her heels and snapped her fingers, causing one of the girls petting Tan to take Gregor by the hand and lead him away, down a hallway marked by closed doors concealing pleasurable shrieks. The greyhound followed, and soon the three of them in the unquestioned largest room in the establishment. A great canopied bed took up much of the room, and in the middle of the floor was a sumptuous maroon rug that looked like it had been cut from the back of a moonbear who had taken a dip in a vat of wine.

The girl—nay, woman—began to undress. She looked to be in her midtwenties, and she was beautiful in all the usual ways, with the exception of a small gap in her front teeth that made her even more alluring, especially when she offered Gregor an unselfconscious smile. "Do you like what you see?" she asked Gregor once her clothes were off. The answer, of course, was "yes," but Gregor couldn't bring himself to say it, for reasons that had nothing to do with her but everything to do with the version of the man he had long willed himself to be—a widower faithful to the ghost of his bonded and to the brother he feared was destined to die.

"I...I'm not here for—"

She interrupted him with a kiss. It was a chaste kiss considering the circumstances, a gentle laying on of lips. He accepted it from her like an undeserving penitent receiving absolution from a Hawk's-Eye in a Stavusian temple, silently and with a stunned gratitude. A far-off voice in the back of his mind screamed that he was doing something wrong, but, a different voice argued, how could it be wrong when it felt like forgiveness? Especially when forgiveness was what he needed most?

The door opened, and the young woman separated from Gregor. Gregor turned to see the madam of the house entering the room, holding a handsome beige robe. "Don't mind me," she said with a pleased smile, and tossed the robe over the back of a wooden chair in the corner.

Gregor came back into his body. "Wait," he said, stopping the madam in the room. "Thank you for the robe. It's all I need. Now I must be going."

The madam laughed like he was speaking nonsense. "Surely you don't mean that. You were just getting comfortable. Now, if you'll allow me to get out of the way—"

"You will show me out this instant!" he insisted. Tan barked in solidarity. Gregor's voice was firmer than he had intended. The women in the room, unnerved by the change in his deportment, exchanged a look that bespoke previous experiences with men like him, and that was when reality truly came crashing down, the truth of the damage he'd done, the sin he'd committed that couldn't be forgiven by a gap-toothed sex worker. Without another word he stepped forward, extracted the brogan's-heads from his pocket, and pressed all five of them into the madam's hand. Then he snatched up the beige robe and threw it on over his red cloak before barging out into the hall. Tan followed behind him barking, while curses and questions alike rung out from behind the brothel's many closed doors.

He found his way out of the brothel and back onto the road. To his relief, the gathered eyes from earlier were gone. Cinching the beige robe tight around his red cloak, he hurried down the road with Tan at his side. Together they searched for the sea.

The road became broader and broader until it swept around the end of the seawall that guarded Saltbend Castle and spilled onto a fine blanket of sand. The beach, to Gregor's astonishment, was empty. The Blacktyde lay before him. Gregor stood staring at the wonder of the saltwater horizon for a moment, his jeyedoshi thoughts aflame. Seeing a wave speeding toward the shoreline, he reached for the water surrounding it and turned part of the wave into a tower. Its frothy tongue topped out at twelve feet. When the water hit the sand, it slapped like a hand. Tan, startled, barked, before running clear of the runaway tide.

I should make a wave to swallow this city, he thought. *Wash away my sins.* Not that he would…or even could…do it. He was the only person in Ragar Or who understood the true extent of his powers. His life, to a large degree, had been an exercise in discovering what he was capable of, while at the same time being careful never to reveal the upper limits of his abilities. Only the Prophet of Wrath and Blackstar Berak had forced him to show his hand in public. "To the degree that you can help it, hide away your strength." That had been his father the king's command, back in the days when Orius Dayborn would lock the two of them away and school

Gregor on what he was. "Most jeyedoshi don't understand their power well enough to use it," Gregor remembered Orius saying while standing before a pile of dusty old tomes, on the day that Gregor's education began. "But you will know what you are. And you will use that knowledge to defend the Dayborn family name."

Only Dayborn wasn't Gregor's name, was it?

He was a Thorn.

Tan made his way back to Gregor's side, perching softly on the wet sand with his long, bird-thin legs. He looked the part of a good listening companion. "The wave scared you? And now, like everyone else, you want to know what I'm capable of?" Gregor asked the hound. Tan's look said *Yes*. Gregor decided to humor him. "If I used all of my strength, I could make a wave large enough to smash into the seawall," he confided to the dog. He looked out at the Blacktyde. "Here's a different frame of reference. If my enemies were out to sea, I could manipulate the elements sufficiently to drown a few of them." He sighed. "My powers are extensive, but not infinite. And the effort it takes to coerce the elements is…substantial. Plus, it leaves me vulnerable. If enough of the king's enemies attempted to overwhelm me at once—" His thoughts drifted to the Firewalker, that powerful jeyedoshi of yore. He closed his eyes and imagined the last of the Corosian kings standing on the same shore, before this same ocean, with the mightiest of dragons—the Wind—at his side. *How strong were you, Firewalker?* In his mind's eye the Firewalker smiled in reply, before fashioning a wave high enough to blot out the sun.

Another bark from Tan. Gregor turned to see the hound tearing down the beach, racing toward a monstrosity.

The sea fingers. From Gregor's vantage of one hundred yards, the marine fungus looked even more repulsive than it had at a distance. Glistening gray-white, the organism sprouted from the tide before branching into distinct *fingers*. This particular fungus appeared to have taken a beached whale in its grasp, and was assisting with the animal's decomposition.

Gregor followed after Tan. His first thought was that the sight of the sea fingers was going to send the dog into yet another barking fit, but instead the hound began sniffing around it. Worried that the dog might take a bite, Gregor shouted, "No!" Fortunately, the dog's better instincts prevailed: Tan backed away from the sea fungus and sat whimpering on the sand.

Gregor approached the fungus with reverence. Stopping near Tan, Gregor patted the dog on the head. This quieted Tan. Together, they stood in awe of the organism. Deep within the fungi's clutch, Gregor could make out the remnants of the whale, which, at this point in the decomposing process, looked like something else entirely: the mass inside had transformed into a marble swirl of red, gray, and white.

"One bite of it would kill you," Gregor said to the dog. Although sea fingers were a rare phenomenon, Gregor had either read or heard enough accounts of what happened to those who ate the fungus to believe that the stories were more than apocryphal. Most memorable of all was an account he had read while visiting the Tomes at White Walls: during the reign of Queen Portia II, a group of nearly one hundred Thralk-Brakturian pirates had chosen to commit suicide en masse by eating sea fingers when they found themselves stranded on Corkset Island with a Thistleton man-of-war closing in. The Thistleton men witnessed the feast while they rowed to shore. By the time they made landfall, each and every Thralk-Brakturian had keeled over dead.

"Yes," Gregor continued, still talking to the dog, whose attention remained rapt, "you would die. The question is...would I?"

Gregor left the dog's side and moved to within arm's reach of the fingers. *What do you think, Father?* He often wished that Orius Dayborn were still alive, and not simply because he had been a more competent king than Micah; it would have been a relief to speak with someone who was as educated about jeyedoshi lore as he was. There were legends, Gregor knew, that claimed a jeyedoshi could eat any natural thing and not perish. But those writings were scant, and speculative. And as for what happened when a jeyedoshi ingested sea fingers, there was nothing at all.

Gregor ripped a piece of the sea fingers from its wet, gelatinous body. Behind him, Tan whimpered. The fungi had a slick and rubbery feel, matching its look. At the same time, it also managed to feel vital, the way a heart might. *Ingest at your own peril,* Gregor thought, staring at it. But he was traveling too fast on the river of impulse to heed his own thoughts. He tossed a blob of sea finger into his mouth.

Having swallowed the fungus, he sat down on the sand. When thoughts rushed at him, he refused them. Tan came and sat down on his haunches beside Gregor, despite the fact that they were now within reach of the incoming tide. *It's not a bad way to die,* Gregor thought, resting his arm on the dog.

Seconds later, he keeled over into the surf.

He was relieved to find that in death there were no dreams.

Nonexistence spat him back into being like a ball of brackish phlegm. In Stavusian temples it was taught that Theostor the Six-Winged welcomed the faithful into the Eternal Realm of Air and Light, but during his short trip into the afterlife, Gregor hadn't had the pleasure. On this side of the eternal divide, however, Gregor was surprised to find his nephew Ajax manning the welcoming party.

"Uncle Bones!" Ajax's distinguished, aquiline nose framed Gregor's field of vision. Over Ajax's shoulder, the setting, blood-letting sun smeared Dunning Harbor's gray sky underbelly. "You're alive. Stavus save us, I thought…we thought…"

Gregor pushed up on saltwater-soaked elbows to see that the we in question meant Ajax, Greta, the two greyhounds, and a dozen knights dressed in the double sun. Somehow the lot of them had found him in sufficient time to drag him from the encroaching surf.

"It was the dog, was it? That brought you to me?"

"It was. We wouldn't have thought to come here otherwise. The citizens of Dunning Harbor won't set foot on the shore so long as the sea fingers—"

Gregor's disturbed expression made Ajax stop talking. Gregor hadn't noticed it upon first reviving, but now, making use of the day's last light, he realized that he could see his nephew's skull, pressing up against Ajax's strangely translucent skin.

"What is it, Uncle? Why are you staring at me like that?"

Gregor put his head in his hands. Collected himself. Hoped against hope that when he looked anew at his nephew's face, he would see only flesh. But when he lifted his head, the sight of Ajax Dayborn remained the same: he was a talking skull.

Shit. I should have stayed dead.

It was the sea fingers. That was the only explanation. Instead of doing him a favor and ending his overburdened life, the fungi had cursed Gregor with the ability to see people's skulls.

Greta's voice entered the conversation. "Are you okay?" she asked, drawing beside her bonded. Gregor averted his eyes, having no desire to see her skull, too, but found that he could stop himself for only a moment.

To his great relief, Greta was unchanged. Hers was a full moon face, highlighted by cherry-blossom cheeks and eyes like a cold blue sky. No sign of the skull beneath.

"I—" he stopped, letting his eyes make the short trip between Ajax and Greta over and over again, finding, each time, that the only skull he could see belonged to his nephew. Finally, he managed a few words. "I don't feel well."

"What happened?" Ajax asked, casting a suspicious look at the sea fingers.

Gregor tried to meet his nephew's eye, but the sight of Ajax's skull made Gregor nauseous. "Nothing." He changed the subject. "I…I failed your father. I—"

Greta took him by the arm. Bade him rise to his feet. "Not here, Uncle Bones. Come, let us return to Saltbend. Anything that needs to be said will be better expressed in a warm room with dry clothes."

The last of the day's light expired on the return trip to the castle. Gregor thought it a blessing; he could no longer see the bony interior of Ajax's face. The three of them walked in silence, flanked by the Dayborn soldiers and the two prancing dogs.

Dunning Harbor looked different at night. Some of its harshness softened in the darkness, and was made softer still by candles and torches flickering to life. As distracted as Gregor was by the strange developments coinciding with his resurrection, he could not help but be taken in by the changing tableau, a city brought to life by the changeover to night. One of the buildings in particular caught his attention. It rose into the air like a tapering circle, and listed to one side, despite its oversized foundation.

It was a unique-looking establishment, but not so unique that it warranted Gregor's level of distraction.

Why does it bother me so?

Gregor pointed at the building. "What place is that?" he asked all who could hear.

One of the soldiers replied. "It's an inn, Revered Sagekind. I believe it's called The Sea Swoon."

Distant bells rang in Gregor's mind, but, try as he might, he could make no sense of the chimes.

Back at Saltbend, the Great Hall was alive with the sights and sounds of the evening meal. Ajax went directly inside to report to his father. Greta tried to usher Gregor past the Hall. He intended to heed her, but, catching sight of those inside the Hall, Gregor stopped cold. By the light of a roaring fire, Gregor saw that a good portion of those partaking of the feast wore their skulls the same as Ajax, like macabre shadows peering out from inside their skin. It was a horror to witness, but also a mystery, because there were many others in the room who looked the same as always: with faces full of flesh, no sign of the skull beneath.

"Come, Uncle Bones. Don't tarry here. I'll speak to the kitchen; they'll bring a nice roasted duck with crushed ilkberry glaze to your room."

Gregor pulled away from Greta and stepped into the Hall. The clanging of pewter cups and plates quieted as he neared the back benches. Stares turned into whispers as men identified the hated Wraith in Red, sea-soaked beige robe notwithstanding. Gregor was an expert at ignoring such stares, and usually chose not to return them, but tonight, he found himself staring back whenever the firelight formed a skull. *Why do I see the skulls of some, and not others?* he thought.

The answer came to him unbidden. *No,* he told himself, *that's fearful speculation.* All the same a pit formed in his stomach that felt like truth. He looked to the head table, searching for his brother, the head of the Dayborn dynasty. Micah was sitting where Gregor expected him, but, in the gloom of the hall, Gregor couldn't see his face clearly enough to make out a skull. Gregor started to approach the table, needing to know, but before he had taken two steps, he felt a presence behind him so strong that he turned around out of instinct.

A giant of a man was standing there. Beside the giant was a plain-faced, tough-looking woman. Greta stood a little behind the both of them, uncertain what to do.

Gregor had never seen the man before, but he knew immediately who he was. Gregor had a mental list of hundreds of people in the kingdom that he had never met but whom he hoped, based on intelligence gathering, to be able to identify by sight. Gregor had rightly assumed that Madrig, Daguss Salk's mute warrior-cousin, would be among the easiest on the list to peg. The man looked like a legendary Ontish warrior of old: big and strong enough to blast through other men, but possessive of an indefinable quality that made it clear he was no mere brute. Only the scar on his cheek was new.

And if Gregor was right about Madrig, then he knew who the woman was too. Jacy: Madrig's common lover, and a fierce fighter to boot. Back at Coffyn Castle, Deglan had reported to Gregor the gossip circulating among the Ontish: that after the victory over the Blackstar Islanders, Madrig had been given permission by his cousin to bond his beloved, and together they had taken off on a sweetmarch to visit the Yubriy tree.

It appeared they had returned.

From the look on Madrig's face, he likewise had recognized Gregor. Gregor watched as the big man studied him with soft, discerning eyes. Staring back, it at last dawned on Gregor that he couldn't see the big man's skull. With a nod devoid of the hatred—though not entirely devoid of the suspicion—that oft accompanied a northman's gaze, Madrig and Jacy stepped past Gregor and walked toward the nobility seated at the front of the hall.

A raucous cheering erupted as the many Ontish in the room rose to meet Madrig. Gregor's already blocked view of the king and queen was lost in the ensuing commotion.

"Come, Uncle Bones. Come," Greta insisted, grabbing Gregor from behind. "There will be time later to make things right."

Gregor permitted Greta to take him by the arm. Together they wound their way back through the castle, toward the Dayborn quarters in the Burnt Tower. While they walked, Gregor's mind itched, aggravated by the skulls and the strange building he had seen in the city—that tapering, lopsided inn.

"Tell me, Uncle Bones? Which dog is Daguss, do you think? And which is Ropske?"

Gregor turned to find that the two greyhounds were following close behind. "I don't know," he answered truthfully. Then he asked Greta a question in turn, one that had haunted him his entire life. "Must all pairs be compared to the Ontish twins?"

"I think so," she replied, with a touch of humor. "Yes."

Despite the trying nature of the day, Gregor loved Greta for that. He stopped in the middle of the hall and turned and stared at the dogs, who stared back at him with a frank directness. While on the Delilah herb, he had been privy to a vision about the two hounds, one that suggested that they were linked to the Twins. He decided the simplest thing to do was to ask them.

"Which of you is Daguss, son of Beoliotius?"

Neither dog moved a muscle.

"Which of you is Ropske?" he tried.

Again, no movement.

He tried a different tack. He kneeled down in the middle of the torchlit corridor, and softly explained to the dogs the story of their land of origin. "You were born in Ragar Or, which translates from Old Ontish as *Land of Twins*. It is said that all twins born in Ragar Or take on the characteristics of one of the two Ontish brothers who helped create and populate this land. From the line of Daguss sprang the Ont tribe, from the line of Ropske the Coros. The Onts eventually defeated and subsumed the Coros, ending their line, but it is said that every time twins are born, the Corosian line is born anew." He looked at the dogs closely. "Were you not brothers born at the same time?"

The tan hound with the chest plate of white—the one who had saved him—gave a short bark.

Greta laughed, which caused Gregor to laugh a little in turn. Talking to the dogs was a silly bit of business, Gregor knew, but, now that he had started, he found that he could not help himself. His absurdity merely matched the absurdity of the world that he lived in.

"Then I ask once more. Which of you is Daguss, and which is Ropske?"

The black greyhound stepped forward. Naturally, Gregor stuck out his hand and rubbed Black on his back. When he made contact with the dog's fur, the vision-dream he had had back in Low Osgood exploded in his mind's eye.

"RETURN FROM THE FAINTING SEA, THAT WHICH WAS STOLEN FROM ME!"

The sight of the long and lean king startled Gregor. Gregor's thoughts, tempest-tossed, struggled to steady, until at last they found their balance on a dawning realization.

The fainting sea.

The Sea Swoon.

He turned to Greta, who, realizing that something was amiss, stared at him in alarm. Gregor told her the simplest truth that he could think of.

"The black one, I believe, is Ropske."

He sent Greta and the dogs away, and took his meal alone. The duck and the ilkberry glaze were cooked to perfection, but he tasted little of it. When the meal was finished, he spent the next few hours sitting on the edge of his bed, contemplating the vision and considering how his visit to the Sea Swoon might go on the morrow.

But the longer he sat, the more he felt compelled to go the inn now.

Sometime after midnight, he heeded the impulse.

The night guard at the barbican gave Gregor a strange look when he requested that the gate be opened, but acquiesced all the same. Moments later, Gregor was back on the main road leading from Saltbend Castle. Footpaths branched off the main road like a tangle of vines. Gregor, supposing one was as good as the other, left the main road and started down an incline, keeping one eye fixed on the listing, serpent-curled building filling up the near horizon.

He could feel his heart beating in his throat. All things considered, Gregor thought of himself as a man who didn't faze easily. But the day had taken a toll. What was most unnerving of all was Gregor's intuition that the day's most extraordinary event still lay ahead of him. He had too much experience to be exhilarated by the notion, and felt instead the way he so often did as the Sagekind: like he was the plaything of a cunning deity, and was being driven to actions by motivations he didn't entirely understand.

The footpath Gregor had chosen connected to the road that the Sea Swoon was on. Gregor, dressed once more in a clean cloak of red, did his best to avoid the sinister-looking shadows prowling the nighttime streets, and was more or less successful. Only once was he forced to resort to snatching the breath from the windpipe of a man who looked like he intended to do Gregor harm. Ten minutes after leaving Saltbend, Gregor found himself in front of the Sea Swoon, trying to reconcile the strange establishment in front of him with the dream-vision's command. The sense of certainty he had felt when he touched Black the greyhound was no longer there.

I suppose the only thing left to do is go inside.

Gregor opened the door to mayhem. Sprawled on the floor—and clutching what appeared to be a tiny book—was a sizable chunk of a man, who smelled, even at a distance, like he had bathed in mead. On the opposite side of the room, behind a crescent-shaped bar, a strawberry-blonde-haired woman was screaming hysterically, wielding her panic like a weapon. Standing close to the bar, a handsome fellow of middling height wore an expression on his face that suggested he wanted no part of what was taking place. And last but not least, standing closest to Gregor, was a man with ropes of silver-brown hair hanging off his head. This particular fellow held a dagger in his hand, as if attempting to underpin his already scuzzy appearance.

To a person, they all turned and looked at Gregor. The woman continued screaming. Gregor processed what she was saying on a slight delay.

"He's a woodkin! A damned Corosian-cursed woodkin! Help us! Help!"

For a brief moment, Gregor thought the woman was calling *him* a woodkin; the word had jeyedoshi overtones, after all, and Gregor had more than once heard the word used in connection to his name. But the woman's screams were complemented by a pointing finger, the direction of which singled out the short, ragged-haired man holding the dagger.

Gregor decided that regardless of the woman's claims, it made sense to disarm the person wielding the weapon first. He turned to do just that—while assessing the elements in the room that might aid him in his cause; there was a fire in the hearth, and, as always, there was the option of the wind traveling in and out of his adversary's throat—but before he could determine a choice of action, the short little man sheathed his dagger flash-quick, and, in the same motion, transformed his posture into a bow.

"A thousand pardons, Revered Sagekind. There was going to be a gutting, but, now that you're here, I don't believe it will be necessary."

The little man's nonchalant panache took Gregor aback. The others, stupefied into silence, struggled to acknowledge Gregor's identity.

"The Sagekind?" the woman behind the bar at last spat out. She wore a look of frightened distaste on her face. "You're…the king's bastard half brother?"

"I am." Gregor rotated his head on a swivel, trying, by means of studying the scene, to ascertain why the vision had brought him here. His eyes caught on the fellow on the floor…and more specifically, on the book in his hand. "What is that you're holding?"

The drunk struggled to his feet. All the while he kept hold of the book with a viselike grip. There was a fearful and confused look on his face. Gregor was suddenly struck by the strange notion that the young man might stuff the book into his mouth and swallow it.

"Show it to me," Gregor demanded, advancing on the man. In response the fellow transferred the book to his left hand, nearly lost his footing on a slick of mead, righted himself, and put his right hand up in the universal sign for stop. Gregor immediately noticed the raised glyphs on the underside of the young man's fingers. "You're a Gorgostrine?" Gregor asked, unable to hide his surprise.

"Yes, your high…yes…Revered Sagekind." The young man's eyes were afire with fright. "The name's Boryl. You must believe me when I tell you that the man behind you is a woodkin. And my *pensta* charged me with protecting this book from all Corosian-cursed kind."

Gregor knew what a Gorgostrine's glyphs were for, but he had never heard of them being used for their intended purpose. "You grabbed hold of him, then? With the glyphs? And he showed you his true nature?"

Boryl nodded.

Gregor turned to get a better look at the accused. Gregor had long speculated that woodkin legends had some basis in fact, but he hadn't expected today to be the day he was forced to make a definitive judgment.

The short fellow took Gregor's penetrating stare in stride. Before responding, he donned a roguish smile. "I'm no woodkin, Revered Sagekind. The name's Wyn Dunkin. A mere musician, am I. A fiddler, to be exact. My friend here is a lutist." He motioned at the handsome man standing near the bar. "Together, we have traveled north in search of the queen. We've written a song for her."

Gregor startled. "A lutist," he stated, trying to keep from looking flabbergasted. *This is why I was sent here.* "Yes. Of course. I would like to hear the song. The two of you—"

The door to the Sea Swoon banged open, interrupting Gregor. Three men entered the Sea Swoon with violent aplomb, looking like death incarnate. Gregor could see their skulls as plain as day beneath their skin. Eager steel swords graced their hips. Gregor's first thought was that they meant to massacre every person in the room. But then one of the men spotted Gregor, and the violence went out of him as his face twisted up in confusion and fear.

"What…are you doing here?"

Gregor recognized him. He recognized all three of them, in fact. He didn't know their names, only that he had seen them traveling with the other soldiers. Salk men—he was almost certain of it. But they weren't wearing Salk colors; instead, they were dressed in rough tunics that made them look like Dunning Harbor locals.

"I'm the Sagekind. I go where I please. But you already knew that. The more pressing question is: who are the three of you, and why are you here?"

The tallest of the three, who had a lumpy head, caught sight of something on the opposite side of the room that compelled his interest. He elbowed his two companions, drawing their attentions to the same. The tenor in the room changed. Lumpy Head gave a *screw-you* glance at Gregor, and then began walking along the outer edge of the room, in the direction of the handsome fellow standing close to the bar. Lumpy Head's hand went to the pommel of his sword as he walked, and the violence returned to his eyes.

"I'm here because a man in this room needs to die," Lumpy Head snarled.

"No!" Gregor commanded, realizing that Lumpy Head intended to kill the handsome man. But Lumpy Head had already started his charge and was pulling the sword from its scabbard.

292

Gregor reached for the hearth flame. The room went dark as he redirected the soul of the fire into the corporeal entity that was Lumpy Head. In response, Lumpy Head let out a terrible scream and dropped to his knees. Gregor held him there, burning him alive. Around Gregor, the world erupted in shouts. One flew at him like an arrow: "Watch out!"

A body slammed into Gregor. He tumbled to the floor. He lost hold of the flame as he fell, the fire slipping from his mind like a fleeting thought. And then a man was atop him—or rather, a skull. The skull screamed profanities and rained fists from above, ceaselessly, unendingly. Gregor, forgetting what it was to be a jeyedoshi, simply tried to survive, putting up his arms to deflect the blows. He couldn't focus to reach for the elements, not with fists raining down upon him and invective spewing from the skull's mouth.

"Death to abominations! Death to the jeyedoshi! All glory to the Twin Ascendant! All glory to D—"

A dagger cored the man's throat. Blood-rain displaced the fists. The visceral awfulness of it brought Gregor back into his body. He pushed the newly made corpse off him.

It was Wyn who had saved him. But now the little man was in danger of his own: the dagger Wyn had used to kill Gregor's attacker was lodged in the victim's spinal cord, and Wyn was having difficulty freeing it. Facing a rear attack from the third skull, Wyn surrendered his weapon to the corpse and dodged away, distancing himself from swinging steel.

Gregor came to his aid. Refocusing once more on the flame, Gregor drew the terrible heat from its heart and sent it slamming into the third skull, whose fiery screams filled the air. Wyn, seeing his pursuer succumb, reversed his retreat and wrenched the sword from the skull's steaming hand. A second later, Wyn speared the man through his chest cavity, causing the man to slump dead to the floor.

Lumpy Head.

Gregor whirled around, only to find that the world had reconfigured itself in his absence. On the opposite side of the bar, Lumpy Head was suffering a brutal beating; Boryl and the handsome fellow of middling height had teamed up and were pummeling Lumpy Head with bar chairs. *They must have ganged up on him when he was incapacitated.* Gregor thought for sure that they would stop after Lumpy Head grew senseless, but instead Boryl brought his bar chair down with such thunderous force that it resulted in a skull-breaking, life-ending *crack.*

Boryl's labored breathing was the only sound in the dirty silence that ensued. The interim ended quick: in a fit of post-homicidal rage, Boryl's ragged breaths transformed into a fitful screaming as he attempted to use up his excess store of adrenaline. Wyn used the opportunity to work his dagger free from the corpse. Gregor, trying to get his wits, noticed a detail that he had missed earlier: a gorgeous rosewood lute rested against a chair close to where the handsome fellow was standing.

The lute was what grabbed Lumpy Head's attention, Gregor realized.

"Did you have designs on the reading material, Sagekind?" Wyn asked Gregor the instant Boryl stopped screaming, nodding at the book the young Gorgostrine had laid on a table. "Because if not, I mean to make it mine."

"You'll touch that book over my dead body, woodkin!" Boryl shouted, snatching the book back up. Based on the unhinged quality of his emotions, Gregor guessed it was the young Gorgostrine's first time killing a man. From the fury in his face, he appeared primed to have a go at killing his second.

The woman moved out from behind the bar. "Listen to my nephew!" she shouted, appealing to Gregor. "If you are a true servant of your half brother king, you will use your…your…"

Gregor knew why she hadn't finished the sentence. He decided to finish it for her.

"My what? My powers?"

Wyn was the only person in the room to respond, delivering a short and choppy laugh. Gregor, angry at the man's insufferable insouciance, turned on him, and, in an attempt to establish a pecking order of power, tried to steal the air from his throat. But when he reached for it, something blocked him. Something natural and hard, like the barkskin of a beech tree. Stunned, Gregor looked at the little man, who returned his look with an impish smile and brought a playful *keep quiet* finger to his lips.

"The rumors are true, then. We all saw it. You *are* a jeyedoshi," the woman said, facing down Gregor, her voice eerily calm. "And that makes you a friend to this fiend, doesn't it?" She turned to her nephew. "This man is more a danger to us than the Corosian-cursed woodkin. Keep the book from them both."

Gregor knew there was no point in denying his jeyedoshi nature. He could not refute what everyone had seen. Plus, as was now unnervingly clear, he couldn't touch Wyn even if he wanted to. The man was immune to his jeyedoshi powers.

"I would not harm a man who only seconds ago saved my life," Gregor lied, nodding at Wyn, who nodded back like a player in a scene.

"But I *will* have a look at that book." Gregor tried to sound like he'd arrived at the decision by choice, and not by default. He advanced on the hulking young Gorgostrine with a hand extended. If there was one thing Gregor knew, it was how to project a natural authority, whether in front of friend or foe. He tried to make it clear to the Gorgostrine that his ultimate designation would depend upon how readily the young man gave up the book.

"I can't... I won't... I promised my *pensta*..." Boryl protested, his breath reeking of alcohol. For a second there was a fire in his eyes, and Gregor thought he was going to put up a fight, but in the next Boryl surrendered the book, opting not to run the risk of meeting the same fate as the half-charred corpses in the room. The woman sighed loudly when Boryl handed the book over, but said nothing.

From the look and feel of the book, it wasn't terribly old. A half-century at most, which was nothing compared to the works Gregor had studied at the Tomes in White Walls; there were books there that preceded Union, more than two and a half centuries past. This particular book's cover was made of orphan wood from the kurmenhi tree, a rare and highly prized wood found solely on the peninsulas. *This is expensive material,* Gregor thought, but at the same time the cover looked unfinished, painted in blue but with none of the ornamentation often found on works of a similar design. There was no title.

He opened the book, and found to his surprise that it was only four pages long. He began reading. Old Ontish tumbled across the page. The first sentence made an incredible claim.

THIS IS AN ACCOUNT OF THE EVENTS SURROUNDING THE APPEARANCE OF THE DRAGON KNOWN AS THE ICE

GHOST, WHO LANDED IN KALANDRAGOTE IN THE YEAR 174, BY GREFFEN OLLSPAER, KING OF KALANDRAGOTE, WRITTEN IN THE YEAR 209.

The preposterousness of it made Gregor laugh. King Greffen was the father of Horos Ollspaer, the current Kalandragote king. Greffen had died in 209, the year the story claimed to have been written. "Who did you say you got this from? Your uncle?"

Boryl nodded.

"Do you know what it claims?"

Boryl gave a shorter, less certain nod. "It claims to be written by an old Kalandragote king. King Greffen Ollspaer. Or so I've been told. I can't read Old Ontish."

The woman, standing nearby, chimed in, "My deceased bonded was a pious man who worshipped the Twin Ascendant above all else. He was given that book when we were first bonded and charged with keeping it safe from all Corosian-cursed kind."

"Who gave it to him?"

The woman screwed up her face in a scowl. She knew that she shouldn't answer a jeyedoshi, but the temptation to talk about the details of her life to a man such as Gregor was too tempting. Gregor noticed for the first time the unnatural gleam in her left eye. *Glass,* he realized.

"A fellow Gorgostrine. One come down from the peninsula. Died soon after he arrived. Whatever he told my bonded about the book, my bonded believed. But my bonded did not share that information with me or my nephew."

Her words rang true. Whoever this Gorgostrine had been, it was clear that he believed the book was authentic. Of course, that didn't mean it was. Gregor knew well the many fallacies pious people were capable of convincing themselves of, especially the ragged, uneducated, and often self-anointed priests of the Twins otherwise known as Gorgostrines. Odds were this was a case of religious nuttery got out of hand, the book being on par with the many sham religious relics that proliferated throughout Ragar Or. If King Greffen Ollspaer had truly written it, it wouldn't be in this young man's possession. It was that simple.

But then Gregor remembered his vision. RETURN FROM THE FAINTING SEA, THAT WHICH WAS STOLEN FROM ME. Before he dismissed the book out of hand, he needed to return to the castle and study it. *But not tonight. Tonight, I need to return to Saltbend and ensure there isn't a conspiracy against the king in progress. Those were Salk men who tried to kill the lutist. I need to get to the bottom of what's going on, before events take on a life of their own.*

The room grew quiet. Gregor was so distracted by his thoughts that he had almost forgotten the others in the room. But then, like a songbird calling him down a forest path, the spellbinding sound of a lute drew his attention.

The handsome man was playing. Gregor looked up, and, within a moment, remembered the real reason that he had been brought here. The songsmith's fingers weaved magic, calling forth from the ether a music that hinted at the divine, the lute the medium straddling the two realms. Gregor was spellbound. Moments later, Wyn joined in with a fiddle, and the song soared to new heights. When the handsome man started singing, Gregor knew beyond a shadow of a doubt that this was the lutist the Yubriy leaf had told him to find.

The song collapsed in a gorgeous hush. The lutist's fingers lingered on the strings before he dropped them in time to his eyes rising, where they met Gregor's own. As the song's spell faded, Gregor once again became aware of the weight of the book in his hand, and the pull of its mystery. He held them both there, the lutist and the book, mystified by their ultimate import.

Johanna Salk

Johanna woke with the sun the morning after Thacker's death. She sat up on the velvety patch of moss upon which she had slept and admired the reach of the morning star's rays, the way they ran through the trees like the strings of a celestial instrument. Her dreams had been predictably dark and full of death, but the sunrise was helping her to forget them. Within minutes the sounds were fading too, those yips and howls that had earmarked both the butchery of the previous evening *and* the dreamscape of the night. But now, at last, they were dissipating.

Easton slept nearby with his sword close to his side, bloodstains on the scabbard. The three-day beard on him looked like a muskrat's pelt, wild and coarse. *He looks nothing like a prince,* she thought approvingly. *He looks…northern.* She wondered if this was indeed true or if she was simply reimagining him in a fashion more suited to her tastes. With his eyes closed, her thoughts went in a wayward direction: for a moment she saw the deceased body of her formerly bonded in Easton's place. Nicholas Raleigh. The man she might have loved, had he been a different man entirely.

And what of this man? Could you love him?

Easton opened his eyes while Johanna was pondering her answer. The red in his cheeks bloomed when he saw her staring at him, which was a surprise: she hadn't imagined him capable of embarrassment. *He's embarrassed to find me awake first,* she thought. *He feels like he should have been on watch.* When he began repositioning the lower half of his body, however, she realized that wasn't it at all. An impulsive glance at his breeches confirmed it. Then her own cheeks were blushing red, and she was turning away while he was turning away, while at the same time an unexpected pressure built in her chest, a pressure that burst into a laugh.

"I'm sorry," she said. But then she laughed again, in spite of herself. She wasn't laughing at him...or it...she was merely laughing at the awkwardness of the moment. But she feared a prince with a fragile ego wouldn't see it that way. When she risked a glance at him, however, she found to her relief that while his cheeks were no less red, there was a smile on his face.

"Apologies, my lady. I like to sleep past daybreak, but parts of me insist on rising with the sun."

A lock of dark brown hair fell over Johanna's forehead, which she swept away. "You have a good humor. It makes it difficult...not to like you."

Easton rose to a sitting position. The trauma of yesterday's events was still writ on his face, but so was the morning sun, and the kiss they had shared. "It's all a bit absurd, isn't it? Life?" He asked the question rhetorically. "If given my druthers, I'd rather smile my way through it."

"You cried yesterday." She didn't say it meanly, nor did she intend it that way.

He nodded. In his dirty orange cloak, he looked like the bastard son of the sun, sitting at the feet of his father. "It's not an easy thing, slitting a man's throat."

"That was your first time?" she tendered. "Ending a man's life?"

Easton gave a barely perceptible nod. "I'm trained for combat. Highly trained. And I know, in my heart of hearts, that when the need arises, I will make a good show of myself. Like yesterday. I don't mind a bit of rough-and-tumble. In fact, I relish it. But there is a difference between the art of combat, and the end result." He looked into the middle distance. "Yesterday was naught but the aftermath. But I did what had to be done. Difficult as it was."

Not knowing what to say, she ceded her response to birdsong. After a bit, she gestured at his left arm. "May I look at your wound?"

He rolled up his sleeve and offered it for her inspection. The pennywolf's bite wasn't deep—Easton's quick swordplay had seen to that—but there was no such thing as a harmless wolf bite. Yesterday, while Easton had been busy digging Thacker's grave, she had gone to work breaking down the products she had taken from the innkeep's cellar back in Doakmont, both the brayosk bark and the edgeplant rhizome. The ground brayosk—bits of poisonous bark included—was now in the glass vial. The ground rhizome she had used to treat Easton, coating the wound for the purposes of staving off a possible infection. The remainder she had stored in a makeshift leaf pouch. From the look of things, the plant was doing its job.

"I should coat the wound again. Do you mind?"

Easton shook his head.

She had enough remaining grind to cover the wound one more time. When she was done, they both appraised her work instead of meeting each other's eyes.

"Thank you," he said. "I can tell that it's helping."

"It is," she responded. She paused. "I've been interested in plants since I was young. In the wonders a person can work with them." Another pause. "The horrors too."

Easton started to say something, then thought better of it. Johanna wondered if his unspoken words were related to the conditions under which they had met, the poison she had prevented him from drinking. She rarely talked about her fascination with plants with anyone, for the obvious reasons. The depth of her interest had always felt a little unnatural, even to her. If she weren't a twin, she might have thought her affinity with the plant world a gift. But instead, it snagged like yet another jeyedoshi hook in the back of her mind.

Bitterboy, tied to a nearby tree, snorted. Easton laughed at the horse. "Someone is ready to get on with the day." He stood up from the ground, brushed off his breeches, and offered Johanna a hand. "Shall we?"

She allowed him to pull her to her feet. For a split second it seemed that he might continue with the motion and pull her into an embrace, but instead he released her at the critical moment, with a small distance still between them.

The terrain changed. The Edgeling Mountains came back into view, but the peaks looked sharper, like the jutting jaw of a carnivorous animal. With the mountains in view, Johanna and Easton headed due west, into a wild and noncontiguous landscape. The open spaces were increasingly broken by rugged patches of wood that had long ago abandoned the idea of forming into proper forests. Here and there the hand of man was present: daub-and-wattle houses popped up like toadstools, and occasionally, on the outskirts of the forests, Johanna spotted ramshackle wooden structures, the lean-tos of society-spurning isolates. But the manmade sights were few and far between.

As they rode, they scanned the sky. But no dragon wings filled the horizon.

The weather was unseasonably warm. Winter, which had seemed to be sinking its fangs into Ragar Or only a couple of days past, appeared to have retreated entirely, giving way to temperatures more customary for mid-fall. Easton had procured wolfskins for them back in Doakmont, but Johanna had only felt the need of them at night. The change in the temperature made it seem like that by traveling west, they were traveling backward in time.

Johanna knew better, of course. In her mind's eye she could see the maps the Wandering Tongue had made her study during childhood. They were in a low-population pocket, but to the south was the Yur Road, which led west toward Qorl and Cordova, while to the north the Edgeling Mountains formed a tapering fortress safeguarding the Blacktyde Sea. As wild and lonely as the land surrounding them was, they were still hemmed in by a very distinct geography.

"Have you been this far west before?" she asked.

Easton nodded while caressing the palfrey's mane. It had taken them some time to find the horse after it bolted the day before. Johanna liked the way Easton looked after the horse, and the way he refused to resent it for not being the equivalent of her own mount.

"I journeyed to Oseiy with my mother when I was an adolescent. We made a tour of the southern cities."

"What were your impressions?"

"Of Oseiy?"

She shrugged. "Sure. Of Oseiy. Or of any of the southern cities."

"I didn't take to Oseiy. It was like a city stillborn. Being that close to the Provish Want…I remember feeling wild with wanderlust, the burning desire to leave. I wasn't the horse thief then that I am now, but believe me, I was tempted." He paused. "Wrain, I loved."

"Naturally."

He gave a wide grin. "I was a boy. Wrain was a big and boisterous city. Living in Union, I thought no city in Ragar Or was the capital's equal. But when I saw all those ships in Winsham Harbor and heard the languages being spoken in the Wrainish streets…I'm not lying when I tell you that I gave serious thought to boarding a ship and becoming a stowaway."

"I can envision you as a pirate."

Easton laughed. "My mother still believes that I'm destined to become one. She used to say to my father, 'This one will end up working the galley oars of a Thralk-Brakturan man-of-war, royal lineage be damned.' She doesn't say it as often these days, but that's only because she's even more worried that it will turn true."

His mother. The queen. Before Low Osgood, Johanna had little conception of what the Dayborn family was like. They existed in that odd headspace nobles reserved for each other: powerful people best imagined in the most dangerous light. But hearing Easton reframed her image of them. Now when she called to mind her memory of Queen Anjay standing in the snow in the cherry tree garden at Coffyn Castle, Johanna saw her differently: behind that imperious and upturned chin was a worried mother, concerned for the safety of her impulsive youngest son.

An arrow of a question came to Johanna. Before caution stopped her, she notched and let it fly. "What if your brother died? Could you tame your wanderlust then? Become the sort of son a father might entrust with a kingdom?"

She thought her question would catch him off guard, but his reply was whip-quick. "Are you suggesting that a king is only king if he sits on his ass? If anything happened to my brother, Stavus forbid it, I would be a traveling monarch, in the vein of Brogan I, or Daguss II. Not that they were the only monarchs to take to the road. Your namesake traveled quite extensively in the early years of her reign, if I recall correctly."

Johanna Salk I. The mention of the woman who had once been the queen of all Ragar Or made Johanna feel queasy. As a child, Johanna had read of Queen Johanna's rule with a nauseous thrill. The early years of Queen Johanna's reign had been uneasy ones: she had inherited the throne from her childless uncle, Daguss II, the monarch who had infamously wrested the seat away from his twin brother Baron Salk by claiming, after their father Theron Redd's death, that he, and not his brother, was the true Twin Ascendant. (Johanna herself was a direct descendant of Baron Salk's eldest son.) Like her uncle before her, Queen Johanna traveled the realm extensively to shore up support, although she wasn't averse to using the sword when fealty couldn't be guaranteed with words. During her reign, she had famously survived an assassination attempt from an Ontish family whose line no longer existed, for the obvious reasons.

"You are saying that you would rule, then? If the crown fell to you?"

Easton twisted his lips into an impish knot. "If my heart was settled, perhaps. But alas, having been spurned by my one true love, I am resigned to my fate as the wandering prince, forever destined to roam these western lands in search of a dragon."

Days ago, his barbed humor would have unsteadied her, but now she was accustomed to it. She thought of a wicked little riposte. "You have forgotten our kiss already?"

He abandoned the lovelorn pose he had struck, and turned in his saddle to look directly at her. "No. I have not."

A moment passed between them. It had an undeniable charge. But the electric current of their connection was undone by a winged shadow passing on the ground. They broke eye contact and threw their gazes to the sky, hearts beating hard. But the source of the shadow was only an eagle flying close to the sun.

After the eagle passed, they kept their eyes apart. A moment later, Easton spoke.

"Did you love him? Your former bonded?"

Johanna furrowed her brow. Was there a note of jealousy in Easton's voice? If there was, it was soft. His interest in her, however, sounded earnest.

"I dreamed that Nicholas would die," she responded, refraining from answering the question directly. "When they brought me into the room, he was lying on his back with his arms crossed on Lord Raleigh's great white oak bed, just as I had dreamed that he would be." Had she in fact dreamed of Nicholas' death? In her memories she had. But now when she thought back, it seemed entirely possible that the idea of the dream had been implanted after the fact, some trickery of the gods. "We were not a natural pairing, he and I. Everyone could see it. But I strove to make it work. As did he. And isn't that the greater part of love, in the end? The effort? The striving?"

"You would know better than I, my lady. I can only say that for myself, falling in love has not nearly been so difficult."

She chose not to scoff at him. "Is this your first time? Falling in love?"

"Yes."

"Then you have nothing to compare it to. For all you know, what you are feeling isn't even love."

Easton considered this. "It is love," he said at last. "Especially if, like you said, falling in love is a choice. Perhaps the choice was simply an easier one for me than it was for you."

She didn't respond to that.

Eventide brought with it a chorus of wolves. They turned north into the teeth of the noise.

"A forest at the foot of Halfhead Mountain," Easton pronounced, pointing at a summit that looked like an angry god had taken an axe to its top and came away with the vertical portion of its eastern face. "That's where Rooster said we would find the woods witch who coaxed the dragon from the sky."

Johanna nodded. They had made fast time, thanks to Bitterboy's driving pace. Most horses knew deep in their bones that they were prey animals, but it seemed to Johanna that Bitterboy must have descended from a lost race of predator equines, lions with hooves. The Rugarder stared ahead at the forest with fearless indifference.

The palfrey, on the other hand, was trembling.

"Let's set up camp inside the tree line," Johanna said. "Before it gets dark."

It was a hardwood forest, full of thick trees that had long been friends with Father Time. The howling wolves were somewhere inside the forest, but so was a waterfall. As they guided the horses through the trees, the melody of the rushing water drowned out the lupine sounds. Soon they found the waterfall's stream. They brought the horses to the water's edge, where they drank their sweet-cold fill. Then, as if trapped in a spell, all four of them made their way upstream, fighting the fading light, searching for the falling water.

They came upon it just as the night sky extinguished the sun. Watching the glimmering sheet of water disappear in the darkness while still being able to hear it struck Johanna like magic. High above, pinpricks of starlight needled their way through the winter branches. Sitting in silence on Bitterboy, Johanna felt alive with wonder.

But then a strangeness occurred. All at once Johanna could hear the howling wolves again. As the howling intensified, the sound of the waterfall receded. Johanna felt suddenly dizzy, and thought that she might fall from Bitterboy. "Easton," she started to say, but her calling of his name was met with the silence that follows a struck match. Or better, a bloom of flame.

Of which there was one. Standing on the crest of the hill from where the waterfall cascaded, a woman appeared holding a torch. The woman had hair like a moving river, and there was a vastness to her that reminded Johanna of the cosmos. Somehow, Johanna could tell that the woman's eyes were blue, in spite of the darkness and the distance. It was difficult to determine the woman's age.

Seconds later, Johanna noticed other eyes pinning them down.

Pennywolves up on the ridge had surrounded them in the darkness. The eyes of the wolves closest to the woman flashed in the torchlight, and in their reflection, Johanna got a sense of their manifold numbers, expanding outward into the unknowable woods.

We need to— Johanna wasn't sure how to end the thought; it was as if they were stuck in a powerful enchantment. The palfrey broke the silence with a fearful neigh. Easton interrupted the horse with a strong and booming tenor, as if attempting to claim the forest for his own. "Are you the woods witch who coaxed the dragon from the sky?"

Was the woman smiling in the darkness? Johanna could see the woman's eyes in the torchlight, as clear as cobalt, but her face was awash in shadows. "I am," the woman replied. Her voice surprised Johanna. It was cultured and clean, the sort of voice one might expect a Winged Woman to have.

"We've been looking for you. We are—"

"A child of the Salks. And a child of the Dayborns."

As unsettling as the moment was, the way the woman said the word *child* caused Johanna to bristle. "There are no children here," she responded curtly.

Was that amusement on the woman's face? The shadows made it difficult to tell.

"My home is on the other side of this hill. Follow the torchlight."

"What of the wolves?" Easton asked.

"They won't bother you," the woman replied. When the woman turned and started to walk away, Johanna watched in amazement as the wolves turned with her and dispersed into the darkness.

The dark could not hide the strangeness of the woman's house. It was a house, made not of lumber, but of living trees. Somehow, someway, the bodies of half a dozen arboreal specimens had twisted and contorted themselves to form an abode. Tree limbs jutted from the exterior walls and roof, making it difficult to ascertain exactly where the house ended and began. No matter how oddly the dwelling had been put together, the whole was clearly greater than the sum of its parts. The top of the house seemed to merge with the tree shelter above, blending in with the wooden darkness. It was a house fit for a forest queen.

The woman stood next to the stoop and waited patiently while Johanna and Easton brushed down the horses and removed their tack. Up close, the woman's age was difficult to place. Her movements were gingerly and slow, suggesting a woman of advanced age, but her face was as clear and placid as Lake Wyglass, and demanded, in its observing, that one reflect on the rare beauty that the woman must have once possessed.

With the horses settled, they followed the woman inside. Johanna's eyes immediately went to the tree-trunk walls. By the light of a crackling hearth fire, Johanna could see an assortment of animal skulls looking down on her, their bone-white remnants silent and still. As Johanna studied them, she was struck not only by the number of the skulls, but the variety. Every manner of animal skull was up on those walls, from the beasts of the forests and the fields to the birds in the air.

"The animals come to me before the moment of their death," the woman said to Johanna, tracking her gaze. "The ones that want to spend eternity on my walls."

"Whyever would they do that?"

"To be with the others," she replied, making a sweeping motion with her hand. "Many of these animals lived short, solitary lives. All of their existences were brutal, as is nature's fashion. My walls are a chance at something…more."

"And what is that?" Easton asked.

"The opportunity to see the world through my eyes."

Johanna looked. The woman's eyes were whorls. Blue and circling, spiraling, drawing Johanna in. *It's a trick,* Johanna thought, but she was too mesmerized to look away. She wasn't even sure how she was seeing what she was seeing, especially in the room's nighttime gloom, but the color and pattern of the woman's eyes were as clear to Johanna as if she were staring at them outside on a sunlit day.

Easton's voice broke the spell. "I am Easton Dayborn, son of King Micah Dayborn. This is Johanna Salk, daughter of Lord Daguss Salk of High Osgood."

"I know who you are," the woman reiterated. Johanna could still see the woman's eyes, but the effect was muted, the iris and the pupil blurred by shadows.

Easton continued, "We have sought you out because we heard it said that you called the dragon from the sky. And we want nothing more than to see this dragon up close."

The woman picked up a cast-iron poker and stirred at the coals in the fire. "And why shouldn't you see the dragon? Stare into his great face and perhaps pet him on the nose? You children of kings and queens? Who is this dragon to deny you what you want?"

"Fine questions, all," Easton replied, his voice filled with ironic levity.

The woman laughed, a gut-cleansing sound. "You're the second son? The one whose ass isn't meant to sit the Union throne?"

"That's right. These cheeks were meant for nothing greater than riding to the ends of Ragar Or in search of wondrous sights. My lady has already been granted a glimpse of the dragon, a fact that I find terribly unfair. We were hoping that you might remedy this inequity between us."

"You've seen the dragon?" the woman said, raising her eyebrows at Johanna.

"At a distance. Yes."

"But it didn't see you?"

"I don't think so."

The woman chewed on this. "You have a sibling, too, do you not? A twin, they say, one your father means to bond to a frostflower?"

Frostflower was a common euphemism for denizens of the Kalandragote city-state. "Yes," Johanna said, surprised that the news had already traveled this far. Johanna felt her sister's name begging on her lips. "Wulfess."

Once again, the woman grew quiet.

Johanna didn't like the way the woman was confirming information about the two of them without giving up anything in return. "We've given you our names. Why don't you honor us with your name?" Johanna asked, hoping to even things.

"Hilya Mifliy," the woman said in Old Ontish, a dark smile spreading on her lips.

"Fairy Palace?" Johanna translated, confused.

"Close enough."

"And what of your Struvan name?" Easton interjected. "Unless you were born in Kalandragote, you are bound to have one of those as well."

"Am I?" the woman asked. But apparently it was a rhetorical question, because she didn't wait for a reply. "Feel free to call me Shayla. Others have."

Johanna tried the woman's name out on her lips. "Shayla. Thank you for taking us in. And for hearing our request. If there is wisdom or knowledge that you would impart to us about the dragon, we would gladly hear it. And if not, we will accept that too. Simply because we are the children of kings and queens, it does not give us rights to your...expertise."

Shayla didn't respond. Instead, she turned her back on the two of them and started a tour of the room, her feet shuffling against the knotty wooden floor. While she walked, Johanna marveled once more at the dwelling. *Who built this place?* Surely it wasn't the old woman. Johanna may have spent her life living in castles, but she was still worldly enough to know that this wasn't the abode of your typical woods witch. The furniture inside the house impressed as well, both the quality and the abundance of it. An oak table that would not have been out of place in a Struvan lord's castle crowned the center of the room, and all around it were chairs that looked like they had been cut from a living tree's back.

"My expertise," Shayla said after a long delay. Now standing near a pinewood table in one of the room's corners, she picked up two candles the color of molten gold. Bringing them over to the fire, Shayla lit each one with a spill and then returned them to the table. Johanna could tell by the smell that the candles weren't tallow. Instead of the familiar animal odor, a cloying and dark scent wafted through the room, bringing to mind honey mixed with soil. Johanna searched after the smoke with her nostrils, trying to make sense of the smell.

"Yes. Your wiszzzdom." The word nearly slipped Johanna's tongue like a hare evading a snare, but at the last second Johanna caught it. *What…?* While she tried to make sense of her sudden difficulties with the language, she began to stagger, unsteady on her feet. She made a step to the left, then to the right, trying to find her balance…while Shayla moved with a heretofore unseen quickness, transporting a chair from the table to Johanna's side, and helping her to sit in it.

Johanna's head lolled back. Shadows danced at the edge of her vision.

In the near distance, Johanna heard a distinctive slumping *thump,* the sound of a body crashing to the floor.

Easton?

The woman stood before her. *Shayla. No. No. Hilya Mifliy.* The woman's blue eyes were like the swirling cosmos. Like Owoervyrn, the sky-black palace. *Fairy Palace.* Lost again. *Blue, like cobalt.* A vague recognition tugged at Johanna's consciousness, but when she tried to capture it, it slipped away.

Words floated from Shayla's lips on a cloud of curiosity. "Go to sleep, child. I know who you are. It's why I brought you here. Now go to sleep, and we will see…if you are like me."

Gregor Thorn

"The king is displeased that you have awoken him. He says that he will see you on the morrow."

Stryder, of the king's personal guard, was a skull. A simpering and sarcastic skull, shot through with enough confidence in King Micah's anger that he felt no compunction in goading Gregor.

"Tell my half brother the king that what I have to tell him is of the utmost importance. Tell my half brother that if he refuses to see me again, I will kill you where you stand and enter of my own volition." Gregor wondered, even as he spoke, if this was how Stryder the skull died: at Gregor's own hand, so that Gregor could storm the king's chambers.

Stryder closed his stupid, half-mocking jaw. The dull fear in Stryder's bone-socket eyes slowly made its way to his feet. Finally, Stryder wheeled around and reentered the king's chambers.

Gregor tried to slow his racing heart. But the escalating events of the evening would not permit it. Tonight was the night that he must save the kingdom, exhaustion and sea fingers hallucinations and a couple of killings in a Dunning Harbor inn be damned. On top of that, he had to face his brother the king for the first time after stealing the air from his lungs, and he did not know if his brother's skull would be on display when they came face-to-face. *No matter what happens, you will show no panic. Only resolve.* If his heart exploded from the stress of the evening's work, then Gregor was determined that no one would know his condition until he was dead on the ground.

"Damn that man to the Bottom Black!" Gregor heard the king from deep in the bowels of the room. A great shuffling commenced in the darkness. Stryder reemerged from the room and hurried away. Saltbend was a dark castle, but there were sconces full of flame in the hallway, with enough light that Gregor could see…

Micah Dayborn appeared in the doorway, the sheerest gauze of the flesh that formed his face barely visible over the haunting structure of his skull.

Gregor's soul wept, even as he reminded himself that he didn't know for certain what the sight of Micah's skull portended, even as he bore the weight of Micah's hate-filled stare, even as he steadied himself to explain to Micah the dark work that had to be completed before the sun came up.

The king, ever fond of wagging his finger, thrust his pointer in Gregor's face. "If you are here to make amends, the middle of the night is not the—"

"I have found the lutist. The one that the Yubriy tree predicted would arrive. He is secured in a room within this very tower. Along with a friend."

The skull that was King Micah went silent.

Out of the darkness, Queen Anjay appeared at King Micah's side.

Her skull was as visible as the king's.

Waves of nausea overran Gregor. *Please. Not the queen too.* It was all he could do to remain standing.

"The lutist has arrived!? When? How do you know that it's the one prophesied by the Yubriy tree?"

Gregor forced himself to speak. "It is he, my queen. I'm sure of it. Last night, I had a vision that I should go to an inn in the city. When I arrived, the lutist was inside, and in possession of a song that he had first written in the Vake. A song that he said he had written for you."

The queen smiled in relief. Gregor could see in Queen Anjay's macabre expression a shadow of what Sephery might have looked like lying in her grave. Another wave of grief-stricken nausea tried to take him under, but he remained upright.

"Good," King Micah said, clearly still angry at Gregor but welcoming of the news. "Come morning, we will go and see the lutist. Until then—"

"Wait, please. There is much more that needs to be discussed." Gregor steadied himself. "While I was at the inn, three men arrived, intending to kill the lutist. Salk men, I believe, dressed to look like peasants. We were forced to kill them when they tried to attack."

The king furrowed his brow. "We?"

"The lutist's friend was handy with a weapon." *The one that is supposedly a woodkin.* "And there was a man at the inn—a young Gorgostrine, believe it or not—who assisted as well."

Queen Anjay cut to the chase. "This all traces back to Daguss Salk's Gorgostrine, Betrard. Does it not? He somehow discovered that the lutist was inside the city, and, despite his assurances to you in Low Osgood, tried to murder the musicians before they found their way to us." When Gregor didn't immediately answer, the queen jumped to the obvious conclusions. "Oh, there is no sidestepping this. This is treason of the vilest sort. And it must be dealt with. Here and now."

The king snarled. "What would you have me do, woman? Accuse Lord Salk? Because it will be damn hard to call into question the Gorgostrine without impugning Daguss. Besides, there is more to this than you know—"

"Betrard must die," Anjay interrupted, remaining insistent. "And preferably in a public fashion, with his crimes exposed. He must be made an example of. Salk must learn that his pets cannot be used against us."

Gregor supposed it was time to let the king and queen know of the decision he had already made on their behalf. "Betrard is dying now, as we speak."

"What do you mean?" asked the king.

"I've had two men keeping watch on Betrard since Low Osgood. After the attack on the lutist, one of my watchers identified the corpses, and confirmed for me that Betrard was seen speaking to the three murderers earlier in the evening. Once this was done, I sent both men after Betrard, and together they stole the Gorgostrine from his sleeping place. They brought him to a room in this very tower. Inside of that room was a bottle of wine infused with gloaming green, and an empty glass. I've studied Betrard, and I know about his propensity for a drink. He wasn't there for five minutes before he opened the previously recorked bottle. He'll be dead by this time tomorrow night."

Anjay jumped in. "Who are you to make these decisions? This man's death is of no use unless he is made an example of."

"Betrard is not dead yet. And he won't be for twenty-four hours." Gregor chose his next words carefully. "Gloaming green poisoning is a terrible way to die. During the final hour, the person feels that they are burning alive from the inside. The pain breaks even the most stouthearted; no one passes before being reduced to a creature less than human. We will use this to our advantage. He will be given the option of suffering to the end, knowing the horror that awaits him, or he can choose a quick death. In front of the nobility." Gregor paused. "By Daguss Salk's sword."

Gregor expected the king to balk, but instead, Micah nodded. "Lord Salk will be happy to take the priest's head once he learns of his perfidy. He recently expressed concerns to me of the man's fealty to the cause of Union."

Gregor's mind spun. "He did?"

"Yes. Soon after we left Low Osgood."

Clever, Gregor thought. Betrard must have reported back to Daguss after Gregor's conversation with the priest in Low Osgood. Daguss, smart man that he was, had been distancing himself from Betrard ever since. *I suppose it's even possible that Lord Salk and Betrard agreed together that Betrard would take the fall. They had to have known that I would share what I knew about the Yubriy leaf with the king.*

Gregor took a deep breath. "You should not interpret Daguss confiding in you as a show of his loyalty." *Time to say what you came to say.* "I believe it's possible, if not likely, that Lord Salk and Lord Heron have been using Betrard the Gorgostrine as a go-between, and that the conspiracy to foil the Yubriy leaf prophesy consisted of both Struvan and Ontish factions." He paused, to see the king and queen's reaction. Nothing yet. "When I spoke to the lutist and his friend, they informed me that groups of armed men wearing the insignias of the feathered houses had been terrorizing the Vake. These men, which the lutist referred to as *murder birds,* razed an Inn in the Vake where the Swans were searching for musical talent, and killed nearly every soul inside. The lutist claims that the murder birds tracked them north, and that they only escaped death due to the help of Madrig the mute and his bonded Jacy."

Queen Anjay skull-haunted visage expressed disbelief. "The warrior Madrig the mute? Lord Salk's cousin?"

"Yes. When the lutist told me that Madrig and Jacy had escorted him into Dunning Harbor, my first thought was that the warrior-mute had conspired to deliver the lutist and his friend up to Lord Salk. But after hearing the story of how the lutist met Madrig and Jacy, as well as how the warrior-mute and his bonded fought to save the lutist from the murder birds, I'm hard-pressed to believe that's the case. More likely Madrig was bringing them to Lord Salk in good faith. But then Betrard got wind of it, or, worse, was told of the lutist's arrival in the city by Lord Salk—"

"—and shortly thereafter the would-be murderers arrived at the Inn." King Micah's stare turned somber. Gregor could see, even more than usual, the great kingly weight pressing down on Micah, a sight intensified by the skull sitting atop his weight-bearing shoulders. The Dayborn monarch was a man who looked half in his grave.

Gregor resolved to do everything in his power to pull the king out of it. "Micah. We must take action. Tonight. We—"

"—Who are you?"

The king's angry, interruptive question nipped at Gregor like an untrusting steed.

"A bastard half brother. Bound to serve."

"And who am I?"

Thoughts—treasonous thoughts—bandied about in Gregor's skull. *You are my brother. My full-blooded brother.* But he kept them from his lips. "King Micah of House Dayborn, the first of his name, Holy Son of the Air, the Twin Ascendant, and the Rightful Ruler of all Ragar Or."

King Micah held Gregor in his stare. Gregor could see their father Orius in his brother's eyes, questioning, as always, if Gregor could be trusted to keep the lie. "I should disown you for what you did earlier today. Proclaim you a jeyedoshi in front of all the lords and ladies of the land. Strip off your shoe. Show the world the whorl on your foot. Throw you to the Ontish wolves."

Gregor clenched his teeth. He understood his brother's anger, of course, but what frustrated him was that Micah didn't seem to understand that Gregor had stolen the air from Micah's lungs not out of disloyalty, but rather from a surfeit of it. Gregor wanted Micah to live, dammit, to triumph over the machinations of those who would remove the Dayborns from the Union Throne, and if that meant that in the heat of a discussion over how to best achieve that goal, he lashed out in anger, well…surely the king could recognize and forgive that, couldn't he?

But even as the argument flitted through his mind, Gregor lost the will for it. He had failed Micah in the most fundamental way. To be the jeyedoshi brother of the king was to swear to forever pretend to be something else. No matter that Micah could discard Gregor's jeyedoshi mask whenever it suited him; for Gregor to use his powers for purposes other than protecting the Dayborn line was to break the sacred pact that Gregor had pledged to their father to uphold, and that was a betrayal above all others.

"I would not blame you if you did. What I did today was…unforgiveable. I know that. And I will accept any punishment you choose to inflict on me. When this is over, if you want to send me into exile, or even take my life…I willingly surrender myself to your judgement." He knelt on both knees before the king, and pushed his face to the floor. "But first let me serve you. Let me strike a blow against those who would conspire against you. Here. Tonight."

A great silence fell. Gregor fought the urge to look up, and instead kept his face pressed to the floor, awaiting his brother's judgement. He ignored the pain in his knees, the urgency in his soul, the voice in his head that wanted to scream at Micah that they were wasting time that would be better spent moving against their enemies.

Submit. Stay down. Stay down. Stay down.

"Stand," Micah said at last.

When Gregor stood, his brother relaxed his skull-haunted face in a way that suggested forgiveness. "Okay. Tell me what you think we should do."

"The Heron? Against us? No, Uncle Bones. I don't believe it."

Prince Ajax was in his bedclothes. Greta too. The white of their garments gave them a pious quality. They both wore the befuddled expressions of the drowsy, having been roused from their chambers in the mid-of-night. The bonded couple, along with the king, queen, and Gregor, were standing in a room in the sprawling honeycomb that was the Burnt Tower.

Gregor resisted the urge to lose his temper. He was convinced that King Micah, despite his never expressing it, had his suspicions of Dante. But Ajax had a blind spot when it came to the Heron, a blind spot carved from the shared experience of coming of age with the eastern lord and being feted as the two dashing young heroes of the realm.

An unexpected voice weighed in. "But he *could* be against us." All eyes went to Greta, but none quicker than Ajax's, who looked at his bonded like she had betrayed him.

"No! He would not betray us! We grew up together. We—"

"—I said he *could* be against us," Greta interrupted, repeating herself. "Not that he is." She gave Ajax a soft smile that hinted at deep intimacies, a trust that allowed her, in front of family, to contradict him. "It's as we've discussed in private. They are all our friends, and our enemies. All of them." She touched him lightly on the arm. "Lord Heron too."

Gregor's heart flooded with a dawning gratitude. *The girl has been working on my behalf in private.* He continued to watch in wonder as the heat departed Ajax's face. Slowly, Ajax worked his head into a conciliatory nod. "I'll allow that it's possible, though not likely. Everything Uncle Bones has suggested is conjecture. Hearsay. And if decisions have to be made on that basis, then it's obvious that our attentions should be focused on the Ontish in our midst. Especially Lord Salk."

King Micah weighed in. "Rest assured, son. We are dealing with the Salk situation. Tonight. As for whether the Heron is plotting against us, I am not yet convinced. But I do think Gregor's suggestion that we send you and Greta back to Union is prudent. The Blackstar Rebellion is no more, and the capital needs a member of the royal line sitting the Union Throne. If something were to go wrong, the Struvans would not rally to

Lord Saylet the way they would to you. Half of my men will accompany you, as will half of the men from the great army the Heron has gathered. They will all be under your command."

Ajax flinched. "I am to assume command of Dante's men?"

Gregor butted in. "They are all Dayborn men, are they not? Ultimately?" He tried to keep the ire out of his voice. "If Dante is truly with us, he will relinquish control. He and half his men will continue north with the king, to accompany us into Kalandragote, and to dissuade the Ontish from engaging in mischief. The other half will be yours. Once you are in Union, perhaps you will be of a mind to send the better part of Dante's men to Wrain, where they can assist with the ongoing Thralk-Brakturian threat."

"Send them to the far south? That is not subtle."

"The ruling family of the realm must have the greatest say in how the realm's fighting men are used. You say that the Heron is our friend, and can be trusted?"

Ajax's expression was at odds with his answer. "Yes."

"Then he will have no objection to you commandeering his troops. Nor with any decisions you make once they are under your stead."

Ajax nodded, though his expression betrayed his uncertainty. In truth, Gregor was equally uncertain. These decisions had been difficult to agree upon. Ever since Low Osgood, discussions had been ongoing as to how large of an "honor guard" would accompany the king into Kalandragote, and how much would stay behind. Until now, there had been an unspoken understanding that the part of Dante's army that didn't proceed up the Brokebone pass would make camp near the peninsula's neck, and remain there until the king returned from Kalandragote, as a show of southern power. But now, awash in a sea of competing conspiracies, Gregor and the king were recalibrating what was best. Micah's first impulse had been to send the entire Dayborn contingent back with Ajax, and let the chips in the north fall where they may. 'I do not care to live to see the worst of your suspicions confirmed,' Micah had said to Gregor; he was willing to stake his kingship on bringing Kalandragote into the realm, come what may. In the end, Gregor had talked him into hedging their bets. They would keep enough southerners in the north to make the Ontish honest, while Ajax reclaimed the capital, and dispersed the Heron's strength.

"I will do it." Ajax sounded like he was talking to himself as much as anyone else.

"Good," answered King Micah. "When you are home, take control of the capital. You secure the south, while I secure the north. By the time I return to the capital for your brother's bonding to Johanna Salk, the realm will know without a doubt that the Dayborns have not only united the kingdom, but that they are in full control of it."

The Hour of the Jailer arrived. Looking out an arched window, Gregor could see the famed constellation reach its apex in the firmament. As Ontish legend had it, Werring, the sky-demon that had hounded Beoliotius, was trapped for eternity behind that tangle of stars. Although Gregor had little taste for either of Ragar Or's two major faiths, he knew when a prayer was too good to pass up.

Help me to trap the enemies of the king tonight, the way the Jailer once trapped Werring.

But for Gregor to trap them, they first had to come to the Burnt Tower. At the present moment, he was certain that Daguss Salk and Dante Heron were buying for time, trying to put together the night's fragmented pieces. *What I would give to only suspect one, instead of both.* If he was only suspicious of one, he could take greater risks, knowing that the Dayborns still had the backing of the other. Instead, he had to make his moves without losing sight of the greater purpose: tying the fate of the two great lords to the king.

"The Heron is here," the queen announced.

And so he was. The puissant young lord glided into the room with an entourage of one: Jakastor Weylcoin. The skulls of both men were visible, but faint. Together, the two men gave off vastly different vibes. Dante wore a mask of insouciant poise, looking, in his pristine white cloak, like the epitome of relaxed self-possession. Jakastor, on the other hand, was coiled with a dangerous energy; he moved with the menacing litheness of a predator cat prepared to pounce. *If talks go south, he's here to bring us to violent ends.* Gregor eyed the sword on Jakastor's hip with unease. He had tried a million times to convince Micah to disallow weapons in the royal presence, but his brother wouldn't hear it. Why? He trusted too fully in Gregor's capabilities.

"Your Highness," Dante began, bowing so swiftly that it almost eluded the eye. "I was surprised to receive a mid-of-night summons. Is something amiss?"

"On the contrary, Lord Dante. Something wonderful has happened."

The king's sweetwater voice held no sway on Gregor's side of the room. There Gregor was engaged in an eyeball tussle with the most dangerous sword in the kingdom. *Jakastor wonders if my jeyedoshi mind is*

327

quicker than his sword. Having seen Weylcoin's prowess with steel, Gregor wasn't as confident in the answer to that question as he would have liked to have been.

Lord Dante's pale blue eyes made a map of the room. "Wonderful! If it please the king to share the news, I would hear it."

King Micah obliged Lord Dante with a disarming pleasantness. "Of course. After the abscission of the Yubriy tree, the royal house found itself in possession of an unusual prophesy. The leaf in question claimed that a lutist would arrive from the Vake with a song for the queen. Based on our interpretation of the leaf, the lutist and his song were to serve as a talisman of sorts against any evil that might come our way." The king paused for dramatic effect. "Tonight, the lutist, and his song, have arrived."

"The lutist is safe? And in your possession?"

"He is."

Lord Dante's ribbon-thin lips formed a smile. "Good. Stavus's light shines upon us." Gregor watched as Dante, usually the essence of social ease, struggled to find a way to duly convey his joy at the news. Seeing Ajax standing in the corner of the room, the Heron marched over to him, and pulled the prince into a warm embrace. When Dante released Ajax, Gregor was surprised to see that tears were dampening Dante's face. "I know it is impolitic to say, but we Struvans walk a dangerous road in the north. To know that the Yubriy tree shines our way is a comfort."

The king cast an is-this-the-behavior-of-a-man-who-is-against-us? side-eye at Gregor. Gregor tried to impart a wait-till-he-hears-your-request look back at the king, but the expression was a difficult one to convey.

"Truer words were never spoken," King Micah responded. "The Yubriy tree shines a light, but, as you said, the road we walk is dangerous. A fact made all the clearer by the circumstances surrounding the lutist's arrival."

Through the faint veneer of the Heron's wormy lips, Gregor thought he could see the southern lord holding his tongue in his teeth. "What has taken place?"

Gregor had convinced the king to phrase his explanation in a certain way, but, to his frustration, Prince Ajax spoke. "Salk's men learned of the lutist's arrival and tried to kill him. Fortunately, the Sagekind intervened, and stopped them."

The Heron made a good show of his astonishment. "Whyever would…you don't think—?" The southern lord's eyes jumped from face to face. When they landed on Gregor's, the Sagekind could not help but answer Lord Dante's half-formed question.

"We have our theories."

The bite in Gregor's words did not go unnoticed. Gregor wanted nothing more than to go further, to mention the *murder birds* the lutist had referred to, but the king, ever wary of alienating Lord Dante, moved the conversation along.

"Theories, yes. But that's all they are. Theories. Still, decisions have to be made, even in the fog of uncertainty." The king gave an inadvertent sigh. Gregor could tell that his brother was growing weary of his kingwork. All this measured, manipulative talking…it didn't suit him. But it had to be done. Micah continued, "And I have reached an important one. Prince Ajax will return to Union posthaste. He will leave at sunrise.

And when he departs, he will take half of the men you brought north with him."

The Heron froze. He looked to Gregor like a marble statue fracturing under the pressure of an unseen force. *Crack,* Gregor hoped. But, once the calculations in Dante's racing mind were finished, the southern lord's notorious self-possession pulled through. "Of course. This is a wise decision." Gregor watched as Lord Dante forced himself to smile at Ajax. "My men are yours."

"They were already the Dayborns' men, were they not?" Gregor rejoindered.

The Heron faced him, and for a split second, all pretenses were dropped. The southern lord showed the Sagekind mean teeth. "Naturally."

King Micah refused to let the bad feelings fester. "Good. Begin the preparations tonight. There is much to be done, and quickly."

"And what of Lord Salk?" the Heron ventured. "Now that he is under suspicion, what does your Highness intend to do?"

"Those are your words, Lord Dante," the king responded. "I have not said that he is under suspicion. But tonight, the truth will out."

Before meeting with Daguss Salk, Gregor went to collect Betrard. Alone.

Of all the skulls Gregor had seen, Betrard's was the most fully formed, with only the faintest veneer of flesh. Even so, the Gorgostrine's limpid visage transformed into a rictus of horror when Gregor informed him that he had drunk from a bottle poisoned with the gloaming green. "Bad way to go," he admitted after a few moments. When at last his expression unfroze, he made a study of Gregor. "I suppose there's a chance you're lying, to scare me?"

"I am not. For your crimes, for what you and I both know that you've done, you must die. The gloaming green assures that. But every choice you make from this moment on will determine if you're left to suffer to the gloaming green's end, or if you are granted a quicker, more dignified release."

Betrard made a sound that was half chortle, half harrumph. His expression returned to its natural resting state of sharp edges. "Werring take you, jeyedoshi. No…Werring fuck you. If you think that I would betray my beliefs to save myself a few hours of suffering…" Betrard trailed off, keeping his face hard. But Gregor could see the tremble in his hands, in spite of how tightly he gripped them together.

Gregor moved closer to Betrard, swallowing him up in a dark shadow. "If you choose to go the way of the gloaming green, understand that we will make a show of it. We will tie you to a stake in the castle's courtyard. We will gather every noble present. We will read aloud a list of your crimes. Then I will sentence you to a trial by Theostor's tears."

Betrard's skull jerked. "What? You would drown me?"

"No. You misunderstand. I'll merely sprinkle a few drops of the *holy water* on you. For show. The crowd will draw its own conclusions as to your guilt when you begin to suffer from the gloaming green. No matter how strong you think you are, by the end you'll say anything to end your suffering. Who knows what I might coax from your lips?"

"Before the suffering starts, I'll tell everyone that I've been poisoned. I will let them know that it's nothing to do with the tears. I'll—"

"It won't matter. When a man is dying, those are the sounds and the images that stick."

The skull ground its teeth together. "What do you want, jeyedoshi?"

"Answers. For myself. A path forward for everyone else."

"What do _you_ think a path forward looks like?"

"Daguss Salk takes your head and proclaims his loyalty to the king."

Betrard gave another bull snort, but at the same time he lifted his head and looked at Gregor. "Fine. If it please you." He continued staring at Gregor with disdain. "Go ahead. Ask what you will."

"How did you come to know that the lutist was at The Sea Swoon?"

"I was sitting with Lord Daguss in the great hall when the mute Madrig arrived and shared the news."

A piece of the puzzle fell into place. "And then what? Who sent the three men to the Sea Swoon to murder the lutist? Lord Daguss?"

Betrard shook his head, the way a person might when they've heard a particularly bad joke. "Come now, jeyedoshi. I'm the one who sent them."

"On behalf of Lord Daguss?"

Betrard pretended to consider this. "On behalf of _all_ the Ontish. On behalf of all Ragar Or."

Gregor paused. They were in one the darkest rooms in the Burnt Tower honeycomb, an interior box poorly lit by tallow candles. But even without windows, the darkness of the night seemed to permeate the room, seeping in through the stones.

"What about the Heron?"

"What _about_ the Heron?"

"Did he know…was he a party to—?"

Betrard interrupted with yet another snort. Contempt was coming off him in waves. "What do you hope will come of this questioning, jeyedoshi? What knowledge would you gain? And if you had that information, what would it change? If you and your *king* have any hope of keeping the kingdom, the answers to your questions are irrelevant." The Gorgostrine stood. "But know this. I, the servant of the Twin Ascendant, am against you *and* your king. Me. And I acted accordingly. As to the others, believe what you want. It changes nothing."

Gregor snatched the air from the Gorgostrine's lungs. He sensed the impotence in his decision the second it was made, but still he followed through, and watched with cold eyes until the priest of the Twins turned blue. Only when Betrard collapsed to the ground did Gregor give it back.

The priest looked as unbothered as a man deprived of oxygen near to the point of death could be. If anything, he appeared to have gained strength. After his equilibrium was restored, Betrard looked Gregor dead in the eye. "Do you know what I realized, while I was lying there, starving for breath? How important it is to the king that I die by Daguss's hand. Because if I do not, everything implodes."

It was the truth. They were fashioning a story. One that had to be told flawlessly. The real truth—and what to do about it—would have to wait for another day.

"The only realization you should place your faith in, Betrard, is that you are a dead man." Gregor's words sounded empty. But he pressed on. "It's time for you to come with me."

"Where are we going?"

"To see your master, Lord Daguss. It's time to get our stories in place."

The last meeting of the night was unlike the others. It took place in the grand room at the bottom of the Burnt Tower, closer to neutral ground. Some of the bravest and strongest knights loyal to House Dayborn— Larin Dove, Braxton Walshing, and Percy Moon—were on hand, ready, from the looks in their recently roused eyes, to fight for the king if the dead-of-night summons demanded it. King Micah directed them to stand outside the room, and enter only if he called for them. Then, along with Gregor, Queen Anjay, and the prisoner Betrard, King Micah entered the room, to see what Salks were waiting inside.

There were only three people inside the room. Lord Daguss, his cousin Madrig the Mute, and Jacy, Madrig's bonded. Of the trio, Gregor could see the faint outline of one skull.

The walls of the room were hung with rich tapestries depicting unsettling coastal tableaux. In one of the tapestries, paletooth sharks circled a sinking longboat, while in another, the grasping tentacles of a kraken blurred a setting-sun horizon. Otherwise, the room was empty. In the window over Lord Daguss's shoulder, a blurry moon hung in the sky like a nebulous egg. Gregor didn't let his gaze linger there for long. Directing his attention to the head of House Salk, Gregor watched as Daguss digested Betrard's entrance and everything that it meant. Whatever Daguss's thoughts or feelings, he was careful not to react. It wasn't until the king was fully in the room that Daguss broke form, standing and giving a bow a little deeper than the one Dante Heron had offered. Standing next to Daguss, Madrig and Jacy offered proper bows, the kind that might convince a king of a person's fealty.

"Lord Daguss." The king's voice was calm. "It has been quite the night."

Lord Daguss nodded. "So I've heard." He gave another head nod at Betrard. "I see you have my man."

Queen Anjay broke in, her voice cutting like a smooth blade. "We have four of them, in fact. Three dead, and this one dying."

Daguss brought a hand to his bone-white beard. "I trust that the lutist is safe."

"He is," Gregor replied. He thought he saw looks of relief break out on Madrig's and Jacy's faces.

"Good," Daguss said. In the span of a whip-thin second, he drew the Clyesian dagger on his hip. It had a striking onyx inlay, and gleamed darkly against Daguss's white knuckles. Daguss nodded at Betrard. "When do you want me to cut the traitor's throat?"

King Micah responded with an almost pleasurable sigh of relief. *Don't,* Gregor thought, but it was too late; his brother started in on the business of convincing himself of the thing that he most wanted to believe. "Tonight, if it suits you. Spill his blood here and—"

"You will do it tomorrow. In front of every Ontishman that we can gather." Gregor stepped in front of Betrard, as if to protect him.

Silence fell like a stone. Lord Daguss ran the flat of the blade against his palm, turning it over and over again. His gaze dropped to the ground. "I fear you are predisposed against me, Sagekind, so I hope that you will not misinterpret what I am about to say. I answer to the king, and to the king only. Do you?"

Gregor, stung by the memory of his recent failings, hesitated. Queen Anjay answered in his wake. "You would kill the perfidious priest now?

But wasn't it earlier tonight that Betrard learned of the lutist's arrival while sitting at your very own table? Why not keep a closer watch on him, then, if you truly considered him a threat?"

Daguss's voice went flat. "I did not know then…and I *still* do not know…why the enemies of union want this lutist dead. The only thing my cousin told me was that a talented musician had arrived in Dunning Harbor with a song composed especially for the queen. My intention was to send someone in the morning to escort the lutist safely to Saltbend. Why in the name of the Twins would I believe that Betrard had designs on killing the man?" Daguss cracked the knuckles of his dagger-free hand. "But clearly the lutist is more important than I knew. If I failed in keeping the gorgostrine from working against the interests of the king, the failure was one of understanding, and not of loyalty." The Lord of High Osgood turned to King Micah. "As I have told you many times in private, my king, I am for union, and union under a Dayborn king. If we are to see this through to the end, and bring Kalandragote into the fold, you must trust and believe me."

Hogwash, Gregor thought. *If ever there was a more skillful liar…* but these thoughts trailed away as he was struck by the possibility that Daguss Salk might, in fact, be telling the truth. What real evidence did Gregor have, after all, that the conspiracy went beyond Gregor's own biases and suspicions? Gregor forced himself to go on the offensive before his doubts took him under. "Forgive us, Lord Daguss, if we find it difficult to believe that the man *you* chose to be the loyal representative of the faith of the Twins wasn't acting on your behalf when he went about his treacheries. Stavus save us, man, you were the one who sent Betrard to the Yubriy tree!"

"A most grievous error."

"Grievous!? Grievous!? It was far more than grievous!" Gregor forced himself to shut up. There was no advantage to be gained in making the accusation so plain.

Daguss intuited why and bridged the gap. "Betrard stole a Yubriy leaf, didn't he? It's the only thing that makes sense."

For a moment, no one replied. But then Betrard broke in, his voice full of hate. "Aye. That's exactly what I did. I had a chance to sever the foul ties that bind this realm together, and I acted on it. And if you"—he made a dismissive motion at Daguss,—"weren't so Werring-bent on playing the part of the *slavish Struvan* cocksucker, perhaps you would remember your last name and do the same."

Acting. It's all acting. They have been planning for Betrard to take the fall, if it came to it. It didn't hurt that the story Daguss and Betrard were spinning was the one the king wanted to believe. And that would win out. *Or maybe they are telling the truth, and I'm going mad. Maybe the sight of the skulls is warping my jeyedoshi brain, and I can't help but believe that every man who isn't me is against the king.*

Across the room, Daguss looked ready with an acerbic retort for the priest, but to Gregor's surprise the queen got the next word in. "Either you are the most duplicitous man the realm has ever seen, Daguss Salk, or you are an incompetent setting loose vipers in the king's midst. Regardless, why my bonded would trust you after this is beyond me."

"You wound me, my queen," Daguss said.

"Not nearly as much as you've wounded the kingdom, sir, by turning a blind eye to this bastard of a priest."

Gregor's heart thrilled. Having oft been the target of Anjay's ire, it was enjoyable to see someone else on the receiving end of one of the queen's harangues. Gregor wanted nothing more than to join in the attack, to chase Lord Daguss from the board entirely, but that was a line, he knew, that could not be crossed. What they needed was to inform Daguss that they were aware of his private treacheries, for the purposes of boxing him into being their very public friend. Castigating him as their enemy wasn't an option. Not with the king determined to travel up the peninsula.

"There's one only way to rectify all this. We will put on a performance, tomorrow, in the courtyard. At the end of it, Lord Daguss will chop off the priest's head in front of every noble currently gathered in Saltbend Castle's walls." Gregor made his voice firm. "In doing so, you will make it abundantly clear that your loyalty lies with King Micah. Do you understand?"

Daguss turned his chin up at Gregor, and instead turned to the king. "If it is the king's will, yes." He paused. When Micah didn't reply straightaway, Daguss continued, "We are at a dangerous crossroads, my king. My greatest fear is that you mistake my Ontish obligations for disloyalty. But that would be as foolish as me mistaking you for a foe of the Ontish simply because the Heron rides at your side. We are not enemies. If we were, I would have never agreed to bond my child to yours." He paused. "For the mistake of the priest, I apologize. If it were my choice, I would kill him now. But if you would rather that I take his head on the morrow in front of the others, only say the word, and it will be done."

Gregor tried to read the man, hoping to get at the truth in his heart. *The man is a Salk. A descendant of the line that once ruled all Ragar Or. We would be naïve to believe that he is fully for us, no matter what he says. And as for bonding his child to the king's, he is bonding the lesser twin, a small sacrifice for an Ontish lord. He is only saying what he believes must be said, in the ways of lords immemorial. But that is only because he knows full well the game being played. If he is indeed against us, he won't show the knife until the last possible second.*

It seemed possible that King Micah was thinking the same. In the aftermath of Lord Daguss's spiel, the king grew quiet. The energy of the room drew to his unspoken thoughts. *Might he have turned on Daguss?* Gregor pondered. It didn't seem possible, but still the silence persisted, until Gregor felt the need to prepare himself for the unexpected, in case Micah opened his lips and violence ensued. But before the king opened his mouth, Madrig the mute stepped forward, and, with dexterous fluency, commandeered the conversation.

The mute's hands moved like a steady storm. Jacy rose beside him and translated every word. "I, Madrig Salk, pledge my life and sword to King Micah of House Dayborn." Madrig finished with a rather forceful gesture. After a moment's hesitation, Jacy translated it too. "I also swear to King Micah that if Daguss Salk is found to be plotting against the king, I will be the first to run him through. This is my solemn oath." Jacy looked away from the king and back again. When next she spoke, it was clear that it was for herself. "My bonded and I are connected as one. His oaths are my oaths. To that end, I swear the same. Except for the last part, I suppose. If Lord Daguss needs a running through, I'll go second." Then the bonded couple bent the knee together.

More acting, Gregor thought. But when his eyes went to Lord Daguss, the proud northern lord had retreated into his moonbear coat. *Could it be...that Daguss didn't know this was coming?*

Micah accepted Madrig's and Jacy's oaths with measured good cheer. "I accept your oaths. Although I cannot imagine a scenario in which you will have to uphold them. Lord Daguss is my true and faithful servant. And though there is no need for him to prove it, what doubters there are in the kingdom will come away convinced when Daguss takes the head of this treasonous priest on the morrow. In the courtyard."

The burned taste of an uneasy peace settled on everyone's tongues. All the same, it held. Or at least it did until the priest opened his mouth.

"I—"

Gregor grabbed the wind from Betrard's throat. He held it hard and fast. As the priest turned blue and slowly slumped to the ground, Gregor addressed the remainder of the room.

"Here is what will happen when we take to the courtyard tomorrow."

Silas O' the Songs

The night was nearing its end by the time the Sagekind set Silas and Wyn up in a room in the Burnt Tower, Saltbend Castle's newest addition. "Rest, if you can," the Sagekind said after his interrogation of them was finished and he had relieved Wyn of his dagger. "Come sunrise, the king and queen will want to hear the song. Be ready." Then he disappeared like a man with responsibilities that they could not possibly imagine.

Wyn sniffed at the air once the Sagekind was gone. "Smell that? That's tension, that is. Middle of the night or not, lots of people in this castle are awake, waiting on news." When Wyn was finished with his sniffing, he lay down on the grand bed and closed his eyes, a contented smile on his face. "I have my issues with castles, I do, but at least there's little chance of the walls collapsing in on you in the middle of the night." Then he fell right to sleep.

Silas stayed up. His drunk was wearing off, and, unlike Wyn, he couldn't easily go to sleep with his dream of playing for royalty so near at hand. Rather than fight it, he closed his eyes and preoccupied his hands with his lute, allowing it to make sense of the world for him. Without thinking, he plucked out songs old and new. Softly, softly. He played number after number, avoiding the newest. The songs eased his overstimulated mind.

Morning came without his noticing it. It wasn't until the door opened that Silas realized the room was ripening with natural light. He looked up and saw a man and a woman enter, two people that he instinctively knew were the king and queen of all Ragar Or. But he didn't stop playing, nor did he acknowledge them. Instead, he transitioned to "The Queen's Burning Heart."

Whatever magic he had conjured the previous night was still with him. Wyn woke up and joined in the song at the appointed moment, and together they made a marvel of the music, summoning the ghosts in the lyrics to their side. The spell slipped only once, when Silas thought of the words written on the leaf pressing against the sole of his foot, but he quickly recovered, and managed to make it seem that the emotion of the music had gotten to him, which heightened rather than undermined the mood.

When he finished, he looked up to find that the queen had tears in her eyes.

"A song to honor Queen Portia, the most honorable of all the Salk queens." She blotted away the tears. "And I am told that you wrote this song as an homage to me?" Her tone made it clear that there was only one right answer.

"Yes, my queen."

"And what is the song called?"

"The Queen's Burning Heart."

When Queen Anjay heard the name of the song, she placed her hand over her chest.

Silas shifted uncomfortably. Last night, the Sagekind had told Silas about the Yubriy tree prophecy, and his belief that Silas was the prophesied lutist. Silas had felt it in his bones that the Sagekind was right. But now that Silas had played the song before the queen, he felt the lie of the alternate lyrics, the ones he had composed to hide the Yubriy leaf's powerful and unsettling message. *I will play the true rendition for her at a later time,* he promised himself.

The king approached him. *King Micah. Of House Dayborn.* Silas expected to feel fear, but the fear never came. Silas could not ascertain if his lack of fear stemmed from some inherent quality King Micah failed to possess, or if the failing was Silas's own, and he lacked the imagination necessary to appreciate the fear a king should inspire. It wasn't that Silas didn't think Micah looked like a king: the man's entire mien suggested royalty, from his tailored clothing to his well-fed form to his thick, crow-black beard. But the many uncanny occurrences of the past few weeks had caused something in Silas's mind to go faulty, and now he felt no fear before the sovereign of all Ragar Or. *If anything, King Micah should be trembling in the presence of the woodkin.* For a moment, Silas had to keep from giving himself over to manic laughing.

The king stopped before Silas and made a study of him. Finished, he grabbed Silas by the shoulders. "You are Struvan?"

"Yes. I am from the Vake, Your Highness."

"Have you played for nobility before?"

Anna Josephine flashed in Silas's mind. "Yes, Your Highness. The Arcs. At Castle Greenwell."

The king nodded as if he had expected it. Then his stare hardened. "Explain to me the origin of this song."

"It came to me when I was standing in a forest."

Wyn entered the conversation, his voice full of its customary glee. "Not just any forest, Your Highnesses. The one where the Yubriy tree is located."

Silas didn't appreciate being spoken for, but based on the looks on the king's and queen's faces, Wyn's words were well received.

"Is this true?" King Micah asked Silas.

"It is."

"And then what?"

Wyn once again beat Silas to the punch. "Pardon, Your Highnesses, but isn't it obvious? A song like this is meant for royal ears. I told my friend Silas O' the Songs here as much when he first played me this song, and that very day we started our journey in search of banners bearing double suns. The humble songsmith Silas O' the Songs is not one to trumpet his own talents, so I, Wyn Dunkin, accompanied him in case the need should arise. To that end, I say to you now: this man, and this song, were destined for you."

The looks on the Dayborns' faces suggested that they liked what Wyn had to say.

"Good," the queen said at last. "The subject matter of the song is a trifle unsettling, but we will not look a gift horse in the mouth." She nodded at the king. "To the peninsula." And then she left the room.

When she was gone, the king started laying out directives. "The both of you are now in my service. You will travel with the queen and I until our travels are done, and then you will return with us to Union. For as long as we are together—and that will be the case until I say otherwise— you will perform this song, and any other song that we request, at our behest. It goes without saying that you will be well compensated for your services." Micah paused. "Later today, you will perform 'The Queen's Burning Heart' in front of a large audience of nobles. Both Struvan and Ontish nobility will be present. Once everyone is assembled, you will present the song as a gift for the queen. You will make it clear to all who are assembled that you journeyed from the Vake to bring the song to us."

Silas nodded while trying to ignore the beads of sweat forming on the back of his neck. The song that he had nurtured in private for weeks and weeks was changing before his eyes, becoming an instrument of the king.

Ah, he thought. *There's the fear.*

Micah gave Silas and Wyn a grave look. "The Sagekind informed the two of you of the Yubriy leaf prophecy?"

"Yes," they said in unison.

The king's expression darkened. "The Sagekind told me about the men who tried to kill you. Men, it would seem, who were following the orders of those who claim to be allegiant to me." The Dayborn king brought a stern finger into the fray. "Know this. Stavus sent the two of you to me for a reason. The Yubriy tree made the prophecy for a reason. Today is the day we root out the traitors in my midst.

"Today is the day we uphold the promise of Union."

Silas stood on a tiered platform in Saltbend Castle's inner courtyard with Wyn beside him. Try as he might, he could not calm his racing heart. He had performed hundreds, perhaps thousands of times in his life, but never for an audience like the one he was about to face.

One more stellar performance. One more, and all your dreams will come true.

The inner courtyard of Saltbend Castle was massive. The winds coming off the Blacktyde Sea had scalped much of the courtyard, leaving the remainder covered in sparse, coastal grasses. Closer to the castle were rows of curved blue and pale-yellow seastone benches. On the opposite side of the courtyard, the castle's outer wall buttressed up against the larger sea wall, providing extra fortification against the elements. Silas could hear the pounding sea beyond. The waves sounded to him like the muffled whispers of the gods.

The guests began to arrive, some of the most powerful men and women in the realm. They filled up the courtyard like daytime candles, their heads aflame with self-importance. Silas knew the surnames of many of the noble families, but never having seen the faces belonging to the names, he wasn't certain who was who. A select few took their seats among the benches. Silas continued with his guessing game until a man in possession of a menacing sort of elegance walked out of the castle wearing a snow-colored cloak.

"Ten silver Salks says that's Dante Heron," Wyn whispered to Silas.

Silas was certain Wyn was right. Everyone had heard descriptions of the powerful young Struvan lord, and this man fit those descriptions perfectly. Lord Heron took a seat on one of the yellow seastone benches.

Soon after, the Salks emerged. Accompanying them: Madrig and Jacy. They came on the heels of a bald-headed man wearing a moonbear coat the same color as his beard, a man who looked like a boulder at the forefront of an avalanche. *Lord Daguss Salk,* Silas intuited. Included in Lord Daguss's retinue was a tall, beautiful young woman wearing a pearl-and-onyx necklace, and an imposing beast of a man nearly of a size with Madrig.

Wyn piped up again. "Our friends. Looks like they found the Salks after all."

Silas once again declined to respond. The original plan the evening before had been to sit and wait at The Sea Swoon until Madrig and Jacy arranged an invite to Saltbend from Lord Salk. With everything that had occurred, Silas was in the dark as to how events had played out on Madrig's and Jacy's end. He tried to catch their eyes, hoping to learn by means of a glance what had transpired. But only Jacy looked his way, and only then for the span of a firefly's shine.

If Jacy's eyes betrayed anything, it was that she had no intention of getting caught long looking Silas's way.

When the last of the attendees had arrived, King Micah and Queen Anjay strode into the courtyard. Shouts filled the air—*The Sun Forever Rises!*—but, to Silas's mild surprise, the voices weren't as strong as he would have expected for the arrival of royalty. The Sagekind, wearing a blood-red cloak, accompanied the king and queen. Flanking the Sagekind were two greyhounds: one black, one tan and white. A stand-in throne seat had been prepared for the king, positioned diagonally so that it was simultaneously facing the platform and the benches. The Sagekind and the greyhounds took up standing positions slightly behind the king. The queen sat on an empty blue seastone bench at the front.

Once King Micah was seated, he looked at Silas and nodded his head. Silas dipped his chin in response and faced the audience. The heat of the hundred-plus stares made him tremble. *Stay focused. Perform. This is the moment you've been waiting for.* He stepped forward. The sound of a flock of seagulls carried in on the wind. Silas struggled to project his voice above the seagulls as the same wind carried his words away from the audience.

"My name is Silas O' the Songs. I am a lutist and a songsmith from the Vake. I wrote a song beneath the boughs of the Yubriy tree for our queen. My friend and I have traveled far to present it to her as a gift." He took a deep breath. "I present to you: 'The Queen's Burning Heart.'"

I am a character in a performance, he thought. The only thing to do was to play his part well. But for the first time in a long time, Silas felt...off. He began to play, hoping that all would fall into place. But it was not to be. The wind was the biggest impediment; it played havoc with the sound, causing the notes to take to the air like birds with damaged wings. Thoughts besieged Silas, stealing his focus from the song. *Why are we outside? Why are we not playing in the great hall?* Every note was a struggle. His singing was fine enough, he supposed, but in its warring with the wind it failed to transcend. His only hope was that Wyn might save him. The little man came in on cue with the fiddle, but Wyn's playing, always so suited to the moment, sounded thin and far away. Together they flailed through the song to its end.

When it was over, King Micah stepped forward. Silas was so distraught that he half-expected the sovereign to announce their on-the-spot execution.

But the king hadn't noticed their difficulties at all.

He had other matters on his mind.

"The arrival of this man, and his song, were prophesied by the Yubriy tree. As such, he and his friend are under my protection. Any man who attempts to harm them risks my wrath, and my vengeance." The king's voice grew cold and hard, like iron. "Last night, an attempt was made on their lives. Today, here and now, we settle the debt incurred by that violence."

Soldiers emerged from the castle. They wore ringmail over leather, gauntlets and greaves, steel swords and steel helms. The crest on every soldier's chest bore two suns. Six of the soldiers carried dead men in their arms, one corpse per pair. The soldiers deposited the dead men in front of the seastone benches. The faces of the dead men turned toward the distant winter sun, their eyes white and grasping, limbs splayed in submission to whatever entity had hold of them in the afterlife.

Silas recognized the corpse with the misshapen head immediately.

With the corpses dumped, the soldiers spread out around the yard. Silas counted fifteen in total. They looked well prepared for any nastiness that might come their way.

The Sagekind stepped forward. It appeared that he had aged years in the intervening hours since the events of the previous evening. From the look of him, Silas would not have been surprised if he collapsed on the spot from exhaustion. But instead of collapsing, the Sagekind opened his mouth and spoke with a commanding voice.

"These dead men are traitors to Union. Traitors to all that our two beautiful faiths teach us." The Sagekind let his dark and penetrating eyes bore into every noble in attendance. "If anyone here knows the identity of these men, let them step forward and say so now."

To the sound of scores of gasps, Daguss Salk heeded the Sagekind's call. Standing up from one of the blue benches, he strode over to the dead men and looked them over with disgust. He jabbed his finger at each of them in turn. "This one's mine. Name's Stroman, I think. These two belong to me as well, though I don't know their names."

Silas shifted uncomfortably on his feet. Something was off about Daguss's and the Sagekind's delivery. Their words had the taint of performance, the premeditated quality of powerful men setting in motion events that would lead to premeditated ends. But as with everything involving the rich and the powerful, it went without saying that only a select few were in on it.

King Micah reclaimed the courtyard. "These men were privy to information that was not theirs to know. Sacred information. The holy writ of the Yubriy tree. They then used that information to despoil the Yubriy tree's intent, which is to UPHOLD THE PROMISE OF UNION!" Veins bulged on King Micah's face. When he resumed speaking, his voice was tempered, but only slightly. "Reason stands that they did not come into this information on their own."

A chill crept up Silas's spine. Was the king accusing Daguss Salk of treason? Silas recounted the Sagekind's questions from last night, after they had returned to the castle. Then he glanced at Madrig and Jacy. They weren't about to get caught up in the accusations, were they?

Daguss Salk spat. An audibly aggressive expectoration. It struck Silas as disdain for the king. Or at least it did until Daguss spoke.

"I know who the traitor is. He's here, right now."

"Name him," King Micah demanded.

Daguss Salk wore a hard, inscrutable expression. "The traitor is the gorgostrine. Betrard."

Hundreds of turning heads keyed Silas in to the culprit. Standing in the courtyard was a rusty nail of a man wearing a gray wool robe that suggested piousness to the degree that piety was associated with poverty. He looked more like a veteran from a war than a priest. On his face was a mean expression, but otherwise he refused to move.

"Seize him," the king commanded.

Soldiers grabbed the holy man by his arms and escorted him roughly in front of the king. The man wore a sneer of defiance. Silas didn't have the foggiest idea how this fellow was connected to the three men from The Sea Swoon who had tried to end his life, but, like everyone present, he was curious to find out.

Lord Salk provided the details. "Last night, my cousin Madrig and his bonded Jacy arrived at Saltbend with news of musicians they had met on the road. Musicians with a song meant especially for the queen. My intention was to send for them in the morning, and present them as a gift to Your Highnesses today. Betrard was by my side at the time. When the Gorgostrine heard Madrig's news, he grew agitated and left shortly thereafter. As King Micah knows, I've had doubts about Betrard's loyalty to the Dayborn dynasty for some time now. My belief is that he was behind the attack on the musicians."

"But *why* would he attack them?" the king asked. "What reason would he have to believe that these musicians were of a special importance?"

The Sagekind strode forward. He wore a face like an executioner. *If this is a performance,* Silas thought, *his is a dark part.* When the Sagekind reached the Gorgostrine, the two men shared a strange, inexplicable stare, one simultaneously shot through with antipathy and a mutual understanding. With the soldiers holding the Gorgostrine still, the Sagekind started searching Betrard's robe, his hands at first roaming the outside before roughly jerking the robe open, exposing the Gorgostrine's shame for all to see. The assembled gasped yet again. But whatever the Sagekind was looking for, he didn't find it.

The Sagekind stepped back. The Gorgostrine, his gray robe open and his flesh exposed, stared defiantly at his red-robed counterpart. But the

Sagekind didn't return the holy man's sneer. Instead, his eyes descended to the Gorgostrine's feet.

"His boots. Take them off."

Betrard, who had suffered the searching of his robe with a motionless dignity, began to fight. He thrashed his legs until the soldiers kicked his feet from out under him and forced him to the ground.

At last, a boot was wrenched free. One of the soldiers handed it to the Sagekind. With a knowing ceremony, the king's bastard half brother reached inside the Gorgostrine's boot and pulled out a large orange leaf.

A Yubriy leaf.

Silas's knees buckled. The great roaring that erupted from the nobles matched the roaring in Silas's head. Shouts flew through the air like arrows, but Silas could make no sense of them. Every sensation in Silas's body was dulled except the ones inside of his boot, where Silas could feel his own Yubriy leaf bunched up against the arch of his foot like a knot of guilt.

The roaring dulled. Out of the din came the Sagekind's voice, reciting the words written on the Yubriy leaf.

"A song first sung in the Vake, prolongs the line of the suns."

Bedlam. Silas felt dizzy enough to faint. But before he could pass out, a hand took hold of his shoulder: the sinewy claw of his fiddling friend.

"Not only are you a Yubriy leaf prophecy, Silas O' the Song, but so is your song!" Wyn shouted triumphantly in his ear.

In the on-the-spot trial that ensued, the Sagekind made the case against Betrard the Gorgostrine.

"Let it be known by every man and woman present that Betrard the Gorgostrine was present at this year's reaping of the Yubriy leaves. It was there that he stole a Yubriy leaf and kept it in his possession. Seeing what was written on the leaf, he waited for an opportunity to commit treason against the king. When he heard of the arrival of these two musicians from the Vake, he conspired with the dead men you see before you to murder the musicians before they could reach the royal family."

Silas, mostly recovered from the shock of the Gorgostrine's leaf, did his best to focus on what was being said. *But what of the murder birds?* he thought. During their interrogation the previous night by the Sagekind, Silas and Wyn had shared nearly everything that had happened to them on their trip north, including their multiple attempted murders by men from eastern, bird-themed houses. But, for whatever reason, it appeared that part of their tale wasn't suited to the present audience.

The Sagekind jutted his chin at Betrard. "Is that not what happened?"

Whips of sea wind lashed the courtyard. Far away, a large wave broke upon the sand.

"Aye," Betrard answered, gnashing his teeth in a perverse sort of delight. "You have the right of it." The Gorgostrine's eyes danced with unspoken words, but he held his tongue.

"This man deserves death!" the Sagekind shouted to the nobles in the courtyard. Then his eyes returned to Betrard, and his voice grew quiet. "You deserve death."

Betrard settled on a *fuck you* sneer in lieu of a response.

A short silence ensued. There was a tension in it not easily understood.

Daguss Salk broke the silence. "With your highness's permission, I would be the one to end the Gorgostrine's life."

Lord Daguss looked like a man who had taken a bite of a bad head of cabbage but was determined to swallow it down. His expression was a dark plateau, his furrowed brow the menacing storm cloud overhead. Silas took a quick glance at Madrig and Jacy. They looked equally troubled.

"Lord Salk. My trusted servant. The man who will sit on my right at the Union Table once we return to the capital. The man whose daughter will bond my youngest son." King Micah's powerful voice cut through the wind, ensuring that everyone heard him.

Lord Salk, however, appeared to be suffering the king's praise with a visible discomfort.

The king continued, "I grant you permission. Cut the Gorgostrine down, Lord Salk. Here and now. Let our enemies see what happens to those who betray the promise of Union."

The cabbage in Lord Salk's mouth looked not to have improved upon the taste, but all the same he drew his sword and advanced on Betrard. The Gorgostrine appeared, for all of his dirty looks, to be strangely resigned to his fate. All the courtyard held its breath, afloat in the darkening dream.

Except for one man. To the surprise of everyone, a wiry, wolfish-looking fellow sprung from a seastone bench and intercepted Lord Salk. The man drew his sword, which in turn drew gasps from the crowd. His green-eyed expression was a mixture of fury and confusion. Words writhed in his mouth like a mash of fish struggling in a net, until all at once they escaped and poured into the courtyard.

"No, Lord Salk! You can't…I won't allow it…" The man was gesticulating wildly with his sword, and looked to be on the verge of either committing murder or crying. "The Gorgostrine Betrard is deserving of the defense of every Ontish house, not the judgement of this, this"—the point of the man's sword suddenly found King Micah, and there was a madness in his eyes that suggested he was beyond caring of the consequences—"this lesser Struvan, this pretender to the crown, this jeyedoshi-harboring—"

"Reginal! No!" Daguss Salk interrupted, his voice a blunt edge. For the first time that evening, Silas was certain that events had gone off-script. Something was happening that the most powerful men in the realm hadn't anticipated.

The one called Reginal looked like he had been slapped. His face grew flush with anger, turning purple-red behind his bramble-briar beard. Accompanying his ire was his sword, its point now menacing the Lord of High Osgood instead of the king. "Werring take you, Daguss Salk. I'll be damned if I'm going to stand aside and let you end the life of a priest of the Twins, a man who was doing what every good Ontish knows needs be done, all in order to appease this cursed Struvan—"

Those were the last words Reginal ever spoke. In a flash, Daguss Salk unsheathed his sword and deposited it in Reginal's chest, substituting whatever the man might have said next with a bubble of mouth-breaching blood. He plunged the sword in up to its hilt. Reginal died with a look of heartbroken disbelief on his face, staring into the Lord of High Osgood's eyes.

Men everywhere stood and reached for their swords. Silas watched with horror as a terrible sizing up took place, the unpredictable math of men weighing mortal combat. It was impossible to tell who was for the king and who was against him. Out of the corner of his eye, Silas saw Madrig and the beast of a man spring from the seastone bench. Madrig moved to the king's side, while the man-beast drew beside Daguss. This took the fire out of many a belly: the standing and reaching quickly resolved itself into a tension-filled inertia.

"The traitor Reginal Burntree is dead," King Micah announced with an eerie calmness. "The traitor Betrard dies next. If anyone else would like to join them, please proclaim yourself now. Those loyal to Union will be more than happy to accommodate you."

Silence reigned.

The danger passed.

King Micah Dayborn nodded at Daguss Salk.

With a workmanlike manner, the Lord of High Osgood withdrew his crimson-covered sword from the corpse of Reginal Burntree and turned his attention to the Gorgostrine.

Betrard had risen to his knees. The Dayborn soldiers who had forced the priest to the ground backed away. Daguss walked forward until he was directly in front of the priest. Their eyes met. Silas couldn't shake the thought that Daguss Salk's expression was a request for forgiveness.

The priest gave him words instead. "Long live the Twin Ascendant," Betrard said.

Silas thought he saw Daguss Salk's lips move, mouthing something back. But it was difficult to know for certain, because in the next instant the Lord of High Osgood raised his sword and lopped off Betrard's head.

Blood fountained onto the ground. Silas stared at the horror numbly. The sight would have overwhelmed his senses were he not distracted by the weight of the Yubriy leaf pressing up against the sole of his foot.

Johanna Salk

In the candle-kept dream, she was bonded to the wrong man.

Her old bond. Nicholas Raleigh.

"Here I am, my pet," Nicholas called to her from the void.

She hissed at him, shocked by the hatred welling up inside of her. "I do not want you. I never wanted you," she shouted. "And do not call me *pet*. I always hated that." A different thought came to her, apropos of nothing. "*Deference* is a weak opening move from a weak man. Don't you know that?"

It was easy to hate Nicholas in the dream. For one, he was dead, with maggots crawling in and out of his eyeholes. For another, he wasn't the man she had once tried to love, but instead a dreamland impediment to her true desire.

"The one you love is here," Nicholas said, now lying on Lord Raleigh's canopied white oak bed, wrapped in a death shroud.

How do you know who he is? she thought. But instead, she asked, "Where are we?"

"The Eternal Realm of Air and Light. Or Owoervyrn, perhaps. Where the dead go."

But that couldn't be. She had only just kissed Easton, at the feet of Thacker the tracker. It was impossible that they had both passed on. She determined to find Easton. Searching, she looked into the void, but instead of finding Easton she found Thacker. Her father's man was standing on a grassy plain, sewing his entrails back up into his body. When Thacker saw her, he shook his head. "Woodkin work. Had to be. I pledged to your father that I would catch up to the two of you, bring you back if circumstances called for it. But now none of us are getting back, are we? You being what you are."

"Where is he?"

"Who? The second son of the setting sun?" Thacker didn't wait for a response. "Look around. You'll find him soon enough."

But when she turned once more to look for him, there was only emptiness. *Where is he?* she thought again, and out of the emptiness came a great and terrible laughter, distant at first but soon echoing all around her, filling her up, feeding on the marrow in her very bones. She struggled against it, to no avail. She was in its grip, and there was nothing that could be done. "Where is he?" she asked again. Her voice was fading, her body slipping into the light…

"He is asleep. The same as you were a moment ago."

Consciousness. Somehow, Johanna had grabbed hold of its slippery-eel tail. Her purchase, however, was not strong. The woman—nay, the woods witch—was circling above her, like a carrion bird against the backdrop of a woodland sky. Sensation slowly returned to Johanna's body, beginning with the unexpected cool caress of nothingness against half her scalp. Confused, she cupped the northern hemisphere of her head with two open palms. The right found the expected bounty of thick brown hair, but the left met with a hard plate of skull-bone.

"What? Wh-why?" She shook her head, trying to make sense of her changed waking world, trying to understand why half her hair was gone, trying to find Easton. Slowly, the room came into focus. On the opposite wall were the many decapitated woodland animals, staring down at her with a distant pity. The smell of dried sprigs and herbs filled her nostrils. Skylights made of empty space filled the room with light. It was all a bit jarring, but she had no time to make sense of the whole, not when Easton was still missing...

It was then that Johanna saw him. Lying in the corner of the house with his hands crossed over his chest, as still as a corpse. She gasped, thinking him dead. But as the air left her lungs, she noted the slight rise and fall of his chest. *He's not dead,* she understood, and with the realization came two tears, one falling from each eye, tracing pathways of relief down her cheeks.

The woods witch made a grumbling sound. "It's as I feared." She filled up Johanna's horizon and took Johanna's chin in her hand. "You love him? Is that it?"

"Let go of me," Johanna replied, and slapped the woods witch's hand away.

The woods witch didn't react to the slap. *Shayla,* Johanna remembered. *She said her name was Shayla.* The world continued to sharpen. Johanna once again touched the barren side of her scalp. "Why did you—?"

"Answer me, child. Do you love him?"

Johanna's eyes darted to the knotty oak table in the corner opposite Easton. Sitting atop the table were items the woods witch had taken from them during their candle-induced sleep. A silver-gray bloom: the forever flower. The sennequi piece Johanna had stolen from Coffyn castle. Easton's sword. And the glass vial with the bits of brayosk bark.

"I do."

"He offered you the forever flower?"

Johanna looked away. Anger blossomed inside her like a bright flame. "I hope you meet Werring in the Sky Ends," she said to the old woman, her voice dripping with contempt.

The woods witch laughed. "He *did* offer you the flower. But you did not accept. If you had accepted, I would have found the *milu sfal* on your horse, not his. But now"—she tapped the side of her nose—"you wish that you *had* accepted."

Johanna's mounting anger was returning the strength to her body. Slapping away the witch's hand had felt fantastic; she wondered how much better it would feel to punch the old woman in the face. *Why don't you? Woods witch or not, she's thrice your age.* The impulse overtook her. She rose to her feet, balled her fist, and moved on Shayla with all the haste she could impart to her body, intent on causing bodily harm.

The woods witch did not flinch. Instead, she followed Johanna with a steady gaze. Johanna was one step away from delivering the blow when, out of nowhere, the floor grabbed at her ankle, causing her to fall. Stunned and confused, Johanna looked back at the spot where she had tripped, and saw, to her astonishment, a tree-limb appendage retreating into the body of the wood. Johanna's eyes shot to the woods witch, the obvious question therein.

"Careful, child," Shayla said. "You know not who I am."

The comment stunned Johanna into a confused silence. Johanna continued looking at the woods witch, and for a moment she thought she saw a much younger woman, a stunning, blue-eyed, dark-blonde-haired woman of inestimable beauty and grace, a woman wearing an expression that suggested intimate familiarity with the vagaries of power. The vision quickly faded, and in its place, Johanna saw the old woman anew, with layers upon layers underneath.

"Who are you?"

The woman walked over to the table with the forever flower and the red queen. She picked up the sennequi piece and studied it. "I was born in Coffyn Castle. And, like you, I was born a lesser twin. When I was seven years old, the king made a law permitting lesser twins to be abandoned by their family."

"Which king?"

The woman looked amused by Johanna's question, but she did not reply to it directly. "Soon after, my family abandoned me in Low Osgood, and I was taken in by a tavern keep. It was a wretched existence. Outside of whipping me, the tavern keep had no greater desire than to work me to the bone. There were many times when I wished that my family had killed me rather than abandoned me to my fate.

"One day, a prophet arrived in Low Osgood. He predicted the king's death by dragon fire. When I heard his message, I became the prophet's devotee. He was speaking my heart's desire into existence: the death of the man who was the origin of all my troubles. But the prophet didn't have the opportunity to spread his message for long: he was arrested within the week. When they tied him to a stake and burned him in the flames, I stood close enough to smell the smoke." The woman turned and faced Johanna. Her eyes were bright blue whorls, doors beyond understanding. "Shortly after, I climbed Simstone Mountain and made my acquaintance with the dragon. The green-and-black one. The wild one. Teriquay."

Johanna was incredulous. "You're not claiming that you are the dragonfeeder, are you? That's impossible."

The woods witch held up the sennequi piece as evidence. "You don't recognize me?"

Johanna wore a dumbfounded expression on her face. She had absconded from Coffyn Castle with the sennequi piece on an impulse; at no point had she connected the wooden carving to the young girl who had once killed a king, the one known to history as the dragonfeeder. But now that she thought about it, it made sense. *The red sennequi pieces are the subversive figures of the world. The lesser. The Ropskes. The Corosian line. The Firewalker. The dragonfeeder. The Yubriy tree. The jeyedoshi.* But even if the sennequi red queen did represent the dragonfeeder, it was far-fetched to believe that the woman standing before her was one and the same. "You expect me to believe that you once rode a dragon and killed a king? That would make you nearly two hundred years old."

The woman's eyes fired with wicked delight. "Let me make a tea of the forever flower for you. Drink it, my jeyedoshi sister, and I swear that you will live as long as me."

"Jeyedoshi?" Johanna's voice trembled. "I am no...jeyedoshi."

"No? That's not what the story of your body says. Here. See for yourself."

The woods witch produced a mean jag of glass from behind a wicker basket in the corner of the room. When she approached, Johanna imagined for a dark moment that the woman meant to plunge the shard deep into her throat, but instead the woods witch stood back a few feet and held the glass up like a mirror, reflecting Johanna's secret inner cosmos, writ on her scalp. The mark of the jeyedoshi. The spiral was no more than an inch wide, but in its tidy infinity Johanna came face-to-face with the secret story of her life, at last uncovered.

Johanna gave a little cry, like an injured animal. "Father always knew. He must have seen it on me when I was a babe. It's why he's spent a lifetime trying to send me south. It's why—"

"—It's why you are what you are. And will forever be. It's time to accept it. Past time."

The enormity of her new reality was too much to bear. Johanna brought her hands to her face and worked her mouth like a fish, searching for a denial. "No... I...I can't be a jeyedoshi. I won't be a jeyedoshi. I am a Salk, a daughter of the realm, a keeper of the faith—"

The woods witch stole the wind from Johanna's throat with unforgiving speed.

"You had best pray to Beoliotius that you *are* a jeyedoshi. Make no mistake, girl. You did not come to my home by chance. I brought you here. And if you are not the person that I have been waiting for, I will snuff out the lives of you and your boy-prince without so much as a second thought."

The woods witch returned Johanna her breath with all the callous care of a shove. Johanna, shocked, kept her mouth shut.

"Come with me, child," Shayla said after the fraught silence had passed, moving toward the door of the tree-magicked abode. "I have something to show you."

Johanna glanced at Easton. She did not want to leave him alone, unconscious, trapped in the witch's candle-woven spell. The woods witch, seeing her uncertainty, laughed. "If your love for him is true, it will keep, will it not? I promise your Dayborn prince will be no worse for wear when we return."

Fingers of fog weaved through the morning trees, binding the forest in a ghostly haze. Somewhere in the eastern sky shone the Stavusian sun. Bitterboy snorted when Johanna and the woods witch emerged from the house, but Johanna considered it a feeble offering, considering what she knew of the horse's true nature. *Even my valiant steed is wary of this woman,* Johanna thought. But there was little time for thinking. Together they trekked away from the house, climbing farther up Halfhead Mountain's sloping face. Johanna looked back once, but from above, it was difficult to distinguish the woods witch's abode from the rest of the forest; it might have been a secluded wooden palace, or a tangle of fallen trees.

In the near distance, Johanna could hear the waterfall gurgling its morning song. But they were moving in the opposite direction, up and away, toward some unknown summit. The woods witch walked the mountain woods like a seasoned goat. Johanna kept apace, but not without considerable effort. Every few steps her hand moved reflexively to her scalp, searching for the mark there. She could not feel it, although that didn't stop her from believing that each subsequent pass would deliver a different result. *It's been there my entire life,* she thought again and again. *Not that it's been of use to me.* If what the woman said was true, if Johanna was indeed a *jeyedoshi,* she was still nothing like the woods witch, with her manifold powers.

Minutes later, they arrived at a clearing in the mountain forest. It was an acre wide, and level, with soft, green moss underfoot. Standing at the edge of the clearing was a bobcat. The creature regarded Johanna and the woods witch with a feral wariness, but did not run away.

The woods witch turned to Johanna. "What would happen if you spoke to the animal?"

"Why…nothing. It might flee."

The woods witch shot Johanna a peculiar look. At the same moment, a brisk wind cut across the clearing. "Or if you attempted to compel the wind? What would happen then?"

Johanna gave an uncomfortable laugh. "The same. Nothing."

"Are you certain?"

Johanna dared not respond. Growing up in High Osgood, she had known early on that her twinship with Wulfess was special in some dark way, but their father's station had shielded them from the uncomfortable truths that other twins had to endure. Eventually he communicated to them that in every twin-pair there emerged a lesser twin and a twin ascendant, but that understanding, as upsetting as it was, paled in comparison to the idea that one of them might be a jeyedoshi, a potentiality Lord Daguss Salk had dismissed the instant he explained to Johanna and Wulfess what a jeyedoshi was. Seconds after divulging the jeyedoshi's historical significance, Lord Salk assured both his daughters that neither had been born with the jeyedoshi mark. They had lived in the comfort of his explanation unquestioningly. Or at least they did until the year they turned eight. The year their mother died.

"Perhaps you've tried it before?" The woods witch's voice rode the currents of the wind. "Reached for the elements, to see if you possessed jeyedoshi powers?"

Had she? A long-buried memory returned to her. Johanna's mother, Esme Salk, was on her deathbed, laboring for breath; Wulfess was kneeling on one side of the bed and Johanna on the other, each holding one of Mother's hands; Lord Daguss Salk was standing at the end of the bed, looking distraught and world-weary. From time to time he murmured dark lamentations, the type that made the girls worry for his sanity, until at last he turned and fled the room, his typically stoic persona undone by grief.

When he was gone, Wulfess spoke.

"Johanna. Listen to me. What if father has been lying, and one of us *is* a jeyedoshi? The jeyedoshi have power over the elements. If it were true, we might help breathe air into Mother's lungs."

The horror of Wulfess's suggestion made it difficult for Johanna to reply. "But we aren't…" she didn't dare say the word. "We don't have the mark."

Wulfess wore a look of the utmost resolve. "I'm going to try," she announced. Johanna watched with a wondrous terror as Wulfess closed her eyes and focused on their mother, willing herself to become the monster that they had been taught to revile. If will equaled results, Lady Esme would have been breathing in seconds. But Wulfess's effort yielded nothing. If anything, Esme Salk's breathing grew even more labored.

Finally, Wulfess gave up, giving in to a grief so great that she threw her head down on the bed with tears and snot running down her face.

A terrible guilt seized Johanna. Before she knew what she was doing, she was reaching out, grasping at the unknown, trying with all of her eight-year-old might to will the wind into her mother's lungs…and in her blind fumbling it seemed for a moment that her efforts had manifested into a miracle.

Lady Esme's wheezing lessened, then normalized.

But Johanna could not hold onto the magic she had conjured. It slipped through her fingers like grains of sand.

Wulfess was so distracted by her grief that she did not notice what had occurred.

Within the hour, Lady Esme died.

The stark truth of that day hit Johanna now. She had always been a jeyedoshi. What she had once dismissed as the fantastic imaginings of a grief-stricken child had in fact been a glimpse through the jeyedoshi door.

The woods witch stirred Johanna from her reverie. "Pay attention, child." Johanna looked up to see that the woods witch's eyes had turned dreamy, and that she was swaying ever so slightly back and forth, like a person in the throes of a good drunk. Johanna noted that the wind was moving with the woods witch, swirling around her body in ever-powerful circles, shaping and reshaping the old woman's moss-green dress…until with the force of a falling anvil Johanna realized that it was the woods witch who was directing the wind, and not the other way around.

The wind died on command, as if smitten by a deity. The woods witch turned to Johanna.

"Now you."

Her first instinct was to spite the woods witch, and not make the effort. But to her surprise she discovered that a different part of her insisted on knowing, here and now, whether she was in fact what the whorl on her newly shaven head proclaimed. To that end, she reached for the wind, attempting to bind it to her will. Now that she knew that she was a jeyedoshi, she was convinced that it would come easily. But to her frustration, the wind stayed out of reach, like a teasing dancing partner. Johanna doubled and then redoubled her efforts, to no avail. No matter how hard she concentrated, the wind evaded her. She grew evermore irked. Her doubts increased, and she began to wonder if perhaps her childhood memory of the deathbed scene had in fact been a folly of the mind.

"Frustrating, isn't it?" Shayla said, laughing meanly. "Try making it more of a conversation, and less of a command. The wind doesn't like being corralled."

The old woman's voice echoed in Johanna's ears like a faraway dream. Johanna did her best to heed the instructions. She stopped flailing after the wind and instead called it to her, teasing the teaser. The wind, amused, took up the dance, and soon a playful zephyr was gamboling to the rhythm of Johanna's thoughts, moving in and out of her horse-brown hair like a dutiful sprite. It was child's play, really. Johanna could sense the true weight of the mighty entity that humans called the wind surrounding her, observing her actions out of the amused corner of its eye, granting her this dance with the equivalent of its pinky finger. Nevertheless, it was a monumental occurrence. She now knew that she held some rapport, no matter how small, with a facet of the natural world.

"Good. Jeyedoshi have influence over all the elements, not only wind. Wind is often the most accommodating. But they can all be persuaded."

Johanna resisted the urge to nod. Directing the wind had been thrilling, but she didn't want to give Shayla the impression that she was falling under her sway.

The woods witch, indifferent to Johanna's comportment, moved on. "Let's try something different." She motioned at the bobcat, who continued to study them from the opposite side of the clearing. "Call the animal to us."

Johanna resolved once again to try. Like with the wind, she focused her full attention on the object of her desire, and tried to engage it in a conversation of the mind. But despite staring at her with a keen interest, the bobcat kept its distance.

"Speak to it. Animals are creatures of the senses, like we are. Try using your voice."

The idea that a wild animal would respond to a verbal command somehow seemed less likely to Johanna than the idea that it would respond to her thoughts. But she spoke nevertheless, to see what would happen.

"Come to me."

The bobcat hesitated, then found its feet. It walked, and then bounded toward her, stopping when it was within petting distance. Once there, it sat back on its haunches, as if awaiting further instruction.

Johanna was amazed. She had long known that she had an affinity with animals, but she had never grasped that the connection might be so direct. *Where does this power end?* she wondered. She nearly brought the question to her lips. But before she did, the woods witch began to laugh, a wild, high-spirited cachinnation. The sound of it was like an insult against everything Johanna had just experienced. She wheeled on the woods witch, a verbal lash ready on her tongue; only to recoil at the sound of the woods witch's laughter transforming into an ungodly thunder-tongue.

Words poured from the witch's mouth that had no connection to human language. Johanna nearly wept at the assault. Not knowing what to do, she held her hands over her ears and prayed that it would end.

At last, the storm of words stopped. Johanna uncovered her ears, thinking it over. Instead, there was a great tear in the fabric of the sky. Johanna's eyes shot heavenward.

Something was coming.

"Listen to me, child. And listen carefully." A great storm roiled in the woods witch's eyes. "We are jeyedoshi, you and I. The daughters of Coros, from the line of Ropske. The keepers of what has been lost. We think foul scorn that a kingdom or queendom can claim to know what is best for its people when it does not know itself. And so we remind it of its frailty, o'er and o'er again, until at last it is broken, and begs of us the answer to the only question that matters."

The roar of a dragon broke overhead, echoing around the mountains. Out of its mouth a fire belch scorched the pristine early-winter sky. Into that brimstone-blossoming cloud the great beast entered and reemerged, soaring on great leathern wings that held aloft its black-and-verdant body. Fully visible now, the dragon circled the fractured summit of Halfhead Mountain. Once clear of the peak, it turned its attention to the clearing. With its mammoth wings flapping, it settled down on the spot, toppling half a dozen evergreens in the process.

Johanna's heart thundered. The dragon was close enough to touch. Hot air poured from the beast's nostrils like steam from a geyser. The woods witch, unfazed, stepped forward and laid hands on the creature's gargantuan snoot. "My love," she said. "Teriquay."

Teriquay? Johanna struggled to believe that she had heard the woods witch correctly. Was the creature before her truly the king-killing beast of old? The dragon, appearing to read Johanna's thoughts, turned its giant left eye on her. Johanna was struck with the impression that she could step through the dragon's eye like a glass door and there meet a side of herself that she had never known before.

The woman used the alien tongue again. This time she spoke the words quietly, her voice sounding more akin to water moving over rocks rather than thunder. To Johanna's surprise, however, the dragon paid scant attention to what the woods witch had to say. In fact, it seemed more interested in Johanna than the woods witch. It kept its towering left eye fixed on Johanna with an unapologetic intensity. Johanna felt herself trembling in the dragon's gaze, wondering what the intellect behind the eye wanted with her.

"She is yours, but for the asking."

Shayla's switch from dragon tongue to human tongue was so subtly done that Johanna thought at first that she had heard the words in dragon. But even after realizing that the words had been spoken plain, Johanna needed help with the translation.

"I don't understand."

Shayla's voice colored with pain, and not a small bit of anger. "When first Teriquay returned to Ragar Or, I thought that she had returned for me. But no matter how many times I ask, she refuses to let me ride her again. She will not converse with me. She is here for someone new. And that someone is you."

Johanna flinched, shaking her head. She peeled herself away from the dragon's gaze, away from the eye that threatened to swallow her whole. "No. I…I may be a jeyedoshi, but—"

"Damn you girl, this isn't some game. You are either here to take my place, or I have no use for you. Now speak, girl, and bind Teriquay to you!"

Johanna was nonplussed. "Speak? Speak what?"

"Dragon!" the old woman thundered.

The sky lizard stirred. Johanna watched as it began to shift back and forth with a palpable impatience, as if desperate to take flight. Odd susurrations issued from its throat. Johanna was at once drawn to the dragon and scared of it, a fright which grew immeasurably as the dragon became increasingly agitated. Breaking eye contact with Johanna, the dragon began kneading the ground and stretching its wings, readying to take to the air.

"Speak, girl!" the woods witch hissed at Johanna. She kept a hand on the dragon as if she might keep it grounded by force. "Command Teriquay to stay!"

Johanna thought the old woman was insane. Commanding the dragon was a distant second on Johanna's list of priorities, behind avoiding being maimed. She started to back away. Her feet, however, tangled as she attempted to escape. Backtracking, she stumbled to the ground, directly in line with one of the dragon's unfurling wings. She cried out "Stop!" in alarm, but instead of heeding Johanna, the dragon unceremoniously lifted

Johanna off her feet and deposited her twenty feet away, knocking the wind out of her lungs.

Screams and curses filled the air, a foul amalgam of Old Ontish, Struvan, and dragon tongue. But it was no matter; the woods witch could not stop the dragon from rising into the air. Once aloft, Teriquay continued rising until it disappeared behind a sheet of death-shroud clouds.

Silence reigned. The woods witch stared numbly into the heavens. Johanna, confused by the crush of events, waited for an explanation.

"If not you, then who?" Shayla said finally. She turned with a rising anger in her voice. "I read of your coming in a Yubriy leaf prophesy many years ago. The highborn jeyedoshi princess who would take my place. And yet here you are, without a word of dragon. So I ask again: If not you, then who? Who is meant to elevate the jeyedoshi to their rightful place of prominence? Who is meant to ride Teriquay now that he will no longer accept me as his mount? Tell me, girl? Who?"

Johanna dared not answer. The woods witch had expected something of her that she could not deliver. Of that there was no doubt. That only question now was what would come of it.

"Come," the old woman said, whirling around and starting back down the mountain. "I won't give up on you yet. First let's see if you will kill your prince."

The woods witch had no interest in Johanna's protestations. Every time Johanna tried to make one, the old woman stole the breath from her throat.

They returned to the woods witch's abode. Inside, Easton remained unconscious. The woods witch lit a cerulean-colored candle and let the smoke waft near his nose. When the Dayborn prince began to stir, the woods witch pinched the wick with licked fingers. The flame hissed as it died.

Easton regained consciousness with Johanna's name on his tongue. "Johanna!" He slurred the word as he sprung to his feet, only to struggle and stumble as he attempted to recover from his candle-induced coma. He went to draw his sword, but it was no longer there. "Johanna!" he shouted again. There was real fear in his voice. But then he spotted her, and Johanna saw the spinning axis of his bewilderment resolve into a slowly rotating confusion. "Johanna?" he said once more, staring at her half-shaven head.

Johanna tried to respond, to echo his name back to him, but the woods witch denied her. Johanna could only stare at Easton. He looked the ragamuffin in his soiled orange cloak and quilted gray doublet, like a lordling gone to seed. *I do love him,* Johanna thought.

The woods witch read her mind.

"You think that you're in love, do you?" The old woman pointed a crooked finger at Easton. She had him pinned in the corner of the room. "Why? Because he offered you the *milu sfal?* Because he's a prince? Because you believe in union?" she scoffed.

Easton had heard enough. He lunged at the woman, only to be stopped in his tracks by an unseen racking pain. The woods witch released him from her hold a split second later, but the necessary impression had been made. "Do not tempt me into killing you, boy. Not before I've had the chance to convince your beloved that the pleasure should be hers."

The old woman's distraction gave Johanna back her voice. "Whyever would I kill him?"

"Because we are at war with the established order, you and I. Salk born or no, you are *not* one of them. You are a jeyedoshi, child, and that means you are forever a pariah, forever an outcast, forever a threat. This boy may claim to love you, but that is only because he does not know the real *you*. The *powerful* jeyedoshi you. Look at your own lord father. He knew what you were. And knowing what you were, I can assure you that every decision he made on your behalf was intended to distance you from your own power. Including his decision to bond you to the king's second son."

Johanna knew that what the woods witch said was true. Johanna looked to Easton, hoping he would have the right rebuttal, but the uncertain look on the Dayborn prince's face suggested that he was struggling to come to terms with the uncovered whorl mark on her scalp.

The woods witch leaned in. "Do not be fooled, child. What they all want, in the end, is our deaths."

Easton at last tried to respond, but the woods witch stayed his tongue. She only had ears for Johanna.

Johanna obliged her. "And what do you want?"

The magic that the old woman possessed formed around her like a storm. "What do I want?" At the sound of the woods witch's voice the house came to life: the unnatural bend and twists of the house's myriad tree trunks and branches writhed like serpents stirred from a torpor. "I want wildness," the woods witch proclaimed. "True wildness, the kind that holds hands with chaos and does not apologize. Wildness is *why* we are here, child. To bridge the gap between what currently is and what has been forgotten."

"Forgotten? What has been forgotten?"

The woods witch laughed a bitter laugh. "Why, everything! Ragar Or means Land of the Twins, and yet it spurns the descendants of one twin to celebrate the other. That is why the descendants of those who rule today hunted down and killed the Firewalker. Why they massacred the Corosian line. But the beauty of the land of the twins is that we are born again and again and again. We lesser twins. We jeyedoshi. The only problem is that most jeyedoshi have forgotten why we exist." She looked at Easton, who was now restrained and gagged by a tree limb. "Take this one's uncle, for example."

"The Sagekind?"

"Yes. No better than a lapdog, he. A jeyedoshi who exists only to serve. If ever he tapped into his true power, the exalted Dayborns would stamp him out like an ant." She nodded again at Easton. "Make no mistake, girl. Should it come to it, your loving prince would do the same to you."

"I thought you were going to stamp me out?" Johanna sniped. "Because I cannot speak dragon."

Shayla's expression grew dark. "And still I might." The woods witch looked like she was pondering a difficult problem. "When first I stood before Teriquay as a young woman, the words were simply there. I thought the language was likewise latent in you, waiting on a dragon to bring it forth. Not to mention how perfectly you fit the Yubriy leaf prophecy that I read years ago. But perhaps there is a fix. Perhaps it's merely a matter of tapping deeper into your jeyedoshi nature."

The old woman walked over to the oak table. She plucked the forever flower from the table's knotty top and brought it to her nose, inhaling deeply. Watching her, Johanna felt a chill run up her spine.

The tree-limb gagging Easton had slipped its place, allowing him to find his voice. "The flower is not yours. It is a gift for my bonded-to-be." He spoke guardedly, cognizant that the woods witch could take his tongue at her pleasure.

The woods witch held the flower in the skylight. The petals shone pearlescent in the glory of the sun. "But she did not accept, did she? That being the case, how do you know that she is your bonded-to-be?"

"Because I know." Easton puffed out his chest a little. "Because the future declares it so."

A storm cloud of anger gathered on Shayla's brow. The woods witch coupled it with a murderous smile. "Says the boy from the dying dynasty. But by all means, let's drink a toast. To the happy couple's future."

The woods witch walked over and stoked the hearth fire. The flames sprung to life with a jeyedoshi-aided-quickness. Then Shayla took a tin pot filled with water and suspended it over the flames. While she waited for the water to come to a boil, she sang a song.

Keeps in cold
Disappears in hot
Life
Love
Hope
Rot

While Shayla sang, the room came to life once more, the many contorted tree trunks and limbs swaying ever so slightly, making the world feel in motion. Even the animal heads on the wall seemed to join in the rhythm. Johanna tried to ignore the distractions and keep her focus on the woods witch. When the water was brought to a boil, Shayla made a show of the forever flower before dropping it into the pot.

"No!" Easton shouted, to no avail. The *milu sfal* dissolved like snow in the boiling water, coloring the liquid a silvery gleam. Setting down the tin pot, Shayla retrieved two wooden cups hanging from tree-branch hooks on the wall. The cups looked so natural as to appear uncarved; it was as if the trees from which the cups were cut had simply produced knobby growths with cup-shaped cavities. The woods witch took the tin pot and poured five swallows' worth of forever-flower-water into the cups.

"Cold water keeps, hot water drinks," the old woman said. "A cup apiece, for the jeyedoshi who cannot speak dragon and her bonded-to-be."

Johanna was direct. "It's poison. You mean for us to die."

"Poison for him, yes. But he was always meant to die. The only question is whether his death will come at my hands or if you will convince him to accept the pleasant passing offered by the cup. For you, however…when a jeyedoshi drinks of the *milu sfal*, they may live a hundred years longer than expected. When you drink it…you will become like me."

Johanna's mind raced. *How do I stop her? How do I save Easton?* She thought of a question to prolong the moment. "But it will not make me an immortal?"

Bitterness clouded the old woman's eyes. "As you can see from the aged woman before you, the power of the *milu sfal* only extends life for so long. Death is coming for me. I can feel it in my bones. But that's after two hundred years of living, child. No, the flower will not make you an immortal. But it will give you time to accrue powers that others could only dream of." Shayla paused. "But first, you owe me a sacrifice, for showing you what you really are." Shayla extended one of the cups to Johanna. "Convince your beloved to drink this now, and together we will watch him die a peaceful death. If you can do that, I will consider you forgiven for your failure to speak dragon tongue. On the other hand, if you do not, I will take it upon myself to see him off this mortal coil. He will meet a more agonizing end, and you will watch him die, all the same."

Tears welled in Johanna's eyes. "Why must he die?"

"Everything comes with a price, my child. Watching loved ones die while continuing to live—that is the jeyedoshi toll."

Johanna shook her head. "That is a price I cannot pay." She held the cup back out for Shayla.

The woods witch refused to take it. "Drink it yourself, then, my jeyedoshi sister. Drink it and we will see just how deep your jeyedoshi blood runs. Drink it, you non-dragon-speaking bitch, and perhaps I'll spare the life of this boy you claim to love."

Johanna didn't pause to think. She knocked back the contents of the cup with five quick swallows, scarcely tasting the amaranthine sweetness of the forever-flower water as it flowed down her throat. On the opposite side of the room Easton screamed a fruitless "No!"

The deed done, Johanna brought the cup back to her side. Stared the woods witch in the eyes. Inside of her body, she could feel the *milu sfal* going about the work of transforming her into a quasi-immortal. A creeping coolness spread through her system: it felt as if a heavy snow was settling over her soul. But she had no time to assess the changes. Not when the current moment still held so much at stake.

"Good," the woods witch said. She moved closer to Johanna, sticking out her nose like a bloodhound after a smell. "Do you feel the hands of time slowing inside your body?"

"Yes," Johanna answered honestly.

The woods witch grinned. But the grin withered and died on the vine just as quickly as it had ripened. Taking its place was a sour frown, and a shaking head. "We're making progress, but all the progress in the world won't do us a damn bit of good if you can't speak dragon. Tell me, child, if I called Teriquay back, could you speak to him now, or would he once more trample you in his efforts to fly away?"

Johanna caught a glimpse of Easton's wide-eyed reaction across the way. She looked quickly away. She was fairly certain the woods witch was baiting her, knowing that the reply would be in the negative. Feeling that a response of any sort would work against her, Johanna kept her mouth shut.

The woods witch interpreted Johanna's silence as she saw fit. "That's what I thought." A mean look entered the woods witch's eyes. "Do you know, child, that when I follow the thread of my life back to the time before I approached Teriquay on Simstone Mountain, the only through line that I can see is the intense suffering that I endured. I lost my family, my friends...everyone, everything. Before meeting you, I somehow deluded myself into believing that you would be *like* me, that...*something*...about your makeup would make us the same. But now I see how wrong I was. Fortunately, I also see the remedy. Before you are struck with the ability to speak dragon, you must be made to suffer. The same as I was made to suffer. You must learn to lose that which is closest to you."

Easton howled with a sudden pain. The expression on Shayla's face changed as she set her jeyedoshi hooks in him, tearing, burning, clawing at his insides, making his existence a misery. The Dayborn prince staggered first to the left, and then to the right, before collapsing on the floor. His facial expression contorted into a nonhuman rictus of agony.

"Stop it!" Johanna charged the woods witch, unmindful of the witch's powers. She was reminded by the forceful shove of the wind, which stormed the house like a marauding army and knocked Johanna off her feet, behaving nothing like the playful entity Johanna had called to dance less than an hour before. Out of sorts on the floor, Johanna sensed the wind hovering over her, a brazen bully awaiting distraction. But then the force directing the attack slackened, and the wind transformed into an impish question mark, curious of the multiple jeyedoshi in the room.

"This is a lesson, child. Lie there and learn it!" Shayla shouted. But in the fury of the woods witch's command Johanna detected a frustration that bordered on fear. The pieces came together as Easton made a valiant charge of his own, rising to his feet only to be slapped back down by Shayla's renewed attentions.

She cannot split the focus of her powers.

Johanna reached for the wind. Her reaching was a question, but it was one filled with urgency and anger, entirely unlike the desperately wanting query that she had tendered no less than an hour ago. The wind responded in kind, handing itself over to her with all the frantic potency of the moment. Together they beheld one another, the jeyedoshi and the element, energies mounting upon energies, until, with a force that frightened Johanna even as she unleashed it, the wind stormed across the room and slammed into Shayla, breaking the woods witch's body against the knotty oak table with the sennequi piece atop.

The red wooden carving spun atop the table, then toppled over.

The suddenness of the woods witch's death was a strange and unsettling thing. The wind fled the house, and in the still and silent aftermath it seemed as if Ragar Or was holding its breath in wonder at what had occurred. But then, starting with the animals on the wall and then spreading to the body of the house, a nervous, agitated rustling commenced that made it seem as if the animals and the house had both come to life. The movement crescendoed in an explosive, ear-splitting roar, the sound of a far-off dragon perhaps, or of the house threatening to implode, or maybe, as Johanna considered in retrospect, it was simply the dull thunk of Shayla the woods witch's broken body sliding from the table onto the floor.

All fell silent again. Johanna tore her gaze away from Shayla's glassy dead stare and found Easton. The Dayborn prince was staring at her from across the great divide of everything that had happened to them over the past twenty-four hours. Reflexively, Johanna's hand went to her scalp, to hide the whorl mark there.

"Don't," said Easton. He donned a smile that was a distant cousin of the shit-eating grin Johanna had grown so accustomed to seeing him wear, an earnest and honest smile that reflected his desire to say something honest and true. "I would see you as you are."

Gregor Thorn

Gregor was awakened by the sensation of a wet nose nudging at his face. He opened his eyes to find the black greyhound stirring him from sleep with all the dispassion of a pious Winged Woman rousing her sisters to morning prayers.

"Ropske," he said.

The black greyhound did not contradict him.

His sleep had been deep and dreamless. *Strange,* he thought, sifting through the sediment of his waking mind for the residue of a dream. But there was nothing. *I suppose that's what happens when a person spends forty-eight hours on their feet trying to save the kingdom.* Though no dreams came to him, he did recall with vivid clarity the haunting images of his most recent waking hours: Reginal Burntree, mouth hanging open in death-shock, blood fountaining from the hole in his sword-plunged chest, and the gorgostrine Betrard, bloody spray shooting from the stump of his newly headless body. *Two of the king's enemies are dead,* he reminded himself, *and the dynasty is safer for it.* But before Gregor could reify his self-assurances, images of Daguss Salk and Dante Heron floated up.

The wrong two are dead, and you know it.

Enough. Up.

Gregor moved to his feet. The room was ripening with a bold and bright sunlight, an unexpected phenomenon in gloomy Dunning Harbor. The sun's rays made a show of the chest of drawers opposite the bed, where Gregor had stashed the book from The Sea Swoon. For the first time in two days, he had time to think about its importance.

It's time I learn what Greffen Ollspaer had to say. He walked over and removed the book from the chest. Opening the book, he began to read its pages, translating Old Ontish into the common tongue. As he read, Gregor began to pick up the thread of a story, a story connected to names from Kalandragote's history that Gregor was passingly familiar with, a wild tale that expounded considerably on what Gregor knew of the Ice Ghost's sojourn in Kalandragote. *This claims that Greffen's twin brother Kaaros was a true jeyedoshi.* Gregor already knew that Greffen Ollspaer's ascension to the Winterworn chair in Kalandragote had been unconventional. The previous king—King Heljah—had been unable to produce an heir, causing the crown to be turned over to his nephew when he passed. This book, if it was indeed written by Greffen, detailed a stunning account of the day the dragon called the Ice Ghost departed Kalandragote, many years before Greffen became king. It suggested, among other things, that not only was Greffen's brother Kaaros a true jeyedoshi, but that the boys' father, Roop Ollspaer—the brother of King Heljah—had desperately tried on the day of the twin-death rite to save Kaaros's life. By…

Gregor stared at the Old Ontish sentence before him, translating it over and over again in his mind.

Wis vawi hylor Kaaros: Na vakno rinflese pla yubriy skwurir lonsti, in kli vakno varit pla hekspi. Hrotwo, sunflul pla kapis hiskwustriv kwimpti, kli vakno spis pla playskin hlyor kli.

"Father said to Kaaros: I will burn the Yubriy leaf, and you will inhale the smoke. Then, during the twin-death rite, you will call the dragon to you."

Gregor tried to wrap his head around what he was reading. In the story, Roop Ollspaer had managed to get his hands on a Yubriy tree leaf and was trying to save his jeyedoshi son's life by imparting to him the knowledge to call the Ice Ghost to his side. *Could this possibly be true?* None of it added up. Roop Ollspaer was one of the most famous Kalandragote warriors of his time, a man who personified the famed strength of the northern kingdom, a man who expanded Kalandragote's borders during the turmoil of Ragar Or's War of the Three Brothers. The idea that he had gotten his hand on a Yubriy leaf, learned the secret of calling a dragon from the heavens, and tried to pass that knowledge on to his jeyedoshi son...it was preposterous. *And where did he even come across the idea to inhale the smoke of the Yubriy leaf? I'm the Sagekind, and I've never heard of that...*

Gregor put aside what the story was suggesting and considered the authenticity of the book. It was a small book, only four pages long, and appeared to have been written in something of a hurry: the handwriting, though handsome, looked rushed. There were tons of historical records back at the Crow Keep in Union, and among them were communications from the Kalandragote kingdom during the time of King Greffen Ollspaer's reign. Gregor wanted to believe that the handwriting before him matched missives that he had seen written by the Kalandragote king, but without one before him, he couldn't be certain. The book was also missing the royal Kalandragote seal. Whether that was significant, Gregor didn't know. Seals were generally associated with letters, not books. Whoever had written this had chosen to style it like a bare-bones story: one written in a rush, which, considering the subject matter, Gregor could understand why.

Especially if the author was King Greffen Ollspaer of Kalandragote. This wasn't the sort of state secret that a Kalandragote king revealed.

Gregor closed his eyes and tried to picture a dragon. A real one, made of fire and scale and flesh. But his mind kept returning to the books in the Tomes and the pictures of dragons drawn there, renderings by Wandering Tongues who, even if they had seen one of the beasts, lacked the talent to convey the reality of a dragon's appearance. *If I were to inhale the smoke of a Yubriy leaf and learn dragon tongue, the dragon that I could then call from the heavens would not be made of paper.* But behind closed eyes, all Gregor could see was paper dragons with scales of colored ink.

He opened his eyes. Looked out the window. In the sharpening sunlight, his imagination conjured for a brief and explosive second the vision his closed eyes had denied him: a massive winged beast dissecting the space between land and sky, threatening, by the sheer fact of its existence, to wound reality. He saw himself on the dragon's back, bending that wounded reality to his will. The chimera soon faded, and Gregor was once again in his own body, facing the decision at hand.

If you were to call a dragon from the sky, you could ensure that your brother would survive the trial ahead. You could ensure that the Dayborn dynasty would continue.

And then a different, smaller voice.

If you were to call a dragon from the sky, you could bring all of Ragar Or to heel.

His hand moved to the pocket sewn in all of his red cloaks, the one closest to his heart. The Yubriy leaf was there: besides the brief stint it had spent in Betrard's boot (placed there under watch of a Dayborn knight sworn to stand beside Betrard in the courtyard and stab him if the gorgostrine showed signs of reneging on his vow), the leaf had made no other trip than the return one to his pocket. Still, Gregor reached up to touch it, to feel it, to *know*. Not because he was going to use it in the way the story suggested, but simply to…

A knock on the door stayed his hand. He put the book back in the chest of drawers and called for whoever it was to come in.

Stryder, of his brother's personal guard, opened the door and entered. The guard's fiery red hair blazed atop a fleshy, skull-showing face. "Prince Ajax and his bonded are ready to leave, Revered Sagekind."

"Greta," Gregor responded. For reasons he didn't fully understand, he wanted to hear the young woman's name on his lips one last time before she left.

"Yes," Stryder responded. "Half the Heron's army is waiting for them outside the city." Stryder gave Gregor a quizzical look. "The king was surprised to have to send for you. You are usually up before the sun."

Gregor shrugged, stood up, and headed for the door. "Even a man such as myself needs rest from time to time." He looked deep into Stryder's skeletal bone-socket eyes as he passed him by. "If you had seen half the things that I have, you might sleep in too."

The sending-off ceremony was in the same bloody courtyard where Betrard and Reginal Burntree had met their respective ends the day before. Sun-kissed and windless now, the courtyard seemed a less malevolent place. There were less people present, too, but those that were there were pressed around Ajax and Greta, clamoring for their attention. Nearby, two mounting blocks ascended to two steeds cloaked in Dayborn finery, the couple's waiting conveyances.

Gregor bore into the press. He hated to see Ajax and Greta go, but a decision had been made. The right one, he was sure of it. *A hug and a handshake, then back to my chambers.* Lord Daguss and Lord Dante were in the muddle, but Gregor sensed that they posed no imminent danger. Standing next to the prince and Greta was Grocian Mock. The Ontish lord in his largeness made those around him look small, all except Greta, who, with a substantial smile and self-possessed bearing, took up a similar space. Greta was engaged in conversation with Grocian, exchanging pleasantries. King Micah and Queen Anjay were on the outer edges of the press, presiding over the goodbyes, two tired-looking skulls. *Skulls, skulls, skulls everywhere.* Gregor glanced to his right and saw the lutist. He watched the young man for a moment, noting his wide hazel eyes and how they called to mind an animal out of its element—

Someone ran into Gregor, placed their hands on *him*, on his cloak…in Gregor's defensiveness he reached for the ground beneath his assailant's feet, commanding it to fracture with an authority he had never before manifested…only nothing happened, *nothing*, it was as if Gregor's orders had been negated by a power higher up the chain…Gregor's eyes caught up to his flailing mind…patting Gregor's cloak and apologizing was Wyn Dunkin, the *woodkin*, stabbing at him with a jokester's grin.

"Sincerest apologies, Revered Sagekind, you were studying Silas O' the Songs with such intent that you barged right into me. But all is well and good. You have my forgiveness."

Nearby, a spirited if studied laugh. Gregor turned and was assaulted by Wulfess Salk's flagrant pulchritude, her beauty like a battering ram. "For the good of the group, I must insist that these two not be kept under lock and key. Everyone traveling north would benefit from a healthy helping of their songs and wit." She let her gaze fall upon every Dayborn in the press, Gregor included.

Gregor, discomfited by the bump-in with Wyn, didn't respond straightaway. It was Greta who took the liberty of replying to Wulfess on behalf of those in the camp of the double suns. "I'm sure Uncle Bones and my good father the king would not deny our friends the pleasure of the music and company of these two men." She gave Gregor a pointed look. "Would they?"

Am I expected to answer? Talking at the moment seemed beyond him. *What do you say to a world full of skulls?* But most everyone had followed Greta's lead and were now looking at him. Despite the long night of sleep, Gregor felt tired and out of sorts, rattled by Wyn Dunkin's immunity to his jeyedoshi powers, and in no mood for the diplomatic overture Greta was asking him to make, no matter how small the gesture might be. Still, he liked the way the word *friends* had fallen from her tongue, with a tenor that suggested she might have exchanged it for *enemies*—so he played along.

"I bow to the good judgment of our future queen." He made a half bow as he spoke. It made him feel ridiculous, but it won the crowd, for a handful broke into applause, and were soon joined by others. And with that the crowd parted, making way for him to reach the center, to say his goodbyes. He shook hands with Ajax, manly and warm. Then Greta had her arms around his neck, her lips close enough to whisper in his ear. "I carry your wisdom with us, Uncle Bones," she said.

Immediately after Gregor said his goodbyes the throng cleared away, until Prince Ajax and Greta were left alone standing alone with the king and the queen. When those goodbyes were finished and the young couple turned to the mounting blocks, Gregor departed the courtyard. The cheers sending Ajax and Greta out Saltbend Castle's gates followed Gregor back to his room.

Guilt was gnawing at Gregor by the time he reached his chambers. *I should have been up before the sun, out in the camps, ensuring that the Heron kept his word. I should have ridden with Ajax and Greta a mile or two outside the city, to see them safely off.* But his thoughts were overkill, and he knew it. He had shored everything up as best as he could the day before. Whatever happened next was beyond him. He couldn't keep everyone safe, not all the time, not unless, not unless...

He once more imagined the Yubriy leaf, nesting in the pocket of his cloak. There was a good chance the story he had read was a fabrication, but if it wasn't? *I really don't have a choice, do I? I must do whatever is necessary to save my brother the king.* If the story was true, burning and inhaling the smoke of the Yubriy leaf for the purposes of learning dragon tongue would simply be another arrow in the quiver. It did not make it incumbent upon him to use it. *What is the point of my being a jeyedoshi if I don't use my powers to save my family? Isn't that what Father trained me to do?* He made up his mind then and there. The book had come into his possession for a reason. He would test the story's theory, to see if it was true. And if it was, if the moment came when he needed to call a dragon down from the clouds, he would not hesitate to do so.

With his mind made up, he reached for the leaf in his cloak pocket. Only…it wasn't there. His heart juddered in horror. He began a frantic searching—his hands roaming every pocket on his person, his eyes scanning the room—but the Yubriy leaf refused to reveal itself. *When did I last—?* He remembered confirming the leaf's presence in the cloak pocket earlier that morning, before heading down to the courtyard to say his goodbyes to Ajax and Greta. *Between now and then…*

His mind went back in time no more than ten minutes past. To the memory of Wyn Dunkin, the *woodkin*, with his hands on Gregor's cloak.

But how? How?

It didn't matter. Time spent contemplating how the rogue had stolen the leaf was time wasted.

Gregor rushed out of his chambers.

"Trust me. If Wyn is in fact disappeared, we are *all* the better for it."

Silas O' the Songs spoke convincingly. As Sagekind, Gregor considered himself adept at detecting when a man was lying, and Silas's genuine befuddlement/ecstatic relief at his musical partner's inexplicable disappearance seemed authentic. What Gregor couldn't wrap his mind around was how the little man had disappeared. It was one thing to evade detection with half a day's head start and a premeditated plan, but to do so in the span of a quarter hour with all the resources of the Dayborn dynasty deployed to track you down…why, it defied logic.

But, as Gregor knew from personal experience, the homely, ropy-haired musician was in possession of abilities that didn't align with the logical mind.

With no other leads having borne fruit, Gregor scrutinized the lutist. Try as he might, he struggled to reconcile the portentous weight of the Yubriy leaf's prophecy with the out-of-his-depths, hazel-eyed man before him. *You?* he kept thinking, staring at Silas. *You are the one who is supposed to save the queen?* He forced himself to consider the notion that there was more to this man than met the eye, that perhaps Silas was in league with Wyn Dunkin, that maybe the two of them were supernatural agents of the Yubriy tree sent to work magic to some unknown end, but his eyes wouldn't attest to the fact.

You? he thought instead, again and again and again.

You?

"Your friend—"

"He was not my friend, Revered Sagekind. He was a thief, and a nuisance."

"A thief?"

"Yes. He stole a song of mine. I can assure you that it did not prick his conscience in the least."

"A different song than the one you sung for the queen?"

"That's right." Silas was sitting on the edge of the bed in his Saltbend Castle chambers, arms wrapped around the rosewood lute cradled in his lap. His face went through a series of conflicting expressions. "I should not speak poorly of him. Stavus knows the man saved my life enough times to repay whatever debt he owed me for the stolen song. Not to mention that he helped me perfect 'The Queen's Burning Heart.' But when a man is as irritating as Wyn Dunkin, it's the annoyances that stick. Think me a liar if you want, but I'm telling the truth. I hope that we've seen the last of him."

Gregor believed Silas. He had only been around Wyn Dunkin a few times himself, but he knew well enough that the fiddler was a man with a talent for making others feel on edge, even when (or perhaps especially when) he acted the fool. *It's his unseen power that does it,* Gregor thought. *It's all nested inside, latent and large, and the only glimpse of it you get is through his you'll-never-know-me grin.*

Gregor gave Silas a hard stare. "I'm choosing, for now, to believe you. I trust you've seen enough of what I'm capable of to know what the repercussions will be if you're lying."

The lutist gulped. *It's good that he's seen firsthand what I am,* Gregor thought. *It will make our relationship more honest.*

Gregor turned to go. If there was more to the man before him than met the eye, well, time would have to reveal that. He was almost out the door when he thought of one last question. Whipping back around, his eyes settled on the floor, near the lutist's leather boots. He considered how to phrase his question as Silas shuffled his feet. If Gregor didn't already know that he had put Silas on edge, he would have thought the lutist didn't like his boots being stared at.

"When we were in the Sea Swoon, the young gorgostrine and his aunt insisted that Wyn was a woodkin. You spent a lot of time with him. Tell me: do you believe there was any truth to their accusation?"

Silas laughed an uncomfortable laugh. "I'm not sure that I even know what a woodkin is, Revered Sagekind." The laughter died, and the lutist's lips formed a no-nonsense line. "But if ever I've met one, it was Wyn Dunkin."

Gregor's frame of mind deteriorated as the day wore on. The packing had begun in earnest for the continued trip north, but everywhere Gregor looked, he was distracted by the skulls of friends, enemies, and those of ambiguous loyalty. Adding to his gloom, the sun disappeared behind a sheet of oily gray clouds that had rolled in off the Blacktyde Sea. Though Gregor could see its yellow smudge behind the clouds, he couldn't help but think that it had in fact departed with Ajax and Greta, and was headed south to Struvan country.

To Union.

His mood darkened even more when the last of the search parties returned to Saltbend Castle to inform him that they had failed to find Wyn Dunkin. Assurances were made that the search would continue, that the rat-faced fiddler would be found, but Gregor knew the truth. Wyn Dunkin was gone, and the sole Yubriy leaf in Gregor's possession was gone with him.

For a short time, Gregor gave serious consideration to leaving without Micah's permission and heading to Union. It crossed his mind that he might burn and inhale one of the Yubriy leaves secured in the Crow Keep, learn dragon tongue, call Ragar Or's newest dragon from the heavens (however that worked), and then fly north to Kalandragote forthwith. But Gregor also knew that it was a foregone conclusion that his brother would reach Kalandragote before he reached Union. Any plots intended against Micah Dayborn would surely be carried out while Gregor was gone, making Gregor's arrival—whether on the back of a dragon or not—a moot point.

In the middle of the afternoon, he stirred from his funk long enough to visit the kitchens. The kitchen maids were cleaning up after the midday meal. To Gregor's chagrin, the woman he chose to ask for food turned out to be the most disagreeable of the lot: she begrudged him for the extra work involved, implying with her every under-the-breath syllable that only a southern Struvan asshole like himself would have the temerity to make Mock servants scrounge up food after mealtime hours. Gregor resisted the temptation to point out that no less than four northerners had entered the kitchen while he was talking to her and walked out with food. He was still waiting on her to hand over hard bread and an apple when a man wearing Mock livery entered the kitchens and approached him.

"Revered Sagekind, there's a man being made to wait at the portcullis who says that he's your servant."

"There is?" Gregor asked in surprise. "Did you catch his name?"

"No." The liveried man, who had a wispy mustache, anxiously twitched his nose. He looked around the kitchen like he didn't want the other servants to hear him. "He's a young man, and the soldiers at the gate are making sport of denying him. But his protestations seemed sincere. I thought you should know."

A young man? Gregor could not imagine who it might be. With a nod of thanks to the servant, Gregor quit his negotiations with the kitchen maid and made for the gate. His stomach growled in protest, but his curiosity was sufficiently piqued that he forgot his hunger, and, for the moment at least, his depression too.

He wound through the castle, sidestepping bustling servants, ignoring Ontish glares. Once outside, he skimmed the now-empty courtyard and headed for the dark passageway that led to the outer castle gate. Listening carefully, he could hear the distinctive lilt of men having fun at another man's expense, a sound that called to Gregor's mind chipped bells being rung.

"You're done talking now, are you? C'mon boy, you might yet string together the right run of words that would convince us to let you pass. Have another go! Who knows, that Struvan accent of yours might grow hawk's wings if you talk long enough. Then you can fly right by!"

A second man gave a barking sort-of-laugh. *Regional and religious humor, the comedic refuge of the crass man.* Their laughter lessened a little as they detected Gregor's footsteps, then died altogether when they recognized his red cloak.

Gregor accepted their silence as surrender. He walked directly between the two men and looked out the open gate. Seeing who it was, he startled in joyous shock. Standing beside a tan rouncey, looking stoic and resolved, was the young knight Gregor had left in Low Osgood suffering from a stab wound to the stomach.

"Deglan Whisk? What are you doing here?"

The young man's reply was vintage Deglan. "I am come to resume my duty, Revered Sagekind."

Gregor laughed. He hadn't heard anything so honest in weeks. *Except perhaps for my conversations with Greta.* To his surprise, the laughter caused tears to well in his eyes. "You are recovered, then?" he asked, regaining his composure.

"I can ride."

Gregor nodded, a touch of sadness returning. In a different world he would have insisted that Deglan return to his bed until a full recovery was made. But in this world, he was grateful that the boy before him was determined to become a man, no matter the peril. He needed allies at this time above all else.

Gregor continued staring at Deglan. The sight of the young man stirred an inexplicable joy in him. It was something to do with Deglan's appearance, his person, his *face*, but Gregor couldn't place why; he only knew that Deglan Whisk reminded him of hope itself. It was as if the young man's visage exuded the essence of life...and that was when it hit him, like a freak bolt of lightning on a cloudless and sunlit day.

I do not see Deglan's skull.

"Revered Sagekind?"

"Yes, my good Deglan?" Despite his attempt at responding, Gregor could scarcely hear Deglan for the cacophony of thoughts now sounding inside his skull. *If, in the end, Deglan lives...if, in the end, Greta lives...then perhaps the future is worth fighting for. Perhaps there is still hope, after all.*

"We are still headed north? To Kalandragote?"

"Yes." Gregor nodded outside the castle gates. To the north, and to the east.

To whatever came next.

"To Kalandragote."

Epilogue One

A young woman and a slightly younger man stood together near the base of a glistening waterfall, in the thick of a forest glen. The dust on their clothes and the fatigued expressions on their faces suggested that recent days had been rough on them, but in spite of this they managed to look both elated and majestic, a byproduct, perhaps, of their youthful optimism. Their right hands were bound together in a makeshift fashion using the reins of a horse. Although the tying of the strap wasn't perfect by ceremonial standards, any citizen of Ragar Or would have known what the strap signified.

The couple were acting out a bonding ceremony.

Two horses—one a fearless Rugarder, the other a careworn palfrey—stood nearby, the only witnesses. Or so the young couple believed. In reality there were pennywolves in the near vicinity, choosing, as their kind often did, to remain unseen. It had been a tumultuous morning for the pennywolves. A tether had been severed between their kind and a powerful entity, and for that they were in mourning. But there was also a wildness loose in the world, both in the skies above and, the wolves intuited, in the hearts of the young man and woman before them. For this the wolves were grateful.

The couple knew nothing of the pennywolves. They only had eyes for each other. Love, that unwitting alchemy, had found a way to work its smagic between them.

Bonding ceremonies were built of words, and the couple spoke these words to each other the best they could remember them. When the young man said his part, he was thinking of a voice that had spoken to him on the day he first introduced himself to the young woman, a voice as clear as a bell, a voice that told him that the woman before him was the true love of his life, his queen.

The woman had experienced no such premonition. But when she spoke her part aloud, she did so with a willing heart, feeling, for one of the first times in her life, that she was making a decision that was truly her own.

I choose you, Easton Dayborn, she thought.

I choose you.

Epilogue Two

Five miles south of Dunning Harbor, in a span of woods sufficiently thick that a man might travel to the center of it and believe himself removed from the affairs of other men, a rather peculiar man had absconded, a man with ropes of silver-brown hair and a pox-scarred, rodent's face, a man carrying a fiddle and bow in one hand and a large, orange, seven-pointed leaf in the other. There was a sense of purpose to the man's stride, but it would be unfair to call it single-minded, for the man was also singing as he walked, a caterwauling and comical tune that made a mockery of, among other things, Ragar Or's two chief religions. The man walked along until he came upon a mossy patch in the woods. Then the man stopped singing, fell to his knees, and dug at the soil until he had made a small hole.

Content with his work, the man picked up the orange leaf—which he had laid carefully on the ground along with the fiddle and bow—and, with a reverence that served as a stark contrast to his seconds-ago singing, laid the leaf in the hole the way one might a loved one in a grave. Then, his hands dark with dirt, the man covered up the leaf with the removed soil and finished by replacing the moss on top.

He stood up when he was finished. A wind kicked up in the woods at that moment, a high-spirited gust that set the man to laughing. As the wind continued its soundless song, the man put the fiddle on his shoulder and played along.

Acknowledgements

Thank you, dear reader, for reading *The Prophecy of the Yubriy Tree,* the first book in my epic fantasy series, *The Song of the Burning Heart.* If you haven't already done so, I hope that you will consider signing up for my newsletter at benspencer.substack.com for updates. Newsletter subscribers also have access to a free novelette, *Last Performance at the Three Dragons Inn.* Additional information is available at benspencerwrites.com. I am eternally grateful for any reviews that you might post on Amazon, Goodreads, etc.

This book wouldn't have been possible without the faithful and steadfast support of my loving wife, Beth. She is a first reader beyond compare. Not only that, she convinces me to keep the faith during my dark nights of the soul while loving me irrespective of the ups and downs of my writing life. I love her more than words can say.

When I began writing the book, I had a very specific vision in mind. My favorite works of fantasy fiction are vivid, colorful, and character-driven. Like every writer who picks up a pen, I want to create works that reflect the type of novels that I want to see in print. I felt like I was on the right track while writing *The Prophecy of the Yubriy Tree,* but it was my daughter's enthusiasm upon reading the completed book that made me feel like I had achieved what I set out to accomplish. Many thanks to Charlotte for her insight and artistic sensibility. I feel fortunate to share a space in this world with her.

I have been at the writing game for a long time now. Throughout all the highs and lows, it's been the true readers who have pulled me through. For those of you who believe in the transformative power of engaging deeply with another person's imagination, I am grateful. As a reader there's nothing that I enjoy more than diving into the pages of a captivating epic fantasy. I hope that *The Prophecy of the Yubriy Tree* made you feel the same way that I feel about my favorite fantasy works. If it did, I hope that you will continue with me on my journey.

We have many miles yet to travel.

www.ingramcontent.com/pod-product-compliance
Ingram Content Group UK Ltd.
Pitfield, Milton Keynes, MK11 3LW, UK
UKHW041437010825
7195UKWH00036B/408